Broken Pieces

Abby Shrewsbury

To the broken. May the light find its way through the pieces, and may the years you're here be kind.

Copyright © 2026 by Abby Shrewsbury

All rights reserved. No part of this book may be reproduced or used in any manner without written permission of the copyright owner except for the use of quotations in a book review.

Write us at: brokenpieces.novel@gmail.com

Cover and Formatting by: H Khan

Paperback ISBN: 979-8-218-87855-9

E-book ISBN: 979-8-218-87856-6

Contents

1. Sam	7
2. Elliot	29
3. Sam	31
4. Sam	36
5. Sam	46
6. Elliot	54
7. Sam	57
8. Sam	68
9. Elliot	75
10. Sam	77
11. Sam	86
12. Elliot	103
13. Sam	107
14. Sam	111
15. Elliot	121
16. Sam	124
17. Sam	131
18. Sam	135
19. Sam	139
20. Elliot	148
21. Sam	151
22 . Sam	160
23 . Elliot	167
24 . Sam	169
25. Sam	178
26. Elliot	186
27. Sam	189
28. Sam	197
29. Elliot	204
30. Sam	207
31. Sam	219
32. Sam	225
33. Sam	234
34. Elliot	244

35. Sam	246
36. Sam	258
37. Sam	266
38. Elliot	284
39. Sam	286
40. Sam	294
41. Sam	303
42. Elliot	305
43. Elliot	312
44. Elliot	319
45. Elliot	322
46. Elliot	329
47. Elliot	335
48. Elliot	343
49. Elliot	350
50. Elliot	357
51. Elliot	365
52. Elliot	370

Acknowledgments

Writing *Broken Pieces* has been the most personal and most challenging creative journey I've ever taken - and I didn't do it alone.

To my family, who helped me learn the power of resilience, love, and quiet strength. Your belief in me - even when I struggled to believe in myself - was a lifeline. Thank you for listening, encouraging, and giving me the space to heal and create. You helped me navigate through grief and healing and pain. Your unwavering support is something I hope to never take for granted.

To my friends, both near and far, who read early drafts, asked good questions, gave hugs, and put up with my late-night writing sprints and spirals. You were the grounding force I needed. You reminded me that I didn't have to do this perfectly - I just had to keep going. You reminded me that my story *matters*. That my heart is worth sharing.

To my book club girls and game night crew - you gave me joy in the middle of the hard chapters. And to everyone who ever asked, "How's the book going?" - you helped it get here.

To Gus and Bo, my built-in support team. You kept me company through so many writing sessions with your warmth, your chaos, and your presence.

To my chronic illness community: this story holds pieces of all of us. Thank you for reminding me that strength doesn't always look like standing tall - sometimes it looks like choosing softness, rest, and hope anyway.

To Kainos, thank you for the work you do every day. You remind the world that every story matters, especially the ones still being written.

And finally, to the quiet voice inside me that always whispered, *keep writing*, even when I wanted to quit - you were right.

SAM

I collected little promises of safety like other people collected hobbies - locked doors, hovering glances over my shoulder, the way I learned to carry my keys like claws. I followed every rule as if it would be enough. My boss called it being overly careful. I called it staying alive.

My morning routine was a ritual of quiet fear: check the back door bolt, check again, breathe. Tell myself again that I'm not paranoid - just prepared, just aware, just... tired.

The coffee shop hummed with anticipation of our morning regulars and traveling guests. My eyes lingered on the front door. Watching. Waiting.

I always wait for the worst to arrive. Not dramatically - just a shadow at the edge of every room, a hand hovering above every choice.

I wiped at the counter as if it was a religious practice. It practically was. I clung to busyness like a security blanket. While it made keeping the shop clean an easy chore, it ironically made it more difficult to find meaningful tasks to do to fill my time. Manufactured productivity worked all the same, though.

A rattle of the back door against the lock sent my heart into my throat. Not even moments later, a key raked into the hole and turned against the bolt, and I sighed a breath I didn't realize I'd held. Bill and Jessa breezed in, completely unaware of the way they'd terrified me. They held armfuls of grocery bags and boxes with ingredients for whatever new seasonal items they would concoct and put out into the pastry case.

"Morning, Sam!"

I smiled softly and half waved at my bosses, still collecting my breath.

"Hey. Don't forget we've got that community fundraiser on Saturday. Are you still going to be able to cover that with Jessa?"

I nodded to Bill with a wavering smile. Crowds weren't really my thing, but Jessa needed help, and it was for a good cause. In just a few days, our downtown area would be full of volunteers and sponsor booths and families throwing a few dollars around to help raise money for our children's hospital programs. Jessa volunteered us to be the coffee and pastry sponsors while Bill stayed open for the hoards of customers that would flood in from the overflow. And after they practically took me in at eighteen, I would do literally anything for my bosses. So, to the crowds we'd go.

The bell chimed above the front door and our first customer of the day stepped through the threshold into the cozy corner shop. The dark gray, late summer sky threatened to chase her through the door but the warmth of the low light bouncing off the leather seats kept it at bay.

She ordered an americano with an extra shot, starting her morning off with a kick.

The ceramic coffee mug scraped across the counter as I pushed it toward the blonde on the other side. The sound made my skin crawl, but I smiled politely at... Bea? Becca? She'd come in before, but I couldn't quite pull her name. She was nice enough. Not rude, just not going-out-of-her-way-to-make-you-feel-special kind of nice, which I definitely understood. A dainty bracelet dangled from under the edge of her sleeve and hung just off her wrist as she went to pick up the mug and carried it to a perch near the window.

I turned to the back counter, combing through my playlist options like my life depended on finding the least emotional song in existence. Something quiet. Something that didn't demand attention. Something that made me feel like I *wasn't made of exposed wires.*

A soft throat-clear behind me shot adrenaline straight into my throat. I spun too fast - my heel sliding, elbow flailing - and caught myself with both palms flat against the counter like I was bracing for impact.

Deep breath, Reynolds.

I forced my shoulders down and pulled together what I hoped looked like a professional smile instead of the wild-eyed panic I currently felt. "I am… terribly sorry! Can I help you?"

He was annoyingly handsome - his dark brown hair neatly groomed into place above arrogant eyes that danced with amusement. Hints of a tattoo peeked from under the shoved up cuffs of his pristinely white button up shirt as he leaned forward slightly onto the counter.

"Yes, thank you," he grinned, voice smooth and confident. "Just a light roast drip coffee, please."

"Uh… sure," I choked out, horrified at how I wanted to melt at his voice. "For here or to go?"

His head tilted ever so slightly sideways, which I took as acknowledgement that we both knew just how much of a fucking train wreck my mind had become. "I'll take it here, I think. Thanks."

"Room for cream?" I asked as I grabbed a mug. The familiar movements steadied me. The scent of freshly dispensed coffee grounded me.

"No cream." His lips tipped into a soft half-smile. "I like my coffee honest."

I blinked at him. *Honest.*

Was that a line? Did lines still exist in the real world?

Don't be weird, Reynolds.

I handed the cup to him over the counter, avoiding the scraping sound I hated so much. "I haven't seen you in here before. Just passing through?"

He wrapped a hand around the mug - strong hands, veins prominent - and took a slow sip. "No, I've driven by a few times. Figured it was finally time to come in." A pause. Softer: "Glad I did."

My eyes were embarrassingly glued to him as he took his seat. Heat crawled up my neck like a warning light. I despised how nervous he made me feel, so I mustered up a smile that hung in the silence for a few seconds too long. Mortified, I turned back to selecting a playlist and made myself a cup of drip coffee to sip on while I worked and tended to new customers. I felt his eyes on me as I moved - not a constant, by any means, but a consistent glance in my direction.

Saved by the chime of the front door opening (the one I failed to hear when he stepped in moments earlier), I turned in time to see... Beth?... stepping out onto the sidewalk. I recognized a not-so-meaningless task and an excuse to remove myself from the awkward occasional eye contact with the handsome stranger, so I made my way to her table to clear the dishes and wipe it down.

Dammit, Reynolds, what the hell is happening to you? Have you gotten soft all of a sudden? A handsome customer shoots you a smile and suddenly all your reservations are gone? Pull yourself together.

Table slowly and thoroughly cleaned, dishes in hand, I turned on my heel to return them to the sink behind the counter. Like something out of an atrocious rom-com movie a hormonal pre-teen would obsess over, I found myself flattened against a customer. *Of course.* The plate fumbled from my hand and bounced between me and a wall of muscle until it clambered to the floor.

"Easy," he said, laughter tucked into the word. He crouched to pick up pieces of the now shattered plate, helping me gather each shard while purposefully brushing his hand against mine. *Definitely* on purpose. "I didn't mean to ambush you again."

I was mortified. I tried to mutter an apology, but I'm not sure any real words left my mouth. Instead, my full on shame spiral sent me scurrying for shelter behind the counter, dropping the dishes and shards in the sink a little too forcefully, and willing my trembling hands to chill the fuck out.

"I'm so sorry," he offered softly, a few steps away from the counter. "That was entirely my fault. Are you alright?"

One last deep breath left me about as collected as I could get before facing him. "Yeah. Just… jumpy. Occupational hazard of being alive."

That earned a real laugh, low and warm. "I'll try to avoid being life-threatening next time."

Next time.

I dared a glance up. He wasn't smirking now. He was studying me - curious, not intrusive.

He stepped back to give me space. "Since I'll probably be back… I should introduce myself. Elliot Flint."

A weird combination of flattery and embarrassment flooded my cheeks. "Sam."

"Sam," he echoed, pleased. He repeated it like he was saving it somewhere important. Then he checked the time, reluctantly setting his empty mug on the bar. "I've got to run, but-" His eyes caught mine again, and something warm fluttered behind my ribs. "I hope I wasn't too distracting."

I snorted before I could stop myself. Sarcasm = safety. "Not at all. I barely noticed you."

His grin widened like I'd said exactly what he hoped I would. "Good. Then maybe tomorrow… I can try harder."

The door chimed as he left, leaving caffeine and chaos in his wake. And me. Gripping the counter and trying to pretend my pulse wasn't still sprinting.

・・・

I got to work early the next morning. Cringing because I knew it had everything to do with the handsome customer that more-than-hinted at returning, I pushed my way through the back entrance of the shop. Bill and Jessa were unsurprisingly already there baking cinnamon rolls and some sort of puff pastry. They greeted me warmly as I pulled my apron from the hook near the door.

"You guys need any help back here?" I asked as I tied the wrap of my apron.

"Umm…" Jessa looked around assessing where they were in the process. "I don't think so, but you can take these to the front with you," she said as she handed me the first big sheet of finished baked goods.

"You've got it!"

The first of the day passed in a whirlwind. The early morning crowd tended to be regulars with a few random tourists or up-all-night college kids, and the welcome buzz of work kept my mind from being overly preoccupied. I was busy at the back counter pouring latte milk when the front door bell rang and I heard a light trodding of feet stepping up to the counter.

"I'll be with you in just a second," I called over my shoulder, focused on the swirly shape I was making with the foam and not spilling anything over the edge of the mug. I may have been getting better, but I still was not great at latte art, especially if I got distracted.

"No worries; I'm not in a rush."

Elliot.

"Oh, shit," I mutter under my breath as I pour too much milk and cause a mini flood to form around it on the counter. I could hear chuckling behind me, and I fought every urge to flip a middle finger up to the pretentious, cocky, gorgeous man on the other side of the bar.

The shape irreversibly ruined, I took a clean rag to the side of the mug to keep it from dripping and turned to hand it to Andrew Wiley, one of our regulars and a friend of mine. He not-so-subtly looked Elliot up and down, then leaned over the counter as if to tell me a secret.

"Don't worry, if I had that to flirt with, I'd fuck it up too," he laughed under his breath.

I playfully hit at him with the rag, my cheeks suddenly flushed with heat. As he gingerly walked his full coffee mug back to his seat across the cafe, I tucked a stray piece of hair behind my ear and stepped back to the order station to find a very entertained Elliot.

"Good morning, Sam." His smile was devilishly crooked, and something flickered in his eyes, making the already-present heat in my cheeks prickle.

"Good morning, Elliot. What can I get for you?" *Shit. Should have played it cool. There are people who have been here 15 times in a row that you can't remember their name, but his you can. Smooth.*

"Just a light roast drip coffee, please. No room for cream. I think he got plenty for both of us," he teased and cocked his head slightly toward where Andrew had sat across the cafe. Thankfully, Andrew was hidden from Elliot's view by the napkins and condiments, because he was practically salivating over him. "Oh, and one of your delicious-looking pastries."

The word *delicious* rolled slowly and sinfully off his tongue. If it wasn't for my stomach turning at how this stranger was making my heart pound, it might have knocked me off my feet.

Could you be more desperate? You're practically salivating, yourself … but also just look at him… holy fuck.

Words, Reynolds. Use your words. It's been quiet for far too long.

"Uh - wuh… ahem. Which kind?"

His sideways smile arrogantly twitched at the corners, but he shifted his weight back and forth ever so slightly, giving his nerves away. "Whichever you recommend."

"Got it; one drip coffee and one pastry for the man who doesn't know what he wants." Pride swept across my face. I shocked even myself with my quick-witted response.

He propped his hands on the counter and leaned in enough I could nearly feel his breathy laugh. "Oh… I know what I want."

Shit. He wants you.

"I want to know if you picked out this playlist." He winked at me as if he knew exactly what he'd insinuated and nodded toward the speaker playing soft music through the shop.

"Oh, uh, that? Yeah, that was me." I fumbled over my words as I slid him his coffee and a blueberry muffin.

"You always have such good music playing when I stop by."

"Well, to be fair, this is only your second time in," I snarked.

His smile turned shy, a blatant sign that I'd caught him off guard. "I just know good music when I hear it," he said, fighting to recover smoothly. The soft, folky indie music played low through the speakers, but loud enough to echo in the silence that stretched just a hair too long between us. "I must say, Sam, I like your music taste. Any chance you'd be willing to send me your playlist?"

I gulped. *Play it cool. Don't be so damn obvious.*

"Oh, so you just want my playlist?"

He grinned, unbothered. "For now."

For now? Fuck me.

I wasn't quite ready to give this handsome, arrogant stranger my number, so I reached under the counter, pulled out a notepad, and scribbled down the name of the playlist: ***I found these songs in a thrifted cardigan pocket.*** I paused just long enough for him to notice the hesitation, then slid the paper across the counter with a casual smile that I hoped didn't look as strained as it felt.

He picked it up and studied the handwriting like it held the secret to the universe, a smile creeping over his face. "Thanks," he said softly, folding it and slipping it into his shirt pocket. "I'll make sure to listen closely."

The cafe door chimed again, and a group of customers filtered in, pulling my attention away.

"Gotta take the next order," I said, tucking my hair behind my ear again. "But… enjoy the music."

Elliot nodded, "I'm sure I will."

And then, just before he turned to leave, he added, "Maybe next time you can tell me which song reminds you of me."

I nearly choked on my breath. "We'll see if you earn a song, Elliot."

His laugh echoed lightly behind him as he pushed open the door, and I couldn't help the ridiculous smile tugging at the corners of my mouth as I turned to greet the next customer.

Cool, Reynolds. Real cool.

• • •

Try as I might, I couldn't shake the contempt that welled in my gut. All day I felt it pulling at me as if I was on the edge of a cliff and, if I dared to make any sudden movements, a shame spiral waited predatorily to catch me at the bottom. Not only did Elliot practically plaster his interest for me on a billboard, I liked it. I wanted him to want me. Flirty banter I could handle. Maybe. But this… it felt different. And it made me want to puke.

The already lukewarm water dripping from the shower head suddenly ran cold, and I began to shiver.

Maybe this is what you need - a cold shower. Maybe you've never wanted to jump someone's bones more. Whatever. There are bigger problems in the world. Plus, you know nothing about this man. Better yet, he knows nothing about you. What makes you think he'd even want you if he got to know the real you?

Defeated that the cold water did nothing to wash away my growing anxiety, I halfheartedly pushed the handle to turn the shower off. There was no sense in freezing to death if it wouldn't at least make me feel better.

Cooper laid at the edge of the door frame as I wrapped myself in a towel, silently judging me for even concerning myself with something so basic as a man.

"I know, bud. Who even *am* I right now?"

He didn't move, just raised his eyebrows at me with a knowing huff.

I fastened my necklace and ran a brush through my hair, wincing when the bristles snagged on a knot.

Steam still curled around the mirror in thin, ghostly ribbons, blurring my outline like even the glass didn't want to look at me straight on. I rubbed a small circle clear with my palm, then immediately regretted it when my own expression stared back: equal parts anxious and ridiculous.

My reflection looked exhausted - eyes puffy, skin still blotchy from the shower, towel barely hanging on.

Real sexy, Reynolds. Irresistible.

Cooper stretched, toenails clicking against the tile. He yawned so wide his tongue flopped sideways, then he wandered toward the bedroom like he'd decided the night was officially over.

"Must be nice," I muttered, following him out. "No moral crises. No awkward flirting. Just kibble and naps."

He glanced over his shoulder as if to say, *sounds wonderful, doesn't it?*

The air outside the bathroom felt cooler, soft cotton brushing against damp skin as I tugged on a pair of oversized sleep shorts and an old guitar shop t-shirt I'd picked up at the thrift store years ago. My body moved through the motions automatically - moisturizer, meds, water bottle filled and set on the night stand, deadbolt checked for the third time of the night - while my brain kept replaying the day like a blooper reel.

Elliot laughing.

Elliot leaning on the counter.

Elliot's hand brushing mine when he reached for his coffee cup.

I sat on the edge of the bed, towel-dried hair dripping down my back, and groaned into my hands. "You *cannot* have a crush. We don't do crushes."

Cooper thumped his tail once from his spot on the floor but didn't lift his head.

"I'm serious," I told him. "We do not have the emotional capacity for a man with tailored shirts and a tragic jawline."

He sneezed, which I decided to interpret as agreement.

I pulled back the comforter and slid beneath it, the sheets cool against my skin. I shivered again. The quiet of the house pressed close: the low hum of the fridge down the hall, a branch scraping lightly against the siding outside, the rhythmic sigh of Cooper settling beside the bed.

For a second, I imagined what it would feel like if someone else were here - someone who didn't make me second-guess every inch of my existence. Then the thought of Elliot *specifically* crept in, uninvited and insistent.

His laugh again. The way he'd said my name so carefully, like it meant something.

My stomach fluttered, traitorous.

"Nope," I whispered to the ceiling. "Not tonight."

I rolled onto my side, facing Cooper. He blinked at me sleepily, tail giving one last lazy thump.

"Promise you'll stop me if I start doing something stupid?"

Another huff. A dog's version of *obviously*.

I reached down, fingers brushing his fur. "You're a good man, Coop."

I flicked off the lamp with a soft click, leaving the room in a wash of moonlight and shadows. For the first time all day, the world felt quiet. Still busy inside my head, sure, but quiet enough that maybe, just maybe, I'd be able to sleep before the overthinking started again.

• • •

Elliot sat perched on a seat at the end of the bar, his entertainment of watching me work made obvious by the stupidly handsome smile on his face.

The man at the register had just ordered an iced espresso with almond milk, three pumps of lavender, and a side of whipped cream in a separate cup.

I watched him walk out the door, double fisting his miniature cup of whipped cream. My face held the kind of expression usually reserved for horror movies. "Tell me you heard that," I said, not bothering to hide my dismay.

Elliot leaned an elbow on the counter, amusement plastered on his face. "He said it like it was normal."

"I swear, it's like they're calling numbers from behind the register." I grabbed the sharpie and started scribbling on the notepad. "Triple espresso, almond milk, side of whipped cream... yep. Bingo."

He perked up. "Wait, you actually play?"

"Not officially," I shrugged. "But mentally? Constantly."

Elliot laughed, eyes gleaming. "Can I play?"

"You're already winning, Lavender syrup and an existential crisis in one breath? That's a double square."

"Alright, well, what else is on the board?"

I tapped the sharpie against the paper, remembering the worst of the worst. "Guy who asks if we sell matcha then orders a Coke. Woman who insists her latte be extra wet. Teenagers filming TikToks near the napkin dispenser. Oh, and the guy who flirts aggressively while ordering drip coffee."

He raised an eyebrow. "Aggressively?"

"You know. Leans over the counter like he thinks he's The Bachelor or something."

Elliot leaned forward - just slightly, but enough. "Like this?"

I couldn't help the laugh that escaped my mouth. I held my hands up feigning defeat. "Okay, yep, you win."

He crossed his arms, a little too satisfied at himself. "I usually do."

• • •

The park hit me like a gut punch of noise and motion.

Booths crowded the walkway, every one of them screaming for attention with neon poster boards and volunteers with the lung capacity of cheerleaders on espresso.

The smell of kettle corn mixed with grilled onions and sunscreen, sharp and syrupy and too much all at once.

Music blared from the amphitheater - something aggressively upbeat - but even that couldn't drown out the chaos: kids shrieking, adults yelling over each other, strollers bumping ankles, gravel crunching under a hundred impatient feet.

Colors and sounds layered and twisted, leaving me blinking against the bright overwhelm as the world surged too close, too loud, too fast.

I shouldn't have come.

But Jessa had been excited about the fundraiser for weeks, and she made it sound like there'd be a quiet coffee tent tucked into a corner somewhere. She even promised a therapy dog or two. This wasn't what I thought she meant.

I stuck close to the perimeter, trying not to make eye contact with anyone holding a clipboard or wearing a matching t-shirt.

"Sam?"

I turned toward the sound of my name and froze.

Elliot stood behind a booth labeled Healing Hands - Family Support Network. A small boy clung to his leg, clearly mid-tantrum, red-faced and teary-eyed. The woman beside them, likely the child's mom, looked like she was on the verge of crying, herself.

"I'll keep him here for a sec," Elliot said to her, his voice low and even. "Go grab some water. Breathe. You're doing a great job."

The woman hesitated, grateful and overwhelmed, then nodded and disappeared toward a concessions tent.

Elliot crouched to the boy's level and pulled something out of his back pocket: a mini tube of bubbles.

"Want to help me make the biggest bubble in the whole park?" He asked.

The kid sniffled and nodded.

He dipped the wand in the tiny bottle and blew a slow, steady stream of bubbles into the air. The boy watched them float, wide-eyed, then reached to pop them with chubby fingers.

There was something about watching him in that moment - knees in the dirt, hair a mess, laughter catching in his throat - that made my lungs feel too small.

Elliot looked up and spotted me again. A smile spread across his face.

"Hey," he said, standing to brush grass off his jeans. "I didn't expect to see you here."

"I didn't either. I mean… Jessa dragged me out." I nodded at the booth. "Looks like you've got your hands full."

He shrugged, glancing down at the boy who was now blowing his own bubbles with furious concentration. "We all need someone to step in sometimes."

Something about the way he said it made my chest ache.

"Do you volunteer at these a lot?" I asked, toeing the gravel with my shoe.

"When I can," he said. "Events like this are pretty close to my whole family's heart."

There it was again. That softness. That pull.

"I should probably find Jessa," I said, suddenly too aware of the way I was staring at him.

He nodded. "If you want to help with the raffle, I'm pretty sure we're accepting bribes."

I gave a short, uncomfortable laugh. "That right?"

He grinned. "You'd be surprised what a well-placed cinnamon roll can do."

I smiled despite myself.

There was a brief lull in our conversation. Not awkward. Just quiet. Like we didn't need to fill the space with unnecessary pleasantries, we were just content being there together.

I glanced around and noticed Jessa talking to a woman she'd just met as if she'd known her all her life. Probably telling some riveting story about pastries. I smiled at her, and she waved me over. I glanced back at Elliot, whose gaze had followed mine.

"See you around, Sam," he practically hummed, his voice low and steady.

"Yeah," I said. "See you."

But as I walked away, I turned back once. He was crouched again, the boy now perched on his knee, pointing to a bubble floating skyward like it held all the answers.

...

"I think Jessa's apple cinnamon buns were the star of the show," I heard from behind me as I loaded the coffee carafe onto our push cart.

I glanced over just in time to see Elliot collapse a folding table like it was made of cardboard. *Show off.* I drew in a breath, trying to find an ounce of social battery left to accommodate someone who had only ever been exceedingly nice to me.

"Yeah," I said. "They kept people focused on the pastries instead of how bad I am at making conversation."

He gave me a sideways smile. "So, if I want to get on your good side, I should bring baked goods?"

"Sure." I stacked cups a little too neatly. "Flattery, too. Bribes are my love language."

His laugh was soft, like he wasn't trying to draw attention, just share a moment with me. "Good to know."

We worked in silence for a bit. Most of the crowd had already cleared out. Less noise. Less chaos. My brain should have relaxed. But somehow the quiet made everything feel sharper. Like Elliot could hear every nervous thought rattling around in my skull.

"You did great today," he said after a moment, wiping down the table. "Way better than most."

I snorted. "I handed out caffeine. Barely heroic."

"Don't undersell it." He stepped closer to grab a trash bag, tone dipping lower. "Being around this many people? Some folks have no idea how hard that *actually* is."

My hands stilled on the cups.

"You say that like you've studied me or something," I muttered.

He lifted a shoulder like it wasn't a big deal. "Or maybe I just pay attention."

No one pays attention. Not like that.

I cleared my throat, grabbing a stack of napkins like they were a shield. "Fun day?" I deflected.

"Well…" He gave me a knowing look. "*I* had a good time. I saw you mentally plotting about seventeen escape routes."

"That obvious?"

"To me? Yeah." His smile softened. "But you stayed. That matters."

My deflection gears jammed. "The buns were good," I said weakly.

"And the company?" he asked, eyes warm.

A loud clang from the metal cart made me jump, and I fumbled a box. Elliot caught it as it hit the ground - steady hands, just barely not quick enough. He held it a moment longer than necessary, grounding us both.

"You okay?" He asked quietly.

I hated how relief punched through me. "Yeah. Just… overstimulated. It's a hazard."

"Of being alive?" He said, echoing my joke from days ago.

The huff of laughter that escaped me wasn't graceful, but real. "Exactly."

Curiosity lingered in his voice when he asked, "Is it the noise? Or the eyes? People calling your name?"

My fingers brushed the edge of my nametag then found my necklace to twist around my fingers. Tightness squeezed my ribs.

"It's… all of the above." I forced a shrug. "Just feels like too many strings pulling at once, all in different directions."

He nodded, serious now. "For what it's worth, you hid it well."

"Trust me, I know I didn't."

"I wasn't looking for perfect," he said. "I *was* looking, though."

The breath I pulled in was too sharp. Too full. I didn't know how to respond to someone seeing me - really seeing me - without demanding the pieces I kept locked away.

So, of course, sarcasm leapt to the rescue. "You're very observant for a guy obsessed with pastries and drip coffee."

"What can I say?" He grinned again, light returning to his face. "I have layers. Like a cinnamon bun."

"Oh my god," I groaned, unable to stop the smile tugging at my lips. "That was terrible."

"But it made you smile," he pointed out, victory sparkling in his eyes.

We kept packing up - slower now, deliberate - like neither of us wanted the moment to end.

He dusted off his hands as we finally finished. "I'll be at the next fundraiser. Obviously."

"Obviously? Don't take this the wrong way, but you're kind of the last person I'd expect to see at something like this."

He feigned shock and offense while a knowing grin crept over his face. "I'll have you know, I have more depth than you give me credit for. And anyway," he reached the end of the sentence a little too casually, "I hope I see you there."

I met his gaze. The hope sitting behind it was too much… and exactly what I didn't know I wanted.

"Maybe." It was all I could say. I didn't really mean *maybe*. I knew, and he knew, that I'd be there.

...

I slouched on my couch with my computer in my lap and a second glass of wine on the coffee table. Cooper snoozed next to me, flopped over on his back like he'd been run over with a truck made of pure exhaustion.

I pulled up my notes app - where I kept everything from my deepest darkest secrets to a list of future dog names to my grocery list to even my favorite overheard quotes at the cafe - and started a new entry titled **Not Saving This One.**

I typed:

> *I don't know why I'm even typing this. Maybe because today knocked something loose in me. The fundraiser was… fine. Better than fine, actually. It was loud and chaotic and full of people who didn't look at me like I was made of glass.*
>
> *But I met a guy recently… Elliot. He came into the shop a few days ago and has been coming in flirting every day since. I know, I know, what am I doing? But he was there (unexpectedly, I might say). And it felt… idk, safe? No, that's too big a word. Comfortable? But maybe that's worse.*
>
> *I'm not used to someone looking at me like a person instead of a problem. Not like this. He kept checking in without hovering. Asking without prying. It was… nice. Which is dangerous. I hate that something in my chest warmed when he laughed at something I said.*
>
> *Anyway, I should stop before this gets pathetic.*
>
> *Deleting soon.*

I took a sip of wine and stared at the screen like it might reach out and strangle me. Part of me - the embarrassed, completely cringing part - hoped it would. I'd never written about a boy before. Never even considered the possibility that one might look my way. But Elliot had.

I let my head fall back against the couch, staring at the ceiling.

He looked at me like I wasn't broken. Like I wasn't something to tiptoe around. No one has ever done that.

I should've deleted the note. Fuck, I know I should have. But instead I closed it gently, letting it linger in my history like it's something important.

Then I finished my wine and pretended I didn't do exactly what I swore I'd never let myself do:

Care.

· · ·

The door chimed, and my head jerked up, hopeful. Not him. Again.

Elliot hadn't been in the day before, and with ten minutes left until close, it didn't look like today would be any different.

I wiped down the counter for a second time, slower than necessary. The playlist was set to low, something moody and mellow, and it filled the quiet with a kind of loneliness I hadn't braced for.

"Expecting someone?" Andrew called from a few tables away, raising an eyebrow like he already knew the answer.

I tried to sound unbothered. "No."

"Sure." He grinned and placed his coffee mug in the return bin. "Maybe he's allergic to consistency."

"Or maybe he's just busy," I said, a little too quickly.

Andrew didn't press.

I glanced at the door again as the bell jingled. A woman with two kids walked in and asked if we were still open. I smiled, nodded, and made their hot chocolates with shaky precision. It was something to do with my hands. Something to fill the space that his absence had left.

Andrew gave a friendly wave and sauntered out the door. The woman and her kids followed shortly behind. The silence returned.

6:59.

I reached for the open sign, flipped it to *closed*, and locked the door.

He wasn't coming.

I sank back against the counter, arms folded, trying not to let it mean more than it did. Maybe he just got caught up. Maybe I was reading too far into nothing.

Still, my chest ached with something unnamed.

I didn't want to want him here.

But I did.

• • •

You had to know it was too good to be true.

I pulled my jacket tighter around me, hoping that if I pulled it tight enough I'd just disappear into the fabric and it'd swallow me whole. It wasn't even cold out, but my body shook slightly more with each step of my walk home.

How could I have gotten my hopes up so high?

After four days straight of Elliot stopping by for coffee and running into him at the fundraiser, his visits stopped as suddenly as they started. It had been another three days since I'd seen him. I may not have known how to respond to him being interested, but I knew as soon as it ended that maybe I didn't really want it to. And that freaked me the hell out.

It's for the best. You know it. The fewer people to see how much of a shit show your life is, the better. If you just - FUCK.

I stumbled over a crack in the sidewalk and caught myself on my hands and knees.

At least you didn't faceplant.

I stood, dusting the grit from my hands and tears taunting to well up in my eyes. I was right. My life was a shit show. And whatever Elliot had made me feel… I wanted no part in it.

Liar.

Elliot

I couldn't be more glad to have stumbled into that little corner coffee shop that random Tuesday morning.

I was running late. I remember that. Had a meeting I didn't want to go to, my head already crowded with things I needed to say and tasks I needed to accomplish. I ducked inside for a caffeine bribe, expecting nothing more than burnt espresso and a few minutes of warmth before the day swallowed me whole.

And then there she was.

Behind the counter, pouring someone's coffee as if the act required quiet devotion. Measuring the cream like it mattered. Stirring gently, as though the cup might bruise if she wasn't careful. Something about her was just... special. Not loud or showy - more like a whisper I almost missed.

Maybe it was the way her golden-brown hair fell forward when she bent to grab a lid, catching light from the front windows. Or the way she tucked it behind her ear with the smallest flick of her fingers, like she'd done it a thousand times and still didn't know anyone might be watching.

Maybe it was her eyes. God - those eyes. Not sad, exactly, but carrying something heavy behind them. The kind of weight you don't talk about unless someone earns it. I remember wondering what put that shadow there. I didn't know it yet that some shadows don't have a single source. They're built piece by piece. I also remember feeling the urge to, whatever it took, be someone who earned the privilege of unburdening some of that heaviness.

She whirled around, startled. Met my gaze, warm and guarded. Curious. Like she was trying to figure out where I might fit in her life, and if she wanted me to at all.

"I am... terribly sorry! Can I help you?"

Coffee. That was the obvious answer. But it felt ridiculous saying something so small when the moment felt bigger.

I ordered just a light roast drip coffee, my mind becoming void of anything other than the sound of her voice. I watched the way she moved. Precise. Quiet. Almost graceful but a little clumsy at the same time.

There was something about her posture. Shoulders slightly drawn in, not from shyness but from habit. Like she was used to holding herself together. Like she'd learned the world didn't always handle certain hearts gently.

And I remember thinking - I don't want to be another thing she braces against.

Funny how life can reroute itself in a single glance, a single smile, a single girl behind a counter pretending she isn't carrying the weight of a world she never asked for.

I didn't know her then. Not really.

But I knew enough to understand this: Something in me shifted in that little corner coffee shop, and it hasn't shifted back since.

SAM

Elliot was already there when I arrived the next morning. At the sight of him, my stomach immediately filled with butterflies raging and swarming at the coffee I'd been sipping on from home. My anger at him for skipping his cafe routine for a few mornings was completely unjustified. I knew that. I was pissed anyway.

He slouched back in an armchair across from the dark brick of the bar. He seemed perfectly content sipping his coffee, scrolling through something on his tablet, and occasionally - intentionally - glancing up to catch my eye. He was obviously making it a point to linger around for a bit. He was a (mostly) unwelcome distraction that I tried to block from my mind. The steady flow of weekday customers helped; feeling his eyes on me as I worked… didn't.

"We've got the next batch!"

I motioned for the woman stepping up to the counter to give me a moment, then slipped through the door to grab the fresh pastries Bill and Jessa had just finished making.

"Thanks, Sam," a breathless Bill offered as he attempted to keep up with Jessa's flurry of activity. "Justin should be here soon!"

As I came back to the front, the woman at the counter impatiently tapping her nails against her jeans seemed to soften at the sight of warm pastries. My eyes focused behind her to realize Elliot's chair had been vacated, his empty mug sitting on the side table. I sighed lightly, wanting to convince myself it was out of relief rather than disappointment.

After taking the now-more-patient woman's order, her rush to get out of there slowing with each bite of the freshly-baked cinnamon roll, I went to clean the space around the armchair.

"Do you have a moment for a quick break?"

Elliot's hushed, husky voice suddenly brushing across the back of my neck scared the hell out of me. I spun to find him now awkwardly close to my face. My pounding heart rattled my chest and echoed loudly in my ears.

"Um…" I stepped around him, the act of putting his dishes away a welcome excuse to put some distance between us. "I guess?"

I waved through the service window to Justin, my coworker who was a couple of years younger than me and a little pretentious.

"Another coworker just walked in the back door, so he can probably cover the front for a few minutes…" I turned back to Elliot, now feeling more secure with the counter between us. "Is something wrong?"

"Nothing at all."

I scrunched my eyebrows upward in confusion. "Uh-okay… I need to let them know I'm stepping away from the front."

"Of course," he smiled, his ego beaming at getting his way.

• • •

Heat crawled over my skin where Elliot had his hand placed softly over the curve of my back to usher me outside. Not touching, just hovering near. I sincerely hoped he couldn't feel the nerves radiating off of me. My pulse quickened. I felt the sudden urge to have my head on a swivel, watching for danger when it very easily could have been right next to me. I didn't *think* Elliot was dangerous. But how could I be sure?

He led me to the park across the street, my feet feeling like cinder blocks as my dread grew with every step. I was damn near ready to bolt when we finally came to a stop at a bench just out of sight of the cafe. He took a seat and peered expectantly up at me above a cocky grin.

My left hand began to shake as I slowly sank down next to him. Content with my compliance, he smiled a little more fully and turned his gaze forward, eyes focusing on nothing. Silence hung thickly in the air between us. Elliot seemed to lose himself in deep thought as I quietly waited, watching for any hint of what conversation was about to follow, but his face gave nothing away.

"Um, I only have a short amount of time…" My voice trailed off, suffocated by the discomfort of breaking the dead air.

"Tell me about yourself, Sam." His eyes remained forward with unwavering resistance to offer any kind of suggestion to where this conversation was heading.

I gaped, unsure at first that I had heard him correctly. My right hand clenched my left tightly in my lap in a futile effort to keep the shaking at a minimum. After a few seconds to process what he had said, the best I could come up with was, "Huh?"

He turned toward me so suddenly that I winced, instinctively squeezing my eyes closed and drawing a quick breath. I fought with every ounce of mental strength I had to steady myself and willed my eyes to open. His intensity had faded slightly. His eyes were softer, concerned, but his continued silence urged me to speak.

"Um… I have a dog… I, uh - I like to read…" I squirmed uncomfortably under his stare. "I'm very confused as to why I'm sitting here right now telling you about myself…"

He returned to his forward-facing contemplation, and my eyes immediately shot away. I bit at the inside of my lip waiting for further explanation.

It's not that far back to the shop - you could always run and take cover behind the counter.

Elliot sighed heavily. "I haven't been by to see you the last couple of days…"

"Yeah, well, buying coffee every morning can get expensive-"

"I haven't been by," he continued quickly, "because I had a last-minute business trip I had to take."

Surely he has a point, right?

"I've been… distracted isn't the right word. Or maybe it is. But I've barely gotten anything done for the last week and a half."

"Elliot, I'm sorry, but I have no idea what this has to do with *me*."

"Don't you get it?" His voice was barely audible, and I struggled to hear him over the passing cars and distant chatter of commuters. "You are the *only* thing I can think about."

He turned back to look at me, but I kept my eyes fixed on my still-shaking hands. Heat rushed to my cheeks and even prickled at my ears. I could only hope I didn't look as ridiculous as I felt.

"Oh…"

"I spent all week thinking about how I wanted to rush back to the cafe and watch you work all day. How I should have just never left in the first place until you threw me out to lock up, all just to come back and do it again the next day. I've been distracted because my mind is… *consumed* with thoughts of you." He was a little louder, more confident. "Look at me, Sam."

I took a deep breath and glanced up at him from under my eyelashes. His powerful stare had almost completely melted away, leaving only sincerity and what you could *almost* mistake for humility in its place. I felt a second wave of warmth flush my cheeks, and my eyes immediately strayed from his again.

"Your eyes are beautiful. Which of your parents do I get to thank for that?"

I stiffened, my teeth immediately clenching into an uncomfortable vice, and my hand trembled more violently. It must have been blatantly obvious, because Elliot reached out to lay a soft, reassuring hand onto mine. It was all I could do not to rudely pull away.

"Neither," I snipped tightly. "I'd... rather not talk about my family."

"I apologize... I didn't know that it was a touchy subject. Sam, look at me. Please?" His other hand ran through his hair, the first real sign of nerves I had seen. It was oddly comforting.

"Sorry," I mumbled, finally getting up enough nerve to glance up again. "I didn't mean to be a bitch."

His mouth pressed into a thin line, his jaw tightening. "You weren't at all."

"I was." I frowned at his pith. "Listen, Elliot. Maybe I like you a little more than I should. But I push people away, and it's for the best. My life is a train wreck, and to ask anyone else to hop on board would be... brutal."

He lightly squeezed my tangled, shaking hands. "You didn't ask me to hop on board. I'm stowing away." I rolled my eyes. It was sweet, albeit cringey, especially since he was ignorant to the weight of what he was saying. "Do dinner with me tonight."

It wasn't a question, but his eyes looked hopeful awaiting my response.

"I don't know, Elliot..."

"What don't you know?"

"A damn thing about you!" I almost smirked at my snarky response, and he sideways-grinned back at me acknowledging that I was doing a shitty job of hiding it.

"Well, that's what dinner is for."

Sam

I pulled at the edges of my dress, entirely uncomfortable with how it clung to me. The bronze slip dress moved like liquid over my body. Lace traced the edges of the bodice and floated over a scar on my upper chest. The dress was elegant in a way that doesn't need to try, but *damn* did I feel like I was trying anyway.

Captious hazel eyes lingered over every scar and insecurity in sight of the mirror in the staff bathroom of the cafe. I sighed deeply and bit back tears. I was terrified. Dating wasn't really my thing, I honestly hadn't even been interested in it, and this was exactly why. Pre-date jitters felt like the onset of a meltdown, and that wasn't a sensation I particularly enjoyed.

"That gorgeous boy who comes in flirting with you every day? Yes ma'am!" Jessa had practically squealed when I told her I was going to dinner with Elliot. "You look great! Have so much fun, and be prepared to tell me all about it tomorrow."

Bill, on the other hand, had been less-than-enthused.

Whether or not telling them about the date had been wise, the only alternative I could see was allowing this stranger to pick me up at my home, and there was no way in hell that was happening.

It shouldn't feel this scary, should it? Maybe you should just cancel. Tell him you're not feeling well. Better yet, tell him you had a 'last minute business trip.'

"He's here!" Jessa all but shoved me toward the door, kissing my cheek somewhere along the way and combing my hair back into place.

"Please be safe…" Bill hovered toward the back of the mostly dark cafe.

I'll do my best.

I tried to gulp down the lump in my throat, but it hung nauseatingly in place. Useless deep breaths did nothing to lower my heart rate as I reached out with a clammy hand to grip the cold door handle and used all the effort I had to pull it open.

I stepped out into the chilly night and immediately regretted not wearing a jacket. A shiver of cold and nerves ran through me and nearly shook me out of my low heels.

"You look… lovely," Elliot mused, opening the door of his overly expensive car.

A 'thank you' got caught in the middle of my chest, and the car door was closed behind me before I could muster up enough air to force it out. He rounded the front of the car, walking with enviable ease.

Breathe, Reynolds. Relax at least a little bit, for fuck's sake. In… two… three… out… two… three.

"Thanks," I finally said as he buckled himself in. "You look nice, yourself."

Elliot pulled the car onto a quiet street, the kind lined with restaurants too exclusive to advertise. I focused on the passing buildings, fingers tangled together in my lap.

"What are you thinking about?" He asked softly.

"Nothing just… I don't do this a lot." *Or ever.*

He glanced over with a crooked smile. "Me neither, honestly."

That felt like a lie, but not the kind that hurt. The kind that meant to make someone feel better.

The car eased to a stop outside a sleek black building with no signage, just golden lights outlining tall windows and the sound of laughter trickling out from somewhere above.

"This is it," he said, stepping out before I could react. He opened my door before I even reached for the handle.

A gentleman. Of course.

I stepped out carefully, suddenly hyper-aware of every inch of exposed skin and the way my dress crept too tightly around my ribs. His hand hovered near the small of my back - again not quite touching just… there.

Elliot confidently led me into a rooftop bar I had never heard of and certainly didn't belong in. My cheap heels echoed against the patterned tile floor that was so pristinely clean our reflections joined each step in unison. People scattered throughout the warm, dimly lit restaurant spoke in hushed conversation over expensive drinks and soft background music.

"Ah, Mister Flint! Wonderful to see you," the maître d greeted Elliot as he would an old friend; he extended a handshake across his body with one hand and gripped his upper arm with the other.

"Christopher! Let me introduce you to Sam Reynolds. She'll be joining me this evening."

Reynolds… you haven't told him your last name. What the actual fuck?

"Lovely to meet you, Ms. Reynolds." A hearty smile pushed wrinkles into his leathery skin as my head spun. His eyes danced with the light of the nearby fireplace.

I gulped. "Thank you… Christopher, was it?"

Did he do research on you? What else does he know?

My hand nervously found my necklace as we waded through the patrons to a quiet table in the corner lit with a candle.

As we were seated, my eyes shot accusatory glances at Elliot. "How the hell did you know my last name, Flint?"

He grinned proudly, unphased by my suspicion. "Sam, you gave me your Spotify playlist. Your name is on it."

See? Nothing serious. Calm the fuck down.

I blinked, and then felt my shoulders relax - only slightly. Right. I'd been careful not to give too much personal information, but I hadn't thought about the username. I guess I figured no one actually paid attention to that sort of thing.

Still… "Creepy," I muttered, even though my lips twitched at the corners.

"Resourceful," he corrected, unfolding his napkin like he belonged in this world of soft lighting and crystal glassware. "Besides, it's not like I ran a background check. *Yet.*"

He winked. I laughed - nervously, sure, but it counted.

Menus glowed pale gold beneath the candles, casting light straight into my insecurities. No prices. Just a pretentious brick of French words and vineyard names that looked like spells from a book of witchcraft.

The waiter appeared with a grin sharp enough to cut me in half. "What can I get started for you?"

Panic. All the Pinot Noirs sounded like endangered birds.

I half-mumbled something about a glass of *Bourgogne*, tongue tied and tripping over the syllables while Elliot charmed the server like they'd gone to school together. He didn't even glance at the menu.

"I'll take the Blanton's gold single barrel, on the rocks," he said, smooth and certain like he ordered top-shelf bourbon before breakfast. "And thank you."

Of course he had a go-to bourbon that probably cost more than my utility bill and a way of saying "thank you" that made it sound like a privilege to serve him.

God, he's smooth. Not in a greasy, overdone way. Just… comfortable. Like he was used to taking up space. Used to being welcomed. And I - well, I was used to scanning rooms for exits.

My palms were sweating and I had to fight the urge to wipe them on my dress. Elliot turned that devastatingly charming smile on me, and I clutched the menu like a floatation device. Clinks of glassware and laughter somewhere behind me stirred my mind into a tizzy.

You don't belong here. With him. In this place.

• • •

Dinner conversations and a little liquid courage worked wonders on my frazzled nerves. The room was still too fancy, but my shoulders weren't living up around my ears anymore.

Thankfully, my family was a conversational landmine we'd carefully avoided. Instead, we debated truly critical topics like which book genre was superior.

"It's obviously mystery," I argued, gesturing with my fork. "You get to solve a puzzle. You get to feel smart. There's a dead body sometimes… It's thrilling."

He arched a brow. "And what does romance give you?"

"A false sense of hope and unrealistic expectations," I answered without missing a beat. "Hard pass."

Elliot grinned as though I'd just issued him a personal challenge. It made my stupid heart turn cartwheels in my chest.

We drifted into talking about work next - safer territory, I hoped.

"So, you really like working at the coffee shop?" he asked.

"I mostly like Bill and Jessa. They…" I hesitated, considering hard whether or not this was something I wanted to open up about. "They practically saved me."

He didn't say anything, just made this face that was a mix of understanding and curiosity.

"I didn't have any work experience and had just gotten my GED. I was broke as shit and needed something… stable. They were that for me. They're honestly that for a lot of kids. Now they're practically all I have…" I trailed off, realizing I was sharing too much. "Plus, I like the routine. And the caffeine doesn't hurt. Anyway, 'barista' sounds cooler than 'anxious girl who hides behind the espresso machine.'"

He laughed, but his eyes warmed with something akin to affection. "You're underselling yourself again."

"And you're *over*selling your corporation," I countered, pointing at him. "We can't both be wrong."

His smile tilted, boyish and smug. "I'm actually not bragging. Well - mostly not bragging."

He took a sip of his - expensive - bourbon then leaned forward, elbows brushing the linen tablecloth.

"The truth is," he continued. "I started the company because no one else would take a chance on me."

That surprised me. He always carried himself like the world opened doors for him just because he existed.

"I was twenty-two," he said. "Wanted investors. They all laughed in my face. Told me I was too young, too ambitious, too wild, too stupid." A pause. "So I built it anyway."

The soft thing beneath the confidence showed itself - a glimpse he probably didn't give to many people. Vulnerability flickered before he tucked it away again. There was something soothing about seeing the seams in his perfection.

"And what *exactly* is it you do?" My eyes narrowed, half expecting some unethical bombshell to totally make me cringe.

"We're a tech startup that works with nonprofits and community orgs for event management and ticketing. Plan fundraisers, register volunteers, manage donations… that kind of thing."

My eyes softened. I wanted to ask more questions, but it all felt a little out of my depth and a touch personal. I let the moment linger a bit before sarcasm stepped in and brought back the levity.

"And now you're a millionaire with a fancy bourbon habit."

"Allegedly," he agreed. "And the bourbon habit is fully justified."

He motioned to the waiter, who refilled our drinks like we were royalty. It made me hyperaware of the fact that I didn't belong in places where wine came without prices.

"So," he said, shifting gears. "If you weren't a barista-slash-superhero, what would you be doing?"

Superhero? God he is sweetly delusional.

"I…" The truth lodged like a rock in my chest. Maybe *before* I would have had dreams, but those dreams were buried deep under too much earth to dig up now. "…don't really think about that."

He didn't press. Thank God. Instead, he nodded like honoring a boundary.

"Well, if you ever remember your answer, I'd love to hear it."

Heat rushed up my neck. I stared very hard at my plate.

He changed the subject, gracefully. We talked about his childhood dog, his favorite late-night diners, the terrible haircut he once got because his friend Caleb dared him. I laughed more than I had in a long time, even if part of me still hovered outside my own body, waiting for the sky to fall.

Then the waiter brought dessert menus.

No prices again. Because of course not.

My pulse quickened. My breathing followed. Nerves crept back up my spine like unwelcome vines.

"Hey," Elliot said, eyes catching mine instantly. "Do you want to step outside, take in the view?" He sipped on the last of his whiskey waiting for my answer.

"That sounds really nice, actually."

He smiled as he stood, extending his hand for me to take. Accepting his offer, I noticed his eyes linger on the scar between my knuckles. He hesitated for a brief moment, his smile wavering ever so slightly, then dropped our grasp next to his side to lead me out onto the terrace.

See, he's actively trying not to bring something up to hurt you. Maybe give the guy a chance. I mean, just look at him. My god, he looks incredible-

"Enjoying the view, Reynolds?" Elliot turned to lean casually against the railing, probably needing to lessen the weight of his ego.

I felt blood rush to my cheeks as my eyes darted away to finally focus on the other view in front of me. "Oh… wow."

From inside, the view appeared to be some odd version of a painting - full of life, beautiful, but incredibly distant. From the balcony, a whole new perspective drew me in as the city came alive below us. It was the man riding his bike in and out of the streetlight glow. It was the dozens of shimmering windows of people living completely different lives. It was the way the steel and glass mimicked a starry night sky when all you could see were dark gray clouds and a hint of the moon above us.

I dropped his hand to grab the banister to the left of him as if it would somehow help me experience it all even more fully. The bustling nightlife, the hum of traffic, the cool breeze sending goosebumps to the surface of my skin, it was just…

"Breathtaking, isn't it?"

"Elliot, this is… so special." I looked up at him, somewhat reluctant to let my eyes abandon the view in front of me.

His eyes drifted across my face, obviously entertained at watching me take in the scenery. A soft smile played at the edges of his lips. "You're simply stunning."

I felt an instinctive pull toward him, like *almost* everything in me wanted to lean in and kiss him. It scared the shit out of me. As safe as I felt in that moment, I knew it wouldn't last. Nothing good ever did. I shivered just slightly, the cool air combining forces with my stirring anxiety, and I quickly averted my gaze away from him.

"Are you cold?" He stood behind me and began softly rubbing his hands up and down my arms. His touch only intensified both my fear and my urge to just say *fuck it* and kiss him then and there.

My breath wavered as I turned toward him, still unsure of what I was going to do. His hands drifted from my arms to the rail behind me, sending panic and my heart rate skyrocketing.

The terrace suddenly felt small and completely empty of oxygen, claustrophobic with the presence of my spiraling thoughts.

I felt all the blood drain out of my head and pool in my feet.

I spun quickly, nearly knocking myself over, gripped the cold metal tightly, and prayed it would be enough to keep me grounded.

Heat rushed over me.

Every muscle in my body stiffened.

My eyes clenched tightly shut.

A hollow ringing sound attempted to drown out the memories threatening to cloud reality.

It's not the same.

"Sam…"

"Hm?" *Breathe.*

"What's wrong? Are you alright?"

So many emotions swirled within me that I could barely keep my feet under me, let alone put words to what I was feeling. I pried my eyelids open to find that my knuckles had gone white with my grip. Elliot's hands were no longer trapping me where I stood, just my legs that began to tremble under the weight of trauma. I struggled to steady my thoughts enough to form coherent words. Silence spurred my shame.

"I'm fine… I'm sorry." I couldn't bring myself to face him.

He paused, attempting to carefully navigate the obviously fragile situation. "Please… please don't apologize."

"I can go…"

"I don't want you to *leave*, Sam. *Of course* I don't want you to leave. I'm sorry if I've made you uncomfortable-"

"No." I braved myself with a slow inhale and turned to look at him again so he could see the truth of my words. "This had nothing to do with you."

His brow furrowed. "You don't have to explain. I just… will you answer one question for me? Please?"

I nodded hesitantly, unsure as to whether I could actually give him the answer he needed. He gently reached his hand toward me, a gesture he wanted to be sure I knew I could refuse. Before even thinking about it, I placed my still-shaking, scarred hand in his.

"Is someone hurting you?"

 SAM

No. Please, not again.

I clambered backward into the corner and clenched my teeth together, steeling myself for the blow to my head. Tears and sweat soaked my cheeks. Sinking as close as I could to the baseboards, I attempted to shield my face with my arms. It was pointless.

His fingers knotted their way into my hair and tugged me upward against the wall.

"Please…"

A menacing grin spread across his face, his eyes hollow and soulless. "Shut up, you little fucking bitch."

He dropped my hair suddenly as if it burned him, my body crumpling to the floor. He loomed over me. My *protector.* My *provider.*

Fingers digging deep into the muscles that no longer even fought to wrestle free, he pinned my shoulders to the ground. Blood oozed from tiny punctures forming under his fingernails. Air rushed from my lungs as he straddled my chest, effectively suffocating my small body under his weight.

Fucking kill me. Do it. End this for good.

"It'll never be over," he sneered with bitter, gin-soaked breath over my face, peering into my thoughts.

No.

I screamed out, but the crushing pressure on top of me refused to let any oxygen back in. I willed my body to give out.

Suddenly… warmth? A comforting sensation as he faded into the shadows.

"Sam? Sweetie?"

I lurched forward, gasping for the breath I so desperately needed. Confusion clouded my thoughts and vision as I scanned the room. Jessa sat calm and concerned on the edge of my bed. Cooper sat whimpering on the floor peering at me from over the pile of covers. Tears flowed freely - a rush of sorrow, relief, guilt…

"Sweetheart… are you alright?"

I shake my head, heavy breaths still working to convince my lungs that they, in fact, had all the oxygen they needed. Refraining from reaching out at the possibility of triggering something else, Jessa offered her arms open next to her. I scooted closer and sobbed into her lap. Screams threatened at my throat if I dared try to offer any kind of explanation. Thankfully, she didn't need one. Not then, anyway.

"Shhhh… you're okay. You're safe," Jessa's frazzled nerves toyed with her soothing voice as she stroked my sweat-soaked hair out of my face. "It'll all be okay."

• • •

My eyes swelled with dehydration and sleep deprivation. Still shaking ever so slightly,

I had cried myself dry in Jessa's lap, the two of us silently acknowledging that only time would calm my panic.

I finally croaked out hoarsely, "I'm so sorry for-"

Jessa shook her head at me lovingly, shushing any apology away from my lips. "You have nothing to be sorry for, sweetie. I'm just so glad you didn't have to wake up from this alone."

I'm used to it.

She paused, contemplating her next words carefully. "Elliot is here."

Fuck. "Uh… what?"

"I may or may not have accused him of some horrible things. Bill was ready to call the cops," she laughed lightly. "Last I knew you were with him. When you didn't show up this morning and he stopped by, I panicked and rushed over here… but he genuinely seemed just as worried as I was. He wouldn't leave until he knew you were okay… do you want me to send him away?"

I coughed, any moisture in my already-dry throat evaporating completely. If I hadn't convinced him that I was irrevocably fucked up, maybe this would. He would be better off without me, and this would help me prove my point.

"You need to go back to work. Thank you for checking on me, but I'll be alright. I'll deal with Elliot, then I'll be in a bit later after I shower this mess off."

"There's no way in hell I'm letting you come in today. And are you sure you're okay to deal with him on your own? You seemed to be doing alright until you went out with him last night…" Worry worked its way over her, and she searched for any kind of hesitation on my face.

"I'll be alright, Jess," I lied. I didn't think I'd ever be *alright*. But maybe this I could handle. "It wasn't his fault." Another lie. Kind of. "How long have you been here anyway? I'm sure Bill is losing his mind."

She pondered for a moment, then sighed. "You're probably right. We've been here almost a couple of hours…"

Hours? Fuck. You've really done it now.

"Go," I urged. "I'll be fine."

Begrudgingly, she shifted her weight and lifted herself off the bed. Cooper cautiously crawled up to take her place, and I twisted my fingers into his fur. With one last glance over her shoulder, she proceeded down the hallway, and my gut turned flips in anxious anticipation for what was coming next.

• • •

Two light taps on the door frame made my heart jump, still uneasy from the night's events. Elliot stood just into the hallway, a conciliatory glass of water extended toward me, hair a bit messy with stress. His eyes appeared weak as he waited for my acknowledgement to come into the room. I still sat in my bed, likely looking like I had been run over. Cooper's stance shifted protectively next to me.

"Come in."

"Sam…" He handed me the drink and crouched next to my bed, causing Cooper to relax. "A- are you alri-"

"I'm fine. Really." I gulped down half the glass of water then breathed deeply in an effort to compose myself. "Thank you for this."

He hovered quietly, apparently needing some comfort himself as he reached out to pet Cooper. I waited for the questions I knew had to be on his mind. I wouldn't give up any more information than was necessary. I had given him as many details as he needed - as many as I thought he could handle - when I told him that no one was hurting me… anymore.

For what felt like an eternity, the only sound between us was the pounding echoing in my head and the occasional sigh from Cooper.

"Did I cause this?" Elliot looked up at me, eyes heavy and filling slowly with tears. Guilt pulled my heart into the pit of my stomach.

"Of course not." I lied. How could he have known putting his arms around me would trigger… this. "This… this is just me."

He sighed, but I couldn't tell if he was relieved or frustrated that he still didn't understand. Maybe a little of both. He blinked tears away, and I lightly placed my hand on his. When all this started, I didn't know what was going to happen, sure, but I knew it would end up something like this… and he was dumb enough not to listen when I tried to get him to run. His thumb lightly, carefully grazed the scar on the back of my hand as if he was expecting for it to still be painful. For the first time since I'd met him, Elliot couldn't seem to bring himself to look me in the eyes.

Silence pressed in, thick enough to choke on. Shame pooled hot in my chest. He wasn't imagining anything close to the worst of it. He couldn't. He didn't deserve to ever know that darkness.

"Elliot, I-"

He held up a hand. "If you need space, you can have it. I'm not going anywhere unless you want me to."

That was somehow worse. Kinder. It cracked something in me.

"How are you not already on your way out the door?" My voice wobbled, suddenly loud in the quiet room, words spilling out faster than I could control. "We hardly know each other. We've been on *one* date. *One* night. and yet here you are - caring. It doesn't make sense."

"I care because I like you," he said softly, matter-of-factly.

I shook my head, rising to pace a few steps because sitting still felt like suffocating. He startled a little at my sudden motion. The edges of my giant tee shirt tickled at my thighs with each step. My stress of the situation grew with sudden awareness that I should have at least put on pants. My fingers found their way through my hair, a feeble attempt at consoling my growing anxiety and quickening breath.

My throat burned as I tried to swallow panic. "I can't give you what you're looking for."

"Then I'll only take what you can give," he said, quiet but sure. "Even if that's just friendship for now. Even if it's just sitting on the floor with you while you breathe."

I paused, my steps faltering. "You'd really settle for that?"

"It's not settling." He exhaled through his nose, grounding himself before he spoke again. "It's choosing the pace that's safe for you. And I'd rather go *slow* than go *away*."

Tears pricked sharp behind my eyes. Tears I refused to let fall. I looked away again in case they did anyway.

"You make me feel..." I rubbed my palms over my arms. Too exposed. "Something I can't handle."

"That's okay. We don't have to rush it."

He rose from the floor timidly as if I was an animal he was afraid he'd startle. Maybe I was. He moved one step closer - slow enough that I could stop him at any moment. I didn't.

"If you need distance," he murmured, "all you have to do is say so."

The room hummed with our breathing. Close enough to feel him there. Far enough to breathe on my own.

"I'm terrified," I whispered.

He nodded. Waited.

I took one tiny step toward him and looked up at his hope-filled face. It was so annoying. Hope.

"I can't promise I won't freak out again," I muttered.

"That's okay," he said. "I have an older sister. I'm pretty good at surviving freak-outs."

I huffed a laugh - unwilling, but real. His shoulders relaxed with the sound, like he'd been holding himself too carefully.

I scrubbed my palms over my face, breath stuttering. "I don't... I don't know how to do this."

"You don't have to," he said softly. "Like I said, we don't have to rush it."

I looked up at him, unsure what to do with the gentleness in his voice. He had his hands carefully tucked into his pockets as if he was trying to make himself smaller for my sake.

"Do you want me to stay? I can make a couple of calls to the office..."

Cooper nudged my leg, sensing whatever crazy shit my heart was doing. I reached out and ran my fingers through the fur on his head, grounding myself in the softness.

Slowly, I shook my head and sighed, not impatient, just tired. "No, I'm okay... honestly."

He studied my face and shifted back a step, giving me space without making it feel like a retreat. "Alright," he murmured. "Just... call me if you need me?"

I half-scoffed, half laughed. "I actually don't even have your number."

His eyes widened with realization and he blinked hard a couple of times. "You're totally right. You've been holding out on giving me yours," he teased lightly.

I chuckled and shrugged. He wasn't totally wrong.

I reached onto my nightstand and pulled out my phone, handing it to him with the contacts app open to put in his details. It felt oddly like I'd suddenly lost all my clothes and I was standing naked in front of him. I wasn't, obviously (thank god), but just the idea of giving him that kind of access to me felt... vulnerable.

He handed it back to me, a text having already been sent to his phone for him to save my number.

"Now... call me if you need me?"

I nodded slowly, knowing full well I had no intention of doing so.

As he moved past me, keeping a respectful distance, I felt something unfamiliar settle in my ribs - something terrifying and strangely steady.

Not safety.
Not trust.
But maybe the first quiet flicker of both.

ELLIOT

The night after our first date, she was missing.

Jessa had given me the kind of ice cold glare that could freeze your blood in your veins. She thought I'd done something bad to her. I had no idea what she meant.

Moments after a quick recap of the night's events, we were both rushing to Sam's house. God, I was scared. What if something had happened? What if she was hurt... or worse?

Nothing felt any better when we showed up. She was screaming. Jessa made me wait in the living room while she went in to check on her.

My whole life I had never felt so helpless. So guilty.

I was wracking my brain for what could have happened - how I could have caused such a horrible mess for her. Then it hit me. She'd had a moment when I put my arms around her on the date. It was enough to cause me to ask her if someone was hurting her, and she'd said not anymore. She didn't give anything else away. And I didn't push her. But now the heaviness behind her eyes was starting to take a little shape. And it was something I wasn't sure I was equipped to help carry. But I wanted to try.

Eventually, probably a couple hours later, I stood in her doorway offering her a glass of water as if somehow I could drown out her problems with a little drink. She was so... fragile.

"Did I cause this?" I'd asked. But of course I did. There wasn't any other explanation, though she tried to promise me it wasn't my fault.

"I can't give you what you're looking for." She'd tried to push me away. Tried to give me an out I didn't want to take. She'd paced back and forth in her too-large t-shirt, hair a mess, face swollen from crying, and she tried to tell me to run.

I couldn't. Wouldn't is a better word, actually. Maybe most people would have. Maybe the smart thing - the responsible thing - would've been to listen to the way her voice cracked and take a step back. Give her space. Protect myself.

But I remember looking at her in that dim light coming from the hall, hands trembling at her sides, her breath catching like every inhale hurt, and all I could think was:

She shouldn't be alone for this.

She shouldn't have to weather whatever storm lived inside her chest without someone - without me - standing close enough to remind her she wasn't made of glass, even if she felt like it.

She'd said "I can't give you what you're looking for," but she didn't understand. I wasn't looking for anything. Not from her. Just... her. However she came. Broken pieces and all.

I remember stepping closer - slowly, like I was trying not to make waves in a clearly-marked no-wake zone. Her eyes flicked up to mine, wide and terrified, as if she expected judgement or disappointment or the kind of fear that makes people run.

But I didn't run.

"Sam." I whispered it because her name felt like something sacred in my mouth. "I'm not going anywhere."

She shook her head hard, tears catching on her lashes. She sank onto the edge of the bed, knees drawn up, palms pressing against her eyes. Her breath came in tiny, fractured pulls. I crouched on the floor beside her, close enough for her to know I was there, but far enough not to cross a boundary.

We stayed like that. For minutes. Maybe hours. Time didn't make sense in that room.

All I knew was the sound of her breathing - unsteady, raw - and the pounding of my own heart in my ears warning me that this girl... this woman could change everything if I let her.

And I remember thinking, with a mix of hope and fear that I still don't know how to name yet: please let her.

Sam

"You look like shit."

I rolled my eyes, but I couldn't help but laugh at the brutal truth of that statement. No matter how long I'd showered, there was no washing away a lifetime of damage. Andrew hovered in my doorway with Chinese food, a bottle of wine, ice cream, and a timid smile on his face. He shrugged and pushed his way past me into the kitchen.

"Bill and Jess sent me, and I brought reinforcements." He stashed the ice cream away in the freezer and began rifling through the drawers and cabinets.

"Well, hello to you, too," I chuckled, pulling a corkscrew from one of the few drawers he had yet to open.

"Bless you, my dear. I'll pour, you spill. Get talking. What's going on?"

"How much time have you got?"

"Oh, girl... that bad?"

I curled up onto the couch with the wine glass in one hand and a container of lo mein in the other, trying to pretend like the heat from the food could melt the tension sitting in my chest. Andrew flopped beside me, balancing his plate on one knee like this was a perfectly normal Friday night.

"I mean, I just had a rough night. Family drama I really don't want to get into. But things with Elliot are... good," I said, carefully twirling noodles around my fork. "Which is exactly why it's terrifying."

Andrew snorted. "Oh, honey. Let me guess - you're waiting for the other shoe to drop."

"More like the whole damn closet to collapse." I sighed. "I'm just... constantly bracing for impact."

He gave a dramatic sigh, shaking his head. "You really are committed to this whole self-sabotage aesthetic."

"I don't mean to be." My voice wavered. "It's just a lot... I don't know if I'm ever *not* going to feel fucked up."

I sniffled and moved a noodle back and forth with my fork, thankful for the company but still uncomfortable with any form of vulnerability. Despite thinking I'd cried all I could multiple times during the day, the practical therapy session over sinfully high-calorie food had plenty of emotions stirring again. Andrew sat across from me on the couch, practically consumed with his food as he weighed what little information I had given him.

"At some point, Sam, you're going to have to stop using whatever the hell happened to you as an excuse to push away any good thing that comes at you. I get it. It's scary as hell. But constantly running from everything good is no way to live. That shit gets tiring. Whatever it is, you didn't make it through all that just to wallow for the rest of your life. And all that man - that *gorgeous* hunk of a man - is asking you to do is give him a chance to be one of those good things. You want to run? Get a fucking treadmill."

I laughed through the tears rolling freely down my cheeks. "I damn well am going to have to after eating all this, aren't I?"

"Hey... trauma calories don't count!"

"I'd have withered away by now if that was true." I shook my head as I took another bite of ice cream.

"But really though... a little unlicensed advice? You should give him a chance. Maybe he'll surprise you. Maybe you'll fall in love. Maybe you won't, but by the looks of him you'll have a hell of a fun time. Don't put so much pressure on yourself and just go for it! If you don't... I might."

• • •

My head swiveled around from the dishes I was washing to see Elliot holding the door for someone as they exited before stepping inside himself. Without a word, I switched tasks to pour him a cup of light roast drip coffee and have it ready by the time he made it to the counter.

"Wow, Reynolds. Rolling out the red carpet this morning, are we?" He smirked at me, but his eyes seemed to be searching my face for how I would react to his presence.

"Well, take this as an apology. This one's on me," I smiled warmly, motioning for him to stop pulling his wallet out.

His smirk grew and his eyebrows scrunched together. "Uh... what do you mean?"

"I'm sorry for disappearing on you yesterday and the whole... nightmare thing. And for trying to push you away. You haven't been anything but nice to me, and I've been... projecting." My fingers knotted together in front of me. "I can't promise it won't happen again, and I can *guarantee* it won't be a walk in the park to try to get to know me..."

"But...?"

"I'm going to do my best not to completely shut you out."

"Is that so?" Elliot hid his excitement behind a sip of coffee, but his eyes brightened, easily giving him away.

"Yes. And on top of this white flag of a coffee to prove it... I want to take you somewhere tonight." My heart raced, but I worked to convince myself it was the *good* kind of nerves.

"And where might that be?"

"You don't get to know."

"Oh, now how is that fair?"

"Well, I think you're going to love it, and I want to see the look on your face when we get there. You took me to one of your favorite places, and now I'm going to take you to one of mine... if you'd like to go, of course."

His eyes narrowed playfully as he pretended to ponder the idea. "Hmm... I'd say that's a pretty decent offer..."

"Great! Pick me up at 7?"

"It's a date."

• • •

I glanced up from the espresso machine, already halfway through steaming milk for a regular's latte. A chill rippled through me, one that had nothing to do with the draft sneaking in behind the new arrival.

A man stepped inside, wearing an altogether too-large pale navy jacket that was far too warm for the weather as the door eased shut behind him. Something about the way he moved caught my attention - not hurried, not casual either. Measured. Like he was walking into a place he'd already imagined. He was... somehow eerily familiar, but I couldn't place why.

He paused just inside, scanning the room like he was studying the aftermath of a crime.

I turned back to the milk I was steaming, unable to shake the feeling that this man wasn't just another patron.

"Morning," I said automatically. "Be with you in just a second."

He didn't answer right away. When I looked up again, he was already at the counter.

"Nice place," he said. His voice was flat but clear. A little too loud for the quiet cafe.

"Thanks. Can I get you started with anything?" My voice shook.

He studied the menu like it was written in another language, but I had the distinct impression he wasn't reading it.

"You work here often?" he asked.

The fuck?

My grip on the milk pitcher tightened slightly. "Most days."

"Huh." He nodded, slow and deliberate. "Bet you get all kinds."

I offered a tight smile. "Something like that."

A pause. A long one.

"Just coffee," he said finally. "Black."

I turned to make the pour. His eyes stayed on me. I could feel it. People watched baristas all the time, but this was different. Intentional. Not curious, but... cataloging.

I slid the cup across the counter. "That'll be two-fifty."

He placed the cash down, two bills and a handful of coins, slowly, like each movement was part of a performance.

"Thanks," I said and reached for the register.

"I'm Marcus. What's your name?" He asked suddenly.

Marcus… motherfucker, why is he so familiar?

I hesitated. "Sam."

"Right… Sam." He smiled like it was an inside joke I wasn't in on. "Short for anything?"

I didn't answer. My old nickname, *Sammy*, swirled in my head.

He picked up the cup, took a sip, and held my gaze over the rim.

"See you around," he said.

The door chimed again, and he was gone.

Bill looked up from his computer nearby. "Weird vibe from that guy, or was it just me?"

"No," I said quietly, watching the empty doorway. "Not just you."

• • •

A blonde woman came through the front door under the familiar chime. I recognized her. Beth? Brittney? Bridget? She'd been in often enough now that I should have remembered, but my brain still felt shaken loose from the earlier encounter with Marcus.

She unzipped her jacket as she stepped inside and offered me that familiar-yet-distant smile she always did. Warm enough to be friendly, but casual enough not to require anything from me.

"Hey, Sam," she said, glancing over the menu. "Got any new seasonal drinks?"

Her voice alone felt grounding. Normal. Uncomplicated. I hadn't realized how tightly my shoulders were wound until they loosened under the comfort of routine.

"Yeah," I managed, grateful for conversation that didn't feel like ripping off fingernails. I tucked a stray piece of hair behind my ear and leaned forward on the counter. "We just rolled out a maple brown sugar latte, and Jessa's been hyping the cranberry white mocha like it's going to save humanity."

The woman laughed. "Oh god, she talked me into the pumpkin brulee cold brew last month and I didn't sleep for eight hours."

I cracked a tired smile. "Yeah, she forgets the caffeine is, uh… potent."

She laughed again, and the normalcy of it soothed the ringing inside my head. No threat. No hidden agenda. Just a woman trying to decide between something cozy and something dangerously sweet.

"What would you recommend?" she asked.

"Honestly?" I stepped closer, lowering my voice as if the other customers didn't deserve to hear my trade secret. "We've got one called the *sweater weather* latte, and it feels like a hug in a cup."

"A hug sounds perfect today," she said, sighing as she dug for her wallet. "It's been one of those mornings."

"Yeah," I muttered before I could stop myself. "I know the feeling."

Her eyes flicked up in quiet sympathy - not intrusive, just a human seeing the opportunity for connection and being healthy enough not to run from it. "Rough start?"

"You could say that." I cleared my throat, redirecting with practiced ease. "I'll get that latte started."

As I prepped the drink, the grinder thrummed to life, a steady vibration against the noise still reverberating through my body. The steam wand hissed, warm and familiar. A rhythm I could fall into when everything else felt askew.

She watched the process with casual curiosity, elbows propped on the counter. "You always look like you're casting a spell when you make these," she said.

I huffed a small laugh. "If only. I'd conjure a nap."

"Oh, same."

I handed the drink over, and she wrapped her hands around the cup like it was something precious. "Thanks," she breathed. "This is exactly what I needed."

She went and took her seat by the window, pulling out her phone and plopping in her earbuds.

Just then, my phone buzzed in my pocket. Customers all busy, heads in their laptops or tablets or books, I pulled it out to check.

Elliot 2:35pm

Saw a guy in the office carrying a cup of gas station coffee. Thought of you and your future crimes against him.

I grinned and rolled my eyes.

He deserves better. Tell him to seek professional help (aka me).

I felt myself uncurling, like the pressure in my chest from such an odd encounter earlier was finally starting to lift.

• • •

"Hey, Sam, can I talk to you for a minute?" Bill awkwardly stepped into the back room as I hung my apron and pulled my jacket on in its place.

"Sure! Is everything okay?"

"Well, I hope so. I'm just concerned about you, hon." He shoved his hands in his pockets, shifting his weight uncomfortably. "I saw you talking to that boy again… what's his name?"

I paused, briefly lost in thought of who he might be referring to. "Oh, you mean Elliot?"

"Yeah... Elliot. You went on that date with him the other night. Yesterday you were down for a spell. Jess said you'd be fine, but... I just wanna make sure you're gonna be alright."

My suspicion melted away as my heart warmed. Often seemingly gruff, the Army veteran seemed to have an entire lifetime buried behind his green eyes. One damaged soul to another, though, Bill was one of the most caring people I knew. Our mutual, wordless acknowledgement that there was no need to hash out haunted memories assured me of my safety in his presence.

"Thanks, Bill." I shuffled his direction and embraced him briefly. "It's just some old memories resurfacing. Elliot's been nothing but a perfect gentleman, I can assure you. What happened wasn't his fault."

Well, not entirely. He didn't mean *to trigger you the way he did.*

He patted the top of my head affectionately. "You're a good kid, you know? I'm here if you need me. I'm sure you're gonna be just fine"

I don't know that I'd go that far...

• • •

Cooper trotted next to me, happy as a clam as he sniffed practically every blade of grass in his path. His tail swayed with every new scent like he was solving the world's tiniest, most important mysteries. I'd gotten off work at 5, which gave me just enough time to come home to change and get him out for a spell before going out with Elliot.

Going out with Elliot.

I still couldn't say it in my head without feeling like I was swallowing a mouthful of marbles.

I tugged my jacket tighter around me as a humid breeze brushed across the complex lawn. The sky was shifting into that soft, burnished shade of the late afternoon - gold melting into pink - and it made the world feel gentler than I deserved.

As we walked, I typed a note into my phone I'd titled **Don't Read Into This.**

> *Some strange guy came into the cafe today. Marcus? Pretty sure that was his name, because he freaked me the fuck out. He didn't... do anything. Just asked too many questions that felt oddly personal in the weirdest way. And what's worse is that he seems SO familiar, and I can't put a finger on why. Hopefully he's just a one-off.*

My thumbs paused over the screen. The familiar prickling crawled up my spine the way it had earlier in the cafe, like someone pressing a tuning fork to the back of my neck. Maybe I was overreacting. Maybe it was nothing. But it didn't *feel* like nothing.

I kept typing.

> *Anyway, I'm going out with Elliot tonight. I'm trying not to cringe just saying that. It's a friend outing. Obviously. Completely normal. But he's... nice. He's been nothing but, honestly. And, fuck me, I tried to tell him to run. I really did. But he's not.*

A cluster of nerves tightened in my throat. Cooper stopped to sniff a leaf that had surely committed a crime, and I took the chance to breathe.

> *Bill asked me about him today. Practically insinuated that Elliot caused that (disastrous) nightmare yesterday. Which, I guess maybe he did. But not intentionally, of course.*

I winced at the reminder. The way my chest had locked up. The shame that had followed.

> *I've got to get a grip. Pull my shit together. I shouldn't be this nervous.*

My fingers hovered a beat longer before I finished:

> *I'm putting this away before I spiral.*

I locked my phone, shoved it deep in my pocket, and shook my head a little too fast like that might successfully rattle the panic out of me. Cooper looked back at me, secondhand embarrassment in his eyes. It's like he knew I was in entirely too far over my head and was silently waiting for me to implode.

"It's fine," I muttered, rubbing a hand over my face. "I'm fine. Totally okay. Absolutely not spiraling."

Cooper's expression said otherwise.

We shuffled our way up the walkway to my apartment, the porch light flicking on automatically as we approached, like even the building knew I needed someone - or something - to guide me inside. Cooper trotted through the doorway first, confident and unbothered, while I lingered a second on the threshold, heart tapping too fast at the thought of what tonight could be.

Then I stepped inside after him.

SAM

I tugged at Elliot's hesitant hand, his suspicion growing as we turned down the alley. The damp, cracked sidewalk scraped under his shuffling feet.

"Reynolds, you didn't bring me here to kill me did you?" He teased, but hints of concern revealed he was more nervous than he wanted to let on.

"Come on!" I pulled harder.

At the end of the alley, we reached a rusting steel door. I looked over my shoulder and smiled at him as I pushed it open. Through the other side of the door and down the stairwell, we emerged into a buzzing room of all the best things. Books lined the walls in library shelves. The bar stood in the center of the floor, warmly lit with reading lamps hanging overhead. Couches held an array of people groups, some reading, some chatting, some laughing their way through board games. A local artist of some sort plucked away at his guitar on a makeshift stage more fit for a poetry reading.

Amazement washed over Elliot's face. "What *is* this place?"

"Biblioholic: Library. Speakeasy. Welcome to *my* favorite place."

He trailed behind me in wonderment, gazing around as I led us to the bar. My pride couldn't be contained. He hovered in tow and drifted in circles and absorbed the atmosphere around us.

"Vodka tonic with lime and bourbon on the rocks, please."

"I had no idea this place even existed…" I wasn't sure whether that was meant for me, or if it was simply an apologetic explanation of his absence to the room.

"Maybe you don't know as much as you thought, huh?"

He smirked playfully, shimmers of intrigue lighting his eyes. Typically a grayish blue, they burned brighter as the light of a new fire or a pool on the driest of days - a kind of blue you'd willfully drown in. "I guess not."

• • •

"Alright," I sighed, gently dropping my books on the table and patting my hand competitively on the top. "Let's see what you've got… *Faulkner?* You've got to be kidding. You're kidding, right?"

Elliot let out a melodramatic gasp, his hand finding offense at his chest. "Don't tell me… *Hemingway?* Get outta here."

An all-out literary debate commenced between us, gleefully cutthroat. Our beloved classics were forced into battle, casualties piling up as Hemingway and Faulkner took center stage. They always did.

"Faulkner's sentences are a nightmare," I argued, gesturing with my glass like a disgruntled professor. "They're a marathon without water breaks. Or commas."

"They have commas," Elliot protested.

"Not enough to prevent hallucinations," I shot back. "By page ten I'm convinced

I've forgotten how to read."

He grinned, eyes dancing. "But that chaos is intentional. It's brilliant."

"Brilliance shouldn't give you a migraine."

"That's just part of the experience."

"So is a root canal. Doesn't mean I'm signing up for it willingly."

He laughed, freely, like he didn't care who heard. The sound did annoyingly hopeful things to my insides.

"And Hemingway?" he challenged.

I clutched my imaginary pearls. "What about him?"

"You can't honestly think his minimalism is superior."

"It is!" I insisted. "He makes silence loud. He knows exactly what *not* to say."

"So does *every* emotionally repressed man."

I gasped, offended on Hemingway's behalf. "You take that back."

He leaned in, elbows brushing the table, voice dropping like we were conspiring about state secrets. "I will not. I stand by my statement: short sentences are a sign of fear."

"They're a sign of skill," I countered. "Leaving space for interpretation takes trust."

"And rambling takes courage," he said, smirking.

"Or narcissism."

"Oh, absolutely narcissism," he conceded, raising his glass to toast to that truth. "But graceful narcissism."

I laughed, the vodka buzzing warmly through my veins. "We're never going to agree on this, are we?"

"Nope," he said, flashing that infuriatingly confident smile. "But I love how hard you're willing to fight for your wrong opinions."

My jaw dropped. "You are impossible!"

"And you're delightful." The compliment lodged right in my ribs and landed so softly it took me a full second to realize he'd thrown it.

I cleared my throat, desperate to redirect heat from my cheeks.

"We haven't even covered fiction yet," he smoothly transitioned in the silence.

"Oh God," I teased. "You're about to defend romance novels again, aren't you?"

"You said they give unrealistic expectations, but you didn't say that wasn't entertaining along the way."

I laughed, full and unbridled on my third glass. It wasn't like me to release so many inhibitions at once. But something about the atmosphere and the company and the warm light made me a little more forgiving with myself. The thought that I hoped I didn't regret it was simply a shadow dancing on the outskirts of the room.

A server came by with our check to quietly suggest we leave. We paid, but ignored her otherwise, still nursing the last of our drinks to hold onto the night.

"Okay, okay. Last one. What have you got next?"

"On the count of three, we show it. Deal?" I nodded. "One, two… three!"

The Great Gatsby.

"Ahh so we agree on something at least," Elliot smirked.

"I'd consider you crazy if we couldn't find common ground here. His other works? Meh. But Gatsby deserves all its glory and then some. 'Simultaneously enchanted and repelled by the inexhaustible variety of life.' It's like he pulled thoughts straight from everyone's minds but made them sound a hell of a lot better."

"I'm just so fond of Gatsby's love for Daisy. It's all-consuming. It's maddening. It's so tangible. He's insatiable, like once he saw her he could never get enough. No matter your conclusions about her… everyone wants a love like that."

I felt the vodka swim a little in my stomach. Did I? Want a love like that? I had been simply surviving for so long the thought hadn't even crossed my mind. But something *all consuming?* That sounded dangerous. Catastrophic, maybe.

I wasn't sure I was quite ready to raise my hand for *that*. But *this* - whatever this was - was nice.

...

Quarter past one found us bursting back into the alley shadows, our own hidden somewhere in the mix. My hand fit neatly into Elliot's as he led us back toward the car. His step light, he appeared younger in the early morning.

Nerves warmed my face, a contrast to the night's cool air. Maybe it was the liquor. Maybe it was impulse. Maybe it was the hours we'd spent laughing at how acquainted our souls seemed to be. Or maybe it was just because he was *so* damn hot. Whatever it was, it stirred enough courage to quicken my pulse.

"Hey, Flint."

He looked over his shoulder. I tugged at our intertwined hands until he closely faced me, his curiosity pressing into a small smile. We hovered a moment, like the night around us eager for nothing but to take its time. His fingers brushed gently at my cheek and found their way to cradle the back of my neck. My hand shook as I reached out and placed it on his chest. I was terrified. But to do anything other than kiss him in that moment would be a sin. A crime against humanity itself. So I did.

...

I. fucking. kissed. him.

My thumb hovered a moment over the little blue arrow before hesitantly sending the message. Within seconds my phone was buzzing with Andrew's call.

"You *whaaaaaaat?*"

"I *made out with him* in the alley by the bar!" If not for my still-tingling lips that managed to last through my night's sleep, I wouldn't have believed it myself.

"Girl, I need details right this second."

I giggled, gossip ready to serve piping hot on a silver platter. "Well, I took him to Biblioholic. We stayed for… damn, nearly six hours. Anyway, we argued about the classics, drank *plenty*, and, well–" two quick knocks at my door interjected their way into my story. I jumped a little, the sudden noise pressing my insides against my skin. "Hang on, someone's here?"

"Ooo okay, love a little mystery for a Sunday morning. Who could it be? What do they want? Just don't die on the phone with me, alright? I can't afford to pay my therapist that much."

The other side of the door at first blush seemed ordinarily empty. I scanned my porch through the keyhole, quickly becoming suspicious of the person who knocked on my door, whoever they were, and the intentions they carried. I grabbed my keys, pepper spray ready for whoever might be ready to ambush me on the other side, and pried open the door slowly. My eyes fell on a curious pop of pink in the corner, a vase of daisies perched next to an envelope with my name scribbled across the front.

"Oh my gosh…"

"What is it? Unibomber? Severed head? Hand?"

"Okay, okay. Enough true crime for you, mister! No, it's flowers… and a note."

"Oh my god!" Andrew squealed, elation piercing through the speaker. "You are *so* in deep with this one now. Well? What's it say?"

"Hold on!" We waited with bated breath as I tore open the envelope. A *Gatsby* quote unveiled itself as I unfolded the little paper.

I hope she'll be a fool... that's the best thing a girl can be in this world, a beautiful little fool.

⋯

Late Sunday morning, the best time for errands. Quiet, fully-stocked aisles braced themselves for the rush of well-dressed, apocalyptic post-church-service scavengers and enthusiastic meal-preppers. Their impending doom was my solace from people I had no desire to be around.

I browsed the shelves for the items on my list at a leisurely pace. With the sight of strawberry Pillsbury frosting, my stroll was slowed to a stop. I stared at the blue canister as an unexplained fondness grew in my chest. At first I wasn't sure why the random product nearly brought me to tears. I stood there for an altogether too long moment before a warm memory flooded back into my head.

The air smelled sweet. My mom spread the pink frosting across a sheet cake. She struggled to keep crumbs from tainting the should-be smooth surface, and she was beginning to become frustrated. A number five candle and some tall ones that sparkled sprawled across the flour-splattered counter. It must have been my sister's birthday. She sighed. I dipped my short, stubby finger in the can, inevitably getting the colored sugary cream in various places up my hand and wrist. It didn't matter. I was on a mission to make my mom smile. It had been a while. She looked up at me just in time, nearly protesting, and I dotted her nose with my frosting-covered finger. Her surprised, joyful smile was brilliant. She threw her head back and laughed, using her forearm to brush dark brown hair away from her face. Then, hands looking like some sort of evidence of a crime against cake, she scrunched her nose and began chasing me around the kitchen. We made the biggest mess and laughed, really laughed, until our bellies hurt.

A few rogue tears fell from my eyes as I blinked myself back to reality. A dark haired child gaped awkwardly at me from a few feet away, obviously weirded out by the ancient twenty-nine year old he was watching simultaneously smile and cry in the grocery store baking aisle.

I just needed some fucking brown sugar.

Elliot

The night she took me to Biblioholic was closely akin to magic.

I remember that clearly - how the air felt different the second we stepped inside. Like the whole place hummed with its own heartbeat. The warm lamps glowing over crooked stacks of used hardcovers. The soft creak of the floorboards. The smell of some fruity drink drifting through the air.

Sam hadn't told me where we were going. She just said, "Trust me," with that secretive smile that always made me feel like I was opening a door I didn't know existed.

I followed her in, and she looked back at me with this spark in her eyes I hadn't seen before. Not joy, exactly - joy was too big a word for her then. It was more like... a flicker. A something. A tiny flame she trusted me enough to light.

She drifted between the shelves like she belonged there, fingers brushing the spines, her steps soft and sure. I watched her move - quiet, careful, reverent - and realized that for Sam, books weren't just things. They were sanctuaries. A kind of holy ground.

That night we had our first argument of sorts. We battled back and forth about Faulkner and Hemingway until the waitress was practically begging us to leave. We bonded over a love of Gatsby and argued again over romance books being worth reading. Even after everything, I still stand by them.

That night was the first time I heard her laugh. Really laugh.

It's also the first time she kissed me.

Came out of nowhere.

"Hey, Flint," she'd said as she tugged on my hand, pulling me back to face her. Her hand shook as she placed it on my chest, a small smile forming and vodka dancing behind her eyes. And then she kissed me. Slow and sweet and everything I never knew I needed.

That night didn't feel like a date. It felt like an invitation. Maybe not to her past, but certainly to her present. To her safe space. To her heart in its own quiet, fragile way.

And I remember thinking, when she knelt on the floor to search for her favorite mystery book, golden-brown hair falling around her face:

If magic exists anywhere in the world... it's in the moments she finally lets me close.

I knew the next day I had to do something. Stay on her mind.

I sent her flowers and a Gatsby quote I knew would get under her skin just enough.

"Elliot, you didn't!" She'd texted me.

"Oh, but I did."

She deserved it. If I could have given her the world, I would have.

SAM

"The flowers were very thoughtful, Elliot. Thank you again. And the Gatsby quote was a nice touch."

He beamed over the steam of his light roast. With no attempt at feigning humility, a sense of achievement pressed his lips into a sideways grin. "I'm glad you liked them."

The entrance chimed as a breezy brown-haired woman stepped in. White sneakers carried an aura of importance as they popped against her tan suit. She eyed Elliot sitting at his new favorite perch at the bar - really he was the only one who *liked* sitting there unless we were quite busy, but it allowed him to talk to me with ease as I worked. In all reality, this put together woman seemed at first glance like someone who would pair well with him. I pulled at my apron and brushed a fallen hair behind my ear as I turned to help her. She ordered her drink to take with her and claimed a spot a seat away from Elliot to wait, smiling warmly at him.

Half-caf americano, who does that? …Well, someone who doesn't have a major caffeine dependency, probably. You could never. And that well composed? All the coffee in the world couldn't get you there.

I bit the inside of my lip, critical eyes lingering on my scar as I handed her drink across the counter. Even her nails were perfectly manicured french tips.

"Thanks for stopping in."

"Thank you. You guys have a good one," she said, intentionally including Elliot in her well wishes and turning toward him before she left. I watched after her as she stepped effortlessly back out to the sidewalk and sipped on her coffee.

Blinking a couple of times quickly, I shook my head slightly in an attempt to rid myself of the deprecatory thoughts that threatened to throw off my morning.

That's who he should have. Someone put together. Someone more… on his level.

My hand fumbled with my necklace as my hip found the edge of the counter. I leaned there silently spiraling while Elliot scrolled on his phone, completely oblivious.

"So, what have you got going on today?" Elliot's question pulled me back into conversation with him, something I suddenly felt a little less qualified for. He glanced up from his phone, a sparkle of knowing concern flickering in his eyes.

"Um… I actually get off work at eleven, so it's a short day for me! I don't really know how I'll spend my afternoon, but I may read a bit and go for a run. How about you?"

"Well, today's schedule seems like it'll be a little hellish. I'm in back to back meetings most of the day, an interview for an article this afternoon, and a dinner to go to this evening."

See? All things you're completely unqualified for.

"Aw, and here I thought you had dressed up for me," I teased, sarcasm attempting to deflect this gnawing feeling of inadequacy.

I fought to stifle it. To suffocate the shame of everything I *wasn't*. I gave my head another quick shake and dropped my necklace.

"Well, since I'm off early, would it help if I offered to bring by some lunch?"

He hesitated a moment, eyebrows raising in thought. "Actually, that would be super helpful and *much* appreciated. But I do have one stipulation…"

"Oh, we're making demands now, are we?"

"Demand, singular," he smirked. "You have to stay and eat with me. It would at least make my desk lunch enjoyable."

...

I pushed my way into the lobby through the tall revolving glass door and was met by a security checkpoint that could have rivaled TSA. Cameras nested all around like nosy blackbirds. Beyond the imposing entrance, Elliot's office was buzzing with energy. Men in suits and women in heels scurried across concrete floors under modern chandeliers. A beautiful wooden reception desk - one that seemed pointless given the security checkpoint - held three young professionals answering phone calls as if each was urgent and important.

"Can I help you?" A towering man made all the more intimidating by his dark, deep set eyes stepped up to me.

"Um… I'm here to see Elliot Flint?" I held up the bag of food I clutched as some sort of reconciliation that my statement sounded more like a question.

"One moment."

He stepped behind a podium to make an unintelligible phone call, glancing up at me suspiciously every so often. Who could blame him? Once again I was obviously out of place.

I spun around slowly on my heel to observe more of the office, taking in all the grandiosity.

"Ahem… Ms. Reynolds?" I jumped at the security guard suddenly standing behind me. "You're welcome to head up to Mr. Flint's office."

"Could- uh… would you mind pointing me in the right direction?"

"Of course, ma'am. You'll go past reception, hang a left, and take the elevator up to the eighth floor. There's another desk when you get there, and they can point you the rest of the way. He also requested that we make you a badge that'll let you come and go as you please, so if you'll stop back by on your way out, I'll have that ready."

I gulped. That felt like an oddly large gesture. "Okay, thank you."

I hurried through the lobby feeling entirely small. The nook for the elevators was just as glamorous as the lobby; modern, but warm and a little darker as it was out of the way of the large front-facing windows. I pressed the call button and stepped into the readily available elevator. The doors nearly closed, but someone's hand caught the middle just before it was too late.

Oh, great. Her again.

The same woman in the tan suit from earlier stepped into the elevator, completely clueless that she was seeing me for the second time. Her manicured finger hit the third floor button, and she smiled at me before returning her stare to her phone. Oblivious to my awkward discomfort, she seemed as relaxed as ever.

Maybe if you cut back on the caffeine you wouldn't feel so fidgety.

"Have a good one," she told me again as she went to step off onto the third floor. My hand raised embarrassingly in a wave that lingered next to my hip.

I fumbled with a piece of hair with my free hand and hoped that the rest of my interactions with the people in the building wouldn't be so cringeworthy. I did have another reception desk to get past, after all.

The elevator chimed, and I stepped out onto the eighth floor, immediately greeted by more soft lighting and modern furniture that probably cost more than everything I owned. A stylish woman behind the sleek reception desk looked up with a practiced smile.

"How can I help you?"

"Hi. Uh, I'm here to see Elliot Flint? He's expecting me, I think."

She typed something into her computer, then nodded. "Right this way."

I followed her down a hallway lined with glass-walled offices, the kind where you could see everything but still somehow felt like you shouldn't be looking. Just before she opened a set of wide double doors, she turned back to me and said, "He's right in here. If you need anything while you're here, don't be afraid to let me know."

I nodded, trying not to trip over my own feet as I stepped into a space that looked like it belonged on a magazine cover. Warm leather, clean lines, and a wall of windows that offered a jaw-dropping view of the skyline. The only thing more impressive was the man sitting at his desk, jacket slung over the back of his chair, and sleeves rolled up to his elbows.

I held up the food bag like a peace offering. "Figured you might be hungry right about now."

"You figured right." He stood, crossed the room with that casual confidence I still wasn't used to, and took the bag from my hand. "Come sit. You're rescuing me from what was about to be a fourth cup of coffee and a meeting with someone who only speaks in buzzwords like *synergy* and *bandwidth*."

We settled onto the couch tucked into the corner of the office, city alive with midday hurry behind him. I peeled the lid off the fries and snagged one before he could steal the best ones.

"What's next on the docket?" I asked.

"An interview with the New Yorker. I'm kind of nervous actually." He looked anything but. "It's a big deal, you know? Getting our name and our cause in something like that."

It absolutely was. It was huge. And there I was, a barista with barely better than fast food for lunch.

"Yeah, it's amazing," I mumbled, avoiding eye contact and trying to suppress the negativity.

"Are you alright? You seem a little… Sad isn't the right word. Just, maybe a little down?"

"I'm okay…" I fiddled with my necklace and munched on a french fry as I pondered whether or not to blame it all on some made up problem. He tilted his head slightly as if he read my mind and was trying to urge me not to. "It's just… There was this woman at the coffee shop earlier. I don't know if you noticed her. But she *definitely* noticed you. And… anyway, she just… she was practically perfect. And I just feel like *that's* more of what you deserve."

My voice was barely above a whisper by the time I finished speaking, and I couldn't bring myself to look him in the eye.

He chuckled. Not maliciously, just amused. "You think this woman is a better fit for me than you are, then?"

I shrugged, keeping my gaze fixed on the fry I'd been holding for a long moment. "Yes. Maybe. I don't know."

"What on earth would make you think that?"

"Elliot, there's… a lot you don't know about me. Things from my past that - I don't know - I guess I feel like they disqualify me from deserving someone like you."

"Someone like me?"

"Handsome. Generous. Someone who has their shit together." I motioned vaguely around the office as if the space alone could prove my point.

He chuckled again, breathy. "What if I told you that woman didn't have what I wanted?"

I glanced up, half shocked out of my mind. "And what is it you *do* want, Flint?"

He took a breath, opened his mouth to speak, but the intercom on his phone buzzed interrupting him.

"Mr. Flint, Mrs. Chelsea Miller with the New Yorker is here to see you."

"Go." I wasn't quite sure I was ready for his answer anyway. "I'll clean up here and get out of your hair."

He eyed me suspiciously. "You're sure? I can push this a bit…"

"I'm sure. Good luck with your interview."

• • •

I sat on my couch, curled up with a book while Cooper snoozed on the other end.

My phone buzzed on the table.

Elliot: 4:53pm

> *Had a meeting in a conference room called "Hemingway." Spent the whole time wanting to argue with you about him again.*

I found myself rolling my eyes again, a habit I was forming every time Elliot texted me out of the blue.

> *You're wrong and you know it. But thanks for thinking of me.*

I sighed and put my book and phone down, feeling a little stir crazy.

"You want to go for a walk, bub?"

Cooper's ears perked immediately. He lifted his head, blinking like he wasn't sure he'd heard correctly, then bounded off the couch in full dramatic enthusiasm, nails scrabbling against the floor.

"Okay, okay," I laughed, getting up to grab his leash. "Calm down, track star."

He wagged his tail so hard his whole body swayed.

I clipped the leash on and stepped outside, letting the crisp afternoon air hit my lungs. The sky was soft and hazy, that in-between color before the sunset fully commits. It felt… quiet in a way I needed.

Cooper trotted beside me with purpose, nose to the wind, tail swinging like he was single-handedly keeping the world cheerful.

We made our way down the block, passing the community garden and the fenced-in dog park where a husky was losing its mind over a tennis ball. Cooper watched with judgemental disdain.

"Same, honestly," I muttered. "Too much enthusiasm."

My phone buzzed again.

> **Elliot 5:01pm**
>
> *For the record, you only ever win the Hemingway argument because you fight dirty.*

I snorted. Cooper glanced up at me like I was embarrassing him in public.

> *Arguments require skill. Yours are just wounded pride and pretty eyes.*

I didn't realize what I'd typed until after I hit send.

I froze mid-step. "Shit."

Cooper tugged forward, blissfully unaware of my impending emotional death.

Another buzz.

> **Elliot 5:02pm**
>
> *Pretty eyes, huh?*

I groaned aloud, dragging a hand over my face.

> *Autocorrect. Stupid, useless thing. Don't you have a meeting to be in, anyway?*

I shoved my phone back in my pocket before I could humiliate myself any further. "I'm never texting again," I muttered. Cooper ignored me, nose buried in a patch of questionable grass.

We looped around the neighborhood, letting the fresh air clear out my spiraling thoughts of inadequacy. The world felt manageable again. I was getting less jittery with each step.

Elliot 5:14

Sure thing. And yes, actually. About to head to dinner now. Wish me luck.

We shuffled into the house, Cooper trotting ahead like he owned the place. I unclipped his leash and tossed him a treat for being semi-well behaved.

"Good walk, dude."

He flopped dramatically onto the rug like he'd just completed a marathon.

I laughed under my breath and picked my book back up from the couch, but before I opened it, I grabbed my phone back out to return Elliot's message.

Good luck. Try not to charm the entire room immediately. It's embarrassing.

I set my phone down again and curled back into the couch, Cooper scooting closer like he sensed my mood shifting.

"You're right," I whispered, smoothing the fur on his ears. "I'm in trouble."

SAM

"How was your interview? And dinner?" I yawned.

It was almost eleven, which was a little past when my head typically hit the pillow. Elliot was on the other end of the phone, road noise a quiet lull in the background as he drove home from the dinner event he'd attended.

"It went well! The dinner was a bit more relaxing than I had anticipated, which was a nice surprise. The investor we were meeting with was much more laid back than I would have expected. He even cracked a couple of jokes! I am *exhausted*, though, after such a long day. Thanks again for talking to me on the drive back. Are we good? From earlier? You still seem... down."

"I *am* feeling a little down today," I admitted. "Honestly? It's not just our conversation earlier... I'm thinking it may have something to do with this weird memory that popped into my mind yesterday that's got me feeling a bit off, and I can't even honestly tell you if it's a good or bad feeling."

"Well, was it a good or a bad memory?"

"Good… It was about my mother. Back when I was a kid, she was making this cake. It kept frustrating her that she was getting crumbs in the icing, and I just dotted her nose with it to cheer her up. We laughed and chased each other around the kitchen and made the biggest mess… it's got me feeling this weird, almost sort of homesick feeling for my mother."

"I know you've said family is a touchy subject… have you called her? Let her know you're thinking about her?"

A pang of sadness hit my gut, and I grabbed at my necklace and twisted it around my finger. "I… I can't. She's… not with us anymore."

A quiet moment of solemn realization oozed through the phone, Elliot's best foot forward now regrettably lodged in his mouth. "Sam, I-"

"Didn't know. Please don't apologize; It's not your fault, Elliot. It's not something you could have or should have known. I just… I guess it made me miss her."

"That's only fair, and I think it's perfectly reasonable for you to have a mix of feelings about it. Everything doesn't have to be black or white, good or bad. It's okay to be somewhere in between."

I smiled softly. "Yeah, I guess you're right. It's all a bit… complicated?"

"That's okay," he assured. "If you want to talk about it, about her I mean…"

I hesitated. I didn't talk about my mother often… or ever, for that matter. It was the kind of thing that made my soul ache.

"We didn't have a lot growing up, but she made everything fun and special. She would take us to the farmer's markets on sunny days and let us each pick *one* thing. She'd braid my hair even though it would fall apart before she could get the elastic on it, all because I loved it. She… did everything she could to make life worth living."

"How did she pass, if you don't mind me asking."

I gulped. My mouth suddenly dried. I hadn't told anyone but Jessa about my mother. How she passed.

A long moment of silence stretched between us as my mind swirled with anxiety.

Elliot didn't push. He didn't clear his throat or shuffle around or fill the quiet with meaningless noise. All I heard was the soft hum of his engine, the occasional click of his turn signal, and my own pulse pounding in my ears.

I gripped my necklace - her necklace - tighter, the metal warming fast between my fingers. My stomach twisted. I could feel the words trying to claw their way out of my chest, the way they always did right before I shut down and swallowed them whole again.

But this time...

He was waiting. Not demanding. Just... open. Available. Steady in a way that made the truth ache in my throat.

You've got to tell him at some point... it might as well be now. The thought alone made my lungs feel too small.

I inhaled shakily. "My father," I whispered.

There was a sudden hiss of breath on the other end of the line, but he didn't speak. Not immediately. He let the weight settle where it needed to settle.

I closed my eyes, forcing the words out before I could lose my nerve.

"He killed her."

The confession fell into the silence between us like a stone dropping into deep water, sinking fast, disappearing before I could reach for it again. My hands shook. I curled them into fists against my blanket.

Still, Elliot said nothing.

I couldn't tell if he was processing or just trying to be careful with something so fragile.

Finally, quietly, he said, "Sam… I'm so sorry."

His voice wasn't dramatic. It wasn't dripping in forced sympathy. It was barely a breath - gentle, steady, and warm. A lifeline instead of a demand.

I swallowed hard. "It's okay. I don't - I didn't bring it up because I wanted comfort. Or an apology. I just… felt this memory for the first time in a long time and it caught me off guard."

"That makes sense," he said. "Good memories can hurt as much as bad ones sometimes."

I let out a shaky laugh. "Yeah. They really can."

"Thank you for trusting me with that," he said softly. "I know that couldn't have been easy."

It wasn't.

But somehow, sharing it didn't feel quite like ripping open an old wound. It felt like setting down something heavy, just for a second.

I shifted against the pillows. "She was really good," I murmured. "My mom. Even when everything else wasn't."

"She sounds incredible."

"She was," I said.

Elliot cleared his throat gently. "Do you want me to stay on the line until you fall asleep?"

I froze.

He quickly added, almost tripping over the words, "Only if it helps. If it doesn't that's okay, too."

It should have been too much. Too intimate. But the offer didn't feel invasive. It felt like someone holding a door open from a respectful distance.

"Yeah," I whispered. "Actually, I'd like that."

His voice warmed. "Okay. I'm here. Tell me, what did you do with the afternoon off?"

"I took Cooper for a run - we hit a little over 6 miles, which was nice! Otherwise it was fairly relaxing."

"That's impressive, Reynolds. I'm glad you got to rest a bit." He paused to yawn. "Hey, before I forget... Would you - uh, be willing to come to a charity gala with me Saturday? I'm giving a speech, and... well my parents were going to come but they're going to be out of town and... anyway I'd love to have you there."

"Wow, and you're calling *me* impressive?"

You aren't near good enough for him... for this.

"Um... I don't think I have anything going on Saturday evening. What time, and what will I need to wear?"

"I'll pick you up at eight. I'd love to get you a dress... It's a black tie event."

My stomach jumped into my throat. "O-okay."

His pride radiated enough to reach me from wherever on the road he was. "Great! I'll pick something out and have it sent over."

I let out a thin, nervous laugh. "That's... wildly unnecessary, you know."

"Probably," he said, smile audible in his voice. "But humor me. I promise I'm good at this part."

"I'll try not to faint when I see the price tag."

"You won't see it," he teased. "I'm not risking you mailing it back out of spite."

"Smart man."

He chuckled, then quieted. The soft road noise filled the line again - steady and peaceful and almost comforting enough to put me to sleep.

"You doing okay now?" He asked after a moment, his tone turning gentle. "Really okay?"

I curled deeper under my blanket, Cooper shifting at my feet like he knew I needed the extra weight. "I think so… talking helped."

"I'm glad."

His voice had softened into something warm and tired, like he was already halfway inside a dream. It made my chest ache in a way that felt dangerous.

"You should get home soon," I said. "You sound exhausted."

"I'm about five minutes out." A pause. "Will you stay on with me until I'm inside?"

"Yeah," I whispered, eyes heavy. "I can do that."

The line went quiet again, but it wasn't empty. It was full of breath and quiet presence and two people trying, in their own hesitant ways, to meet in the middle.

I heard the turn signal tick, the engine downshift, a car door open, then shut.

"Alright," he said softly, almost like he was afraid he'd wake me up. "I'm home."

"Good," I murmured.

"Goodnight, Sam."

"Goodnight, Elliot."

Cooper sighed dramatically like a warning that I was heading into emotionally uncharted waters.

I didn't hang up until he did.

And when the call ended, the silence didn't feel quite as heavy as it did before.

• • •

"*He's* buying the dress?" Andrew gawked over his coffee. "That's sexy as fuck."

"You mean terrifying, right?"

"No ma'am! Uh-uh. I'm calling it right now, he's going to pick something *stunning* because that man adores you. Gonna be looking like the whole damn four course meal."

"I'm less of a stunner and more of a blend into the background kind of person, though, Andrew," I sighed. "And… I have a few scars I'd rather not have showing. I'm just… worried."

"Honey, you've got to show off your battle scars. Embrace those bitches and-"

The bell rang as the door opened, cutting him off. I was thankful for the excuse for an escape from that conversation until I faced around and saw Marcus standing rigidly in the doorway. Uneasiness hit me like a greyhound bus.

I tried to keep my hands steady as I placed the milk pitcher I was steaming on the counter.

He smiled.

I stiffened. Forced myself to unclench my jaw.

"Afternoon," I managed, gripping the edge of the counter. "What can I get started for you?"

He didn't answer. Just strolled to the counter with the kind of casualness that felt like a lie.

"I like your necklace," he said finally. "Reminds me of this girl I used to know."

I gulped. I'd forgotten to put my necklace back on after my shower that morning. My stomach dropped.

I looked down, hoping maybe I was misremembering, but no - bare collarbone, just the edge of my apron strap.

He watched me realize it. Didn't say a word. Just smiled again, wider this time.

"Maybe I was thinking of someone else," he added quietly.

Not a fucking chance.

My skin prickled. I reached for a rag and started wiping the already-clean counter. "You here for coffee?"

He tilted his head, like I was a puzzle he was slowly putting together.

"Just browsing."

"Not really a *browsing* kind of place," I said, sharper than I intended.

He chuckled. I reached for the phone behind the counter. Didn't touch it; just wanted him to see my hand near it.

That seemed to amuse him more.

"You're funny, Sam."

He turned slowly, walked to the pastry case, and crouched as if examining the scones. But I could feel his eyes flicking back to me through the glass. Watching.

After a beat, he stood again. "Not hungry after all. Maybe next time."

The bell chimed as he left, and I stood frozen in place for a full ten seconds after the door swung shut behind him.

Andrew was oblivious, head in his laptop and headphones back over his ears by the time Marcus had made his way to the register. To him, he was just another customer.

But he was more than that. I just… still couldn't place why.

• • •

I frantically pulled a big t-shirt over my still sopping wet head. "Just a second!"

Rushing to the front door still toweling my hair, I flung it open to find a delivery man wide-eyed at my sudden and flustered appearance.

"Um, Sam Reynolds?"

"Yes, that's me," I claimed breathlessly.

"Delivery for you from an… Elliot Flint. Please sign here."

I felt myself blush as he handed the fancy package through the doorway to me, fumbling and still damp from a shower. Thanking him, I carried it into my room and placed it on the bed.

I pulled at the black silky ribbon to loosen the bow. The box alone appeared expensive, and my stomach felt heavy at the speculation of how much money Elliot may have dropped on a dress for me. With a steeling breath, I lifted the lid to find a jewelry box and note settled atop tissue paper begging to be unwrapped.

To go with that necklace you always wear. - E

My heart fluttered at his attention. I pried open the jewelry box carefully to find a pair of dazzling earrings - tear drop diamonds hung delicately from the daintiest of gold chains somehow anchored to the findings. Nerves shook my hands ever so slightly, and I set the jewels off to the side. A texture much akin to rose petals brushed my fingers as I began to unfold the tissue paper. I gulped and clutched the deep forest green velvet gently to lift it to my shoulders. The fabric tumbled exquisitely, nearly reaching the floor. Examining the shape, my mouth suddenly parched. A v shape reached from the wide straps down to nearly the center of my abdomen and back.

Holy shit, Flint.

・・・

My fingers knotted together in my lap and I stared out the window at the passing buildings. Never in my life had I worn something so expensive to an event so lavish with people so important. Anxiety swam in my stomach like it hadn't waited the full thirty minutes after lunch.

Six scars. Six scars that are exposed across your chest and back and arms just waiting for him to notice. You really think he won't ask about them?

"What are you thinking about?" Elliot reached over and placed a hand on mine.

"Nothing… just nervous, I guess."

"Well, what are you nervous about? Maybe I can ease your mind."

"All of it. The people. The pictures. The grandiosity of it all…"

"Hm," He pondered a moment. "The grandiosity will wear off, I'm sure. As for the pictures, you look *ravishing*, and you have nothing to worry about. And there will be quite a few people but… *'I like large parties. They're so intimate. At small parties there isn't any privacy.'*"

A thin smile crept across my face at the *Gatsby* reference, my lips pressing together in an attempt to stifle it. My cheeks grew warm.

"See? It's going to be a lovely evening." He gave my tangled hands a light, reassuring squeeze as he pulled the car up to the valet.

We stepped out of the car, the cool evening air sending a slight shiver through me. Elliot placed his hand at the small of my back over a just-concealed scar and, even though he couldn't possibly realize its presence, it set my nerves prickling. Soft velvet tickled over my feet shackled in strappy heels as we walked.

"We've got a brief stint of posing for pictures, then we'll head inside. Are you sure you're alright?"

I inhaled slowly, preparing my white lie and attempting to make sure it was convincing. "Yes, I'm good. Let's go."

Photographers imprisoned a carpeted walkway against a wall of event logos. Their camera shutters nearly deafening, the scattered flashes left spots in my vision as an additional peril to my wavering legs.

Ah, yes, the intimacy of large gatherings.

Elliot leaned close to kiss my temple.

"You're doing great," he whispered. The shuttering erupted at the gesture, then waned as the cameras had finally satisfied their appetite for a moment.

We took the brief reprieve as our cue to escape and stepped through heavy doors for refuge inside the banquet hall. Instrumental music poured over speakers concealed somewhere throughout the room. Small globe-shaped bulbs hung in rows over candle-lit tables casting a warm glow over the event. It seemed as if even breathing the air was expensive.

Pull yourself together. Smile. You've got this.

• • •

By the time the speaking portion of the event had started, I wasn't even sure I could remember my own name after Elliot had introduced me to so many new faces. Our seats were located at a table tucked into the front corner of the room for his easy access to the stage. It just so happened to be the perfect location to catch the gaze of inattentive guests, too, our every action observed as caged animals. As warm as my heart felt for Elliot as he made his way to the podium, my smile failed to reach my eyes while I clapped.

"Every three minutes, a child somewhere in the world is diagnosed with cancer. Just over twenty years ago, my brother Nathaniel was one of those children."

I stiffened. He'd mentioned a sister, but nothing about a brother. Elliot took a deep, steadying breath before continuing.

"Nate was one of those kids who just *loved* being around people. It didn't matter what we were doing, if we were doing *anything*, he wanted to be a part of it. When he got sick, we saw that begin to change. He didn't have the energy, and even when he would have a good day he was more an observer than an active participant. It wasn't long into his sudden illness that we received the diagnosis: medulloblastoma. For those of us without medical degrees, this meant he had a tumor growing in the back of his skull and progressing down to his spinal cord. At first, his prognosis was positive. After about two months, however, his cancer had spread aggressively in spite of the best efforts of our doctors, and the outlook was grim. At the tender age of fourteen, just three months following his diagnosis, Nathaniel passed away."

Dear god, you're kidding. This man who oozes "easy life" has more depth than you ever dreamed. He lost a brother? As a child?

Elliot wiped a tear that threatened to fall from his eyes. It made me want to reach out. To offer him a hand like he'd offered me so many times already.

"Almost daily something happens that I'd love to be able to share with my brother. His life may have been short, but he had a profound impact on my family and our loved ones. Now, I'm no doctor. I can't attest to the science behind all of this. But what I can say is the work of the men and women here at the American Childhood Cancer Research Center is life-changing, and your funding can help them work toward a future of families remaining whole. Thank you for your work. Thank you for your dedication to finding a cure. And thank you, from the bottom of my heart, for your support of families like mine."

A tear slid down my cheek as the room erupted with applause. My heart sat low in my chest, weighed down by a peculiar blend of guilt and sympathy. I hadn't known any of this about Elliot yet. His willingness to share with me - with a room full of people - what had to be a deeply personal and emotional story simultaneously ignited inspiration and fear within me.

You've barely scratched the surface of your trauma with him, and now here he is bringing you to an event where his is on display for all to see. You know that means he's probably more than willing to share an even more personal account with just you. How does it feel? To have someone open up to you and be so cold that you can't do the same. Not even a little bit.

"That was beautiful, Elliot." I wiped my lonesome tear away and kissed his cheek as he came back to sit down.

"Thank you, and thanks again for coming with me." He reached for my hands that I hadn't realized were clasped in my lap.

Look at him. Look at all this. He's too good for you. You don't belong here. You're playing dress up for the night, but even the most expensive of dresses can't disguise your damage.

Elliot glanced over at me as the next speaker began some much-too-scientific explanation of the research she was overseeing. I forced myself to maintain eye contact and mustered up a small smile in concern that he'd think I was burdened by his story - or worse yet, apathetic. He returned my smile and began drawing circles on the back of my hand with his thumb, each one accompanying another browbeating thought of inadequacy.

• • •

Elliot and I settled on a bench just outside the glow of a street light. A thin mist sprinkled the cool air and hung in space like a near fog. If I was alone, it would be eerie. It almost was anyway, but Elliot made me feel… secure? Drops of moisture were starting to accumulate at the nape of my neck as we quietly sat on our perch. It was as if anything much above a whisper would disturb the night around us.

"Tell me about him…" I paused, then added, "If you want to, that is."

He pondered the question lightly as if I had asked him about the weather. "He was a great big brother."

"So he was older?"

"The oldest. He was five years older than me. My sister, Ashley, she's three."

"So you're-"

"The baby, yes." He chuckled and shook his head. "Nate always gave me a hard time about that. Calling me *golden boy* and all."

I laughed. Elliot *was* a golden boy. Everyone's dream child. Handsome, successful, intelligent, kind…

"We were just boys, you know? We'd rough house and get in trouble and gang up to terrorize Ashley…" He sniffled a bit, tears welling in his eyes. "He was so much fun. The most adventurous person I've ever met." He gave a soft, incredulous laugh. "And I've met a lot of people."

He turned to me like that point mattered. Like I should understand that his brother hadn't just been wild for a kid - but exceptional.

"He would've had so much fun out in the world. As an adult, I mean. I used to imagine us backpacking through Europe or blowing all our money on something stupid in Thailand. He would've dared me to jump off every cliff we passed." He smiled, but tears began to fall slowly down his cheeks.

I reached for something to say, but came up short. "Elliot, I'm so sorry."

It felt insufficient. Probably because it was. I knew all too well that words like that get dulled when you've heard them too many times. Still, I meant it with every ounce of me. There's no sense in a god - or whoever - taking away a boy from his family before he even had a chance to grow up.

He nodded, slow and quiet.

"We make it," he answered honestly. "It's not easy. But nobody has it easy."

Ain't that the damn truth.

I nodded, too. But my throat tightened unexpectedly.

There he was - *Elliot* - with his neat smile and solid life that I didn't feel at all equipped to understand, and even *he* carried ghosts. Maybe that's just how it goes. We all carry someone. Or something.

He glanced sideways at me. "Sorry. I don't get to talk about him much. Like *really* talk about him. I didn't mean to dump all that on you."

I shook my head almost too quickly for the moment, but I needed him to understand.

"It's not dumping. And even if it was, I asked for it. It's more like... letting me learn about you."

He smiled at that. Just barely. The kind of tired, grateful smile people give when they've just let you see something sacred.

He reached his hand over my left one and thumbed over the thin, pale mark that curved behind my knuckle.

"Where'd that come from?" he asked softly.

I froze.

"This?" I gave a quick, breathy laugh. "Stupid really. Cooper was little and got caught in a barbed wire fence. He was fine, the little brat. But I came out with battle scars. Probably should have gone to the ER that day, but I didn't."

It wasn't Cooper. It wasn't barbed wire. And it definitely wasn't an accident.

Elliot didn't press. He just nodded and continued tracing his thumb over the raised skin. I couldn't tell if he bought it or not. Either way, the lie burned between us like static. He had trusted me with his brother. I wanted so badly to give him something back. A scrap of truth. A story. A scar. But I couldn't. Truth hung like putrid vomit in the back of my throat. He handed me something vulnerable and real, and I handed him a lie.

• • •

As soon as I got home - before I changed, before I took my makeup off, before I even took Cooper out - I whipped out my laptop and collapsed onto the couch to journal. I couldn't keep it in. I opened the notes app and titled my next entry, **You Bitch.**

> *Why? Why the fuck would I LIE to him? He trusted me. He opened up about something real and painful and carved straight out of the softest part of him, and what did I do?*
>
> *I panicked.*

I retreated.

I threw up a wall so fast it practically cracked the foundation.

All he did was ask. Gently. Carefully. Like he was holding the question with both hands. And I fed him that half-truth like it was nothing. As if he didn't deserve better.

The scar was right there. He touched it like it mattered, like he wanted the truth, not the prettied-up version I hand out to strangers and doctors and anyone who gets too close. And instead of trusting him with an inch of honesty, I chose fear.

He deserved more than that.

He looked at me like he was waiting for something real. And the awful thing is, I wanted to give it to him. I did. My throat just closed up and the story snagged on old wires inside of me, and instead of trying, I backed away.

I told myself I was keeping things simple. Safe. Controlled. But now I'm so mad at myself I could scream. Or cry. Or both.

Mostly I just want to take it back. Just rewind and try again and tell him the truth. No, not all of it - I'm not suicidal - but maybe a little piece of something real. Something that doesn't make me a walking red flag.

Fuck, I'm such a mess.

I slammed my laptop closed and tossed it to the other end of the couch. Cooper nudged my leg through my gown trying to signal that he wanted to go out, but I sat with my head in my hands for a long moment.

"How the fuck do I do this, Coop?"

He nudged me again.

"Okay, okay."

I strolled over to the hook by the door and grabbed his leash. He danced at my feet. I clipped his leash to his collar and pulled the door open, the fog still hovering low like a blanket someone forgot to pull back from the earth.

We stepped out into it, and I clutched my phone tightly in my hand.

Cooper swerved back and forth looking for the perfect spot to handle business. I flipped my phone over in my hand and pulled up Elliot's messages. The cursor blinked like an invitation.

I contemplated typing out a confession right then and there. Saying all the word vomit that was on my mind. But that wouldn't be right.

I typed:

> *I hope you're home safe. Tonight was… a lot, but in a good way. Thanks for making it easier.*

I paused before I hit the send button. It felt… exposed. Like I'd left the shower curtain open or something. Then, before I could spiral out about it any more, I pressed send and locked it again, turning it over in my hand. The air around us felt thin and thick all at the same time as if I couldn't get enough, or maybe I was drowning in it. There I stood, dress and heels still on, waiting for my dog to shit, guilt eating me alive. I think I would have been less scared if a real-life monster came out of the dense fog and chased after me.

Then, a buzz.

Elliot 11:42pm

> *I'm home, don't worry. A lot is kind of our thing, huh? I'm glad it was the good kind tonight. Goodnight, Sam.*

And the pit in my stomach grew.

Elliot

She let me in.

Just a little, but enough to know she trusted me. Maybe without meaning to.

She'd been off all day. Quiet in that way she gets when her mind is chewing on something sharp. Brought up some woman that she thought was a "better fit" for me.

It was laughable, honestly. The idea that anyone could give me what I'd already found in her. And anyway, I know now that wasn't the only thing weighing on her mind. And either issue alone would have been enough to stir her mind into a spiral, much less the combination.

I remember asking her why she thought this woman was a better fit, and she'd shrugged - small, dismissive, almost embarrassed - and told me that her past disqualified her from deserving someone like me.

We got interrupted by work. I should've canceled the interview. Stayed there. Made sure she knew that, no matter what ghosts she thought she carried, she was the only one I wanted.

Then she told me about her mother.

She was doing me a favor - talking to me on a long drive home so I wouldn't fall asleep at the wheel after a hellish day punctuated by an investor dinner. And then, somewhere between exits, she let that truth slip into the open.

And... fuck, I just didn't know how to respond.

If I had been with her, maybe I could've reached out. Offered a hand. Something. Anything. Instead I was on the interstate in the dark, gripping my steering wheel while she unraveled one of the deepest wounds of her life on the other end of the line.

So I just listened. Let the silence stretch long enough for her to fill it only if she wanted to. God, I hope she felt it as space and not distance.

She told me her father killed her mother and all I could come up with - after a full minute where my throat wouldn't work - was, "I'm so sorry."

It felt... feeble. Like the thin curl of smoke rising from a candle that had already burned itself out - there, then gone before it meant anything.

But she didn't fall apart. Not then. It awakened something deep in her, an ache I could practically feel through the phone, but it didn't cause her to crumble. She stayed steady. She was always stronger than she ever gave herself credit for.

It wasn't long after that she came with me to the cancer research gala. And god did she look stunning. I'd sent her the dress and some jewelry earlier in the week, and when she walked in... she took my breath away.

She came because my parents couldn't be there. Because she didn't want me to go alone. And I got to share Nate with her - really share him. And she held the memory of him like it was fragile and precious. Like she understood what he meant to me without needing the whole story.

I don't think she ever realized it was the first time I'd truly opened up to someone I was dating about him. I might've mentioned my brother in passing before, but I'd never shared the real Nathaniel. Who he was. What losing him took out of me. And somehow... She made it feel safe to share the memories.

I remember the drive home after the gala.

The city lights flickered across her face in the passenger seat, soft and warm, and she kept looking out the window like she was afraid to disturb the moment.

She didn't talk much on the way back. She gets quiet when she's overwhelmed, and I didn't push her. I just let the silence settle around us like a blanket, comfortable and calm. It felt... easy. Easier than anything had in a long time.

At one red light, she glanced over at me - barely a second, barely a shift of her eyes - but it was enough. There was gratitude there. Something tender. Something that made my chest tighten so suddenly I thought maybe I'd forgotten how to breathe.

I remember thinking, "God I'm in trouble."

Because it wasn't the dress. Or the way she'd stood beside me through the speeches. Or even the soft way she'd asked questions about Nate, careful and gentle, like she didn't want to bruise a single memory.

It was the way she held things.

Her pain. My pain. The world. All of it, quietly, without fanfare. Without asking for anything back.

It wasn't long after we got to her house that I knew.

She stood on her porch, fingers curled around the skirt of that dress, hair falling loose from the clips. She looked up at me like she didn't understand why I'd chosen her as my date. As if she didn't realize she'd made the entire night bearable simply by existing in it.

She said, "Thank you for letting me come."

And something in me broke.

Because she still thought she was a burden. Still thought she was taking up space she wasn't invited into.

I wanted to tell her she saved the night. That her being there meant more than anything the donors or board members had to say. That the only thing that made that room full of strangers tolerable was knowing she was somewhere in it.

But I didn't say any of that.

I just watched her - standing there under the porch light, small and brave and so much stronger than she knew - and the truth hit me with full force.

I'm falling for her.

Not in the cinematic, fireworks kind of way. But quietly. In the way life shifts when you're not paying attention.

I'm falling for the way she listens. The way she tries. The way she lets me see her edges but still thinks she has to apologize for them. I'm falling for her softness and her storm. For the shadows behind her eyes. For the pieces she's still terrified to hand anyone.

And I remember gripping the steering wheel when I drove away, heart pounding so hard it hurt, thinking one thing over and over: please don't let me ruin this.

Because whatever this was, whatever we were building... it already mattered more than I meant for it to.

And god help me, I didn't want to lose her.

SAM

I rolled over in bed and stared at the clock on my bedside table. 3:52 glowed bright blue, mocking me. I'd been restless since lying to Elliot. It ate at my gut and nauseated me.

Such a beautiful night. And you ruined it. What kind of relationship starts with lies? Not a good one, that's for sure.

Cooper twitched next to me snoozing the night away. I sighed and rolled onto my back. *Might as well just get up.*

I heaved myself forward and up out of the bed, a heavy task on account of all the shame I was carrying. My worn pair of running shoes slid on - maybe if I couldn't sleep it off, I could try to outrun it. Cooper sighed heavily from the bed, not yet ready to get up in the early morning hours.

"Come on, dude," I said, patting my leg. "Let's go."

He jumped out of the bed and made a slow, long stretch of his body. Following me down the hallway, we readied ourselves at the door for our run. Unfortunately, the repetitive pounding of my feet against the pavement only compounded the self-depricating thoughts.

It's just a little scar. What harm could a little white lie like that actually do? Besides, at least it was a believable lie.

Ha! 'Believable lie.' Where in your life would you have run into a barbed wire fence? Much less, when have you ever let Cooper off leash? He probably saw right through you. And right after he shared with you about his brother. Are you kidding? Of course you hurt his feelings! You're such a bitch.

• • •

"How was the gala?" Jessa sang teasingly at me as I trudged around the corner of the counter.

"It was beautiful," I yawned honestly. "Elliot had an eloquent speech about his brother who passed, and I think they raised a lot of money for research and such."

Bill's eyes narrowed. "You get enough sleep kiddo?"

I rubbed at my eyes and pulled on my apron. "No. But I'm okay. Just need some coffee."

Jessa grabbed a mug from the shelf and dispensed some drip coffee into it before handing it my way. A cautious smile hinted that she might be catching on that there was more at play, but she kept it to herself.

Bill shuffled to the back, and I turned to Jessa in a hushed voice. "Hey, so when someone tells you something personal and instead of reciprocating you lie and say something totally incorrect… when you *want* to tell the truth you just… can't, what do you do?"

Jessa studied my face for any inkling of what I might be talking about, but I just shrugged at her.

"Well," she wiped her hands with her towel and placed it back over her shoulder. "You wait until you can. And then you do."

I nodded slowly and sipped on another drink of coffee.

You're going to need multiple of these to make it through today.

"Sam, what are you referring to?"

The front door chime interrupted Jessa's next question, and I gratefully ducked away from our conversation. Elliot strolled in, bright eyed and bushy tailed like he'd had the best sleep of his life.

"Man, drinking on the job, Reynolds? How do you let her get away with this?" He laughed to Jessa, who smiled widely at him. "You okay, Sam?"

I took another swig and set my mug down to the side of the register. "Yep! Just sleepy, that's all."

He smiled his sideways, cocky grin. "The party life a little too much for you?"

"Must be it," I rolled my eyes. "Your usual?"

"Actually, yes, plus a half sweet vanilla latte please. To go. I'm meeting Ashley today to help her with some stuff around her house."

I raised my eyebrows at him. *Helpful and handsome. Hmm.* It was like he peered into my thoughts, his cockeyed smile turning up at the corners.

I took in his charm - the way his eyes lingered on me, the way his smile wavered just slightly as he searched my face, the way his hand made its way through his hair as he leaned forward against the counter. If I didn't already feel guilty enough, his presence amplified things tenfold.

You're such a horrible person.

"You sure you're alright?" He asked, quieter this time to make sure he was only audible to me.

"Yes," I deflected. I grabbed my coffee mug and held it up to him as if it was proof that I was telling the truth. "I'm sure. Just didn't sleep well after being up late is all."

Lies. Lies. More lies.

Jessa handed a carrier of drinks over the counter to Elliot with a warm smile. "I heard you had a wonderful speech last night, dear."

He chuckled shyly, rubbed at the back of his neck, and glanced at me. "Well thank you. It sure helped to have a friendly face in the crowd."

He smiled - one of those soft, earnest ones that didn't ask anything of me. And yet, somehow, it felt like he was asking everything of me.

You don't deserve his flattery. I looked away, pretending to check the register.

"Anytime," I said quietly.

He raised the drink carrier slightly as a parting gesture and nodded to both of us. "See you soon."

As the bell jingled behind him, I exhaled the breath I didn't realize I'd been holding.

Jessa didn't say anything else. Just watched me from the corner of her eye as she started wiping down the machine.

I picked up my coffee again, now lukewarm and bitter, and took another long sip.

He'd given me his truth. And I'd given him fiction dressed up as honesty.

I wasn't even sure which of us I was trying to protect anymore. But I knew this: if he ever asked again - really asked - I didn't think I'd be able to lie a second time.

Not to those eyes.
Not to that face.
Not to him.

SAM

"Sweetie, I don't know how to tell you this…" Jessa sighed over the phone speaker. My heart skipped a couple of beats, fearing the worst.

Am I about to lose my job? Are Jessa and Bill okay?

"Elliot asked about you."

My mouth ran dry. "What do you mean?"

"He stopped by today while I was locking up. He… he wanted to know about your past."

My breath caught in my throat. "Um… okay, what did you tell him?"

"Sam, *I* only know the bits and pieces you've told me, but even so, it's not my story to tell."

I finally let out a sigh, but rage bubbled up inside of me. I mustered out through welling tears of frustration, "He had no right…"

"I know, sweetie, but listen. I can tell he cares about you. He just wants to know you're okay."

"Jessa, I've *told* him that no one is actively hurting me. He *told* me he'd be patient with me. *This* is not being patient. Besides, how do you tell someone about the kind of abuse I went through? About the group home? About how fast I was left to figure out this world on my own? About the one time I trusted someone and they wound up *dead* because of it?"

My words were flooding out, hurried and aching.

"Sam, take a breath," Jessa said softly.

I did. Shaky, but full.

I couldn't pull words together with all that was swirling around my head. It felt like an act of betrayal. Like someone had cracked open a safe I hadn't wanted to give out the combination to.

My mind spun - wild, frantic, loud. All the things I'd trusted him with, all the things he didn't know… and suddenly the things he shouldn't know.

He went behind my back.
He dug.
He pried.

He went looking for demons I wasn't ready to introduce.

A hot wave of nausea rolled up my throat. My fingers trembled around the phone.

"Sam?" Jessa's voice softened, like she could feel the storm brewing on my end. "Talk to me."

But talking felt impossible. My thoughts were colliding too fast to separate. The world felt too tight around me, too bright, too close.

I pressed a palm to my forehead, sweat beginning to bead up and forced air into my lungs.

It wasn't just betrayal - it was exposure. A door kicked open inside me that I hadn't checked the lock on in years.

And god it hurt.

It hurt in a way I hadn't expected from him.

"Maybe I shouldn't have said anything, but I wanted to let you know…"

"No, I'm glad you did."

"Listen. I know you don't owe anyone your story. But you can't pretend it doesn't eat away at you when you keep it in from someone you care about."

I went silent. She was right. I postured myself as a person who didn't need anyone else. But the truth of the matter was that the walls I built around me were becoming a prison. Hot tears rolled down my cheeks.

"Sweetheart? Are you there?"

I wiped at my face and deeply inhaled through my nose to collect myself. "Yes, I'm here."

"I love you, you know? And I'm here for you."

"I know, Jess. Thank you. I love you too."

• • •

"Good morning!" Oblivious, Elliot beamed at me as he waltzed up to the counter.

"I need to talk to you," I snapped, tearing off my apron as I steeled myself for a fight. "Not here."

He pressed his eyebrows together in complete ignorance, and for a brief moment

I relaxed, suckered into his gray-blue eyes full of concern.

"Jessa, I'll be right back," I hollered around the corner. She gave me a thumbs up that seemed to equate to a *go get 'em tiger*, and I took it as the resolve I needed.

I grabbed Elliot's upper arm and pushed him out the front door, the friendly chime mocking us as we hastily pushed past the sidewalk and across the street to the park. I'd been stewing all evening and morning waiting for him to show up. Maybe that was wrong. Maybe I should have called. Maybe I didn't care.

"Sam, what is it? What's wrong?"

"You asked Jessa about me." I released my grip of his arm and whirled around to face him. He may have had a whole foot and a half on me, but with the indignation rising in me I knew I could bring him to his knees if I wanted.

He searched my face as realization made its way to his. "Sam, I-"

"No, you've done enough talking. It's time for you to listen," I said, cutting him off. I motioned between us. "I don't *have* to do this. I was doing *just fine* before I met you. *You're* the one asking *me* to open up. *You're* the one who wants something here. And you *told* me you would be patient. I trusted that. I trusted *you*. When everything in me screamed not to. And what do you do? You betrayed that trust by going to one of the only people who has had my back in my life trying to use them against me? Expecting a tell-all about my life?"

I breathed in, realizing I hadn't taken a breath the whole time I'd been yelling at him. My left hand trembled—anger, fear, I didn't know. But I refused to let him see it.

"Sam, stop, please-" He took a deep breath in an attempt to collect the massive dump of rage I'd just thrown at him. "Yes, okay? I asked about you. But only because you make it *so* hard to know if you're okay, Sam. Do you realize that? I'm *worried* about you."

I scoffed. "Worried about me? Elliot, you hardly know me. Why do you even care so much, huh?"

He looked almost offended by the question. "For one, Sam, I *am* a human. Despite what you may think, I'm not some ostentatious asshole. I care. I have a heart. And second... I don't know, okay? I don't know what it is about you. But since the moment I met you I wanted to know more. You're just-"

"Some mystery to crack before you'll be on your way again?"

He lowered his voice. I could tell his feelings were starting to become more fragile. "It's not like that. You know it."

Tears stung my eyes. I took a shaky breath and looked down at my feet, willing the tears back behind my eyes.

"I don't know what else there is to say... I'm hurt."

He hung his head lower and lifted my chin to meet my gaze in earnest. Regret filled his eyes. "I'm sorry. I didn't think about that being a breach of trust, but you're right. It was."

"Fuck yeah it was, Elliot! You don't understand what a big deal it is that I'm even entertaining the idea of opening up to you."

"Sam, that's not fair. Of course I do."

"Respectfully, Elliot, you don't." I crossed my arms, clenching my trembling hand under my armpit. I needed him to *not* see what kind of hold this had on me. "And I understand that you won't get it until you know... I'm just... I'm not there yet."

He reached out a trepidatious hand but settled it back by his side when I kept my arms crossed. His weight shifted from one foot to the other, and I thought he might turn to walk away. And part of me wanted him to. That would be par for the course of my life, anyway. But he hesitated... then he stayed.

"How can I make this right?"

"You can't... not today."

· · ·

The rest of the day dragged by like a wounded animal, limping from one hour to the next. I wanted nothing more than to go home, bury myself under a blanket, and drown whatever was left of my dignity in a glass - or three - of wine.

Jessa didn't ask. Not at first. She hummed along to the shop playlist, made faces at regulars when their backs were turned, and let the silence between us do what it needed to do.

It wasn't until the *Open* sign flipped around and the clatter of the last dishes faded that she finally spoke.

"How was your conversation with Elliot?"

Her tone was light, but the question still made my shoulders tighten.

I sighed and leaned back against the counter, apron hanging loose around my waist. "Brutal."

She tsked and shook her head, sweeping stray coffee grounds into a pile. "That boy…"

"I don't really know what to do with him," I admitted. "He's-" I exhaled, searching for a word that didn't sound pathetic. "Too much and not enough at the same time. He wants answers I don't have - ones I can't give him yet. And maybe I don't deserve the patience for him to wait to find out."

Jessa gave me that look - eyebrows up, lips pressed together - the one that said she'd heard the lie I was trying to slip past her. "You think you don't deserve patience?"

"Don't start with your therapy voice," I muttered, untying my apron and sauntering toward the door to the back room.

"Then don't run from this," Jessa said, stopping me in my tracks. "You're going to have to decide how you feel about him to determine where you go with this information. He overstepped a boundary, yes. It's okay to be hurt by that. But for what it's worth, I don't think he's going anywhere. He strikes me as the type who'd sit on your porch all night just to hand you coffee in the morning."

I laughed, just a little. "He doesn't need to see me in the morning."

"There she is," she said warmly.

I rolled my eyes and pushed my way into the back room. Jessa followed.

"I mean it, though, Sam. Maybe this stung a little. But you have to decide whether or not you're going to let yourself be loved."

• • •

I toyed with the phone in my hand. It felt stupid to still be so upset about Elliot, but I was. And I felt like I needed a friend, but I didn't want to be *that* girl - calling just to talk about stupid boy drama.

Andrew won't care. He lives for this stuff… but you'll change his opinion of him. You don't want him to hate him… or maybe you do. Maybe that makes it easier.

I hated how cynical I was. I wished for a moment that I could be *normal*. Not this fucked up, trauma-beaten, secretive version of myself that I was. I wished I could *enjoy* Elliot. He was just trying to learn more about me, after all. Was that such a bad thing?

Yes. You haven't given him the permission to know that stuff yet. It's none of his business.

I flipped my phone upright in my hand and pulled up Andrew's contact, my finger hovering over the call button.

Normal people call their friends.

"Helloooo," Andrew answered in a sing-songy voice, music cutting in and out in the background.

"You're busy, I'll let you go."

"No ma'am! I'm just cooking some dinner. What's up?" The music turned down but remained on, low and soft behind his voice.

"Well… I- uh." I didn't know how to get into it. "It's about Elliot."

I heard a clatter and suddenly Andrew seemed closer to the phone - more engaged. "Oh? Do tell."

"He asked Jessa about me."

"...Okay?"

"No, like, *asked* about me."

"And again I say, *okay?*"

I rolled my eyes and flipped my hand out in exasperation. "He was prying, Andrew!"

"So? Don't you want to know everything there is to know about him? This is what we do when we like someone, sis. We stalk them and figure out their entire life story. You know, his family-"

"So I'm just being dumb?" I cut him off, really not wanting the low down on Elliot's family life. I felt guilty enough for lying to him after learning about his brother. I didn't need more ammo for humiliation to shoot my way.

"No, Sam. You're not being dumb. He should have stalked you online like the rest of us do with our crushes."

"Yeah, well, he probably tried. I'm not online."

"Oh yeah... well, it's definitely a bit of an invasion of privacy, sure. I'll give you that. But at least he cares."

At least he cares.

• • •

I wrestled with my feelings all the way to bed and then some. I tossed and turned for over an hour debating whether I'd been too harsh, said too much, pushed too hard. He did cross a boundary, but maybe Andrew was right. He cared. And that had to count for something, right?

Glancing at the clock next to my bed, I sighed deeply. It was late. But I didn't want to go to sleep with this internal war going on. I wasn't sure I *could* anyway. I grabbed my phone off the charger and stared at my recent messages. Part of me wished I had heard from Elliot by now, but I'd asked him for space - practically screamed at him for it - and I couldn't blame him for giving it to me.

I clicked over to my notes app instead and titled this entry: **Okay But Hear Me Out.**

> *We fought today. Fuck, like actually fought. I yelled at him for going to Jessa behind my back to ask about my past. But, I mean, that's justified, right? He deserved that? I can't begin to put to words how pissed I was… Am. Idk.*
>
> *Andrew seemed to think it wasn't a big deal. But it felt like a big deal to me. Like he violated some unspoken peace treaty between us about my past.*
>
> *I don't think this is actually the case, but it FELT like he was trying to prove I wasn't enough. Like he needed some excuse to leave, and he decided to go to the one person on this earth who actually knows a few things about me to gather ammunition. And I guess I got defensive.*
>
> *Maybe I should have reached out earlier instead of letting it simmer all night and morning long. That probably would have been the healthy thing for me to do. Asked him why he felt the need to do that instead of assuming and yelling at him. It's just… so tough, you know?*
>
> *It's late but I think… I should text him.*

I slid the notes app closed and clicked back over to messages.

I wasn't sure what to say. Couldn't think of how to wrap all my thoughts into a simple text. My need for boundaries with my appreciation for his feelings. I hovered over the keyboard for a long moment. Finally, I settled on a quick:

> *Hey. I'm sorry. Talk tomorrow?*

I swiped away to find a playlist to put on to fall asleep to, hoping it would help me relax. I genuinely believed Elliot would be asleep by the time I'd come around to messaging him, but he almost immediately responded.

Elliot 11:53pm

Please. I'm sorry, too. Dinner at my place?

I didn't respond in the moment. I'd reply in the morning. I was already drifting off to sleep with a wave of relief flooding my veins.

Elliot

15

Our first fight was a brutal one.

And it was my fault.

I had asked Jessa about her past, because... god, she's impossible to read when she's hurting. I only wanted to know she was okay. I thought it was harmless. I thought caring about her that much was harmless.

She didn't take it too well.

Now looking back on it, I guess I can't blame her.

I walked in the coffee shop, all smiles as if my whole world wasn't about to threaten to crack in two. But the second she looked up at me, something flashed across her face - anger sharp enough to cut, stunning enough to steal my breath. If I hadn't been so taken by it, I would have been scared. Maybe I was.

I remember her grip on my arm - firm, not cruel, but absolutely unforgiving. She practically flung me out of the cafe, simmering with a rage I couldn't quite understand. Boiling over, really.

She yelled. Not nonsense, either. These were words she'd been storing up, letting them steep until they were strong enough to burn. And, god help me, I stuck to my guns for a hot moment.

At first, I was pissed. I couldn't fathom why she wouldn't just... let me love her.

Then, I saw it.

The hurt. The embarrassment. The fear.

And my stomach dropped because I realized I'd been the one to put that look on her face.

"Am I just some mystery to crack before you'll be on your way again?" she'd asked me. And, fuck, that one stung.

Now I get it.

Then? It felt unfair. Like every tiny step we'd taken toward trust had been tossed out the window. But even in the middle of it, even as she threw walls back up between us, I wasn't walking away. Not from her. Not from whatever this was becoming.

Finally, when I unclenched my own pride, I asked what I could do to make it right.

"You can't... not today."

And she walked off - more guarded, less soft - and it took everything in me not to chase her. To not beg her to let me fix it, to let me prove I wasn't going anywhere.

I went to work that morning with the ground pulled out from under me a bit. Did my best to busy myself with work that mattered. But my mind raced with thoughts of her.

Her laugh.

The way her eyes caught these flecks of gold when she was excited.

The scar on the back of her hand she said came from a barbed-wire fence... still don't know if I believe that one. I never remembered to ask again.

By noon I was going stir-crazy, wanting nothing more than to break into the space she'd demanded, scoop her up, and tell her she didn't need to be afraid of me.

I typed out a message:

> Sam... I'm sorry. What can I do?

And just stared at it. Blinking cursor. Unsent.

I didn't want to push her. Whatever my question had triggered in her, it went way deeper than just me.

And as the day dragged on, I found myself praying - actually praying - that I hadn't ruined this. That she'd still want me around. That I hadn't crossed some invisible boundary I could never undo. And for the first time I realized I was imagining a future I didn't want to lose.

Finally, way past when I'd expect to hear from her, my phone lit up.

> **Sam 11:52pm**
>
> Hey. I'm sorry. Talk tomorrow?

Relief. It flooded over me like a levy broke. Of course we could talk tomorrow. Of course it was fixable. Of course I could get over myself.

Hell, I would've grovelled if she asked me to. And I think that was the moment I knew. This was becoming something bigger. Something I wasn't ready to name out loud yet, but felt down to the bone.

16
SAM

Jessa's words were heavy on my mind as I walked, following my phone's directions to Elliot's place for dinner.

You have to decide whether or not you're going to let yourself be loved.

I struggled to reconcile my feelings for him with what he'd done. But then again, had it really been that bad?

My heart and mind battled back and forth like a pendulum. Quite frankly, he pissed me off. And it wasn't just because he'd asked, either. It was because he *cared* enough *to* ask. In all honesty? It terrified me.

My feelings for him had only grown. My initial impression of someone who hadn't seen a single struggle in his life - someone who wouldn't be able to handle when things became difficult - was wrong. The more I learned of him, the more I realized he was fully capable of dealing with hard things. And it made me want to understand him better.

You can't ask that of him if you're unwilling to share yourself, you know.

I couldn't remember the last time I'd longed for happiness. Safety, sure. Security. Maybe even contentment. But happiness? That was always too risky. Because true happiness requires vulnerability - for you to be willing to open yourself so much to something or someone that it has every possibility of wrecking you entirely. I learned early on that not many people were worth the risk, but I was beginning to wonder if Elliot might be.

Stepping into his building from the chilly autumn weather felt like a warm embrace. Inside stood a desk attended by a man who looked to be in his late forties, his blond hair falling over companionable brown eyes.

"Good evening. How can I help you?" I guess I looked as lost as I felt.

"I'm here to see Elliot Flint for dinner."

"Ah, yes, he's expecting you, Ms. Reynolds. You'll take the elevator on the far left; it's the only one that goes up to the penthouse. And if there's anything I can assist you with during your time here, please don't hesitate to call down."

The penthouse? He just keeps getting more out of your league.

I thanked him and turned to the bank of elevators, the furthest left designated with slats surrounding it as if to pronounce its importance above the others. The ascent to his floor was quick enough to give me the sense of near-vertigo. Or maybe it was just butterflies.

The aroma of fresh pasta immediately wafted in when the doors dinged open at the top floor. Concrete floors mimicked his office, but the decor elements he had chosen leaned more welcoming and homely. Brilliant textures complimented the space well - the worn-in leather of his couch, the natural wood table, the thickly knit blanket draped over the armchair, the crackling fire of the fireplace. Even the soft music playing in the background added a blankety smooth, nearly tangible texture. A handful of stairs stood across the room leading to a wall of glass extending to what I assumed to be a hallway and overlooking an expansive balcony with a swimming pool.

Elliot smiled widely as I stepped in. "Ah, just in time. Dinner's nearly ready!"

"It smells incredible," I greeted him with an awkward sideways embrace, not sure exactly where we stood. "And your home is stunning."

And so is he. Would you look at how adorable he looks in that apron?

He turned to the stove and I took a moment to appreciate his appearance. His tattoo poked out under his rolled sleeves - one of my favorite looks of his, but with a new twist. Apparently date night meant the top couple of buttons on the front of his shirt found their way undone, the tattoos beneath his collar bones peeking out just so. The slightest hint of chest hair poked through the bottom of the v shape the shirt made. His dress pants hung lower on his waist than I imagined they did earlier in the day, and they drifted above bare feet on his concrete floor.

Boy, is he a sight.

He lifted a spoon from the sauce, cupping his hand underneath to avoid dripping any on the floor, and motioned for me to taste test.

"My god, can you do *everything?*" I hadn't even cleared my mouth before the flattery spilled out.

His head inflated with ego, his devilish smirk returning to his face. "Careful, Reynolds. I'm a dangerous man with a compliment."

"I don't doubt that a bit." Heat rushed to my cheeks, and I slipped out of my jacket, hanging it on the back of a barstool. "Can I help with anything?"

"Actually, would you mind pouring us some drinks?" He nodded toward a well stocked bar.

"Bourbon. Rocks, right? Any particular kind?" I eyed the array of bourbon bottles - enough to be impressive, but not so much to be a collector of any kind.

"You've got it! Surprise me."

I gathered a glass from the top shelf of the bar and got ice from the fridge door.

Henry McKenna 10-year sounded fancy enough. I gave it a hefty pour and slid it down the counter to him. He looked up, gave me a knowing wink, and took a sip.

I perused the bar, completely lost in the fancy labels I hadn't seen before, and settled on a bottle of wine.

"Do you mind?" I held the bottle up.

"Of course - go ahead."

I guessed at a drawer to find a corkscrew and found it in the first one I opened.

You organize things in a similar way, it seems. That's a good sign,

The bottle opened with a high pitched *pop* and red wine poured into my glass. I raised it to take a sip but was stopped in my tracks as Elliot grabbed his bourbon and spun on his heel to face me.

"Cheers," he stated, tilting his glass toward mine. "To us."

To us fighting? To us yelling at each other? What version of us?

"To us, I suppose."

We both sipped at our drinks. Elliot's eyes danced in the dim light of his home, and I could tell he was pleased with himself that I had still agreed to come after our fight. He was acting… normal. It scared and fascinated me at the same time.

"Dinner will be ready in five," he said, turning back toward the stove. "Make yourself at home until then,"

I slowly moved around his home taking in the atmosphere and sipping my wine. Black and white family photos speckled the space. Two people I assumed to be his parents smiled back at me with a younger looking Elliot between them. They looked… normal. Happy. It was hard to believe looking at that photograph the loss they'd endured. Then there were other photos of Ashley's med school graduation, some friends it looked like from college, and one I assumed had to be really old of him and Nathaniel.

Shows that you really can't judge a book by its cover.

I moved on, noting the record on the player had switched off. I set my glass down and flipped the record to the other side, then hit play. Soft music filled the air again. Elliot's hand slipped into mine from behind, startling me at his sudden presence. My breath caught in my throat and my mouth went dry.

You've got to get the fuck over this at some point, Jesus.

"Dinner's ready," he all but whispered. "Sorry to scare you."

I took a steeling breath and turned toward him, keeping his hand in mine. "Thank you for cooking."

He inhaled deeply in return, turning to lead me to the table. "Anything for you."

My cheeks flushed. He easily had that effect on me.

He pulled my chair out for me, and I thanked him as I sat. The plate in front of me smelled of garlic and herbs and fresh cheese… it looked as delicious as it smelled. Elliot grabbed both of our glasses for a refill before he sat himself across from me.

"I wanted to say I'm sorry again, Sam." Elliot reached for a sip of his second glass of bourbon. "I didn't mean to upset you like I did."

I nervously stabbed at the food on my plate. "You just did it because you care, right?"

"Of course, Sam. What other reason would I have?"

"Elliot, I don't know. The people in my past tended to use anything they knew about me against me. It's hard for me to open up. To really trust someone with any information about myself."

He reached a hand into the middle of the table and held it face up - a gesture I oddly wanted to accept. "And I'm sorry. I should have trusted that you'd tell me in your own time."

"That's the thing. I'm sure I will… but… I've never done anything like *this* before."

But you make me want to. Maybe not when you do things like *that*. But I want to. It's just going to take some time."

He chuckled, seeming to understand where I was coming from. "I'll be patient. I want this to work. From now on, I promise, I'll come to you if I have questions."

"That's all I can ask for."

• • •

I giggled hysterically as Elliot leapt and waved a dish towel back and forth in front of the smoke alarm. Smoke curled through the open living space from the mouth of the oven, our forgotten dessert thoroughly charred.

"I guess among the very few things you *can't* do is bake a dessert, huh?"

He stopped jumping at my teasing and turned to me, disapproving face falsified by the curve hinting at the corner of his lips. I busted into laughter again, causing him to lose his annoyed facade and join in. He weakly tossed the dish towel up at the smoke alarm.

"Well, I guess we'll see if I can turn the whole building out to the street for a bit," he chuckled. "I'm sorry we won't have dessert to finish dinner off with, though."

"Oh, I got dinner and a show, I think I'm just fine. Thank you again for cooking, by the way."

"Anytime! I love it, honestly, and getting to cook for you is just an added bonus."

I stood to clear our dishes, but Elliot stepped in my way and grabbed them from my hands. "No ma'am. You don't get to clean on date night."

My face prickled warmly, a shy smile working its way onto my face. I leaned against the counter, fiddling with my necklace nervously as he rinsed the dishes in the sink.

"What's up?" He eyed my hand that immediately dropped the chain at his attention.

"I…" *You can do this.* "I wanted to say I'm really enjoying this. I mean… this is really hard for me. Obviously. But I'm enjoying getting to know you."

He turned toward me, drying his hands in a dish towel. Grinning at me almost sheepishly, he lifted me to sit on the counter. "I'm enjoying this, too. It's not easy to let someone in, but I'm going to be here waiting to be the first through the door whenever you're ready."

I pulled him in close and pressed my lips to his, pasta breath and all.

• • •

I smiled over my shoulder at the concierge as I stepped onto the sidewalk. My hands tugged at my jacket to bundle around me and shield my smile - from what, I don't know.

What if you tell him everything? What if he stays? What if… there's the slightest hope that you could be happy?

A few weeks prior, I would have mocked the thought. I would have sworn that being alone was a conscious decision I had made rather than a trauma response and an attempt to avoid feelings, good or bad. But things were changing. Elliot was changing things. The chance for life settling into some semblance of normalcy set aflame the smallest flicker of anticipation in my chest.

I was so consumed with my date night high that I didn't notice the woman walking past me as she paused.

"Sammy?"

SAM

I stopped dead in my tracks. Dread crept over my skin at the sound of my old nickname, and my hand shook violently. Heart beating in my throat, I turned slowly on my heel.

My chest ached as if it was slowly filling with concrete. There she stood, a bony storm of blonde hair, lanky limbs, and faded clothing. Her once vibrant blue eyes now heavy with fog and sunken into her flushed face. She was a weathered and worn frame of my sister. Only a year apart, we couldn't have chosen more different paths for our lives. We were different now. When we were young, it was easier to find common ground, especially under the circumstances… It wasn't so easy anymore.

"Hi, Laurel." The chill in my voice made even me shiver.

"It's been a bit…" She trembled as her hardened hands moved up and down her arms. I hesitated, bracing myself for what she may want. "I- I uh… I'm glad I found you. I've been wanting to talk to you about something."

"I don't have money to give you."

"No, I know… that's not it. I… it's Uncle James." That word made my blood stick in my veins, my head attempt to float away. "He's *alive*. found me. Wants to apologize for leaving us like he did."

You don't have to listen to this.

"How did *you* find *me*?" My stomach threatened to jump out of my throat. I crossed my arms, grabbing them with each opposite hand in search of any kind of comfort I could find.

"Didn't you hear me? James is alive. And he wants to-"

"*Stop*, Laurel. I don't know what the fuck you think an apology is going to do after all this time. He's the one that left us to deal with Charles. Because of him we witnessed what no child should have to."

"Don't you want to-"

"No! No, I don't. What do you expect to happen, L? Because I can tell you how this will go down. He's going to stir up a bunch of shit neither of us want to relive, all to tell us that *he thought Charles was a good guy* and *no one would have dreamed he'd do such a thing*. But we did. Because we got the brunt of it. I'd really rather not hear another glowing review of our father."

"It wasn't *all* bad, Sammy. There were good times. Don't you want to remember the good times?"

"Drugs have obviously made you fucking delusional. I don't want to remember any of it. I'm sorry, I have to go now." I pushed past her without bothering to hear a response. I needed to get out of there.

"Wait, Sammy!"

Just keep walking.

I gasped for breath, my lungs feeling completely devoid of air. Sounds of passing traffic echoed in my head.

Get somewhere safe.

I wracked my brain for where I even was.

My head swirled searching for any form of coherent thought. A street name. A nearby store. Anything.

Spots blurred my vision and my fluttering fingers went numb. I blinked hard and rubbed at my face.

Shadows seemed to close in around me.

Elliot's. Just get back to Elliot's.

I stumbled my way a few blocks back to his building, drunk with panic. I pushed through the doors, the warm air suffocating as it washed over me.

"Ms. Reynolds? Are you alright?" The front desk man stepped around to come to my aid. I shied away from his touch.

"I… I-just…" I continued fumbling my way toward the elevator, the concerned man following closely as if expecting me to fall. "No."

The elevator doors opened instantly as I pressed the call button. I jammed my finger into the button for Elliot's floor and flattened my back against the wall. The image of the concerned door man was pinched as the doors closed again. I slid down the wall as the elevator ascended, clutching my knees to my chest.

It wasn't all bad, Sammy.

Don't you want to remember the good times?

When I finally reached Elliot's floor, he had settled with a book on his couch. He glanced over the edge of the pages, confusion furrowing his brows as he searched the elevator. He stood from his seat. His eyes found me and alarm replaced his confusion. His book hit the floor as he rushed to my side.

"Sam? What the hell happened?"

It wasn't all bad, Sammy.

There were good times.

Don't you want to remember the good times?

• • •

I sipped at a soda in an effort to settle my still swimming stomach. My foot bounced restlessly, shaking my leg and the couch cushion I didn't remember making it to. A swarm of emotions took turns victimizing my thoughts.

"I'm sorry."

"There's nothing to be sorry about, Sam." Elliot was barely seated on the edge of the armchair, his elbow resting on his knee to hold his head up. Stress wrinkled his face. "I just… I don't entirely understand. We were laughing and talking and kissing not even forty-five minutes ago. Last time I saw you in a state like this, we had been on a date the night before. Are you sure this has nothing to do with me?"

My eyes fixated on my bouncing leg. "I swear… and I promise it's not always like this…"

He rubbed at his forehead then ran his fingers through his hair. "What happened when you left?"

I swallowed hard.

It's now or never.

"I… I have a lot to tell you before you're going to understand."

SAM

My first memory of my father screaming at me was at five years old. If only it could have remained as bad as I thought it was then. He'd yell. He'd watch my sister and I in disgust as we did as children do - played, sang, ate snacks. His disdain solidified this notion within me that I'd always fall short… that we weren't enough. Mom seemed to fade into the background after that. I never asked, but maybe he beat her, too. I'll never know…

I think it was about a year after that when the hitting started. Pulling our hair, excessively disciplining us for the smallest things, even pushing us to the ground. I was still convinced we had done something to deserve it, that something remained innately fucked up about us, and if we could just *fix it* we'd be worthy of something more than a militant home.

But then… then it turned into some wicked game. A chess match of misery, and he always got his queen. This soulless, empty grin would emerge as he hit me, and it would widen with every scream. Each outburst proved another reason to hit me harder, to spur his calculated malice. He'd scream *shut up, you fucking bitch*, then continue to give grounds for me to scream more.

I'd occasionally hear him beat Laurel. I was always first, though. *Age before beauty*, he'd say. That said, my head was usually pounding enough by then that I didn't often have to endure hearing too much.

In public, it was always *kids being kids*. Doing all the things that brought him to violence - falling on our bikes, skinning our knees on the playground, bumping into tables. People believed that shit, so I thought they'd never believe anything else. After all, this was *Charles Prickett*. Family man. Guy's guy. Fucking church elder. Employee of the month, August 2001.

Only one person ever had guts enough to say anything about it... to ask if we were okay. Uncle James - my father's brother - pulled me and L aside one night and asked a lot of questions. For his own brother to be asking... It was our sole chance to get help. We tried to take it. We told him everything and clung to him, our savior, to take us with him when he left. *These things take time*, he'd said. And that was the one thing he didn't have.

My father walked him out of the house that evening, arms shackled together. Humming along, buzzing with gin, they strolled out brothers, and my father came back, hours passed, eternally alone. Laurel and I were both sitting on my bed when the door flung open. He no longer hummed or buzzed. A dormant volcano now rattling with rage, his steps smoldered underneath him. We cowered as the smoke billowed up, his fingers slowly working at his belt buckle. Once removed, he extended it out to me - not an offering, but a demand.

Hit her.

Hot ash landed at every fiber of my being, igniting a fire of my own in the name of repudiation. Tears boiled down my face and my jaw steeled. Unmoving, I glared up at him. Laurel sobbed quietly next to me as if trying to go unnoticed. My father and I stared each other down for what seemed like an eternity. Pure hatred stirred in my gut until spit launched from my mouth at his face. His silence was deafening. As he abandoned his original plan, I reached entirely new levels of terror.

The leather of his belt sang a vitriolic whisper across his fingers as he stretched it between his hands. He moved deliberately slow. His still damp head cocked sideways.

He reached down, hand clenching my ankle, and dragged me off the edge of the bed. Not without fight, he cinched me to the bedpost, my hands instantly blueish in their struggle. My eyes squeezed tightly shut.

Watch, or she gets it worse.

The memory is carved into my mind, tragically like a broken couple whose initials linger in an old tree. I thought that would be the worst experience of my life. Again, I was wrong.

It wasn't long after that, maybe a few months, that my mom rushed in one night telling me and L, sixteen and fifteen at the time, that we were leaving. She was flushed with hurry, the three of us feverishly gathering just necessities as we had the first glimpse of hope, maybe ever. Nothing was mentioned of what suddenly sparked her decision to leave, but we weren't about to question it. We were free… almost.

My father ripped his way through the front door. The ramblings of a mad man spilled from his mouth in a fury, hardly legible. His gun appeared to fight at his grip as it tussled back and forth through the air. I couldn't cry. I couldn't move. Laurel clung to my arm and sobbed into my shoulder. Across the room, my frantic mom now stood statuesque, eyes following my father's every movement. The door hung open. It taunted us with fresh air.

I'm not sure how long we stood there, too afraid to move as my father paced and screamed and cursed. Then, the heaviest of silence fell. Even a misplaced breath threatening to detonate his instability. His head swiveled menacingly toward my mom. He looked as if her very existence offended him.

You.

He raised his gun. Cocked. Loaded. Ready. Her eyes found mine. He fired. Bits of her found the wall behind her. She's gone instantly. Her body fell to the floor. Laurel screamed, still buried into my shoulder. I was frozen, all but a lonely, falling tear.

He faced me.

All because of you, bitch.

The barrel found his mouth. A loud pop. And then it was over.

At least for him.

It wasn't long before I was ripped from my sister and whisked away to the police station as a witness to my parents' murder-suicide, barraged with impossible, tone-deaf questions. Did my father exhibit abusive behavior toward my mother? Did he *actually* abuse us, or was he just a disciplinarian? Did I ask anyone for help or confide in anyone during the years of alleged abuse? Did I *really* not have anyone willing to take me in for the night? Did I *actually* watch as my father shot my mother then blew his own head off?

That night found me curled up in a twin-sized bed in a group home some fifty minutes from my taped off childhood house. I'd been allowed to go back and gather a few items once they had cleared the bodies from the scene, and I'd walked away with no more than a duffel bag of clothes, my childhood stuffed bunny, and my mother's necklace. I never saw that house again.

Overcrowding sent my younger sister elsewhere. Apparently no home had enough square footage to hold *two* fucked up teenagers experiencing unspeakable trauma. I kept in contact as much as I could, but her recreational drug use turned to habit turned to more stress I wasn't able to cope with, especially from afar.

Within a week of me being in that home, one of the kids attempted to sexually assault another, one was arrested for stealing, and one had found out the story of my parents and tried to manipulate me with the fear of it getting out. Then a twelve year old kid named Ricky was found hanging from a noose he'd tied around his closet rail. So I ran.

I took odd jobs and bounced from shelters to cheap motels until my family's estate was finally split between me and my sister. It wasn't much, but enough to get a stable living space. She, of course, withdrew hers almost instantly. Addiction was a leech that drained every bit of her away. I spent the next year attempting to get Laurel help. Rehab centers, treatment facilities, and even an overdose scare in the ER (the only one I knew about, at least). I hadn't seen her for three years after that; I hadn't heard from her at all in two.

…how the hell was I supposed to tell Elliot *that*?

SAM

"Elliot, please," I said, voice splintering as panic squeezed my throat. I didn't know what to expect from him - shock, confusion, disbelief - but the silence was worse. Crushing.

It's too much. You're too much for him. Of course you are. You had to know this was coming.

He stepped back, hands lifting to his head as if trying to physically hold in the flood of emotions threatening to drown him. His breathing was uneven. Not loud or aggressive, just shaken. Like the ground beneath him had cracked open.

"I don't know what to say," he breathed. Not angry. Just broken by something he couldn't fix.

"I didn't mean to overwhelm you," I whispered.

"You didn't," he said quickly, chest rising and falling too fast for that to be true. "It's just... I hate that this happened to you. I hate that you're still carrying it. That you always will. And I *hate* that I can't take any of it away."

His voice cracked on that last word.

I swallowed, hands trembling. "You're scaring yourself," I murmured.

His eyes flicked up. "Yeah... yeah, maybe."

Slowly, I reached out and touched his arm. "Sit with me?" I asked. "We don't have to talk."

He nodded, like he wasn't sure he deserved comfort but he needed grounding more than pride. He sank into the chair, me onto the couch. Not together, but with each other still. Not touching. Not even looking. Just breathing. Holding space for something so massive no one should have to carry it.

Maybe that's why it felt so hard. Opening up.

Because I sure as hell didn't want to carry it. Why would I willingly place it on someone else to have to bear the burden, too?

Minutes passed. Maybe hours. His eyes were red when he finally spoke again - soft and careful.

"Thank you for trusting me," he said hoarsely. "I can't pretend to know how much that cost you."

He was right.

"I know you'll need time to process, just... please d-don't walk away?"

His watery eyes shot up at me so quickly I flinched in response. He rose slowly from his seat and crouched before me, gently stroking my cheek. Tears began to fully fall from his more-gray-than-usual eyes.

"Walk away? Are you kidding me?"

"Well..." I didn't know what else to say. My whole life almost everyone walked away. It's just a product of being this fucked up.

My eyes fell down to my still-shaking hands, but Elliot gently lifted my chin until my eyes had no choice but to meet his again.

"I'm not going anywhere. I fall more and more for you every day, Sam. And I'm going to do whatever it takes to make you understand that you're worth staying for."

...

A light mist danced in the exterior building lights against the night sky. My head ached and pushed against the backs of my eyes, heavy with every type of exhaustion. The slightest tremor still ran through my body as I moved to get up.

"What are you doing?" Elliot jumped up, arms outstretched like my legs were going to give out. Though I wasn't sure they wouldn't, I was the tiniest bit annoyed at how codependent it all seemed.

"I need to go home. Cooper's been there alone most of the day, and I need to let him out. It's getting late…"

"I'll drive you."

"Elliot, you don't have to do that." *You should let him.*

"Dammit, Sam, do you think I'm going to let you walk in the cold and rain *alone* after all of this? I'd be out of my mind. I don't even like the idea of you being alone at all after this."

I paused, letting the idea play out in my tired mind. Before I could contemplate much at all, he was gathering my jacket and his keys.

"I… I just… I appreciate the offer, and I'll take you up on the drive. But, Elliot… I want you to know that… even though it's not always this crazy… this is my life. I've learned to deal with my trauma and figure it out as I go. I'm not… I do know how to take care of myself…" I looked up at him and sincerely hoped my eyes weren't pulsing as much as they felt they were. I needed to be convincing.

"I'm quite sure you do, darling. But it shouldn't have to all be on you. You deserve to let someone else take care of you, at least every once in a while."

It was everything I could do to fight off sleep on the drive over. Exhaustion tugged at my eyelids. The unusual quiet made the road noise seem louder than it should in such a nice car. I couldn't tell how Elliot was processing it all. It was a lot, I knew.

Some people say that when you share with someone you feel closer, but I didn't feel that necessarily. It wasn't that he was *leaving,* but even as bad as it was - everything I told him - it still just didn't feel like I could possibly communicate quite how bad it all truly had been. And even still it hurt that it broke him.

At least it was out there. It may have been a surprise wrecking ball to the walls I'd built around myself, but at least they were down. I didn't have to hide anymore. And that was a brand new feeling for me.

Pulling up in front of my apartment, Cooper's nose appeared through the blinds and pressed against the window.

We shuffled up the walkway in sleepy silence. Though the late night air was crisp, I fought drowsiness - every step feeling heavier and more forced than the last. I slowly picked through the four keys on my ring before sliding the wrong one into the door.

"I'm sorry," I yawned, sloth-like in my motion to fix my error.

Elliot chuckled and shifted his weight. I could tell he was worn down, too, but he was doing a decent job trying to hide it.

We made our way into the entryway and I tossed my keys onto the counter. Grabbing Cooper's leash off the hook by the door, another yawn escaped and sent a shiver through my body.

"I'll take him," Elliot said, taking the leash from me before I could argue. "We'll be right back, won't we, bud?"

As much as the idea of being cared for made me uncomfortable, gravity was in full effect on my body and it felt as if the earth might swallow me up at any moment. I dragged myself to the couch and curled under the blanket.

I woke to the sofa disappearing under my body, my weight being lifted into the air. I hadn't realized I'd fallen asleep, and I had no idea how long it had been. Moaning in protest, I tried to squirm and wriggle my way out of Elliot's grasp, but my body argued with every movement. My eyes refused to pry their way open.

"I'm just moving you to your bed so you'll be more comfortable, Sam."

"Coop-"

"Cooper's been taken out. I found his food and fed him, then took him out again. He's just fine. You need to rest."

Golden boy.

The light switch flicked on causing my shut-eyed view to glow a bright pink. My face turned a little from the harsh light toward Elliot's chest, my eyes clenching further.

The bed pushed against my weight as he gently laid me down.

"I… I can't leave you alone tonight, Sam. I'm going to be out here on the couch if you need me."

"Mmm. Stay."

"That's what I'm saying…"

My hands clasped behind his neck, pulling him toward me with what little effort I had left. "No, stay."

My lips pressed into a frown when he stood, breaking my grasp and ignoring my request. The light switch flipped off. After a brief sound of shuffling, the bed dipped below his weight and I smiled softly, already drifting in and out of sleep. I rolled over and snuggled closer to him. Normally repelled by the idea of physical touch, I felt an odd comfort nestled in the crook of his arm. He nestled his lips in the edge of my hairline.

"Goodnight, darling," he whispered against my forehead.

I couldn't will myself to respond. Barely even an *mmm* made it out before I drifted back off to sleep.

• • •

I stirred from my restless sleep, still surprised at Elliot's presence. It shocked me every time I woke, mainly because I kept thinking he'd come to his senses during the night sometime and flee. But there he was. Sleeping. Peaceful. I watched the rise and fall of his chest and allowed it to lull me almost back to sleep - until he groaned and rolled toward me, eyes fluttering open slowly.

"Mmmm…morning."

"Good morning."

"How long have you been awake?"

"Not long," I lied, feeling like I had barely slept a wink. "Elliot, I'm so sorry…"

He rubbed at his sleepy eyes and yawned, still pulling himself out from under his slumber. "For what?"

"For… everything. I'm sorry I dumped everything on you. I'm sorry you had to drive me home. I'm sorry I asked you to stay…" I trailed off, not even knowing what else to be sorry for, but feeling the guilt nonetheless.

"Sam," he sighed into my forehead as he pressed his lips to my skin. "I don't know what I'll have to do, but I'm *going to* get you to understand that you don't have to apologize for someone *wanting* to take care of you."

A few surprise tears welled up in my eyes.

"What is it, darling?"

"I just guess I've never really felt like anyone truly *wanted* to take care of me…Not like this." I gulped, fighting back the wetness in my eyes. "For the longest time, it's always just been me taking care of me."

He sighed again, patiently, and began twirling a piece of my hair around on the pillow between us. Silence filled the space. It was like he knew I didn't need a response to come to the conclusion that it didn't have to be that way anymore… if I decided not to run.

Before I had the chance to think myself into a tizzy, he shifted his weight and was up out of the bed. Only then did I notice he was still in the clothes he had surely worn to work the day before.

"Do you want coffee? Breakfast? I know a place," he winked at me.

I tossed the covers back and sat up taking in the shambles that made up my outfit.

"Not to hold out on you, but I think we both need a shower and a change of clothes before we make it out into the public." He looked down in shock as if the idea hadn't occurred to him, either, that we'd both been about twenty-four hours in the same clothes. "I have to work at eight anyway."

He glanced at his watch, "How about this? You shower. I'll take you to work, and I can get my coffee to go since I'm such a mess."

I gave a breathy laugh and shrugged. It was a good plan. "I guess that works for me."

• • •

The storm rolled in quickly - thick gray clouds swallowing the morning sun and a steady downpour lashing the windows like the sky was punishing us for existing. We'd barely made it inside when Bill and Jessa started darting in and out the back door in a frantic blur.

"What's going on?" I asked as Bill set a soggy box down on the counter.

"Delivery guy just set all our beans outside," he said wiping at his face under the dripping ball cap he was wearing. "There are 15 giant boxes."

"I'll help"

"Me, too," Elliot chimed in, pushing up his sleeves.

I glanced over my shoulder, already halfway through the door. No time to argue. Not with rain in my shoes and beans on the line. "You don't have to…"

He didn't even answer, just walked behind me through the door into the monsoon. We trudged into the rain past Jessa who was scurrying inside with two big boxes stacked so high there was no chance she could see where she was going. Elliot held the door for her then turned to help grab from the big stack of boxes in the alleyway.

We silently worked at the pile of boxes until they all made it inside and the four of us were soaked to the bone. We stood in the back, puddles growing beneath us, grateful there were no customers brave enough to try to come in during the downpour.

"You know you didn't have to do that, right?" I stared at Elliot, his hair plastered to his forehead in a way that was *far* too attractive.

"Of course I should have. Don't want you to suffer the horror of a caffeine shortage," he winked.

"You're right - you might've just saved lives," Jessa joked.

He shrugged modestly, pushing sopping hair off of his forehead. "All in a day's work."

"Thank you both," Bill said, towel in hand attempting to dry off. "We'd still be bringing boxes in if it wasn't for your help."

"It's no problem, Bill. Really," Elliot replied, a small smile affirming that he was being honest.

We made our way to the back side of the front counter and I grabbed a towel from beneath to toss it to him. He caught it mid-air, smirking like he expected applause.

As he rubbed the towel through his hair, I took in the sight of him - dripping, slightly disheveled, utterly at ease. That familiar cocktail of lust and panic churned in my gut.

"You're really something, you know that?" I said before I could stop myself.

He peeked out from behind the towel and arched an eyebrow at me. "Something good, I hope?"

I rolled my eyes. "To be determined."

Thunder cracked loudly, rattling the front windows. I glanced outside and shivered. Elliot followed my gaze.

"I should probably wait out the storm a little bit," he said smoothly, avoiding bringing attention to my jumpiness. "You mind if I stick around?"

I should have said yes. I should have made some joke about health codes or wet dog smells. Instead, I nodded.

"Coffee?" I asked, reaching for a fresh cup.

"Only if it comes with more sarcastic commentary from you."

"Oh don't worry, that's complimentary."

I handed him the cup and watched as he wrapped both hands around it, grateful for the warmth. He looked up at me with something soft in his eyes - something that made me want to do something reckless. Like curl up in his arms and admit I wanted to stay there. Maybe it was because he *really* saw me now. But he felt… safe.

"Elliot?" I said quietly, pulling his attention away from the cup of coffee in his hands.

"Yes?"

"I'm glad you were here today," I admitted, my heart in my throat at the honesty.

"Me too," he replied softly.

Elliot

I was riding a high after she came over for dinner the night after our fight.

She showed up wearing this worn-in leather jacket - soft looking, like she could have rolled out of bed wearing it. She hovered in the elevator doorway at first, uncertain, skeptical even, and I remember thinking I'd do anything to make her feel welcome. Safe. Like my home could be a place she could finally let her guard down in.

She shook off the cold, slid her shoes off by the door. Always considerate. And the way her eyes moved over me... careful, almost reverent, as if she wanted to commit it to memory in case she never let herself get this close again. It did something sharp and warm to my chest.

I cooked. We drank a little. I apologized - because I should have.

"You just did it because you care, right?" she'd asked.

There was something in her eyes I didn't know how to touch. Some bruise life had given her long before I ever showed up. A wound with edges I couldn't see.

But of course I asked because I care. Because by then I was already falling for her, even if I couldn't say it out loud, And all I wanted was to know her more. Really know her. Maybe that was selfish of me, though. To ask without first having the permission. To ask anyone but her.

Dinner was easy in that soft, tentative way we were just beginning to find - talking about our days, the shift in the weather, the books on our nightstands. I don't remember most of it. What I do remember is the fire alarm going off because I burned dessert. Her laugh - bright, startled, delighted - echoed through my kitchen, bruising my pride but making me grin like an idiot.

Somehow she ended up on the counter, kissing me like she'd made a choice she wasn't sure she should enjoy. Arms looped around my neck like a safety net.

It was so nice.

Until it wasn't.

After she left, I floated around in this warm little bubble. Cleaning up. Putting on slower music. Grabbing a romance novel to wind down with. I curled onto the couch and...

That's when the elevator dinged again.

At first, I didn't see anyone. Then I saw her - tucked into the corner by the wall, shaking. Tears sliding down her face. Curled in on herself like she expected someone to strike at any moment.

The book fell from my hands. I rushed to her, scooped her up, brought her to the couch, set her down where the most pillows were like that could soften whatever had ripped her open. She shook so violently I was afraid she was going to vibrate right out into the floor. Silent tears. Hiccuped breaths. A storm I couldn't see through.

I tried giving her space. Sitting over on the chair across the room and just... watching without crowding. I tried giving her a soda to sip on, hoping the little bit of grounding would help. It did. Barely.

My mind went to war with itself. Had I pushed too far again? Triggered something? Was it me?

"What happened when you left?" I finally asked.

That's when she told me about her sister. About the abuse. About the group home. About... all of the things I still don't like to think about.

It was so much all at once.

I'd known about her mother. About her father being the one to kill her. I'd suspected as much to know that he wasn't a good man. But this - hearing the whole truth at once, the scale of it - it rattled me. I felt like I'd been shoved into deep water, told to swim or die.

I stayed quiet too long. I wish I hadn't. I hope to god she didn't think I was contemplating running. It wasn't that at all. Not even close. It was just... all so heavy. The kind of heavy no one should have to carry alone for as long as she had.

And then the anger hit. White-hot. Blinding. A man that cowardly, that vile... hurting little girls. His own daughters. I still can't wrap my head around it.

And then there's James. Resurfacing after all this time. After he failed them so miserably...

"Elliot, please," I remember her saying, barely a breath.

It broke something open in me. Because it wasn't just her voice. It was like I saw her from back then. Frightened. Small. Alone.

But she wasn't alone.

I didn't know how to help her carry all of that, but I knew with absolute clarity: my new life's mission was to try. To help her lay it down piece by piece, until she didn't have to hold it alone ever again.

Sam

The rain and the lunch rush had died down, and I finally had a second to breathe. Jessa had made a run to the shelter with pastries and coffee, and Bill was on a supply run. Elliot had retreated to his house for a shower and a change of clothes. For a rare moment, it was just me, the quiet hiss of the espresso machine, and the gentle hum of indie guitar strumming through the speakers.

That's when I saw him.

Marcus.

The same too-large jacket, same heavy stare. He was standing just inside the door like he'd forgotten why he came in. His eyes swept the cafe slowly - too slowly - and then landed on me.

I tried to keep my hands steady.

"Sam," he said smoothly. "Didn't expect to see you here."

Where else?

"This is where I work, Marcus," I said, keeping my tone level. "What do you need?"

He leaned an elbow against the counter - closer than he needed to be - and glanced around like he owned the place. "Just passing through. Thought I'd grab a coffee. Say hey."

My spine stiffened. "We're busy."

We *obviously* weren't.

Marcus ignored the comment.

"Is there something you need?" I asked again, louder this time.

He tilted his head. "Maybe just a conversation. We never really got to finish ours."

"We didn't need to," I snapped. "You made your point."

"That's the thing, though," He said softly. "I don't think I did."

The air thickened. My fingers curled into fists at my sides.

"Hey man," Bill called. I hadn't heard him enter the back door, and his sudden presence was both a jolt to the system and a welcome surprise. "We've got a no-loitering policy. And no harassing the staff. You need to go."

Marcus didn't look at Bill. Just stared at me, gaze unblinking, like he was committing something to memory.

"Okay," he said, finally turning toward the door. "But I'll be around. People like us? We always circle back."

As he pushed the door open, a gust of wind swept through the shop, scattering a few flyers and napkins from the bar. He didn't look back.

Bill turned to me. "You good?"

No. Not even a little.

"Yeah," I lied. "Fine."

His gaze still fixed on the front door, he shook his head. "Just… be careful with that one. He's off. Lock the doors when you're alone, okay?"

• • •

At closing time, Elliot hung back by the window while I locked the front door to the cafe. "Hey, I know a little truck down the street with great tacos. How about we take a walk before we leave?"

I turned toward him, the pit in my stomach still present from the encounter with Marcus earlier that afternoon. "I'm not really hungry."

"You don't have to eat. But… I thought maybe you could use a walk."

I sighed lightly and nodded quietly.

The pavement still glistened with leftover rain, and the breeze carried that post-storm smell - like wet dirt.

We walked in silence at first. He didn't ask what was wrong. Didn't prod. Just walked beside me, matching my pace, hands in his jacket pockets.

About halfway down the block, I finally spoke. "Thanks for not asking."

He glanced sideways at me, then nodded. "I'm learning. Sometimes the best thing you can do is shut up and keep walking."

That made me huff out a quiet laugh. "You really are too good at this."

"I'm just winging it, honestly. Hoping I don't fuck it up."

"I'd say you're doing fine."

We stopped at a corner where a bright blue taco truck was parked, already gathering a small crowd. The smell of spiced meat and fresh cilantro drifted toward us like a peace offering.

"Are you sure you're not hungry?" he asked.

I paused and glanced at a man walking by shoving a taco into his mouth. "I could eat."

He ordered for both of us. Nothing fancy, just two tacos each and a sparkling water. While we waited, we leaned against the brick wall beside the truck, shoulder to shoulder, quiet again.

"You don't have to talk about it," he said, not looking at me. "But I want you to know I'm around. Not just when things are easy."

I nodded. "I know."

I meant it. I didn't want to mean it, but I did.

• • •

I laid on the couch, one arm draped over my eyes, the other absently scratching behind Cooper's ears. He huffed and nuzzled in closer, content with the slow rhythm of my hand on his fur.

The TV was on but muted - some crime doc I'd seen before playing in the background. I wasn't really watching. I was stuck somewhere in the quiet space between *what happened* and *what it meant*.

Elliot hadn't asked what was wrong.

He hadn't touched me without permission. Hadn't offered empty words or tried to fix me. He just walked beside me. Bought me tacos. Let me sit in the stillness without making me feel like a burden for needing it.

It shouldn't be rare. But it was.

I stared at the ceiling. My heart still felt like it was waiting for the other shoe to drop, like maybe today had just been an illusion. Some glitch in the matrix where a man could be kind without an agenda.

Because that's what kindness had meant before - *bait*. Be nice, draw her in, break her down. It was a pattern I knew by heart.

But today... today didn't fit the mold.

I didn't even tell him what happened with Marcus. I didn't have to. He still stayed.

I shifted on the couch, restless. There was a knot in my chest that wouldn't loose, like I wanted to cry but my body had forgotten how.

I closed my eyes and let Cooper's soft breathing fill the room.

Tomorrow, I'd have to act like nothing had changed. Like the ground hadn't shifted a little beneath me. But tonight... I let myself remember what it felt like to walk through a storm and not feel alone.

• • •

I woke up to sunlight slanting through the blinds - warm and golden, the kind of morning that felt like a clean slate.

But the ache in my chest was still there.

Cooper laid sprawled out across the foot of the bed like a living throw blanket, snoring gently. I stretched under the covers, trying to shake off the haze of sleep and the remnants of yesterday's thoughts.

My phone buzzed from the nightstand. A notification - just a sale email from some store I didn't remember subscribing to. I picked it up anyway, thumbing through the lock screen. Before I knew what I was doing, I opened my messages. Elliot's name sat at the top of my recent texts.

I hadn't messaged him first. Not once. He always made the first move - checking in, sending something stupid and funny, asking about a new roast of coffee he should buy for his house.

My fingers hovered above the keyboard.

> *Thanks for yesterday.*
> *You didn't have to, but I'm glad you did.*
> *I... needed that.*

I typed. Deleted. Typed again.

God why is this so hard? It's just a stupid message.

He wouldn't even expect anything deep. He'd probably send back a heart emoji or some sarcastic line about tacos saving lives. But still, I hesitated. Because if I sent the message, I'd be admitting that it mattered. That *he* mattered. That I wasn't just surviving anymore - I was starting to care.

And caring made things messy. Vulnerable.

I sighed, locked my phone, and set it face down on the nightstand.

"You're ridiculous," I muttered to myself, swinging my legs over the side of the bed.

Cooper let out a grunt of protest, still half asleep. I padded into the kitchen to start some coffee. Maybe I'd text him later.

Maybe I wouldn't.

The morning passed in pieces.

I cleaned the kitchen. Took Cooper for a long walk around the block. Folded laundry I didn't remember washing.

I kept busy, because if I sat still too long, I'd think about the text I didn't send.

I'd think about the look in Elliot's eyes when I said I was glad he was there. About how natural it had felt to stand beside him, like I wasn't a puzzle missing half its pieces.

I flopped on the couch, phone in hand, debating whether it was too early for a second coffee when my screen lit up.

> **Elliot - 11:34am**
>
> *Hey! Hope you're enjoying your day off.*
> *Also, pretty sure that taco truck changed my life.*
> *No pressure to respond. Just... thinking of you.*

I stared at the message for a long time.

No pressure.

He always knew exactly how to say just enough. Not too much. Not too little. Just enough to make me feel like I could finally exhale.

I didn't reply.

But I read it again and smiled softly to myself before I tucked the phone under my thigh like hiding it would quiet the flutter in my chest.

Desperate for another cup of caffeine, I busied myself with the familiar routine of making coffee in my Chemex. Grind the beans. Boil the water. Dampen the filter to clear out the paper taste before you put the freshly-ground beans in. Slowly pour the water over everything as it foams and blooms. Voila, fresh cup of coffee.

I picked up my computer from the coffee table and opened it up. My notes app was still open - the last thing I'd written was an **Overheard at the Coffee Shop** entry of someone who'd said, "My cheeks were starting to twitch and I thought 'ah, not again.'" Completely random and unhinged. The way I liked it.

I hit the little plus sign to create a new note and titled it: **IDFK What to Call This One.**

> *This week was supposed to be easy.*
>
> *I wanted normal. I've EARNED normal. For once in my life, things were actually good. Elliot and I had made up, the fight blew over as quickly as it had started, and we were... laughing, kissing, dancing lightly to the vinyl he had playing.*

> Then Laurel showed up. And fuck, she looked wrecked. The dark circles. The track marks… That's not even the worst of it.
>
> James is apparently alive. After all this time, it wasn't that Charles killed him that night. Just threatened him within an inch of his life and scared him shitless enough to walk away from two little girls who had begged for help. How the hell was I supposed to forgive that? See him again?
>
> I trauma-dumped on Elliot that night. I mean the biggest crash out I could conjure. And he… stayed. I don't really know what else to say, because it's as simple as that. He quite frankly handled it like a champ. Shocked? Sure. But wouldn't anyone be?
>
> He called me "darling," by the way. And I didn't hate it.
>
> I'm beginning to think he's one of the good ones. I honestly wasn't even sure those existed. Maybe they do.

I hesitated, taking a long swig of coffee. I wasn't sure if I wanted to put this next part in writing. That'd somehow make it more true. But I continued:

> Exact opposite of that, though… That guy showed up again at the cafe. The creepy one? I don't want to write his name this time. I don't like seeing it on the page. Writing it makes him real, and I very much want to believe he's not.
>
> Maybe it's all a coincidence. Maybe I'm being dramatic. Maybe my brain is inventing problems because of how well things are going with Elliot and my trauma feels the need to sprinkle in a little spice.
>
> But I can't shake it.
>
> The way my stomach dropped. The way my fingers went numb. The way I felt sixteen again for a split second.
>
> Elliot texted me later that day and I ALMOST said, "I think something is wrong." But I didn't. Because I don't want him looking at me the same way everyone else has. I don't want to be the girl with shadows in every corner.
>
> He deserves someone who isn't always half a heartbeat away from running.

I shouldn't drag him into this. Not until I know what "this" even is.

I guess for now it's taco trucks and falling apart and unloading boxes in the rain.

I feel unhinged. I'm sure I'm overthinking it. All of it. Just… Fuck, I wish this week had been simple.

I closed my laptop and stared at the silver logo reflecting bits of the room in a distorted shape.

"God, I hope I'm not too much for him," I said out loud to no one.

Cooper lifted his head and looked at me like I'd disturbed his sleep.

"Listen," I said, pointing at him. "I'm having a crisis. You could at least offer moral support."

He blinked once. Slowly. Judgmentally.

"Wow. Rude."

He settled his chin and the house grew quiet again. Too quiet. The kind where every thought grows teeth.

Elliot made me feel like maybe I wasn't a disaster after all. Marcus made me feel like I should triple check the locks. The combination was giving me emotional whiplash.

I sighed and sank deeper into the couch. "I'm not too much, right?" I tried out loud. "I'm a lot but not… too, too much."

I couldn't tell if I believed it. But maybe saying it out loud was a step in the right direction.

SAM

The morning rush had just thinned, leaving behind the soft hum of the grinder, the occasional hiss of the steam wand, and the comforting clink of mugs against saucers.

I wiped the counter with practiced ease, humming faintly to the playlist I'd queued up - folky, easy stuff. I felt… lighter today. Still wary, sure, but not as tightly wound. Like maybe I could breathe a little deeper.

The bell above the door jingled.

Of course it was him.

Elliot walked in, a paper folder tucked under his arm and that familiar calm trailing in with him. He was wearing a plaid jacket over a light blue button down that made his eyes look soft. Stupidly soft.

"Morning," he said with a cautious smile, as if unsure what version of me he was walking into today.

"Hey," I answered, setting the rag aside and leaning against the counter. "No taco truck today. Hope that's not a dealbreaker."

He laughed. "You sure? I'm ready to chase that thing across town."

I smiled before I could stop myself. It felt easy. Natural.

"What can I get you today? Your usual?"

"Dealer's choice," he said, sliding his card across the counter. "Surprise me."

"You're brave."

"I'm optimistic."

I rolled my eyes, grabbing a mug and beginning to pour brown sugar syrup. "Big talk for someone who drank drip coffee for two weeks straight."

"Hey," he said, mock-defensive. "You've corrupted me. Now I have opinions about espresso and foam ratios."

"Next thing you know, you'll be talking about mouthfeel," I winked at him.

"God, I hope not," he grinned. "There's a limit."

I handed him the drink and our fingers brushed for just a second. I felt it - just a spark - but it didn't make me flinch this time.

"Busy day ahead?" he asked, taking a slow sip.

"Not really. Done here by three."

He nodded, then hesitated. "No pressure, but I've got a stack of contracts to read this afternoon. I was going to swing by the park and get some air while I worked. You and Cooper want to join?"

I paused. Not because I didn't want to. But because it wasn't enough. I wanted more.

"I was actually going to cook tonight," I said, surprising even myself with how casually it came out. "Something simple - like grilled cheese and soup, nothing fancy."

Elliot raised an eyebrow, careful not to let his surprise turn into excitement.

"Sounds like my kind of fancy."

Bullshit mister penthouse.

"You could… come over, if you want. Hang out. Watch a movie or something. Only if you're free."

Only if you're free. Only if you want to. Only if this isn't a mistake.

He smiled - not smug, not too eager. Just warm.

"I'd love that."

I busied myself pretending to check the espresso machine to hide the way my chest had suddenly gone tight.

"Cool, just… text me when you're done with work for the day."

He nodded, taking the lid from me. "Looking forward to it."

I nodded, too. Not because I had to, but because I meant it.

· · ·

The smell of tomato basil soup filled the kitchen, thick and comforting. The simmering pot popped occasionally, tiny bursts of sound that felt too loud in the quiet. I turned the tv on and pulled up Spotify, selecting an *autumn vibes* playlist that was chill but not depressing. Cooper snored from his usual spot against the door, tail twitching like he was chasing something in his dreams.

I moved slowly, half focused on stirring the soup and half on not checking the clock every three minutes. The grilled cheese sandwiches sat on a plate nearby, perfectly golden. Maybe too perfectly. I'd redone the first batch because they didn't "look right." Whatever that meant.

Get a grip, Reynolds. It's grilled cheese, not a wedding proposal.

A soft knock at the door made me jump. Cooper's head shot up, ears perked. He stood by the door, nose pressed to the crack like he could inhale Elliot from the other side.

"Yeah, yeah, company, I know." I wiped my hands on a towel.

When I opened the door, Elliot stood there, hands shoved into his jacket pockets. I hugged him, introductions still feeling awkward to me, but he kissed the top of my head and I relaxed a little. He smelled faintly of rain and cedar, like he'd walked through weather to get here even though the sky hadn't bothered to drizzle.

"Hey," I said.

"Hey yourself." His smile was small but easy, like we'd both silently agreed not to make tonight harder than it had to be. "Something smells amazing."

"Soup and sandwiches. I warned you. Culinary masterpiece."

He stepped inside, glancing around the apartment like it was sacred ground. "I'm honored to witness it."

He crouched down to greet Cooper, who had gathered his favorite ball in his mouth as if he was presenting Elliot the great gift of fetch.

I chuckled at the sight. "You know, he seems to like you."

"See? Positive reviews. I can't be *that* bad then, huh?" Elliot rose finally as Cooper trotted off.

I rolled my eyes but my lips curled into a smile at the edges.

I handed him a bowl and a spoon, gesturing toward the small table near the window. "Bon appetit, or whatever people who burn toast usually say."

He smiled, taking a seat. "It looks great, actually."

He took a spoonful, winced slightly when it was too hot, then laughed at himself. "Okay, that was *my* fault."

The sound of his laugh made something unclench in my chest. We ate quietly for a few minutes, the music and soft scrape of spoons the only noise between us. It wasn't awkward at all, just simple. Nice.

"Can I ask you something?" He said finally, voice gentle.

I paused mid-bite, narrowing my eyes. "Depends on the question."

He smiled softly. "Fair. Nothing heavy. Just… how are you *really* doing?"

My instinct was to deflect. To say *fine*. To make a joke. Instead, I found myself exhaling. "Better than I was? Still figuring out what that even means, I guess."

He nodded like that was an acceptable answer. Maybe it was. "Figuring out's a full-time job."

"Tell me about it." I leaned back in my chair. "You're probably the same way, though, right? Always fixing something?"

"I used to think that was noble," he admitted. "Now I just think it's exhausting."

I laughed a small laugh. He was right. It was exhausting. "So, what, you're retired from heroics?"

"Trying to be," he said. "I'm learning it's okay to just… sit with things. With people."

"Even messy ones?"

"Especially messy ones."

My heart did that annoying tight-skip thing again. I glanced down at my bowl before the moment could get too loud.

He reached over - slow, deliberate - and set his hand flat on the table near mine.

Not touching, just there. Present.

"Thanks for dinner," he said finally as his spoon rattled lightly in the nearly empty bowl. "It's the best thing I've had in weeks."

"Either that's a lie or your cooking is tragic, and I know *that's* not true."

He laughed and shook his head. The conversation meandered from there - old college stories of his, movies we pretended to hate but secretly loved, Cooper's habit of stealing socks and hiding them under the couch cushions. With every new topic, the sharp edges of life dulled a little more.

By the time I stacked our empty bowls in the sink, I realized I hadn't thought about what could go wrong in over an hour.

Elliot leaned against the counter, watching me dry my hands. "So... movie?"

"Sure," I said. "But if you pick something pretentious, I reserve the right to fake falling asleep."

"Duly noted. How about *How to Lose a Guy in 10 Days?*" He wiggled his eyebrows like he was issuing a dare.

"Wow, you really are a romantic, huh?"

He shrugged. "Call me predictable."

We settled on the couch. Cooper decided to curl up next to Elliot, which felt like the sweetest kind of betrayal. The room dimmed with the setting sun til all that was left was the flicker of the TV. Halfway through the movie, I felt Elliot's arm stretch across the back of the couch. Not touching me, just a quiet offer of closeness if I wanted it.

I did.

I nestled into his arm and could practically feel him jump out of his skin with amazement that I'd accepted his invitation for personal touch. It made me want to kiss the smug look off his face, but there wasn't one. He just smiled softly and kissed the top of my head again.

And for the first time in a long time, it felt like progress.

Elliot

I remember the morning after Laurel showed up - after the whole mess with James cracked something in Sam that she was trying so hard to ignore. I made a quiet promise to myself then: I was going to do everything in my power to make her smile again. Not to fix what I couldn't fix, not to shoulder what wasn't mine, but to be a soft place to land.

So we slipped into this gentle rhythm. Quiet dates at her house whenever she felt up for the company. Long walks with Cooper, the three of us moving in step like we'd been doing it all our lives. Endless hours spent over espresso at the cafe. It was the kind of time that didn't feel wasted or routine. It felt... necessary. Like oxygen. Pretty sure that's when we fell in love with my favorite taco truck, too. We must've gone there once a week, laughing over how they knew our order before she even opened her mouth.

And despite everything, she wasn't falling apart.

She was aching - quietly, steadily - but she kept taking these small steps forward. One moment at a time. One day at a time. And somehow, that made me admire her more than any grand gesture ever could.

We built this routine without meaning to: me showing up at the coffee shop in the mornings before work. Unhurried date nights after long days. Then we'd go home separately, text each other goodnight, pretend it didn't hurt a little that the day had to end.

I missed her every second I wasn't with her. I tried not to hover - god, I tried. She needed space to breathe, not someone clinging to her grief. But loving her, even before I could tell her that... It made me want to stay close. To know she was okay.

It was the simple things that made staying away impossible.

Like the morning I walked into the cafe and she wasn't there. It hit me harder than it should have. This sudden, irrational fear something had happened. Her coworker, that pompous-ass guy who thinks steaming milk makes him a philosopher, gave me this look like I didn't have the right to ask where she was. Dickhead.

But then he told me, begrudgingly, that Bob and Jessa had sent her to drop off pastries and a pot of coffee at the homeless youth shelter.

She hadn't even mentioned it to me. She'd just gone. Faced one of the shadows from her past head-on like it was nothing. Like surviving it once hadn't already cost her more than most people give in a lifetime.

I remember standing there with my hands around a paper cup (specifically because she always gave me a real mug) speechless. Proud.

She was simply amazing.

SAM

A few days later, the afternoon lull had settled in - a brief hour where the espresso machine wasn't crying for help and nobody was demanding something dairy-free, sugar-free, and joy-free.

Andrew had claimed his usual seat across the cafe, laptop open, headphones on… until they weren't. I was wiping down the front counter when my phone lit up with a new message.

> **Elliot - 3:24pm**
>
> *Survived lunch with a board member and only mildly wanted to fake my death. Hope your day is going better than mine.*

I bit the inside of my cheek and smiled.

"You're smiling," Andrew said, loud enough for the handful of customers to hear. Subtlety was *not* his spiritual gift.

"No I'm not," I said quickly, too quickly, and turned away to hide the heat flooding my cheeks.

"Liar," he sing-songed. "That was a full-on, texting-a-boy smile. I've seen it. I've *done* it."

"I was smiling because you're ridiculous," I deflected.

He stood and wandered over to the counter, one eyebrow raised and a devilish glint in his eye. "Sam Reynolds. Are you in *love?*"

"Jesus Christ," I hissed. "Keep your voice down."

"I *knew* it," he whispered dramatically, leaning on the counter like we were conspiring against a common enemy. "I mean, look at you. All pink-cheeked and glowing. It's kind of gross, honestly."

I rolled my eyes but the tightness in my chest hadn't gone away. He was joking, but the truth was still creeping in.

"What?" he said, eyes narrowing. "Why do you look like you just remembered you left the oven on?"

"I don't know," I said, fiddling with the corner of a napkin sticking out of the dispenser. "I just… is he *really* going to stay?"

"Sam."

"What if he regrets choosing me? Or thinks I'm… too much. Too broken. Too something."

He blinked, his playful expression softening into something quieter. "Hey, don't do that."

"Do what?"

"Act like there's an expiration date on being loved." He shrugged, suddenly serious. "You don't have to apologize for wanting something good."

I looked at him, caught off guard by the shift in tone.

"And for the record," he added, smirking again. "If he *does* regret it, I will personally key his car."

That earned a tiny laugh from me.

He grinned. "That's better. Now go text him back something vaguely suggestive. It's the only way to stay in power."

Andrew flitted back to his seat, looking far too proud of himself as he popped his headphones back on like he hadn't just dismantled my emotional walls with a latte in hand.

I stared at my phone, Elliot's message still glowing on the screen. My thumb hovered for a second, hesitating. Was I *really* going to take dating advice from a man who once ghosted someone because they used too many emojis?

But still.

I typed:

> *Glad you survived. I assume there was at least mediocre coffee involved?*

Pause. Then another text.

> *Also… what would you say to grabbing drinks tonight? You, me, Andrew, maybe rope in a couple of your people, too?*

I stared at it. My heart thudded.

It wasn't a dirty text. It wasn't even that flirty. But for me, it might as well have been skywriting.

I hit send before I could talk myself out of it. I also texted an already-busy-again Andrew.

> *Alright, you win. Drinks tonight.*

Across the coffee shop, his phone buzzed and he peeked at the screen, then up at me with a raised eyebrow. I shrugged.

"I'm taking your advice," I mouthed at him.

He grinned like the puppet master he was and gave me a triumphant thumbs-up.

My phone vibrated almost instantly.

> **Elliot - 3:41**
>
> *That sounds like a great idea. I'll text Ashley and Caleb and see if they're in. What time?*
>
> **Elliot - 3:42**
>
> *Also... mediocre coffee? Rude.*

I smiled. Okay. Maybe this wasn't so scary. Maybe tonight would be... good.

• • •

The bar was louder than I expected. Not chaotic, but buzzing with a kind of kinetic energy that made my nerves rattle a little in my chest.

Andrew and I slid into the booth first - him with the confidence of someone who could talk to wallpaper and make it blush, and me doing everything I could not to look like I regretted this already.

Elliot arrived a few minutes later, flanked by two people who could've walked straight out of an Abercrombie ad.

Ashley, his sister, was bubbly in a non-annoying way, with kind eyes and a laugh that made you want to tell her secrets. Caleb, Elliot's college friend, was all easy charm, a little loud, a little cocky, but not unkind. Just... the kind of person who talked with his hands and never asked you anything he didn't already have a funny answer for.

"This must be Sam," Ashley said, sliding into the seat beside me with a genuine smile. "I've heard so much about you."

"Oh god," I muttered. "Good things, I hope."

She grinned. "Annoyingly good. I was starting to think he made you up."

Elliot took the seat across from me and gave me a soft look, the kind that could melt steel. His knee brushed mine under the table, just enough to make my pulse trip.

Andrew immediately launched into a story about a customer I'd had that day who tried to order an "upside-down, dairy-free cortado with foam," and the conversation spiraled from there - jokes, casual questions, teasing jabs that made me feel a little like I'd stumbled into someone else's friend group, but in the best way.

It was… nice. Comfortable. Almost normal.

Until Caleb leaned back with his third beer and elbowed Elliot. "Man, I gotta say, this is a new one for you. A woman who listens to your board meeting stories and doesn't fake a family emergency? I'm impressed."

Elliot laughed, albeit uncomfortably. "What can I say? Sam's a better actor than most."

I smiled tightly.

Caleb meant it as a joke. I knew that. I *knew* that. But a quiet thought burrowed beneath my ribs: *They're all waiting to see how long I last.*

I reached for my drink. Something crisp and citrusy, thank god. I was about to excuse myself to the restroom, just for a second to breathe, when a new arrival slid into the booth beside Caleb - a friend of his, I gathered from the nods around the table.

He leaned in to whisper something that made Caleb bark out a laugh, and in doing so, his breath hit me like a wall.

Gin.

Not the classy, botanical kind, either. No lime. No tonic. Just straight, cheap gin.

The sharp sting of it pulled something taut in my chest. The booth walls pressed closer. My skin felt like it didn't fit. I tried to laugh at something Ashley said, but my throat had closed around the sound.

Just a drink. Just a smell.

But it wasn't.

It was *his* breath. *His* slurred words. *His* rage.

The room blurred. Someone bumped the table and my glass wobbled. My hand shot out to steady it, but I knocked it instead.

Fuck.

A little splash of cocktail spilled on the table, and suddenly every nerve in my body screamed to *run*.

Elliot reached over, his hand brushing mine. I flinched.

"Hey, you okay?"

I nodded, too quickly.

"Need some air?"

I nodded again.

"Come on," he said, already sliding out of the booth.

I let him lead me out - out of the bar, out of the buzzing warmth, out into the cool night. The minute the door shut behind us, I felt my knees begin to buckle. He caught me before I could fall completely, steadying me with both hands.

"Breathe, Sam. You're okay. Just breathe."

I tried. Fuck, I tried.

The cool night air hit my face like a balm. My lungs pulled in a shaky breath - then another. I gripped the edge of the brick building with one hand and pressed the other to my chest.

Elliot stood close, but not too close, his hands loosely in his jacket pockets.

Flashes of abuse flickered in my head like a bad film reel. I breathed deeply, trying everything I could to focus on literally anything else. The air I *was* breathing. The concrete underneath me. The creepy little bug carrying a random crumb like it was on a victory lap.

"Better?" he asked gently after a long moment had passed.

I nodded, slower this time, still staring at the pavement.

"Was it something someone said?"

"No," I rasped. Then paused. "Yes. I don't know. It was just… the smell." My voice was brittle, barely audible. "Gin."

He nodded slowly, understanding flickering across his face like a shadow. "Want me to go back in, say you weren't feeling well?"

I didn't answer right away. The thought of going back inside made my stomach twist. But disappearing without explanation felt worse - like leaving behind some version of myself I'd finally started to recognize.

"I don't want to be rude," I murmured.

Elliot tilted his head, voice soft but firm. "Sam, you don't owe anyone an explanation."

I met his eyes. He was present. Without pity. Without judgement. Just… there.

"Okay," I said, voice steadier. "Can we just go?"

"Of course."

We walked in silence back inside - just long enough for Elliot to gather our things and exchange quiet words with Ashley. I caught the moment she looked over at me, concern softening her expression, but she didn't say anything. Just nodded.

On the walk back to my place, the quiet settled between us. The kind of silence that said everything without speaking.

His hand brushed mine once. I didn't pull away.

By the time we reached my door, I'd stopped shaking. Mostly.

"You want to come in?" I asked, not even sure what I meant by it. Just that the idea of being alone made my chest tighten all over again.

"If you want me to."

I nodded, keys trembling just slightly in my hand.

Inside, the air felt still and familiar. Cooper thumped his tail sleepily at us from his spot on the couch. I gave him a quick rub behind the ears before collapsing onto the edge of my bed, my jacket still on, the weight of the night starting to settle.

Elliot stood in the doorway, unsure. "Do you want me to stay out here or…"

"No," I said too quickly. Then softer, "Just… stay with me for a little while?"

His shoes were off before I'd finished the sentence. He sat beside me, close but careful. His hand found mine again. Warmer this time. Steadier.

"Do you want to talk about it?" he asked.

I shook my head.

"Okay."

He didn't ask again.

Instead, we sat. Just breathing. My head on his shoulder. The city outside grumbling through the windows.

Eventually he kissed the side of my head, murmured a quiet *goodnight,* and settled in beside me, fully clothed, fully present, fully calm.

I turned off the bedside lamp, the room swallowed by soft shadows.

But the quiet didn't stay gentle for long.

25
SAM

Stop! Please! Don't come any closer! Haven't you done enough?

He made his way toward me again, the evil grin widening with each step.

"I'm coming for you, Sammy," he hissed through gritted, yellowed teeth.

I tried to crawl away, but the rough bottom of his golf shoes pinned my right arm to the floor. I fought back the scream that rose in my throat, knowing that it would only bring him more pleasure. The pressure on my arm increased with each second that dragged by, and I prayed somehow, someway there would be an end to this torture.

I could feel my skin splitting beneath the spikes of his shoes. I momentarily wondered if he'd put them on just to cause me more pain, but the thought was interrupted when he grabbed my other arm and yanked me from the floor out from under his shoe with a long scrape.

"You little bitch. You're nothing more than that. And you never will be." His rancid breath blew over my face with each whisper.

Tears streamed down my face, and I tried not to let his words get to me. They weren't true. I knew they weren't. But when it's beat into you it can be hard to believe otherwise. Suddenly he dropped my arm, my body crumpling to the floor beneath my weary muscles.

"Stand up you fucking bitch. Get up! Now!"

Drops of sweat and tears made the cold floor slick against my damp forehead. I cried. I'd lost the ability to do anything else hours ago. My throat was raw from the screams that had clawed their way out of my throat and into the dense air around me.

He laughed darkly and bent to press his lips against my cheek. The smell of gin curled menacingly under my nose. "Oh, Sammy. I'm much closer than you think."

My eyes snapped open. I was gasping for whatever oxygen I was struggling to find. Elliot was bent over me, worried and working furiously to try to get me awake. My body trembled and my cheeks were damp just as they had been in my night terror.

"Elliot," I croaked. "I'm okay."

I squeezed my eyelids together in an attempt to dull the aching in my head.

"Sam..." Just noticing that I had woken up, Elliot pulled me into his lap and cradled me in his arms. His heart beat feverishly against his chest. I glanced up from under my eyelashes and saw nothing but pain in his eyes. Worry lines had formed between his brows, and his lips were firmly pressed into a frown.

You couldn't count on all your fingers and toes the ways you can hurt this man.

The only thing that could possibly quiet the insecurity gnawing at me was to make sure *he* was okay.

"I'm okay, Elliot, really. It was a bad one, but I'm awake and here now. You're here. I'm okay."

The tension around his eyes relaxed ever so slightly, but the worry lingered. He didn't release me, just held me tighter, his hand splayed across my back like he could shield me from whatever hell had clawed its way into my sleep.

"I didn't know what to do," he whispered. "You were thrashing, Sam. Crying. Saying things I couldn't make out."

I buried my face against his shoulder, ashamed of the mess I'd become. "I'm sorry."

"No," he said immediately, pulling back just enough to look at me. His voice stayed gentle, but firm. "Don't apologize for this. Ever."

My lip trembled. "I *am* sorry, though. This is… a lot."

He brushed a damp strand of hair off my cheek. "You're not broken, Sam."

I flinched at the word he pulled straight from my thoughts. "You say that now."

"I'll say it tomorrow, too. And the day after that. For as long as you'll let me."

His words sliced clean through the fog, startlingly tender. Too good. Too kind. Too much.

But I didn't tell him to stop.

I let myself lean into the warmth of his arms; let my weight rest on him for a little while. The storm inside me had quieted, but only just. I knew it would come back. Knew the memories didn't dissolve with dawn. But right now, in this sliver of night, he was here. And I didn't have to survive it alone.

"Can I stay a little longer?" He asked after a long moment of silence.

"Please." I closed my eyes.

He shifted us gently so we were lying side by side again, arms still wrapped around me like a lifeline. I could feel my breath slowing, syncing with his.

"I'm not going anywhere, Sam," he whispered.

And I believed him.

At least for tonight.

· · ·

Warmth.

It was the first thing I noticed. Not sunlight, not sound, not even pain - just warmth. A steady rise and fall beneath my cheek, the brush of breath across the top of my head.

I blinked into the soft gray of early morning and realized I was still tucked into Elliot's chest, his arm wrapped protectively around me like a barrier between me and the dark.

We'd fallen asleep like this.

He was still here.

For a moment, I didn't move. My eyes fluttered closed again as I let myself feel it - his hand on my waist, the weight of his presence, the quiet peace humming under my skin. My muscles didn't ache from tension like they normally did after an episode like that. I wasn't dizzy with dread. Just tired. Spent. And - god help me - safe.

"Hey," Elliot murmured, voice gravelly from sleep. "You okay?"

I groaned into his shirt. "Too early to know."

He chuckled softly, his chest rumbling against my cheek. "Fair."

I eventually peeled myself away from him, mostly because my bladder demanded it. When I came out of the bathroom, he was sitting up now - hair sticking up in five directions, shirt wrinkled, looking like every woman's emotionally available fever dream.

"Morning," he said, voice still hoarse.

"Don't say it like that," I muttered, rubbing my face. "You sound way too cheerful. It's offensive."

He smiled, unfazed. "Can I make you coffee?"

I squinted at him. "*You* making the coffee sounds like a safety hazard."

"I'm capable," he said, climbing out of bed and stretching. "How hard can it be?"

"Famous last words," I mumbled, but waved him toward the kitchen anyway.

He disappeared down the hall, and I followed slowly, dragging my blanket with me like a disgruntled ghost.

It took about thirty seconds before I heard a cupboard open, then another, then the distinct sound of something metal clanging against tile.

"Where do you keep your - uh - filters?" He called.

"Near the coffee. Revolutionary concept," I deadpanned, sinking onto one of the barstools.

He found the filters. Eventually. Then stared at the Chemex like it was an alien artifact.

"Do you… boil the water first, or-?"

"Oh my god," I groaned, standing to take over. "Move. This is painful."

He stepped aside, hands raised in surrender, laughing. "I was *this* close to figuring it out."

"Sure you were," I said, filling the kettle. "Next time I'll let you burn down my kitchen just to prove it."

"Noted. For the record, though, I make an excellent french press at home."

"Of course you do. Mr. Single-Origin."

He grinned at that, leaning against the counter while I went through the motions - grind, pour, wait. My routine. My rhythm.

"You always hum when you make coffee?" He asked after a minute.

I shot him a bleary side-eye. "Only when someone ruins my morning cup with noise and bad technique."

He laughed. "So… always?"

Despite myself, a smile tugged at my mouth. "Apparently."

He reached over to grab the mugs as I poured."Truce? I'll handle clean-up if you let me redeem myself with breakfast sometime."

"Define breakfast," I said, passing him his mug.

"Something edible that doesn't come from a drive-thru… or the cafe."

I gave a sleepy shrug. "We'll see."

We stood there in the quiet after that, sipping and breathing, the morning stretching softly around us.

"Thank you for letting me stay," he said finally. His tone was different - steady, careful.

I leaned against the counter, eyes half-lidded but honest. "Thanks for not running."

He didn't smile this time. Just met my gaze and said, "Not my style."

My heart fluttered. And for once, I didn't fight it.

• • •

The bell above the front door jingled midmorning, and I looked up from the register just in time to see Andrew breeze in, wind-tousled and smelling faintly like cinnamon gum.

"You look like hell," he said cheerfully, sliding onto a barstool at the counter.

"Good morning to you too," I muttered, beginning to make his usual order. "And thank you for that *warm* and *affirming* greeting."

"You're welcome. I'm a gift." He leaned in, lowering his voice just enough to make it clear this wasn't just another drop-in, "Seriously though… you okay?"

I swallowed, carefully folding a dish towel. "I'm here. Working. Functioning."

"That's not what I asked."

I hesitated. "I had a rough night. But… I made it through."

Andrew nodded slowly, eyes searching my face for more than I was offering. "Elliot texted me."

I raised an eyebrow. "He did?"

"Just said you'd left early and he was staying with you. He didn't give any details - classy move by the way - but I figured…" he trailed off and shrugged. "Just wanted to make sure you were alright."

Something in my chest softened. "I didn't know he'd reach out."

"Yeah, well," he said, suddenly more focused on tracing the top of his mug with his finger. "He seems like the type who doesn't bail when things get complicated."

"He's… been good to me."

Andrew looked up again, and this time his expression was stripped of all the usual bravado. "I know I mess around a lot, Sam, but for real… if you ever felt unsafe or like you needed to get out of something… I'd help you. No questions asked."

The last person you asked for help disappeared off the face of the earth, never to be heard from again. Even if you need help… best not to ask.

My eyes stung. "I know,"

"But," he added, his grin creeping back in like sunlight through a window. "I don't think you need rescuing from Elliot. Dude's a golden retriever in a cashmere sweater. I think you're safe with him."

A quiet laugh escaped me. "A golden retriever?"

"Loyal. Eager. Weirdly into eye contact."

I shook my head, but couldn't stop smiling.

Andrew reached across the counter and gave my hand a brief, reassuring squeeze. "You're doing good, Sam. Don't let your brain convince you otherwise."

"I'll try not to."

"Good. Now," he said, leaning back with a mock-stretch. "Can I get a cinnamon scone, or are you still emotionally fragile and liable to burst into tears if I ask for carbs?"

I grabbed the tongs and pointed them at him. "One cinnamon scone, coming up. But *only* because I'm emotionally fragile."

"That's what I like to hear."

Elliot

26

The night at the bar started off easy. Normal.

It was really something special seeing Sam settled between a mix of her people and mine. Everything just fit neatly into place like a puzzle you'd suddenly found the missing piece to. It was my first time really hanging out with Andrew, and the guy was a riot. I understood immediately why Sam kept him around. He had this uncanny ability to take any situation and make it worth laughing at.

And Ashley - god, Ashley glommed onto Sam like she'd been waiting her whole life to meet her. Sam was overwhelmed at first, stiff in that way she gets when she's trying not to run. But a couple drinks later, something softened. She loosened up into this girly, sassy version of herself I'd never seen before. Watching the two of them banter was... honestly kind of adorable.

Then Caleb had to be a dick. One offhanded comment about Sam and the whole table froze. I wanted to deck him. Didn't. But I wanted to.

It wasn't even Caleb who broke the night open. It was his friend - some random nobody - who reeked of gin, practically knocking Sam off her feet.

I watched it wash over her like a storm rolling in off the coast. Fast and dark. No care in the world how much fun everyone had been having. Her posture changed, breath shortened, eyes went someplace far away.

She tried to control it. To shove it back down into the hole it crawled out of. But then she reached out and accidentally spilled her drink, and it was over. Panic flared behind her eye like a startled wild horse.

"Need some air?" I asked.

She just nodded.

I walked with her outside, arms half-raised and ready to catch her if she fell. And she did, right there on the sidewalk. I placed her back on her feet and stepped back enough to give her a moment, some time to collect herself.

Her breath came in sputters and the color had drained from her face. She looked like she was fighting her own body for oxygen.

God, what I would have given to take the whole damn thing away. But I couldn't. So I stood there, hands shoved in my pockets, close enough to be there but far enough not to crowd her.

It took a while. Her breathing slowly leveled out, the tremors eased, and when she finally looked up at me, eyes shiny, tears clinging but refusing to fall, she whispered, "Can we just go?"

I gathered our things, said a quick goodbye to the table - without bothering to explain - and walked home with her in silence.

I offered to stay on the couch. I didn't want the couch. I wanted to take her in my arms and hold her til the fear let go of her throat. I'm still so grateful she let me.

She fell asleep fast, drifting off in the exhaustion of holding herself together. I stayed awake, basking in the simple sound of her breath, finally even and peaceful, at least for a moment.

I remember thinking: I can't protect her from this.

I rubbed my hand over my face, surrendering to whatever life was about to throw at us. She stirred then, twitching, mumbling, caught in whatever memories had dragged her under at the bar. And then it got worse. Screaming. Writhing. Crying. A nightmare trying to physically claw its way into the room with us. I jumped up, shaking her gently, panicking because I had no idea what to do. No idea who to call. No idea how to save her from something I couldn't even see.

She woke with a gasp - scaring me shitless- and I realized I'd been pacing, helpless and out of my depth.

"I'm sorry," she'd whispered, like she'd done something wrong. Like she was a burden

She wasn't. God, she wasn't.

I told her so. All but begged her to believe it. Maybe she did. Maybe she didn't. But for that night, just for the moment, she let me say it. Be there.

And for me... that was everything.

Sam

Cooper roamed around Elliot's place like it was full of unexplored magic. He paced and sniffed and investigated. Elliot and I hung back by the elevator door, watching and laughing.

"He's checking for threats," Elliot said seriously. "Probably suspects I'm secretly running an illegal cat sanctuary."

"He'd be thrilled," I smirked, stepping inside. "He thinks he's the mayor of every building he enters."

Elliot leaned casually against the wall, arms folded, watching me as I stepped out of my shoes and shook off the wind from the walk over. His space was so *him* - clean, thoughtfully designed, but not sterile. A shelf of vinyl records stretched below the window to the right. Two different throw blankets tossed haphazardly over the back of the couch. Bookshelf full of old literature and poetry and tech manuals.

It was the kind of space people built when they expected someone to stay.

"You hungry?" he asked, pushing off the wall.

I nodded. "Starving, honestly."

"Excellent. Because tonight's menu is my famous veggie stir-fry. And by famous I mean I've never poisoned anyone with it."

"High bar. Can't wait."

He moved into the kitchen and I followed, slipping onto a stool at the island as Cooper flopped dramatically on the rug like he'd trekked across a desert to get here.

I watched Elliot work - grabbing vegetables, chopping with practiced ease, occasionally dancing a little to the music playing low from a speaker in the corner. Something soft and mellow. His movements were fluid, natural. Comfortable.

I didn't know if I'd ever be that comfortable in someone else's space.

"What?" he asked, glancing over at me with a grin.

"Nothing," I said, but felt my lips tug upward. "Just still surprised you know how to cook. I figured someone like you would survive off meal prep containers and overpriced juice."

"Ouch." He tossed a slice of red pepper at me. "I'll have you know, I am a man of many domestic talents."

"Like…?"

"Cooking. Laundry. Alphabetizing my vinyls. Giving incredible shoulder massages."

I rolled my eyes, popping the pepper slice in my mouth. "Sure. Let me know when you start offering those shoulder massages to friends."

He gave a slow, sideways glance. "Are we just friends, Sam?"

The question sat between us. Not threatening. Not pushy. Just honest.

"I don't know what we are," I admitted, staring down at the counter. "But this…

being here… it's good. It's more than I thought I'd get to have."

He didn't press. He just slid a bowl in front of me, steam curling up from perfectly sauteed veggies, and sat beside me with his own.

"Then we'll take it one dinner at a time."

We ate in easy silence, Cooper snoring softly on the rug. My fingers brushed Elliot's once as I reached for my glass of water, and instead of pulling away, I let them rest there. Just for a moment.

It wasn't a grand declaration. It wasn't a confession.

But it was peace. And for me, that was everything.

• • •

It happened in seconds.

One minute Cooper was sniffing the edge of the concrete near Elliot's building's dog relief area, tail wagging, completely innocent. The next, he was on his back, wiggling around like he'd found the holy grail of dead things.

"Oh, for *fuck's* sake," I groaned. "Cooper - no! Stop! That's disgusting!"

By the time I pulled him up by his leash, it was too late. Whatever he'd rolled in was… potent. A smell so vile it felt like a personal attack.

I pinched the bridge of my nose, gagged once, and muttered, "You're fucking lucky I love you."

We shamefully made our way back through the building and up to Elliot's penthouse. Of course, he smiled up at us from the couch as soon as the elevator doors slid open.

"You won't keep that grin for long," I muttered.

He raised a brow as Cooper ran over to him and placed his front paws flat in the middle of Elliot's chest. As soon as he caught a whiff, he stopped short, mid-laugh, eyes watering. "Oh, wow. That's… impressive."

"Impressive?" I gaped at him. "My dog marinated himself in roadkill."

Cooper trotted proudly around the apartment, tongue lolling, looking very pleased with himself.

Elliot grinned and, because he's apparently made of sunshine, said, "C'mon. We can fix this. I've got a shower big enough for a small horse."

Of course you do.

Inside the bathroom, the concrete floors carried through, but warm brown cabinets and silver fixtures bounced off the pristine white sink and toilet. It looked like something out of a spa brochure. White towels folded with military precision. A rain showerhead the size of a dinner plate. A giant plant in the corner stretching up almost to the ceiling.

Cooper shook once, and a splatter of mystery goop hit the floor.

"Don't you dare," I warned, glaring at Elliot when he started to laugh again.

He bit his lip, trying and failing to look serious. "Right. Serious dog emergency. Got it."

He wrangled Cooper into the glass shower, which immediately became a splash zone. I tried to hold him still while Elliot fiddled with the controls.

"Is there a *dog* setting?" I asked, already soaked from the first shake.

"There's a *rainforest* one," he said helpfully, pressing a button.

Water came down in a heavy, warm sheet, drenching all three of us.

"Elliot!" I sputtered, hair plastered to my face.

He laughed so hard he had to brace himself against the wall. "Okay, okay! *Too* rainforest."

Cooper took this as permission to shake again, drenching the rest of the bathroom.

I groaned. "This is a nightmare."

"This," Elliot said between chuckles, "is the best thing that's happened in my house all year."

"Glad my humiliation entertains you."

"You're adorable when you're mad."

I glared, though my lips betrayed me with a twitch. "You're cleaning the floor."

"Deal."

Elliot grabbed the bottle of Dawn dishwashing soap - the closest thing we could find to dog shampoo in his house. He worked the suds into Cooper's fur while I rinsed, our arms bumping now and then. At one point he looked over, soap on his cheek, hair damp and sticking up.

"You know, I think we make a pretty good team."

"Yeah," I said, pretending to focus on the dog. "Until he decides to shake again."

As if on cue, Cooper did.

We both shrieked, scrambled, and slipped - Elliot catching my arm before I hit the concrete. Water dripped from his chin, both of us hacking in a half cough, half laugh kind of way.

"Maybe next time," I managed as we wrung out the last of the suds, "we hire a hazmat team."

"Or I just build him his own shower."

I smirked and rolled my eyes. "Of course you would."

Elliot had bought a basket of toys for Cooper to keep at his house. A sweet gesture,

Cooper had picked his favorite and ignored the rest. Elliot didn't seem to mind, he just laughed and handed it over when we finally got the dog dry enough to stop dripping.

Cooper flopped onto the rug, gnawing happily, tail thumping slowly.

I sank onto the floor beside him, exhausted, damp, and smelling like wet dog. "Next time, we're just going to my place."

Elliot sat down next to me, equally soaked. "Deal. But admit it - this was kind of fun."

I eyed the puddles spreading across the concrete floors. "Define fun."

He grinned. "This. You, me, chaos, and a very proud dog."

I rolled my eyes again, but couldn't stop the smile creeping in. We sat there like that for a while - two drowned humans, one content dog, and the faint echo of laughter in a house that suddenly felt a little more like home.

• • •

I exhaled into the comfort of routine as I stepped into the warm buzz of the cafe the next day.

Bill was already humming some old blues song under his breath, and Jessa had a bandana tied around her head like she was ready to paint a house. I hung my bag on the hook behind the counter, tied my apron into a crooked bow, and reached for the day's first cup of coffee.

"Morning, Sam," Bill said as he loaded a tray of croissants into the display case. "You seem different lately. Did someone finally convince you to start getting eight hours of sleep?"

"Something like that," I said, half smiling. "It's just… been good recently."

"You look… lighter," he noted.

Before I could respond, Jessa popped her head around the back cooler door. "Oh, hey. Forgot to tell you. That weird guy came in yesterday. The one who always asks for you. What's his name? Mark? Marvin?"

My stomach dipped.

"Marcus?" I said, too quickly.

"Yeah, that's the one," she nodded. "Asked if you were working, then didn't order anything when I said you weren't. Just sort of… lingered. Made me nervous. Not illegal or anything, just… weird."

Bill stopped and looked up. "He asked for Sam again?"

Jessa shrugged. "Didn't seem dangerous. Just… off."

A familiar tingle crept up the back of my neck. That cold-fingered kind of anxiety that didn't need evidence to feel real.

"Did he say anything else?" I asked, keeping my tone light.

"Nope, just said he'd 'catch you later,'" Jessa said, her voice already trailing off like it wasn't a big deal.

But it felt like a big deal. Or… maybe I was just being paranoid.

I cleared my throat and forced a smile. "Well. If he comes back and I'm not here, tell him I'm at the FBI witness protection office, would you?"

Jessa chuckled. Bill didn't. Instead, he gave me a long, unreadable look before turning back to stocking the pastry case.

"Hey, we've got a new cardamom syrup coming in today," he said a few moments later. "Think you can handle the taste testing?"

"Obviously. It's the hardest part of the job, but someone has to suffer for the craft."

The tension lightened. Customers trickled in. We got busy. The espresso machine hissed its comfortingly aggressive steam. The smell of warm pastries and sharp coffee filled the air. And I let myself enjoy it. Even with the unease lingering beneath the surface, I let myself enjoy being okay - for now.

SAM

"My day was good," I told Elliot as I kicked my shoes off by the elevator door. "How about yours?"

Cooper ran up to him as if he was welcoming him to his own home. "Hey buddy... Long," he replied. "I spent all day in meetings."

"How about we order in tonight, then? Just relax and do... nothing."

I made my way over to where he reclined on the couch and sat on the edge next to him. He placed a kiss on my forehead. "That sounds great."

"Pizza?"

"Sure," I nodded, grabbing my phone from the coffee table and pulling up the best pizza place nearby.

He grinned, moving toward the kitchen to grab two glasses and a bottle of wine.

I placed the order, then leaned back into the cushions, trying to ignore the flutter of nerves in my stomach. The kind that weren't bad, just… new. Like the way he always looked at me when he thought I wasn't paying attention. Like how his voice always softened a little when he said my name.

Elliot handed me a glass and settled next to me again, closer this time, thighs brushing. His shirt was half unbuttoned, his sleeves casually rolled, and the light from the lamp caught the edge of his cheekbone just right.

My god.

"You've got that look," he said quietly.

"What look?"

"The one that says you're thinking really hard about something, but pretending you're not." He nodded toward my hand that had instinctively, habitually made its way to my necklace.

I dropped it.

"Maybe I'm just tired."

"Mmhm." He took a sip of wine. "Or maybe you're trying not to say something."

I took a long sip of my own, buying time. "Maybe I am."

He turned toward me slightly, one arm slung along the back of the couch. "You don't have to say anything… I'm not pushing."

"I know," I said, and I meant it.

That's why it scared me. Because he *wasn't* pushing. Because ever since I yelled at him about pushing the *one* time he did, he didn't. And somehow, it made me want him more.

We sat in silence for a moment, the kind that settles like a blanket. My foot brushed against his knee, and instead of pulling away, I left it there.

"I like this," I said softly.

"What's 'this'?"

"You. Here. This space." I glanced around the room, then back at him. "It feels… safe."

His expression shifted - softer, deeper. "That means everything to me, Sam."

He reached for my hand, threading his fingers through mine with gentle confidence. His thumb ran slow circles against my skin, grounding me. I scooted closer, just a little, until our legs touched fully. He didn't move. Just watched me.

"I'd like to stay," I said before I could change my mind. "Tonight, I mean. If that's okay."

His hand squeezed mine just slightly, then let go to brush a loose strand of hair behind my ear. "Of course it's okay."

We sat in the quiet for a moment. Not awkward. Just close. His hand lingering on my cheek.

"Sam… I don't want to rush you. You know that, right?"

"I know," I whispered, leaning into his touch. "I just… don't want to feel alone tonight."

He nodded. "You won't."

His kiss was soft. No pressure, no expectation - just warmth and steady affection. When I leaned into him, he pulled me closer, his arms wrapping around my waist like a promise. For once, it didn't send my heart rate skyrocketing.

We stayed wrapped up on the couch longer than I expected. I let my head rest against Elliot's shoulder as Cooper snoozed at our feet, the warm weight of Elliot's hand in mine. The pizza box sat half-eaten on the coffee table, the wine nearly gone.

I didn't want to move. Didn't want to break the spell of quiet contentment.

But part of me also did.

"Do you want to go to bed?" I asked, voice barely above a whisper.

Elliot looked down at me, cautious. "Are you tired?"

"Yes," I admitted. "But... not just that."

His expression shifted, and his eyes scanned mine carefully, reading every word I was too afraid to say.

"Okay," he said, soft and steady.

We moved slowly, wordlessly, cleaning up enough to feel like we weren't leaving chaos behind. Elliot reached for my hand and led me down the hallway to his bedroom.

"Hey," he stopped as we neared the edge of his bed. His other hand made its way to cradle the back of my neck. "I want you to know we don't *have* to do anything. Just being with you like this is more than enough for me."

"I know," I said, squeezing his hand. "But I want to."

A breath he hadn't meant to hold escaped from his chest. He nodded, his voice tender. "Then let's go slow."

He kissed me again - soft, lingering, no pressure. Just warmth and the steady promise of safety.

That's what made me want to. For the first time in my life, I felt fully safe. Fully seen. Like every scar, every wall, every hard-earned inch of healing had brought me here - not to this moment, but to *him*.

We moved toward the bed together, slowly peeling away layers of clothing between long pauses and quiet touches. I didn't feel rushed. I didn't feel small. I didn't feel afraid. I felt... chosen. Known.

When his arms came around me, it didn't feel like I was being consumed. It felt like I was being cherished.

We climbed beneath the covers, tangled but unhurried. There was no performance. No pretending. Just two bodies drawn together by something deeper.

And when it finally happened - when I finally let him all the way in - I didn't break. I didn't run.

I stayed.

And afterward, when my head rested against his chest and his fingers traced slow, comforting patterns across my back, I felt the unfamiliar warmth of safety settle somewhere deep in my bones.

. . .

The smell of coffee pulled me from sleep before sunlight did.

I blinked groggily, the pale morning light bleeding through Elliot's curtains. His side of the bed was warm but empty, and for a brief second, panic flared in my chest.

But then I heard the sound of a cabinet door shutting in the kitchen. The low buzz of a man humming an off-key version of something familiar. Cooper's soft snore from the floor beside the bed.

I sank back against the pillow.

I'm still here. He's still here. Nothing broke.

A few minutes later, the bedroom door nudged open and Elliot appeared - boxers hanging low on his hips, hair sleep-tousled, holding two mugs of coffee like he was offering peace to a queen in exile.

"Morning, beautiful," he said with a grin that was far too awake for this hour.

I groaned. "Ugh. You're one of *those* morning people, aren't you?"

"Oh, absolutely. Sunshine and all." He handed me the mug and perched himself on the edge of the bed. "But I did get that bag of coffee you told me to get."

I took the mug gratefully and breathed in a deep sniff before I took a sip. "You're forgiven."

He leaned over and brushed his lips against my forehead, "Good. I don't want to be on your bad side before breakfast."

I laughed, the sound scratchy from sleep. "Smart man."

Cooper stirred and trotted toward the bed, nose nudging at Elliot's knee like he was ready for his share of the morning, too.

"I made breakfast," Elliot added, petting the back of Cooper's head. "Well, eggs and toast. The pancakes may look like they made it through a war zone, but I promise they'll taste okay."

"Is that so?" I smirked.

He raised an eyebrow. "Only one way to find out."

I pulled back the covers and swung my legs over the edge of the bed, the air chilly against my bare skin. One of Elliot's sweatshirts was lying across the chair in the corner, so I grabbed it and tugged it over my head.

It hung halfway down my thighs, cozy and soft, and when I turned around Elliot was staring like I'd just cast a spell.

"What?" I asked, suddenly self-conscious.

His smile curved slowly. "You look… really good in my clothes."

I rolled my eyes as I shoved the too-large sleeves up my arms. "You're ridiculous."

"And yet here you are, making yourself at home in my hoodie. I think that makes us even," he winked.

We made our way to the kitchen, Cooper trailing behind like our sleepy little chaperone. I hopped up onto the barstool while Elliot plated food and passed it across the counter.

There was still something quiet inside me - like I was still waiting for him to realize the real me was far too fucked up to bother with - but maybe it wasn't as loud this morning. I felt safe. Full. Like maybe letting him in hadn't been a mistake after all.

"You okay?" Elliot asked, watching me over his cup of coffee.

"Yeah," I nodded, and this time I meant it. "I really am."

Elliot

I remember the moment she said it. "I like this."

Her voice was quiet, almost shy. Like she was testing the weight of the words in her mouth before letting them land between us. She looked around my living room then back at me with those earnest eyes that always seemed to ask if I was safe to trust.

"You. Here. This space. It feels... safe."

God. I don't think she ever knew what that did to me.

Safety had never been something I expected to be for another person. But she said it like it was the simplest truth in the world.

"That means everything to me, Sam," I told her. Because it did. More than I could put into words.

When I reached for her hand, she let me take it, our fingers threading together like we'd done it a hundred times. My thumb found that familiar rhythm against her skin, and she leaned in ever so slightly - this small, quiet gesture that felt louder than any words I've ever heard.

We sat in the quiet for a while. Not speaking. Just breathing in sync. Her cheek resting against my hand. My heart doing that ridiculous thing where it felt too full and too fragile at the same time.

I didn't want to rush her. I needed her to know I'd wait forever if she asked.

"I know," she whispered. "I just… don't want to feel alone tonight."

I promised her she wouldn't. Quietly. Reverently.

I kissed her then. Soft. Careful. The way you'd touch something precious without risking breaking it. She leaned into me, and I felt her melt in a way she didn't realize she was capable of. And I held her closer. Arms around her waist like a steadying anchor.

We stayed curled up on the couch long after the pizza had gone cold. Cooper snored at our feet. Her head rested on my shoulder. My hand stayed tangled with hers because I couldn't bring myself to let go. It felt like the kind of moment you want to bottle and keep somewhere safe.

When she finally whispered, "Do you want to go to bed," I felt something shift in my chest. Not lust. Not expectation. Hope.

I searched her face. She let me. And whatever I saw there - fear, longing, trust - told me everything I needed to know.

We cleaned up together, almost ceremonially, like we were making space, not just in my home, but in whatever fragile thing existed between us.

Down the hallway, right before the bed, I stopped her. I cupped the back of her neck and searched her face again, making damn sure she knew we didn't have to do anything.

"I know," she said. "But I want to."

The breath left me in one long exhale I didn't realize I'd been holding. I nodded and kissed her again. Soft. Patient. A steady promise that she was safe with me.

The rest happened gently. Carefully. Slowly peeling back layers of clothing like the pages of a book we were afraid to rush through. I didn't want to take anything from her. God knows enough had been taken already. I just wanted to be someone she didn't have to guard herself against. In any way.

And when she finally let me hold her - truly hold her - it didn't feel like desire fulfilled. It felt like grace. When we moved together, it wasn't about the sex. It was about trust. About the way her breath hitched but didn't break. The way she searched my face like she was memorizing proof that I meant every quiet promise I'd ever made.

Then she stayed.

That's what I remember cherishing most. Not the heat. Not the sex. But the staying. Like for once, she'd stopped running. Stopped fighting. Realized she could rest in the assurance of me.

Afterward, she rested her head on my chest, her breath warm against my skin, her body soft and unguarded in my arms. My fingers traced slow patterns across her back - more to soothe myself than her, I think. Because holding her like that felt holy. Like being trusted with something irreplaceable.

And in the soft, dim quiet of that room, with her head tucked against me like she belonged there, I felt something settle deep in my bones. It wasn't triumph. Something quieter. Deeper. The warmth of being chosen by someone who had every reason not to choose at all.

I remember thinking, for the first time in the very specific words, how much I loved her.

Sam

The little diner on the corner Elliot had recommended was only half full, the low hum of conversation mixing with the clatter of cutlery and the scent of warm bread. It was the kind of place where the vinyl booths cracked in the corners and the waitress called you *honey* whether she knew you or not. Familiar. Comfortable.

Safe.

Jessa stirred a packet of sugar into her tea like she wasn't in any rush to say much, which somehow made it easier to talk.

Still, I stared at the menu longer than necessary.

"You didn't bring me here to read about tuna melts," she finally said, glancing over her glasses at me. "Spill it, sweetheart."

I set the menu down and folded my hands on top of it. "I feel… ridiculous."

"You're talking to the woman who once spent an entire therapy session crying over a kitchen sponge. Try me."

I let out a half-laugh, half-sigh. "It's Elliot. Things are... good. Really good. Like, scary good."

She smiled. "I gathered that based on the way you practically float into work these days."

"I just... I don't know what to do with this. With *him*. With someone who actually shows up and doesn't flinch when I'm not shiny or easy or... fixed."

"Sounds like you *do* know what to do. You're letting him in."

I swallowed hard. "That's the problem, Jess. It's starting to feel safe. And safety... doesn't feel safe to me. It feels like waiting for something to go wrong."

Jessa's expression softened in that way only she could manage - like she'd just seen something precious and fragile in my words, and was holding it gently in her palm.

"Honey, when all you've known is surviving, peace feels like a trick."

I blinked hard. My throat tightened. *Yeah. That.*

"But it's not a trick," she continued. "It's a shift. It's your heart learning it doesn't have to live in fight-or-flight anymore."

I looked away, tracing the chipped edge of my mug with my finger. "I don't know how to stop bracing for impact. Part of me believes him when he says he's not going anywhere, but another part... is waiting for him to get tired of me. Or scared off. Or hurt *because* of me."

Jessa reached across the table and laid her hand gently over mine. "Let me tell you something I know for sure: people who love you don't walk out when it gets heavy. They learn how to help you carry it. And Elliot? That boy looks like he'd carry a mountain if you asked him."

I laughed, wiping at the corner of my eye. "He kinda already does."

"Then trust him to keep showing up. And trust *yourself* to be worth showing up for."

The waitress stepped up then and dropped off our sandwiches. We both reached for our napkins at the same time, and Jessa smiled like she always did when she knew she'd landed a truth too big for me to process in one sitting.

"You've survived hell, Sam," she added quietly. "You're allowed to enjoy the sunlight."

I took a bite of my sandwich, chewing slowly, the words settling deep into my bones. Maybe she was right. Maybe peace wasn't a warning sign.

Maybe it was the reward.

• • •

Cooper trotted around the dog park with his favorite ball in his mouth like he was bragging to the two other dogs that were there (who couldn't have cared less). He brought it back to me, slobber dripping onto my jeans as he dropped it in my lap.

I chuckled and threw it again for him. I knew it would take at least ten minutes before he brought it back again, so I pulled my phone out, notes app ready and waiting for a new entry. I called this one: **Emotionally Compromised, Thanks for Asking**

> *I don't even know where to start.*
>
> *Last night was… god, I don't have a word that fits. "Good" feels too small. "Safe" feels too heavy. "Perfect" feels like a trap. All I know is that he held me like I was something meant to be handled very carefully. Like I wasn't something sharp he needed to walk on eggshells around.*
>
> *For the first time in my life, being touched didn't feel like bracing for impact.*
>
> *Nothing tense. Nothing stolen. Just warmth and breath and the kind of quiet that doesn't ask anything of me.*
>
> *And afterward, when I panicked a little - because of course I did - he just… stayed. Didn't rush me. Didn't fill the silence with questions. Just traced circles on my shoulder until I could breathe again.*

I didn't know people like him existed.

And now that I do, I'm terrified.

I talked to Jessa about it today. About how I'm scared I'm going to ruin this before it even has the chance to be something. She said I'm allowed to have good things without an apology to the world.

I'm trying to believe her. I WANT to believe her.

Elliot looks at me like he's choosing me on purpose. Like he sees the mess and the scars and the whole disastrous package and still wants to be here. It doesn't make any sense. People don't stay when things get complicated. I think I've about learned that lesson in every language.

And maybe that's why it's so hard. Because I can feel myself leaning. Wanting. Softening in ways that feel reckless.

There was a moment last night, just a heartbeat, where I thought, "Oh, this could be something real." And the thought almost knocked the air out of me.

It still does.

I don't know what to do with a feeling that big. I don't know how to hold it without crushing it or dropping it or pushing it away before it asks anything of me.

But I can't pretend it's not growing.

I'm scared. But for the first time ever, I don't want to run. I don't know what it means yet. I just know it feels… like the start of actually wanting something.

• • •

I made my way up the stairs to Ashley's flat. Her walk-up was just a few minutes walk from Elliot's, and she'd all but begged me to come for a girl's night.

I hadn't seen her since that night at the bar, when I got triggered to all hell and bolted like a scared animal. I was embarrassed, but the fact that she still wanted to hang out - to get to know me - made me feel slightly better.

I hesitated just outside her door, smoothing my hand over the hem of my sweater like it made a difference. Part of me still wanted to bolt - not because I didn't want to see her, but because I wasn't sure I could stand the warmth of being wanted when I felt so jagged on the inside.

Before I could second guess it again, the door swung open.

"You're here!" Ashley's face lit up. She pulled me in without giving me the chance to overthink it and wrapped me in a hug that smelled like lavender and dry shampoo.

"I didn't bring anything," I said sheepishly, stepping inside.

"You brought *you*. And… split ends. And Cooper! That's more than enough."

I rolled my eyes as she took my coat and motioned toward the couch, which already had a blanket thrown over the back, a bottle of white wine sweating on the coffee table, and two clay face masks laid out like we were teenagers at a slumber party.

Not your kind of teenager. Regular teenagers.

"I told you I was going full cliche tonight," she said, plopping down beside me. "Now sit. Drink. Let me judge your skincare routine."

It was exactly the kind of night I didn't realize I needed.

"I don't know how you function with this little hydration," Ashley whined, handing me a ridiculous pink tumbler with *marry me, I'm hydrated* printed on the side. I took a sip then set it on the coffee table, replacing it in my hand with the wine.

"I function just fine," I protested, taking it. "Besides, wine counts."

She raised an eyebrow. "Says the woman with the circulation of a Victorian ghost."

I grinned, curling my legs under me on the couch. "Okay, valid."

Ashley's apartment was minimal but warm - plants she kept alive with a terrifying amount of commitment, the smell of eucalyptus and clean linen, light hardwood floors that were clean as a whistle.

"I feel like I haven't seen you in forever," she said, sitting beside me with her own glass. "How's golden boy?"

My cheeks warmed.

"Good," I said, too quickly.

Ashley tilted her head. "Too good?"

"Is that a thing?"

"You tell me."

I sighed and stared into my glass like it might give me the answer. "It's just… I feel safe with him. And that's a first for me. And it's terrifying. But…" I took a deep, steadying breath. "I feel like I could see a future with him. Marriage and babies and all of that kind of thing…"

Ashley blinked. "You want kids?"

I felt myself curling inward, trying to make myself smaller. "I didn't know… now I kind of feel like I might."

"That sounds like growth if you ask me."

"Yeah." I let out a breath, unsure whether to laugh or cry. "I guess it probably is."

Her face softened a little bit. "Have you ever felt this way?"

I shook my head and took a long drink of wine. "Never."

She offered a small smile. "You know, I always hoped Elliot would find someone special. I mean that. Not some basic bitch with a ponytail. Someone… genuinely good. Someone with some depth. And I know he has that in you."

I sighed. "God I hope so. I try to be… for him."

She nudged me. "You're so much more awesome than you give yourself credit for, you know?"

My eyes stung suddenly. "But… what if I'm not? Or what if I royally fuck things up?"

She leaned back, taking a sip of her own wine. "You know, my fiancé… we dated in med school on and off. Every time things got calm, I panicked. I didn't know how to just… receive something good. Like I had to keep earning it. I self-sabotaged like a pro. Broke up with him the night before his boards. Real classy move. Love is hard."

"Yikes," My eyes widened a bit. "But you're still together?"

"He forgave me… eventually. And, with lots of therapy, I learned how to accept love without needing to prove myself. But I'll never forget how it felt to torch something just because I couldn't believe it was mine. I hope you can learn to let Elliot be there for you before you have to face that feeling, yourself."

I sank further into the couch, her words curling around something in me that had no name. We sat in silence a moment, and I swear she was stretching it out just to make sure I felt the gravity of her story.

Then, finally, Ashley clinked her glass gently against mine. "To safety. And to not running from it."

"To not running," I echoed.

• • •

I stood in the elevator going up to Elliot's apartment, gift bag dangling from my wrist and immediate regret coursing through my bloodstream.

This was too much. It was just a notebook. But it felt too personal. Too… over the top.

I should've gotten him a bookstore gift card. Or a mug. Or literally anything that didn't involve handing over my heart wrapped in leather.

But no. I had to go sentimental. Because apparently I love suffering.

Cooper whined in anticipation beside me as we ascended. The doors slid open to Elliot in a soft gray t-shirt and matching sweatpants, hair a little messy as he read on the couch. He looked up and lit up when he saw me. I mean, actually lit up. I'm pretty sure the literal color of his face changed.

"Hey," he said, warm and easy, getting up and sauntering over to me. "Come in."

He hugged me and pressed a kiss to my forehead. There were cupcakes on the counter and a half-empty whiskey glass.

"You already celebrated?" I asked, a little disheartened.

He shrugged. "Not really. Mom called and sent cupcakes. Andrew texted. That counts."

I rolled my eyes. "It does *not* count. That's the saddest birthday I've ever heard!"

He laughed, leaning against the counter. "Well, this is adulting. And anyway, you're here now, so upgrade achieved."

My heart was doing gymnastics. I thrust the gift bag at him too fast, like ripping off a bandage.

"This is for you," I said, voice squeaking like a broken clarinet.

He blinked, surprised. "Sam… you didn't have to get me anything."

"I know," I said quickly. "It's nothing big. It's stupid. I don't even know why I-" I stumbled over my words. "Just open it before I combust."

He smiled softly and reached through the tissue paper into the bag, pulling out the journal.

Black leather.

With a strap that wrapped delicately around it.

Simple.

Understated.

The exact opposite of how it felt to give it to him.

He turned it over in his hand, thumb brushing the textured spine. "This is… really nice."

My stomach dropped. "It's dumb. It's like - I dunno. You take notes and stuff. For work. Or your-your brain. I just thought maybe you'd, um… like it."

The panic rose fast. I could feel it trying to flood my lungs.

He opened it, flipping quickly through the pages but not realizing I'd written a note on the first one. "Sam, hey."

He looked up at me. Intentionality in his eyes.

"This is perfect."

My heart stuttered.

"I mean it," he added. "I love it."

The words hit me harder than they should have. I looked away, because the warmth on his face was too much, too direct, like staring into the sun.

He leaned down to kiss me. Soft. Slow. The kind of kiss that made my bones feel unreliable.

When he pulled back, his forehead rested against mine. "Thank you. Really."

I nodded, trying not to melt into a puddle on the concrete floors. He set the journal carefully on the counter like it was something precious.

"Okay," I said, clapping my hands. "Birthday boy. What's the plan? Cupcakes? Whiskey? Quarter-life crisis?"

He grinned. "All of the above."

"Brave choice," I said, grabbing a cupcake with chocolate frosting.

He handed me his whiskey glass, got a second from the cabinet, and poured us each a large splash from a bottle with a label I couldn't pronounce.

"To thirty-two," he said, tilting his glass toward mine.

"To surviving thirty-one," I countered.

Our glasses clinked, and the sound felt like it settled something warm into the room. He drank first, then I did, and the whiskey traced heat down my throat in a way that made me quietly laugh at myself.

He smiled, eyes soft. "You never get used to the burn, do you?"

"Maybe by the time I'm thirty-two," I teased lightly.

"I look forward to that," he replied like it was a promise instead of a joke.

I peeled the cupcake wrapper slowly, trying to look casual even though my hands wouldn't quite steady. He leaned beside me, close but not crowding - familiar in a way that made my pulse jump.

"Any wisdom to offer in your old age?" I asked, nudging him with my shoulder.

He took a moment to think without making it a big performance. "I learned I don't need a lot of people around me... just the right ones."

He looked at me then, and it wasn't dramatic. Just real. Quiet. A truth spoken like he didn't mean to reveal it.

I didn't know what to do with the warmth that swept through me, so I tore my cupcake in half and handed him a piece. "Here. For your emotional vulnerability."

He laughed under his breath, acceptance in his eyes. "Bribery. I see how it is."

"Whatever works," I said.

Cooper let out a little huff and trotted between us, tail wagging like he'd been waiting for acknowledgement. Elliot crouched to rub behind his ears, voice soft, gentle in a way people don't usually speak unless they feel safe.

"You missed me, didn't you?" he murmured to the dog. Then, glancing up at me. "I missed you, too."

It wasn't a line. Just words, offered simply. And I felt them land in my chest like a leaf in a pool, soft enough not to disturb anything around it.

For a second I thought he might kiss me again. Or say something. Or… I don't know, something would tip us over some invisible line we'd been walking along for weeks.

And, fuck me, I wanted him to.

Instead, he broke the quiet moment with a smile that almost came off as shy. "This is the best birthday I've had in a long time."

"Yeah?"

"Yeah." He lifted his glass. "Thanks for being here."

I swallowed, because my heart was suddenly too loud in my chest. "Of course," I said. "I wouldn't have missed it."

It was nothing.
It was everything.

And if either of us had been braver, something else might have happened right then. Something big and terrifying and honest.

But neither of us said it. Not yet.

Instead I raised my glass, too. "Happy birthday, Elliot."

We drank. Laughed til our faces hurt. Split another cupcake. Got a little tipsy, leaning shoulder-to-shoulder on the couch, his knee brushing mine like it was accidental.

And the whole time, that unsaid thing hummed between us. Not frightening or heavy, just waiting. Growing. Whether I was ready or not.

SAM

I set the donation bin down with a soft thud and brushed my hair out of my eyes. The community room at Healing Hands buzzed with quiet chaos - kids coloring, toddlers waddling around with half-eaten crackers, volunteers trying to look competent. The usual.

Elliot stood beside me, looking wildly out of place in dark jeans, a henley shirt that probably cost more than I made in a week, and a dark suede jacket. He had that polite work event expression on: half smile, eyebrows slightly raised like he was waiting for someone to tell him where to stand.

I shot him a questioning glance, and he leaned close to whisper, "I just saw a toddler eat a crayon. A whole crayon."

"That's basically a food group," I laughed.

Across the room, Carla, one of the organization's admin, waved a hand at me. "Sam, sweetheart, the reading corner's getting a little chaotic. Think you could wrangle someone into storytime?"

"Sure," I called back. Then I slowly turned to Elliot.

He stepped back like I'd brandished a weapon. "No."

"Oh yes," I said, already smiling.

"Sam, No." He pointed at himself. "I don't… perform."

"You don't have to *perform*. Just read the words on the page. Oh, and do the voices of all the characters," I giggled.

"Children are harsh critics," he muttered. "I've seen *Les Mis* audiences go easier on performers."

I laughed - really laughed - because he was actually nervous. The man who could give speeches to hundreds without breaking a sweat was afraid of maybe ten kids in a beanbag circle.

"I thought you did this all the time?" I shot him a questioning glance, and he shrugged.

"Yeah. Blowing bubbles and racing cars and building towers. Not reading. That's terrifying."

"Come on," I coaxed. "They'll love you."

He hesitated. I softened my voice. "Elliot… they need gentle voices and patient faces. And you've got both. You'll be great at this."

Something in his expression thawed, just a little.

"You really think so?"

I nodded. "Yeah, I do."

He swallowed like I was handing him a sacred task instead of a picture book.

"...Okay," he said finally. "Which one do I read?"

I handed him *The Gruffalo*.

He gave me a look, but followed me to the reading corner anyway. A few kids spotted us and scampered over, plopping down on beanbags with wide eyes.

Elliot sat, knees up by his chest because the tiny chair nearly folded him in half. The visual alone made two kids - and me - giggle.

He opened the book like it was a legal contract.

"Alright," he said softly. "Who wants a story?"

Eight little hands shot up.

His shoulders dropped. Something in him relaxed, a subtle unclenching. And then he started to read.

He wasn't overly theatrical or loud. He read gently, like the words were meant to be held instead of performed. The kids leaned in closer with every page.

By the end of the story, the kids clapped (enthusiastically, off-beat, adorable). Elliot looked stunned, like he hadn't expected the approval of people under four feet tall.

My chest tightened unexpectedly.

As the group dispersed, he met my eyes with a small, shy smile I hadn't seen on him before. "That was…" he cleared his throat. "Not terrible."

I nudged him with my elbow. "You were great."

He shrugged, a little embarrassed. "They're sweet."

"Yeah," I whispered, catching the way one of the kids waved goodbye to him. "They really are."

We walked back toward the supply table, an empty donation bag waiting for us.

Elliot glanced down at me, quieter than usual.

"Thanks for making me do that," he said. "I… didn't know I'd like it."

I smiled. "I did."

And for the first time, maybe ever, I felt something warm and steady bloom in my chest. Something soft, and maybe dangerous, and very, very real.

⋯

I kicked my shoes off the second I stepped inside, the weight of the day catching up to me all at once. Cooper trotted up to me, dramatically waving his tail and yawning as if he'd had a long day, too.

"Real tough one for you, huh?" I muttered, tossing my keys into the ceramic bowl on the counter.

He huffed at me in response - offended, probably.

The apartment was quiet in the way I liked best. Not empty, just… still. The faint vanilla scent from the candle I'd blown out that morning lingered in the air. I half-cracked open a window to let the cool evening breeze flow through my living room.

I changed into one of my oversized t-shirts - threadbare, soft, safe - and collapsed onto the couch beside Cooper. He didn't move, just scooted an inch closer so his head was on my thigh.

"Thanks for being a good boy today while I was gone," I said as I scanned the floor for evidence otherwise. But no, he'd been great.

The warm memory of Elliot reading to the kids tugged at me, one of the girls declaring he "looked important," then immediately asking if she could have a piggyback ride. And Elliot, stiff at first then melting into something sweeter than I think he realized he was capable of.

The warmth in my chest startled me.

My phone buzzed loudly against the coffee table. Cooper's ears flicked up at the sound. I reached for it.

> **Elliot 8:39pm**
>
> *You make it home okay?*

A smile pulled at my lips.

> *Cozy and comfy now. Thanks for checking on me.*

I went to put my phone down, then picked it back up to type again.

> *By the way. Remember the little girl you gave that piggyback ride to? Olivia? She told me you read like a "sleepy robot."*

I chuckled to myself and put my phone down. I tried to read, but my eyes kept drifting over the same sentence until Cooper side-eyed me like even *he* knew I wasn't paying attention.

Then there he was, lighting up my screen again.

> **Elliot 8:45pm**
>
> *I can't tell if I'm charmed or deeply wounded.*

My laugh, real and loud, startled Cooper. He glared at me like I'd violated a treaty.

> *Both. Always both.*
>
> *For what it's worth… you did great today. The kids loved you. Even the brutally honest ones.*

He typed. Stopped. Typed again.

> **Elliot 8:47pm**
>
> *Thanks, Darling.*

I loved them, too.
And… I loved watching you with them.

My breath hitched.

Too sweet. Dial it back.

The typing bubble appeared almost immediately this time.

Elliot 8:48pm

No.
Goodnight, sleepy robot.

I groaned into my hands. Set my phone down, face warm, heart doing that traitorous thing it started doing sometime recently every time he did something sweet. Cooper nudged my hand with his snout - I couldn't tell if he was demanding pets or asking if I was okay.

"Yeah," I whispered, scratching behind his ear. "I think I am."

Sam

Elliot was walking me home from some fancy Italian restaurant down the road he'd taken me to. I was grateful for the walk, stomach bloated with carbs. The night air was cool, crisp enough to tamp down the warmth lingering in my cheeks from the wine I *definitely* shouldn't have finished.

"Remind me next time," I groaned, "that I'm five-foot-nothing and can't eat half a loaf of bread before the pasta arrives."

Elliot shoved his hands into his coat pockets, grinning. "I tried to warn you."

"You didn't warn me," I shot back. "You encouraged me. You said, and I quote, 'Get the tortellini. It'll change your life.'"

He laughed, the sound echoing off the brick storefronts we passed. "And? Has your life changed?"

"Yes," I said dramatically. "I'm going to explode on this sidewalk, and you'll have to explain it to the authorities."

"I'll tell them you died doing what you loved: aggressively consuming carbs."

I bumped my shoulder into him. He bumped back, slightly harder like he thought I could handle it.

The streetlamps washed the pavement in pale yellow. Shadows of trees swayed across our path. Cooper would have loved the smells out here, I realized. I'd have to bring him tomorrow.

Elliot cleared his throat lightly, the sound cutting through my quiet spiral of thought. "You seem… relaxed tonight."

"I'm full of bread," I said. "Nothing can hurt me."

His smile softened. "No nightmares lately?"

I hesitated. "No."

"Good," he murmured. And he didn't push it. He never pushed.

We walked a few more steps in comfortable silence. My boots scuffing, his longer stride adjusting to match mine. Every now and then his hand brushed near mine at his side. I finally folded my hand into his, swinging lightly between us with every step.

"Do you ever notice," he said suddenly, "how the neighborhood smells different at night?"

I tilted my head. "Like what?"

"Like…" He inhaled dramatically. "Like someone somewhere is making cookies."

I sniffed. "That's not cookies. That's the pizzeria on Sixth."

"No, I'm pretty sure someone is stress baking."

I laughed, louder than I meant to.

We turned the corner to walk up to my door. The closer we got, the more something fluttered in my chest. Anxiety. Anticipation. Uncertainty. I never really could tell the difference.

I slid my key into the hole and pushed the door open, the smell and warmth of home wafting over me. Cooper trotted up to us, saying a quick hello to me before passing me quickly for Elliot. I did my best not to be offended.

We fell into a silent routine - music on the tv, books in hand, leaning back on opposite ends of the couch.

"I have something to ask you… it may feel like a big ask." Elliot said, his tone suddenly shifting as he rolled Cooper's ball around between his hand and his leg. He wasn't often nervous, at least to the point that it showed. His anxiety gave *me* anxiety.

I stiffened and gripped the blanket shared between us closer to my body. "Okay…?"

"Will you have dinner with my parents? Uh, with me, of course."

I was torn. Part of me felt honored he'd even ask. A bigger part of me wanted to bolt. "Elliot, I don't know…"

He looked up finally, nervousness and a glimmer of hope filling his eyes. "I'm not going to force you to go, of course. I'd just… I'd really appreciate it if you would."

I took a sharp inhale then leaned forward to grab my water from the coffee table. Something to stall. Give me time to think.

What if it all goes horribly wrong? What if they hate you? Worse yet, what if they see right through you? What if Elliot's told them everything? What if he hasn't and they bring up your family?

He waited patiently, still swirling the ball around on his leg. Cooper stared at it anxiously waiting for him to decide to throw it.

"When?" Begrudgingly, I kept myself tense, braced for the impact of whatever came next.

He looked back over at me, hopeful, slowing the swirling of the ball on his leg.

"Friday."

I couldn't believe I was even considering it. There were so many possibilities of things going terribly wrong. But I wanted to *know* Elliot. As much as it scared me, I wanted to be a part of his life. And that meant doing things like meeting his family.

I closed my eyes and took a deep breath in. "Okay."

"Okay?"

"Yeah… okay."

• • •

Three nights remained until I was supposed to go to dinner with Elliot and his parents. I stared at my closet and sighed, crossing my arms. Nothing felt right. After all, how do you say, *Sorry, I have nothing to offer your son but my very fucked up self and I know I'm not good enough for him so I have no idea why I'm here* with an outfit?

"I have *nothing*, I swear."

I held my phone up to my half-full closet in defeat. Andrew rolled his eyes on FaceTime and sighed loudly. "What *ever* will we do? I don't suppose a shopping trip is in order…"

I cringed, but he was right. We had to shop. I needed something new for this occasion. Something classy but fun. Something that looked nice enough to fit in with Elliot's people without breaking the bank. Something that could hopefully apologize for my entire existence before I ever said a word to his parents.

Lot of pressure for a dress.

• • •

"You are a smitten kitten," Andrew said nonchalantly as he perused the rack of dresses in front of him.

I shook my head, complete denial taking over as much as I was cringing at his rhyme. "Andrew, no, I-"

"You can't deny it. I've *never* seen you like this. You've never even looked a man's way, much less spent time dress shopping for dinner with *his parents.*"

He was right. And I hated it.

I kept my mouth shut and continued sorting through the dresses in front of me, many of which were far too revealing for what I needed.

"Something with a high neckline," I said, pulling a tan number out of the row. "Like this, but maybe a little longer."

Andrew nodded, mission accepted, and kept rummaging.

"Have you ever done dinner with a partner's parents?"

"Oh, honey, parents *love* me," he laughed. "As a matter of fact, two of my ex's moms still send me Christmas cards."

"Got any advice?" I was only half joking.

"Don't be *too much* yourself. Like… okay be yourself, just… less snarky."

No pressure or anything.

He pulled out a blue satin dress and pressed it into my hands. "This is the one."

I held it up in front of me, weighing how many scars I thought it might hide. I wasn't used to dressing up often. I'd done so more in the past couple of weeks with Elliot than I probably did in my entire life. If it wasn't for the fact that I felt that I needed to hide so much of myself, I might actually enjoy it.

"At least try it?" He begged.

The dress shimmered like ink under moonlight - sleek, midnight blue satin that clung in all the right places and flowed in others. It hugged my waist before falling into a graceful, swaying skirt that brushed my calves with each step I took out of the fitting room. The neckline was softly draped, high and elegant, gathering just enough near my throat while leaving my shoulders bare.

"Stunning," Andrew said, giving a light golf clap. "I told you."

I swayed awkwardly. It had nearly enough coverage for my liking, but a few scars still slipped out from under cover.

Maybe they won't notice.

• • •

I was restocking the syrup shelf behind the counter - well, pretending to. My hands moved the bottles, but my brain was across town, already spiraling over the dinner Elliot had invited me to tomorrow night.

His *parents*.

He'd been nervous to ask me, but he was acting like it was such a casual thing. *Nothing big, just dinner*, he had said. *My mom always cooks too much, and my dad will probably try to impress you with his trivia knowledge.*

But it *was* big. I hadn't met anyone's parents like this. Ever.

I dropped a bottle of vanilla syrup. It didn't break, just clattered against the tile with a hollow *thunk* that made me flinch away.

"You alright?" Jessa called from the espresso machine.

"Fine," I lied, crouching to pick it up.

I heard the familiar *shhhh* of the steamer pause mid-whirr. A moment later, she rounded the counter, towel slung over her shoulder, gaze narrowed in a way that meant she wasn't buying it.

"Sam."

I stood and tucked the syrup back into place like it was the most important job in the world. "What?"

"You've been jittery since your shift started. Not caffeine-jittery. *Elliot-jittery*."

I sighed and leaned my hip against the cabinet. "He invited me to dinner with his parents."

Jessa's face softened. "That's sweet."

"It's terrifying."

She waited, arms folded, not pushing - but not backing down either. That was her gift. She never needed to pry because her silence was loud enough to make you want to fill it.

I folded my arms, mirroring her without thinking. "I'm just... I don't know if I'm ready for that kind of thing. His parents? That's, like... real. They're going to want to know who I am, and I don't even know how to answer that. I've built walls around myself for so long... I don't even remember how to walk through a front door like a normal person."

Jessa didn't jump in. She let me finish unraveling first.

When I finally looked up, her face was calm. "Sam, meeting someone's family isn't about giving them your whole life's story. It's about showing them the part you're learning to live in."

I blinked. "That's vague and sounds suspiciously like something you read on a throw pillow."

She laughed. "Maybe. But it's true. You don't owe anyone your pain wrapped up in a powerpoint. You just show up. You be kind. You eat the casserole. You don't have to bleed at their table to be real."

I looked down at my shoes. "What if I disappoint them? What if... I disappoint *him?*"

Jessa stepped forward and touched my shoulder lightly, grounding me. "Honey... Elliot already *sees* you. If he's inviting you into his world, it's because he wants you there. Not because he wants to fix you. You're allowed to show up imperfectly."

My eyes stung with the beginning of tears I refused to let fall.

"Is it okay if I'm scared?" I asked, quieter than I meant to.

Jessa nodded. "Of course it is. Just don't let that fear convince you that you're not worth loving."

• • •

My finger hovered over the little blue arrow.

Elliot, I'm sick. I'm sorry.

I hesitated, guilt stirring in my stomach. I couldn't do this to him. But I couldn't do… *this,* either.

Sighing heavily, I chucked my phone onto my bed without hitting send. My phone screen lit up with the "undo text" box, and I clicked to wipe away my blatant lie.

Coward.

I paced the length of my bedroom, arms crossed so tight it felt like I was holding my ribs together. My reflection in the mirror looked pale, jumpy, a little too much like the girl I thought I was finally leaving behind.

This wasn't about him.

It wasn't even about his parents.

It was about the walls I'd carefully mortared shut finally showing a few cracks, and what it might mean to let someone see what was on the other side.

It wasn't often Elliot asked something of me. He'd gone behind my back to Jessa the once, but ever since he'd been nothing but gentle and patient. He didn't push. Didn't ask too much of me.

And now he was asking for something so *simple*. Dinner. With his parents. At their home.

Not a trap, not an ambush. Just a table, some food, some polite conversation, and probably a homemade dessert.

It should have been easy. But it felt like stepping onto thin ice, unsure if the surface would hold.

Cooper padded in from the hallway, tail wagging softly, like he could sense my nerves. He rested his head against my leg and looked up at me, eyes dark and steady.

"You think I'm being ridiculous?" I whispered, running a hand down his back.

He huffed.

I took a breath.

Maybe it wouldn't be perfect. Maybe I'd say the wrong thing or panic halfway through dessert. Maybe I'd freeze, and Elliot's parents would stare, and the room would close in around me.

But maybe I'd survive it.

Maybe I'd even *enjoy* it.

I grabbed my phone again and typed something else before I could think too hard.

> *On my way. Can't wait to meet them.*

I hit send. Then I sat on the edge of my bed for a full minute, heart hammering in my chest, trying to convince myself that I'd done the right thing.

I didn't know if I was ready. But maybe I didn't need to be. Maybe Jessa was right and just showing up was enough.

33
SAM

"Sam, breathe, darling." Elliot and I were riding in his car on the way to meet his parents. It was just a casual dinner at their house, but I was petrified.

Never in my life had I dreamed I'd be close enough to a man to meet his family.

I inhaled deeply and closed my eyes trying to force myself to relax. *Could you act more* normal *please?* "I'm just nervous, that's all."

"They're going to love you. Don't worry. It's going to be great." He reached across the car and grabbed my hands, his thumb soothingly tracing over them.

The car rolled to a stop in front of a three story Victorian style home with a porch that wrapped all the way around the bottom level. It was elegantly large, but not looming. Definitely luxurious, but not overstated. Like his family *had* money, but they didn't have the *fuck you* attitude to go with it.

"Here we are," Elliot said, opening my door.

Always the gentleman.

I stepped out, careful not to crease the dress I had worn. As we walked up the stairs, my heart rate grew quicker and I could feel my face grow hot. I couldn't remember ever being this nervous before such a mundane situation in my life. But there I was, practically trembling on the porch.

"Hey," Elliot said, grabbing my hand and turning me to face him. "Please don't worry."

He placed a calming kiss at my temple before knocking on the door. Each rap amped my nerves all the more.

A beautiful dark haired woman answered the door. She was stunning. She had Elliot's eyes and tan skin, yet both slightly lighter. Her red cocktail dress flowed effortlessly down her body. It had to have been custom made or tailored the way it hung just right on every curve. A smile widened across her stained lips revealing brilliantly white teeth.

"Come in! Elliot, how are you?" She hugged her son and turned to place her arms around me as well. "You must be Sam. I've heard a lot about you."

My cheeks reddened. "Hello, Mrs. Flint. It's so nice to meet you."

"Please, call me Catherine. We're glad to have you, dear." She turned and led us into a living room where a peppery gray-haired man stood by a wood burning fireplace, wine in hand. "This is Elliot's father, John. John, honey, this is Sam, the girl Elliot's been telling us about."

I could feel the *wink wink, nudge nudge* in her tone. I glanced up at Elliot, also struggling to hide his nerves, but he gave me a literal wink and folded his hand into mine, squeezing it ever so slightly. "All good things, don't worry."

"Sam, it's so nice to meet you!" John stepped forward and leaned in to kiss my cheek, a surprisingly warm gesture that I somehow didn't mind. Maybe it was his kind eyes or the wrinkles around his nose or the way he had his sleeves scrunched up like Elliot always did, or maybe I was deep in shock, but whatever the case, I embraced it. I smiled warmly, albeit a little shakily, at him as he backed away to hug his son.

"Can I offer either of you some wine?" Catherine's smooth voice hummed through the air.

"I'd love some," I said, anxious for something to anchor myself with.

"Bourbon for me, please."

Elliot and his father began engaging in some small talk about a sports game I had no interest in, and I felt my nerves begin to fire erratically. Catherine appeared just as quickly as she had gone, effortlessly gliding through the house, and she handed me a glass of red wine.

I felt so out of place, which seemed to be the norm for me around Elliot. Everything about him was so… grand. Even the quiet luxury of his family home mocked my humble beginnings.

Humble beginnings? How about humble existence? Everything about you is inadequate compared to him. Then and now.

I gulped eagerly at my wine, my left hand beginning to shake by my side.

"Catherine, your home is lovely," I mustered up, sounding more confident than I felt.

"Thank you so much! We've been blessed to love this place for years." She lacked Elliot's cockiness. Everything about her screamed humility and grace.

I couldn't help but notice the difference between their home and Elliot's penthouse. Elliot's place was very… beige. Boujee, but neutral. John and Catherine's place was bursting with life and colored family photos and plants and paintings.

I wasn't sure where to look or what to say next, and the pressure of the moment was beginning to get to me. I overheard words here and there from Elliot and John's conversation like *center* and *offense* and *guard* and I had no idea what any of it meant, but they were invested. Catherine looked as if she was about to ask me a question, but I wasn't quite sure I had the resolve to formulate an answer just yet.

"Um, would you mind pointing me to a bathroom please?" I asked so quietly I was surprised anyone heard me.

"Of course! It's just down the hall, second door on the left."

I excused myself and scurried down the hall. Door locked safely behind me, I leaned back into it, closed my eyes, and groaned quietly.

How are you this embarrassing? You have got to chill the fuck out. Pull yourself together, Reynolds.

I leaned forward and pushed myself off the door, turning the sink knob as I pivoted to look in the mirror.

"You've got this," I whispered, lying to myself.

I let the water trickle over my fingers.

Just a minute more, then you're back out the door.

A light tap startled me out of my pep talk.

"Sam? Are you okay?" Elliot's voice was hushed from the other side of the door.

"Yeah- uh. I'm okay. I just needed a minute." I toweled the water off my hands and unlocked the door plastering a smile on my face.

"I'm sorry. Dad and I get so caught up. I thought you seemed a little uneasy, so I just wanted to check on you." He kissed my forehead for a lingering moment then pulled away. "Are you sure you're okay?"

"Yes, Elliot," I sighed impatiently. "I've just... this is the first time I've ever done something like this."

He smiled his crooked grin that settled my soul, and he squeezed my hand. "Well, you're doing great. Just... be you. They'll love you."

You keep saying that.

I was nervous as we sauntered back down the hallway - worried John and Catherine would be quietly judging the fact that Elliot just had to check on me in the bathroom within the first ten minutes of my arrival. They weren't though. They were midway through a conversation about one of John's patients who had decided to try at-home dry needling his own knee. Needless to say, it didn't turn out well. Elliot and I folded in seamlessly, as if we'd never left to begin with, and my shoulders began to relax a little.

Catherine and John were an amazing couple. The kind you observe quietly and think - *they know something the rest of us don't.*

John reached out and took Catherine's hand as she passed behind him, and she gave him a look that could have spoken entire volumes. I wondered how long it had taken them to get there - how much life had passed between them to build something that soft and certain.

"Would you two like to go ahead and eat, or perhaps sit a while?" Catherine asked, stepping into the living room with the ease of someone who *enjoyed* making others feel at home.

"Sit, please," I said, grateful for the suggestion. "I could use a breath."

John chuckled. "That's what I say every time she cooks. 'Let me rest while I emotionally prepare.'"

"Oh hush," Catherine said, smirking.

I eased back into the loveseat with Elliot, still unsure how to hold my body like I belonged in such an elegant space. But his arm curled naturally behind me, and that helped a little.

"How did you two meet?" I asked, curious.

"Oh, now *that's* a story," John said, setting down his glass. "I was a third-year med student. She was working in admin at the hospital, running laps around half the people on payroll and making twice the impact."

"He's still mad I wouldn't go to lunch with him the first time he asked," Catherine said with a sly smile.

"The first *three* times," John corrected. "She claimed she was too busy, but she always made a point to walk by my station."

"I had to make sure you weren't killing anyone," she shot back.

I laughed, the nerves in my shoulders loosening for the first time since we arrived.

"But seriously," John said. "One day I brought her soup when she was sick. That was the crack in the armor. She never looked at me the same after that."

"Because it was awful soup," Catherine added. "But he made it himself, and he sat on the floor outside my office until I promised to eat it."

Elliot glanced at me with a raised brow. "Sound like anyone you know?"

I smiled. "Maybe."

I felt my heart flutter, and I wasn't sure what to do with the warmth it stirred in me.

"Now," John said, rubbing his hands together. "Cards?"

"Oh no," Elliot groaned.

"Oh yes," Catherine chimed. "She has to play. It's a rite of passage."

I looked between them, amused. "What are we playing?"

"Rummy," John said. "Loser clears the dishes."

"You're on."

Half an hour later, I was grinning from ear to ear as I laid down my final set. "That's game."

John let out a low whistle. "Well, I'll be."

Catherine narrowed her eyes at her hand. "I think she hustled us."

Elliot dropped his cards with dramatic flair. "You betrayed me."

I shrugged, trying and failing to suppress a smug smile. "I play a lot of game nights at the cafe."

"Sam," John said, leaning back in his chair. "You ever consider joining the family professionally? We could use that killer instinct."

Laughter filled the space, warm and easy, and for a moment I wasn't thinking about the past or the jagged pieces of myself I usually tried to keep hidden. For a moment, I was simply there. Present. Whole.

Elliot reached under the table and gently laced his fingers through mine.

Yeah. Maybe this is something I could belong to after all.

• • •

"They really do like you, darling," Elliot said as we pulled out of the driveway for the forty-five minute drive back to his place.

"I like them, too. They're very nice. And they seem to love you a lot," I smiled. They seemed to love each other a lot, too. A rarity these days.

"They do. We've all always been super close, especially since Nate died."

"Something like that will either bring you closer together or rip you apart," I shrugged dryly. He reached across the car and squeezed my hands that I didn't realize were knotted in my lap. "I... sorry. That was insensitive."

"No, it's true."

Do it. Open up. Share with him.

"Laurel, my sister... We used to be so close. But there was so much trauma there that we just... we can't seem to deal with it in a healthy way together. I feel bad... I'm her big sister. I'm supposed to be there for her. She just makes it damn near impossible."

Elliot was quiet for a moment, the sound of the tires humming against the pavement filling the space between us. His thumb traced slow, grounding circles on the back of my hand.

"She's still your sister," he said gently. "No matter how messy it gets."

"I know," I whispered. "That's the worst part. I don't stop loving her, even when I wish I could. Even when that would make everything easier…"

He glanced at me, and something in his expression softened - not pity, but understanding. Recognition.

I looked out the window, blinking back the sudden sting behind my eyes. The flat fields blurred past in a wash of green and dark.

"I think she blames me," I said after a while. "For not protecting her. For leaving. For all of it."

Elliot didn't interrupt. He let me say the things I never said out loud, the ones that curled up in the back of my throat every time I thought of Laurel.

"And maybe she's right," I added quietly. "I don't know."

He squeezed my hand again - not tight, just enough to remind me he was still there. Still listening.

"I think," he said slowly, "that you survived something terrible. Nobody expects you to have done so perfectly. You made it out. That's what matters."

I closed my eyes for a second, the weight of his words settling into my chest like warm stones.

"I'm trying," I whispered.

"I know."

We fell into silence again, but this time it wasn't heavy. It was the kind that settles in between two people who understand that words are sometimes too small for the things they're trying to carry.

I turned to him and offered a soft smile. It was all I could manage - but it was real. And he smiled back, as if it was more than enough.

...

The silence between us on the way home had gone from comforting to constricting - like there was something left unsaid. I couldn't put a finger on why, but it was in the way he suddenly avoided eye contact or the way his hand abandoned mine about twenty minutes out from his home.

You overstepped. He doesn't want to hear you complain about your sister. She might be a deadbeat, but at least she's alive. You should've just kept your mouth shut.

I chewed on the inside of my lip for the last ten minutes of the drive, surprised it hadn't split open with how nervously I bit at it.

When we paused at a red light, Elliot tapped the steering wheel lightly with his fingertips. He looked at me briefly, flashed a small smile, and then turned back to watch the light. His hand ran through his hair, which he only ever did when he was anxious.

By the time we pulled into his parking spot, I was about to explode with worry.

"Elliot... is something wrong?" I asked as we stepped into the elevator.

"Everything's perfect, darling. Why do you ask?" He turned toward me and looked gently into my eyes. Something was on his mind, and I knew it.

"What are you thinking about?" He always asked me that question, so I figured it was about time that he answered it himself. I was getting close to panicking.

He closed his eyes and a soft grin spread across his face. "You."

His eyes opened again, full of affection.

"Elliot?"

Before I could say anything else, he grabbed my chin and tilted me up toward his face. He pressed his lips into mine, a deep yearning pulling me ever closer. Something about this kiss calmed my nerves. A gentle affection radiated from him.

"Sam…" He pulled away slightly as his hands made their way to either side of my head. "Sam, I love you."

The words landed in my chest with a softness I wasn't ready for. I blinked, trying to remember to breathe.

He loved me?

He looked into my eyes again and I realized why he had been quiet. That's why his hands were trembling just slightly against my skin.

I wanted to say it back. The words were already there, tucked in the corners of my heart. But for a split second, I hesitated.

What if you say it and something breaks in you? What if you can't take it back?

But then I looked at him really looked at him. Not the charming grin or the ocean-colored eyes, but the man who saw past every wall I tried to rebuild.

He helped me realize who I was. He helped me see that I didn't have to let my past take charge of my life… tell me who I was supposed to be. He showed me I was worthy of affection and that the way my father treated me didn't have to define who I was. In a matter of weeks he'd gone from a stranger to the safest place I knew. He saw past my scars, past my fucked up emotions and my flaws and loved me. He really loved me.

A tear slipped down my cheek. I reached up, wrapping my arms around his neck like I might fall if I didn't.

"I love you too," I whispered.

His lips found mine again and his hand dropped to the small of my back. We didn't care that the elevator door had dinged open minutes ago. We didn't care about anything else in that moment aside from getting lost in each other.

Elliot

I remember the night Sam met my parents - the moment it happened... the exact second I knew I couldn't hold it in anymore. Not eventually. Not someday. As soon as humanly possible.

She slipped into my parents' home with this cautious grace, like she was testing the air first, making sure she wouldn't break anything fragile by existing there. But little by little, she softened. She laughed at my dad's terrible jokes. Let my mom fuss over her drink. And when she beat all of us at Rummy, she smiled this big, surprised smile that made something inside me ache in the warmest way.

It was unbearable - how much I loved her. How much I needed her to know it. Like the words were a lit fuse inside me.

God, I was nervous.

Not because of the words themselves - I'd been feeling them long before I even admitted it to myself. But because I didn't want her to run. She'd been through enough fire. I didn't want to become another thing she felt she had to survive.

The car ride home is burned into me. She told me a little about her sister - just a fragment, a crack in the armor she rarely let anyone see behind. And hearing that hurt... not because she was telling me something painful, but because she had to live it at all. I could feel how deeply it cut her, how helpless she felt watching someone she loved so much slip away.

There was nothing I could fix. Nothing I could offer except presence. So we drove the rest of the way in silence - the good kind. Heavy. Warm. Full of everything we weren't saying yet.

But when we stepped onto the elevator and she turned to me and asked if something was wrong, I felt the bottom drop out. I hated that my quiet had made her doubt herself. Made her think she'd misread me. The last thing I ever wanted was for her to feel uncertain with me.

So I did what I could: looked her in the eyes, brushed her cheek, kissed her. And god, that kiss...

It was all the words I hadn't said yet. It was every moment I'd bitten my tongue. It was all the love I'd been holding in my chest like a secret I was finally ready to hand over.

By the time I pulled back, I was close to tears. And then the words just... came. They didn't feel forced or dramatic. They felt inevitable. Like they'd been waiting for this exact moment to slip free. Like I didn't know why I hadn't said them a thousand times before.

I told her I loved her.

I watched as she took it in. She blinked hard, grounding herself, then opened her eyes back up to study my face like she needed confirmation that she hadn't imagined it. I saw the shift, the careful guard she always kept up tremble, soften, and fall away just a little.

And then she said it back.

It felt like everything in me exhaled all at once. Like since I met her I'd been held underwater, baptised in the concept of her, and I had finally, finally just come up for my first breath.

35
SAM

I watched quietly as Elliot sipped his coffee, his tracksuit pants hanging low off his hips.

When I'd asked him to come stay the night, I wasn't expecting the not-so minor freak out I was having after the whole *I love you* thing, though I should have known better by now. Maybe it would have been better to take some time to myself. To process. To *not* be awkward as fuck. But here we were.

I had this nauseating mix of wanting to jump his bones and simultaneously wanting to hide under the covers because I was suddenly worried.

What if we said it too soon? What if he regrets it? What if he was just caught up in the moment?

He glanced up at me over the rim of his mug, and his eyes crinkled in that way that made me feel like I was *seen*. Not observed - seen. Like he knew the exact brand of chaos ricocheting through my head but chose not to name it.

"You're staring," he said gently.

"No I'm not," I lied, immediately turning my gaze to the wall like it had something fascinating to offer.

He chuckled, set his mug down, and padded toward the couch where I was curled up under a throw blanket. Cooper shifted to make room as Elliot sat beside me, one leg tucked under the other.

"I know you're freaking out a little," he said casually, like we were discussing the weather. "It's okay. I kind of am, too."

I perked up a little at that, intrigued.

"You are?"

He nodded. "Yeah. Because it's big. Saying 'I love you' isn't small for me." He leaned back against the cushion, head tipped toward mine. "But I meant it. I wasn't caught up in anything. I knew. And I know."

I took a deep breath.

My fingers played with the edge of the blanket in my lap, "I've never had something feel… good and terrifying at the same time."

"Sounds like maybe that's progress, though," he said with a soft smile.

"Sounds like emotional whiplash."

He let out a quiet laugh and didn't push. Just reached over and brushed a strand of hair behind my ear, like it was the most natural thing in the world.

A comfortable silence settled over us for a while, broken only by Cooper's occasional doggy sigh and the hum of my too-quiet apartment.

"I used to think I'd never let someone stay the night," I said suddenly, my voice barely above a whisper. "Not because of anything weird. Just… it felt too vulnerable. Like I needed a contingency plan or something."

Elliot didn't flinch. Didn't make it a *moment*.

He just nodded once, eyes still on mine. "What made you change your mind?"

I hesitated and broke eye contact. "You didn't make me feel like I needed one."

His expression softened so much I thought he might melt into the cushions. He didn't reach for me. Didn't move in. But the warmth between us said everything.

• • •

I curled up on my couch in a stolen shirt from Elliot, soft and comfy and probably out of my budget. It still smelled a little like his detergent. That clean-cotton-and-amber scent that made my chest tighten in the stupidest, most annoying way.

Cooper hopped up beside me, circled once like a ship docking badly, then plopped down with his head on my thigh as if he owned me. Which, fine, maybe he did.

The apartment was quiet in that post-happiness haze: dim lamp glow, remnants of my makeup smudged under my eyes, the echo of this morning still stuck in my skin. Him in the kitchen while I made coffee. His fingers brushing my back. The way he said "I love you" like it wasn't terrifying, like it wasn't the emotional equivalent of handing me a live grenade gift wrapped to perfection.

I pulled my computer into my lap, the cold metal kissing against my bare legs, and opened my notes app. The blinking cursor stared at me, daring me to name what I was feeling. So I typed the title: **Love? In This Economy?**

And for the first time all day, I let myself breathe. Really breathe. Shoulders unclenching, chest loosening, like the act of putting words on a page made the world tilt back into place.

> *I can't believe those words came out of my mouth.*
>
> *No - scratch that - I can't believe they came out of HIS.*
>
> *He said "I love you" like it was the most obvious thing in the world. Like he'd been carrying it around and waiting for the exact right moment to hand it to me. And I said*

it back. Before my brain even had time to process or flash the usual warning signals.

For once, my fear didn't outrun my truth.

It felt... good.

Which is obviously horrifying.

I keep replaying the moment. The way his face softened. The way he kissed me. Every time I think about it, my heart does this annoying fluttery thing that makes me want to crawl out of my own skin.

And then this morning. God. Waking up next to him felt like something out of someone else's life. Someone steadier. Someone softer. Someone who hasn't spent her entire adult life bracing for abandonment.

We made coffee. He kissed my hair. I leaned into him without thinking. I didn't realize how badly I'd wanted that kind of quiet until I had it.

And that's what scares me the most.

Because wanting him this much means losing him would break something in me I'm not sure I could put back. But none of that showed on my face. At least I hope not. I let myself have the moment. The warmth. The safety. Him.

Fuck, I'm so happy.

And fuck, I'm so scared.

He loves me. And I love him. It feels impossibly big.

But for a few hours today, I let myself believe I deserve it.

• • •

The smell of cinnamon and sugar hit me before I even turned the corner into the kitchen. Jessa had already been up for a while for a Monday, judging by the two trays of muffins cooling on the counter and the smear of flour on her cheek.

"Morning," I muttered, shrugging off my raincoat. The clouds hadn't opened up yet, but they were threatening.

She gave me a glance over her shoulder, eyes scanning me like she was doing some sort of emotional MRI. "You look like you had a good weekend."

I blinked. "That obvious?"

She turned fully now, hands on her hips, and grinned like she'd just won something. "This have anything to do with Elliot?"

Heat shot into my face faster than a kettle hitting boil. "I - what? No. Maybe." I dropped my bag on a chair. "I don't know."

"Oh sweetheart," she teased, crossing to the counter and plucking a muffin from the tray. "You have this boy-induced glow all over you."

"You really get on my nerves sometimes," I mumbled, sinking onto a stool.

She smiled and slid the muffin toward me. "Start talking."

I stared at the cinnamon crumble topping like it might save me. "We… might've said something Friday."

Jessa's eyebrows shot up. "Something like…?"

I groaned into my hands. "Don't make me say it."

"Oh, I'm *absolutely* making you say it."

"Fine," I said, muffled. "We said we loved each other."

The kitchen went still. even the rushing clouds outside seemed to pause. Then, Jessa squealed. Actually squealed. It was like being attacked by joy incarnate.

"Oh my gosh, Sam!" She grabbed my shoulders and shook me gently. "That's huge!"

"I know," I said, voice small. "Believe me, I know."

Her expression softened immediately. The teasing evaporated, replaced by something gentler, like she'd remembered who she was talking to.

"How do you feel?"

I leaned back, staring at the ceiling hoping it would answer for me. "Terrified," I admitted. "Really, really good… and really, really terrified."

"That makes sense," she said, sliding onto the stool across from me. "Love's supposed to feel like that sometimes. Especially when you haven't been given many safe places to put it."

My throat tightened.

"I didn't plan on saying it," I whispered. "It just… fell out. And he looked at me like he meant it."

"Because he did. You can see it all over that boy's face."

I swallowed hard. "What if it's too fast? What if I mess everything up? What if I break him?"

"Oh, honey." She reached across the counter, taking my hand. "He chose you. All of you. Not the easier version you keep trying to convince people you are."

I blinked away the stinging in my eyes. "I don't know how to do this."

"Then let him help you learn," she said. "That's what love is."

I let out a shaky breath, the tension in my shoulders easing just a fraction.

The clouds outside finally opened, rain tapping softly against the building.

Jessa squeezed my hand once more, then stood to grab another tray from the oven. "Now eat your muffin before you faint. You look like you've been emotionally wrung out and hung to dry."

I cracked a laugh. "Thanks. Really."

"Anytime, sweetie," she said, giving me a warm smile over her shoulder. "And Sam?"

"Yeah?"

"I'm proud of you."

And somehow, that meant almost as much as the words from the other night.

∙ ∙ ∙

Ashley had declared it "mandatory morale night," which was her polite way of saying she and Andrew were dragging me out of the house whether I liked it or not.

So I found myself squeezed into the corner booth of Biblioholic, a candle flickering between the three of us and a flight of fruity cocktails sweating on the table. Cooper was at Elliot's with a frozen peanut butter treat. I was only mildly jealous.

Ashley lifted her glass. "To getting Sam out of her cave!"

"Cheers," Andrew added, already halfway through his second whiskey sour.

I clinked my glass against theirs. The drink was pink and smelled like vacation, and I took a sip that was definitely too big.

"Whoa there," Ashley laughed. "Pace yourself."

"It tastes like juice," I argued. "Dangerous juice, but still."

The booth buzzed with low music and the murmur of other tables. Ashley recounted a disastrous encounter with a patient who'd decided to sneak a ferret into the hospital while Andrew kept shaking his head like he didn't believe it had happened.

When Ashley got up to order another round, Andrew leaned across the table. "You doing okay?"

"Yeah," I said, and for once, I meant it. "Actually… I think I am."

He nodded approvingly. "Good. You deserve a night where nothing explodes."

Ashley returned with a tray of drinks - very bright blue.

"Oh no," I whispered.

"Oh yes," she grinned, sliding one of them in front of me. "Electric lemonades. Don't smell them. Just go."

I sniffed it immediately. It smelled like battery acid and childhood. I made a face that made both of them laugh.

We sipped. We laughed harder. At some point Andrew showed us a photo of him at age thirteen with braces and a middle-part haircut from hell. Ashley nearly spewed her drink everywhere.

My drink disappeared faster than it should have. Warmth bloomed in my cheeks. The bar lights got a little softer.

Ashley squinted at me over her glass. "You're tipsy."

"I am *hydrated*," I protested, though the word came out sloppier than intended.

"Sure," Andrew said. "And I'm the Queen of England."

I set my glass down a little too hard. "You know what? I love Elliot."

Ashley half laughed, half scoffed. "We know, babe."

I blushed, a mix of all the different types of alcohol we'd consumed swimming in my cheeks. "I just… it's a new feeling."

Her face softened. "We're happy for you. Right, Andrew?"

"Right," he said as she nudged him in the stomach. "Happy and not at all jealous!"

I laughed and had the sudden urge to pee, feeling like I was about to explode with affection and urine. I slid out of the booth, the bar rocking underneath my feet.

"I'll be right back."

I shuffled my way to the bathroom, peed, took way too long to button my pants, and stumbled out to the sink. My reflection swayed in front of me. I sighed and let my hands steady me on the counter. I felt something stir in me while I stared back at myself. Something... mushy..

I wasn't delusional, I knew I wasn't the sweetest person alive. But I thought maybe, just maybe, I could try. For him.

I pulled my phone out of my pocket, the screen blurring a little. Typed:

> *Hey. I love you. And I think you're really cute. Like... annoyingly hot. Just thought you should know.*

And I hit send before I knew what was happening. Content with my decision - for now - I washed my hands and found my way back to the table, where Ashley and Andrew were deep in discussion about his dating life, complete with sound effects and hand gestures.

I laughed as I slid into the booth, nearly falling flat on my face.

Andrew paused, looked over at me, and grinned. "*Why* do you look like you just confessed to a felony you *definitely* committed?"

My mouth fell open and I gaped at him. "I have... no idea what you're talking about."

Ashley's eyes narrowed. "Uh huh. What did you do?"

"I..." I took a sip of what was left of my electric lemonade. "May or may not have texted Elliot."

Ashley hit Andrew with the back of her hand like she was making sure he'd heard it, too. "Sam, you're *drunk*! What did you say?"

Heat rushed to my face. I couldn't remember.

I pulled my phone out again, words dancing around on the screen. "Uh... I may have confessed my feelings for him." My eyes widened and I looked up too fast. "Guys, help!"

"Maybe he didn't see it. Can you unsend it?" Ashley offered.

I looked down again, horrified to see the bubble with the three dots flickering in the corner, taunting me.

"Fuck."

We all sat in silence - the first time that night any of us had shut the hell up - and watched in horror as the dots kept rippling in the bubble.

> **Elliot 10:26pm**
>
> *Should I frame this text for when you deny ever sending it?*

"Goddammit," I muttered, raking my hand over my face and turning my phone toward them. "How bad is this?"

"You totally gave him the upper hand," Andrew said.

I peeked through my fingers, and Ashley was nodding in agreement.

"Wait, he's typing again!"

I spun my phone back to face me as his message popped up.

> **Elliot 10:27pm**
>
> *Please hydrate immediately before you say anything else cute that will ruin me.*

"I'm about to go throw your phone in the fryer," Andrew said, snatching it from my hand.

Ashley gasped like she'd been personally victimized. "Oh my *god*, Sam, he's flirting. He's flirting back. You're fine!"

"I am absolutely *not* fine," I groaned. My head thunked onto the table. "I'm going to have to move to another country. Somewhere with no cell service. The mountains. The tundra. Antarctica."

Andrew held my phone hostage above my head. "Relax, Frostbite Barbie. The man loves you. Anyone with eyes loves you. You're the only one panicking."

Ashley grabbed my arm. "Okay, okay. How do you want to respond? Something cute? Something safe? Something that doesn't make you want to die?"

"Nothing," Andrew said. "She responds with nothing. Radio silence. Put the device down, Reynolds."

Ashley ignored him entirely. "Sam. Sweetheart. Look at me."

I lifted my head.

"He loves you," she said gently. "And you love him. This is not a disaster. This is literally what happens when adults have feelings."

Andrew snorted. "I'd barely call them adults."

"Shut up," she hissed.

I swallowed hard, feeling my heartbeat in my ears. Panic was starting to set in. "But what do I *do?*"

Ashley held up one finger, the universal sign of drunk girl authority.

"You say nothing. You drink water. You go to bed. You let sober Sam deal with this tomorrow."

"That is," Andrew conceded, "shockingly good advice."

"I know," she said proudly.

He sighed and shoved a glass of water toward me. "Here. Hydrate before you tell him you want to name your hypothetical children Beatrice and Horatio."

"I would *not-*"

"You *so* would."

Ashley leaned in. "Sam. Babe. Listen. If a man texts *that* back? He's already gone for you. You can't ruin this."

I stared at the water like it held ancient wisdom. Maybe it did.

"Okay," I whispered. "No more texting."

"Good girl," Ashley said, patting my cheek like I was a toddler who'd finally put her shoes on the right feet.

Andrew slid my phone into his back pocket. "This is mine now."

"You can't just seize my property," I protested.

He smirked. "Watch me."

Ashley and Andrew slid out of the booth, and she extended her hand out to me. "Come on. Bedtime. You've emotionally overextended yourself."

As they ushered me toward the door, I caught a blink of my phone lighting up in Andrew's pocket - another text from Elliot I couldn't read.

And surprisingly, that didn't make me want to puke.

It made me… warm. Hopeful.

God help me.

SAM

I stepped into Elliot's home the next evening and greeted Cooper, who seemed to have fully adjusted to his home away from home. It warmed my heart but stirred some discomfort deep within me. Like I knew we'd just hit a major milestone in our relationship but I was prepared to take two steps backward at the drop of a hat.

I looked up as I slid off my shoes. Across the living room, up the handful of stairs, and out the balcony doors, there was an unfamiliar glow. I padded cautiously toward it, my sock feet slick on the concrete. As I got closer, I realized the hue was candlelight flickering in the late autumn breeze.

The cloth-covered table stood between the pool and the banister, a cluster of candles in the middle next to a photo frame that I couldn't quite make out from inside. Elliot crouched next to the table, still shifting things around as if to make it *just right*. He wore a set of crisp white sneakers in contrast to his black trousers. A white t-shirt hung just out from under a plush gray sweater, and his silver watch face gleamed in the candlelight.

I stepped out into the cool night air feeling entirely underdressed and underqualified. I shivered, only partly because I was chilled. Anxiety was a caged animal inside me, angry and ready to demolish anything in sight.

Why?

"Darling, you're home!" Elliot smiled as he looked up at me and raised from his crouched position by the table. "Come. Have a seat."

I swallowed hard and willed my feet forward, habitually greeting Elliot with a small embrace. That's all it felt like, though. Habit. Going through the motions. I didn't feel... present anymore.

I took in the table as I got closer. The frame in the middle was a black and white photograph of me and Cooper - my favorite one. Takeout from my favorite Chinese place was spread out at either place, and a glass of wine sat next to my meal, bourbon next to Elliot's.

"What is all this?" I asked, trying hard to feign calm.

"Just because," he said casually, completely oblivious to the swarm of inadequacy he'd set off inside me. "I got this framed to put up in the house so you and Cooper could go on the wall. I just... wanted to do something special for you is all. By the way, *annoyingly hot?*"

He pulled my chair out for me, then sat across the table, that boyish smile tugging at the corner of his mouth like he had no idea I was moments from spontaneous combustion.

"I-" I started, then stopped.

Just because.

The words echoed in my head like a taunt. That's what people said before they left. Before they broke things. Before they made you love them and *then* decided you were too much work.

"Sam? You okay?" His voice was soft, but the question punched hard.

I forced a smile and stared down at the photo frame. Cooper was still young, his ears floppy, his tongue out, his eyes as bright as the day had been sunny. My own face was turned toward him in the shot - laughing, unguarded.

I didn't even recognize myself.

"You didn't have to do all this," I said quietly, hoping it would come out as gratitude. But it sounded more like a warning.

"I know," Elliot said, still smiling gently. "But I *wanted* to."

I reached for the wine glass and took a too-large sip. I nearly choked on it as my throat tightened.

"I just... I don't know how to be this version of me. The one who gets this. Gets you." I gestured vaguely around the table. "I feel like I'm watching my life happen instead of actually living it."

Elliot sipped at his whiskey then tilted his head. "Is that such a bad thing?"

I stared at him, blinking away the stinging behind my eyes. "It's a *terrifying* thing."

He didn't flinch. Didn't look away.

A silence hung between us. The kind that needed to be filled with words we couldn't find. I looked at him and saw someone who meant it - every part of it. And instead of relief, that scared me more than anything.

I wasn't ready to lose him. But I wasn't sure I knew how to *keep* him, either.

I took another sip of wine, this one slower. More intentional. Then I set the glass down and looked back at Elliot, who still hadn't moved, still wore that patient expression like he had all the time in the world.

"I don't want to mess this up," I said finally, barely above a whisper.

"You won't." He said it with such certainty it cracked something open in me.

He was so casual about something I felt was so epic. It was practically life or death for me, this anxious feeling I had with him. And he was so flippant about how big of a deal it all was. I could tell that, in his mind, we were simply slated to find each other and fall in love and that was the beginning and end of the story. But to me it felt more complicated than that.

"I might," I argued finally, picking at the edge of the napkin in my lap. "Not because I want to… just because I don't always know how *not* to."

"I know," he said. No judgement. No fear. "And I'm not going anywhere."

The candlelight danced between us, casting shadows on the table and softening the lines of everything. I took a deep breath and let it out slowly, the tension in my shoulders easing just enough for me to lean my elbows on the table and actually smile.

Calm the fuck down. You can't run. Not from him. Not now. Trust him. Enjoy this.

"You framed that picture," I said, glancing at the photo again. "That's one of my favorites."

"I figured," he shrugged. "You look… happy in it."

"I was. Cooper had just eaten a squirrel's tail."

Elliot laughed, full and bright. "That's disgusting."

"It was," I smiled wider now, surprised at myself. "But… I guess that's what joy looks like for me. Messy. A little weird. But real."

"I like your kind of joy."

He reached his hand across the table, palm up. I hesitated only for a moment before sliding mine into his. His fingers curled around mine like he'd been waiting for the invitation.

We sat like that for a while - eating, laughing, soft music floating out from the balcony speakers. He teased me lightly about my drunk text the night before, but I didn't mind. I didn't overthink every word. I didn't count the exits or calculate escape routes. I just... was.

...

The first thing I noticed was the smell of coffee.

The second was the absence of warmth next to me.

I stretched under Elliot's comforter, the crisp sheets cool against my skin in all the right ways. Morning sunlight filtered through the window blinds, casting quiet stripes across the bed and my bare shoulder.

Cooper let out a soft huff from the foot of the bed, curled up into the tightest circle he could manage. I gave his side a sleepy pat, then reached for my phone. 8:26 am.

Footsteps padded across the concrete floor, followed by a familiar creak of the door. Elliot peeked his head in.

"Morning, sleeping beauty," he grinned, a mug in each hand. "I didn't want to wake you. You looked way too peaceful."

"Peaceful?" I mumbled, sitting up and rubbing my face. "I probably looked like a troll."

He crossed the room and handed me one of the mugs. "A very cute troll."

I narrowed my eyes at him but took the coffee anyway. "That's a weird thing to say to your girlfriend."

His grin deepened. "So you're my girlfriend now?"

The question caught me off guard. He wasn't teasing - his voice was gentle, hopeful, a little careful.

I glanced down at the coffee and took a sip to buy myself time. Warm dark roast, single-origin coffee. Maybe he could work a french press after all.

"Guess I am," I said finally, quietly, eyes still on the rim of the mug.

When I looked back up, his smile was softer, steadier. "Cool."

"Cool?" I raised an eyebrow.

He leaned down and kissed me, slow and sweet, his hand resting lightly against my jaw.

"Cool," he repeated against my lips.

Cooper groaned dramatically from the bed like he couldn't bear another second of our domestic bliss. We both laughed.

The morning drifted forward in warm, unhurried time - shared coffee, stolen kisses, unbrushed teeth, and the kind of quiet that felt earned. Safe. Like we were building something brick by brick, moment by moment.

And for the first time in a very, very long time, I didn't feel like I needed to apologize for feeling happy.

We settled on opposite ends of the couch - Elliot with some romance book, me with my computer in my lap. I hadn't ever really journaled with anyone else in the room, but I'd been having a lot of firsts lately. My heart beat hard in my ears. I took a deep breath and navigated to my notes app, titling this entry ***Oops, I Spoke Feelings***.

> *This week's recap:*
>
> - *Elliot made a whole-ass dinner on the terrace*
> - *Like romance movie level???*
> - *Who does that?*
> - *For ME?*
>
> *Then the real crime… I called myself his girlfriend. With my mouth. In front of him. Casually, like I've said it a thousand times. And he smiled?? Like that was completely normal and not me having an identity crisis?*
>
> *Anyway, I'm currently experiencing heart palpitations not caused by caffeine.*
>
> *I love him. Like… disgusting levels of mushy type of love.*

This is fine. Totally fine.
(Absolutely lying to myself)

"Whatcha working on?" Elliot asked, not even looking up from his book. Not invasive. Just curious.

I blushed and half-closed my laptop like a boy caught looking at dirty images.

"Nothing," I said too quickly. "Just some marketing stuff for the cafe Jessa wanted some help with."

The lie felt innocent enough. There was no reason for Elliot to know I was journaling. Much less about him. How embarrassing for me.

He hummed softly, still reading, flipping a page with that unhurried calm he always carried around. "Mmm. Tell her I'm charging consulting fees next time she steals you after hours."

I snorted despite myself, tension leaking out of my shoulders. "You wouldn't charge Jessa anything. She'd kill you."

He smirked without looking up. "You're right, I *am* afraid of her."

Cooper trotted over to Elliot for a head scratch, the little traitor. Elliot obliged, one hand still holding his place in the book.

"You okay?" he asked casually. Still not prying. Still giving me space to breathe.

"Yeah," I said, surprising myself at how true it felt.. "I'm good."

I closed the laptop and set it on the coffee table. Elliot reached over and rested his hand on my leg - light, warm, and grounding. Nothing demanding. Just… there.

And the softest, stupidest part of me melted.

I leaned into him until my head rested on his shoulder. He didn't react with surprise, just shifted so I fit better against him, like it was the most natural thing in the world.

The sun glowed outside the terrace windows, throwing soft shadows across the room. His thumb brushed absentminded circles against my knee. Cooper snored lightly at our feet.

It was wild to me that a few months ago I'd been perfectly lonely, doing life pretending like I didn't need anyone else. But now I settled against the chest of a man who loved me - truly loved me. We breathed the same slow, steady air. Our hearts beat against one another through our chests. And I let myself exist in the moment. Let myself want it. Let myself have it.

Even if that still scared me more than anything else.

37 SAM

Elliot strolled in, still on his phone from work. I glanced up from my book and smiled at him. He dramatically rolled his eyes and pointed at his phone as if he'd rather be doing *anything* else. I chuckled, and Cooper jumped off his spot on the couch by my feet to greet Elliot. He gave him a quick scratch on the head and turned to kick off his shoes.

I hadn't seen Elliot much in the other seasons, just late summer and early fall, but I already imagined him in autumn to be my favorite. The layered outfits, the ankle boots, the scruff of his hair in the wind…

He winked at me as if he could tell I was internally objectifying him.

How does he do that? Always know what you're thinking?

My phone buzzed on the coffee table. I ignored it. Elliot made his way down the hall to his bedroom, already half undressed in his search for more comfortable clothes.

Another buzz.

I sighed, half-grumbling as I reached for it.

I expected a spam notification, or maybe Andrew sending me another ridiculous TikTok.

Instead, the unknown number on the screen stopped my heart.

Hey, can we talk?

My breath caught. Then I saw the initial at the bottom.

- L

That was it.

No explanation. No apology. No update on life or excuse or olive branch.

Just a match dropped in the middle of my peace.

I blinked at it, my chest tightening slowly like a fist curling inward.

Just like that, the warm room felt too bright. The air too thick. I tucked my phone under the blanket and tried to regulate my breath.

"Everything okay?" Elliot's voice startled me from behind, no longer on the phone, and now just in a pair of tracksuit pants.

"Yeah," I lied, and leaned back against the cushion before he could see my face.

I could hear him rummaging through the fridge behind me. He set off talking about his day negotiating contracts, and I wanted to listen, but his words jumbled in my head.

Can we talk?

"Sam?"

"Uh, yeah?"

"I said, are you good with pasta for dinner? I don't think we have anything else around here…" He faded off, rummaging through the fridge again.

"Pasta's fine." I replied, though the idea of eating anything made my stomach churn.

I sunk lower onto the couch and clutched the blanket closer.

Can we talk? What could she possibly want to talk about now?

"Sam?" I looked up, Elliot standing beside me now, looking down at me in a ball on the couch. "You sure you're okay?"

His eyes searched mine.

I nodded, but my voice caught before it could make it to my mouth. "Just tired."

He didn't believe me. I could tell. But he didn't call me out. He just sat down and reached out, resting a warm hand on my thigh. Not pushing. But I couldn't tell him.

He wouldn't understand. He has the perfect relationship with his sister, and his dead brother of course can do no wrong. He'd push you to fix it. Worse yet, he'd probably make some good points about the whole thing. You can't tell him.

I felt like I was underwater. Like my body was still sitting on the couch with him, but my head had drifted far away and the more I tried to stay present, the heavier it felt - like grief and memory were coiling around my ankles, tugging me under. All the way to the memory of Laurel's laugh, her tears, her voice when it used to call my name like it meant something.

Maybe I should answer her. Maybe I shouldn't.

What if I let her back in and everything fell apart again?

What if I didn't - and it already had?

⋯

The espresso machine hissed behind me, but I barely heard it. My hands moved on autopilot - grind, tamp, brew, steam - but I couldn't remember what I was even making. A caramel latte, maybe?

"Sam," Jessa's voice snapped me back to the moment. I looked down. The cup I was pouring milk into was already full, and warm foam now pooled at the base like some kind of sad coffee moat.

"Shit, sorry." I grabbed a towel to clean up the spill.

"You've made three drinks wrong this morning," she said, not unkindly. "You're not here."

I avoided her eyes and dropped the towel in the sink. "Just tired."

Jessa tilted her head. "Tired I can believe. But this?" She gestured gently at me. "This is more than tired, Sam."

"I'm fine," I lied, maybe too quickly.

She dried her hands on her apron and leaned her hip against the counter. "You know what I've learned about keeping things bottled up?"

I raised an eyebrow.

"It doesn't protect you. It just poisons everything else."

I looked away, guilt now pressing into my lungs.

She softened. "Whatever it is, hon, you don't have to face it alone. You've got people now. Real ones."

• • •

Elliot set two bowls of steak tips on the coffee table, a flicker of pride in his eyes like he'd just won "most domestic man alive." I forced a smile as I curled up on the couch beside him.

"Smells amazing," I said.

He glanced over. "You okay?"

"Yeah, just… long day," I said, same script, different stage.

We ate in silence, the clink of forks and the distant hum of the dishwasher the only sound between us. He tried a few times - comments about a podcast, a funny text from Andrew - but I barely registered them.

Finally, he set his bowl down and looked at me.

"I miss you."

I blinked. "What?"

"You're here, but not really," he said gently. "You've been somewhere else for the last… couple of days? And if you don't want to talk about it, that's okay, I guess. I just… I want to know how to be there for you."

God. He always says the right things.

"I don't know why I'm like this, " I whispered. "I'm not trying to shut you out."

He reached for my hand. "I know. But even if you don't have the words yet… I'm still here."

My fingers curled around his instinctively.

Still here.

My mind carried me back to Jessa's words earlier in the day. *It just poisons everything else.*

I bit at the inside of my cheek to fight back the sudden stinging in my eyes.

Elliot, obviously concerned now, moved to where he was kneeling in front of me, eyes burning my paper heart to dust.

"Sam, I'm not trying to push, but… I can feel something shifting. You're pulling away. And I just got you. I want to understand what's going on."

It just poisons everything.

I didn't want to say it out loud. Saying it would make it real. But it was already real—already coiled around my ribs like a vice.

"Laurel reached out," I whispered. "I haven't answered. I don't know if I'm going to. If I want to."

His eyes softened. Something between sympathy and pity flashed over his face. He recovered quickly, though, a soft conciliatory smile pressed into his lips. "You don't have to do anything you don't want to do, Sam."

"I just… don't know *what* I want. Like you've said before… she's still my sister, no matter how messy things get."

He sighed. "I didn't mean it like that… You don't owe her anything you're not ready to give," he said quietly. "You're allowed to protect your peace."

I leaned forward, resting my head on his shoulder. I didn't say thank you. I didn't need to.

He just wrapped his arms around me, steady and sure.

Still here.

• • •

The penthouse was quiet. Too quiet.

Elliot had already left for work, his side of the bed still faintly warm when I stirred that morning. Cooper snored softly from the foot of the bed, occasionally twitching like he was chasing something in a dream. I curled deeper into the comforter, letting the warmth and stillness stretch longer than I usually allowed myself.

After a long moment had passed, I carried myself - wrapped in Elliot's comforter

- to the kitchen to try to muster up enough courage and caffeine to face the day. He'd already left coffee in the french press and a note in his careful handwriting.

> *Have a good day, darling. Call if you need anything. Still here.*

Still here.

I still wasn't used to someone meaning that.

Last night's conversation echoed in my chest. Elliot hadn't flinched. He hadn't pushed or pressed more than he should have. He just... stayed.

That should have been enough to ground me. To start the healing. And maybe, for a second, it was.

A soft drizzle tapped at the windows, the kind of morning where time stretched and sagged around the edges. The kind where you're *almost* okay.

I reached for my phone - muscle memory. Just a quick scroll.

At first, it was nothing. Spam. Weather. A notification from the news app I always forgot to disable. Then:

Unknown Number: 8:21 am

> *I don't want to fight. I just want to talk like adults. You weren't perfect either, Sam. Maybe we both need to own some things. -L*

I froze.

The cup of coffee didn't make it to my lips. My hands suddenly felt too large, too clumsy. I set the mug down before I dropped it.

There it was - the twist of the knife.

It wasn't a scream. It wasn't a threat. It was worse.

It was subtle, manipulative. Almost reasonable. The kind of message that made you question your memory. Your truth.

You weren't perfect either.

Of course I wasn't. No one was. But that wasn't the point.

She knew that wasn't the point.

I may not have been perfect. God knows I wasn't. When I ran from the group home, I didn't have resources. Hell, I didn't even have shoes without holes in them. I had nothing. No money, no plan, no adult who gave a damn. It wasn't until a whole couple of years later that I met Jessa and Bill. At the time, I was sixteen and starving and terrified, not a savior with a plan.

And yeah, I'd left her. Left her in a hell we were both drowning in, but she'd made choices that detonated the rest of her life. The consequences swallowed her whole.

But that didn't make her message true. It didn't rewrite history. It didn't make sixteen-year-old me responsible for the ruins of her adulthood.

Yet she knew exactly where to aim her words - right at the softest part of me. The part still convinced I should have been stronger, smarter, better.

The part that never forgave myself for surviving.

Shame pooled hot in my stomach. Guilt whispered maybe she was right. Maybe I had abandoned her. Maybe every terrible thing after that was somehow my fault.

But it shouldn't be about me. It should be about the man who abused us.

I stared at the message, rage and shame battling somewhere deep in my chest. Did she actually believe that? Or was it just another way to pull the rug out from under me?

I didn't respond. I couldn't.

But I also couldn't put the phone down.

A part of me wanted to scream. Another part of me wanted to write her a novel explaining every ache she left behind. And another - maybe the most dangerous part - wanted to believe her. Maybe I was no better than Gatsby, trying to build something stable on a foundation that never really held.

...

I walked into the cafe just after ten, a full hour later than scheduled. The shop was already buzzing - college kids in hoodies hunched over laptops, moms in leggings juggling toddlers and caffeine, the usual suspects.

Andrew spotted me immediately.

"Look what the cat dragged in," he called, closing his laptop.

"Yeah, an hour late. I'm going on break," Justin said, already halfway through the kitchen door.

"Good morning to you, too," I grumbled to them both, slipping behind the counter and grabbing an apron.

Andrew narrowed his eyes as I tied it around my waist. "You okay? You look like you got hit by a very stylish truck."

"Thanks, that's exactly the look I was going for." I tucked my hair into a ponytail and avoided eye contact.

He didn't buy it. He was too sharp for that.

"You want me to ask if you're good again or just assume you're emotionally constipated this morning?"

I gave him a flat look, but my lips twitched at the corners. "I'm fine. Just tired."

He raised a brow. "Fine as in *actually* fine, or fine as in *one wrong word and I'll burst into tears on the espresso machine?*"

I snorted. "Somewhere between those two, probably."

He nodded sagely. "So… chaos."

"Controlled chaos," I clarified.

Andrew stepped back and shoved his mostly full latte across the counter at me. "Here. You're not allowed to spiral on an empty caffeine level."

I took it from him and offered a soft, "thanks."

He leaned against the counter, his arms crossed. "Do you wanna talk about what's got you weird, or should I keep guessing until I land on your exact emotional trauma of the day?"

I took a sip of the latte.

"I got a text," I said quietly. "From someone I haven't heard from in a long time."

Andrew didn't say anything - just nodded as if to tell me, *go on*.

"She didn't apologize. Didn't ask if I was okay. Just… twisted it all to sound like I'm equally to blame for everything."

I let that hang in the air a moment.

"I hate that," he said finally. "When someone hurts you and then tries to make it seem like it was mutual. Like your survival was just as bad as their abuse."

That stopped me. I looked over at him, heart pounding. I hadn't said anything about abuse.

But he just kept talking, voice quieter now. "It's a mind game. Makes you doubt what you *know* you lived through."

I swallowed hard, unsure if I wanted to cry or hug him or both. "Exactly."

Andrew shrugged like it wasn't a big deal, but his eyes were serious. "People like that, they don't want peace. They want access. Big difference."

That sentence punched me in the gut. *Access.*

"She wants to talk," I said.

He tilted his head. "Do you?"

I stared down at the latte, tracing the rim with my finger. "I don't know."

"Well," he said gently. "Just don't forget: you don't owe anyone the version of you *they're* most comfortable with."

I looked up at him. "When did you get so damn wise?"

He grinned and shrugged. "I watch a lot of Oprah."

I laughed, an honest one this time. "Thanks, Andrew."

He patted my shoulder. "Anytime."

The shop was thinning out. The espresso machine hissed out a tired sigh, and I was grateful for the moment of peace. I was wiping down the counters when Jessa came through the door from the kitchen.

"Sweetie, I was worried sick. Are you okay?"

I turned to her, guilt piling up in my stomach. "I'm okay. I'm sorry I'm late… just a lot going on right now."

She eyed me suspiciously, visibly trying to decide whether or not it was the right time to push. I smiled warily.

"What's going on, Sam?"

"It's stupid."

"I seriously doubt that."

I hesitated. "Laurel texted me."

She blinked slowly. "First time in a while, right? What did she want? More money?"

"It's been years," I whispered. "Well, I ran into her a few weeks ago, but she's actively reaching out and asking to talk now. She didn't say anything terrible. She just... twisted things. Like always. Like maybe I'm the one who's overreacting. Like maybe it was all my fault, too."

Jessa didn't rush to respond. She sipped from a mug, then stepped closer, speaking gently. "You know, that's the thing about manipulative people... they don't always need to yell or threaten to do damage. Sometimes the most toxic ones come in the most quiet, polite packaging."

I blinked hard, trying to hold the tears at bay.

"She said she just wanted to talk," I muttered. "That we both needed to own some things. And I - fuck, I don't know. Part of me feels like maybe she's right."

Jessa placed her mug down and touched my arm - light but grounding. "Sam. Listen to me. There's a difference between taking responsibility and taking blame. You've done so much to try to heal. Don't confuse her discomfort with your guilt."

I swallowed, throat tight. "I haven't answered her."

"You don't *have* to."

"I don't even know what I'd even say if I did."

"Then don't force it. Not yet. Maybe not ever."

I nodded slowly, chewing on the inside of my cheek.

"And Sam?" she added, waiting until I met her eyes. "You are not that girl anymore. The one who had to survive in silence. You are not alone now. You've got people in your corner - me, Andrew, that sweet man of yours who'd probably slay a dragon for you."

A half-laugh caught in my throat. "He's... been amazing. Which I think is making this worse. I don't want to ruin what we have."

"You're not ruining anything," she said firmly. "You're reacting to something traumatic. That doesn't make you broken, it makes you human. And if he *really* loves you, he'll weather this storm right alongside you."

I let out a long, slow breath. Maybe the first one I'd truly taken all day.

• • •

Whatever her name was - Becky? Bailey? - came in with a warm smile and a cute little purse that complimented her outfit perfectly.

"Hey, Sam," she said, growing my guilt of *still* not remembering her name. "How are you today?"

I took a deep breath. "Fine," I lied. "And you?"

She set her purse on the counter as if it weighed a million pounds. "Ugh, I am dealing with some work drama, and it is driving me up the wall. So, I took a break for a coffee run. Save me?"

I laughed and shook my head. "I'm no superhero, but I'll do my best. What'll it be today?"

She looked over the menu, then looked up with hope in her eyes. "You still have the stuff to make that sweater weather latte? I know it's not on the menu, technically, but I'm desperately craving it."

I began going through the motions of getting her drink ready. "Of course. I've got you, girl."

Girl? What are we, fifteen?

She sighed deeply, exasperated. "Thank you so much. We were supposed to be working on this project together, me and some of my colleagues, right? I did the slides *and* the research. This asshole Jeremy just… stood there and scrolled TikTok like a teenager. Anyway, fast forward to today, and we present to the leadership team. At the end, he says, 'Thanks everyone, I worked really hard on this.' Can you believe that?"

I shook my head, feigning disbelief at this problem that seemed to really rock her world but was so insignificant in the grand scheme of things. I didn't want to be rude, so I just listened.

"He's such a prick… sorry."

I laughed at that. "You're not going to offend me with language, that much I can assure you."

I handed her latte across to her and offered the most genuine-looking smile I could muster. "I hope things get better. Thanks for stopping in."

She hesitated, almost like she was ready to dump some more work drama on me, but she turned on her heel to leave.

• • •

The door chimed just as I was wiping down the already spotless espresso machine. I didn't look up - somewhere between overstimulated and underwhelmed.

"If I have to spend another minute around interns who think *vibes* are a legitimate diagnosis, I will combust. I need caffeine and human conversation." Ashley leaned against the counter with feigned exasperation.

I chuckled - maybe on another day it would have been a full-fledged laugh. But today was… off.

"Dr. Ashley gracing my humble shop? What'll you have?"

"Hmm…" she glanced over the menu half-heartedly. "Whatever you're drinking today. Two of those please… one for you, obviously. You look like you've had all the caffeine you've ever drank drained out of you."

I shook my head and smiled, just enough. "Yeah," I said. "Just… not a great day."

She stilled for a beat. "Want to talk about it?"

I hesitated. I'd been doing a *lot* of opening up. It wasn't *bad*, per se. Just… terrifying.

But for some reason, with Ashley, it didn't feel impossible.

"Let's just say my past is trying to claw its way back into my present." I scooped ice into the shaker with the espresso. "It's… exhausting."

Ashley accepted her brown sugar shaken espresso when I slid it toward her, watching me with that physician's mix of concern and calculation. But then she softened, stabbing her straw through the hole and taking a sip.

"Damn," she said, eyebrows lifting. "This is good. Whatever emotional crisis brewed this up… keep having it. Just don't let it totally kill you."

That almost earned a full laugh from me. "That your official medical advice?"

"Absolutely not. I left my white coat in the car." She studied me for another second. "I know I'm not Elliot," Ashley added gently. "But I'm still here. So if you need a buffer, or a late night distraction, or someone to tell you you're not crazy… I'm game."

I looked up and met her eyes, the corner of my mouth tugging upward. "Thanks, Ash."

She bumped my cup with hers. "You got it, Sam. And hey… for what it's worth? You're doing better than you think."

• • •

I sank deeper into the water in the giant bathtub at Elliot's. My breath made ripples over the edge as it escaped my nose unevenly. Not usually a bath person, I was chilled to my core and needed the warmth to envelop me.

Elliot poked his head around the door, cautious, weary. "Sam?"

I glanced up at him, then back down at the water. I tried to be as motionless as possible and make the surface of the bath still with me.

"You don't have to talk to me about it… but I think you should talk to someone."

I nodded just slightly.

I didn't want to push him away. I didn't know how to let him in.

"You want some company?"

He stepped into the bathroom more fully, his shirtless chest rippling with each breath. His sweatpants hung loosely around his hips, dipping slightly in the middle. Various tattoos speckled around his upper body - the olive branches under his collarbones, the swallows on his arm for his mother, the tiger on his right ribs for his brother, the snake over his left hip because it "looked cool."

God he's so stunning.

I nodded, fully this time. Slowly.

He sat next to the tub on the floor, his knees cracking slightly as he went to sit. His hand extended to me through the water and grabbed mine.

"Want to talk about it?"

I thought about it for a moment. Thought about his propensity for always knowing just what to say. Thought about how selfish it felt to complain about my sister when his brother didn't even get the chance to grow up and disappoint him. Thought about Jessa and Andrew urging me to open up to him.

"I just wish…" I faded off. Surprising me, tears began to fall. Freely.

Elliot reached up with his other hand and gently thumbed away my tears, which were quickly replaced with new ones as I sobbed. There was so much I wanted to say and yet words were too small to hold the weight of all my wishes.

He didn't speak right away. He didn't rush to fill the silence or ask for more than I could give. I wasn't sure I could give anything in that moment - and somehow that was okay. He just sat there, one hand wrapped around mine beneath the water, the other gently wiping away the tears that refused to stop falling.

Eventually, his fingers found a slow rhythm, brushing softly against the back of my hand. He lowered his chin to rest against the edge of the tub and exhaled softly, his breath shallow and warm against my arm.

The quiet between us was thick with understanding, with patience. Like he knew I was unraveling and he was perfectly content just to sit beside the thread.

"I hate how small it still makes me feel," I finally whispered, my voice hoarse. "Like I'm sixteen again and it's all still happening."

He didn't move, but his grip on my hand tightened just slightly. "That makes sense," he said simply. "This isn't something you can just walk away from."

I looked over at him. His eyes were closed now, his face relaxed but open, like he wasn't just listening - he was holding every word like it mattered.

"I keep thinking I'm gonna be able to move on," I said. "That I can heal. But then she shows up, just a name on a screen, and I'm right back in the wreckage."

"Sam." He lifted his head to meet my eyes. "Healing doesn't mean you never hurt again."

A sob escaped me, sharp and sudden. He didn't flinch. He reached for me - slow, deliberate - and cupped the side of my face in his dripping hand.

"You're *not* broken," he said, voice firm now. "You've just been carrying too much alone."

His words knocked the breath out of me. Not because they were dramatic or grand. Because they were true.

I nodded slowly, water dripping from the ends of my hair as I leaned forward and rested my forehead against his. His other hand rose to the back of my neck, grounding me there with him.

We stayed like that. For how long, I'm unsure. Until the water grew cold.

Eventually, I started to shiver, and his voice broke the silence.

"You want to get out? I can warm you back up."

I half-laughed, half-sobbed. "You offering to be my heating pad?"

"I make an excellent one, actually." A crooked smile. "I'm practically a furnace."

I let the smallest smile crack through my exhaustion. "Give me a minute."

He nodded, standing and pressing a soft kiss to my temple before stepping out to grab towels. And for the first time in days, I felt like I wasn't drowning.

Maybe not healed. But held.

Elliot

Things... started to change.

Not huge, catastrophic shifts. If anything, it was the quiet things I noticed first. The ones most people would miss if they weren't looking closely. But I'd gotten good at reading Sam - her silences, her breaths, the way her eyes moved when she was trying to hold something together.

She'd been sitting next to me on the couch one night, book in her lap, blanket tucked around both of us. And then she just... drifted. Eyes fixed somewhere far away, jaw tightening like she was bracing for impact from a memory I couldn't see. I said her name softly, and it took her a second too long to come back.

That's when I knew something was wrong.

It kept happening. These tiny moments where it felt like her mind was slipping somewhere I couldn't follow. I told her some dumb joke Andrew texted me (one that would've usually made her roll her eyes and laugh despite herself). But she didn't even smile. Just looked past me, like she was trying to make sense of something she couldn't quite say out loud.

I tried to give her space at first. God knows she deserved that more than anyone. But every time I asked if she was okay, she gave me the same soft, automatic, half-hearted "Yeah, I'm fine," that told me she wasn't.

That's when everything cracked.

I pushed. Not in a harsh way, but in an I-love-you-too-much-to-watch-you-crumble-silently way. And finally, she let some of it out. Laurel had texted her out of nowhere. And she didn't know what to do about it - didn't know if she should respond or ignore it or let it burn a hole straight through her chest the way it had been for days.

She felt guilty. Said Laurel had brought up that they both needed to "own some things." That she wasn't sure what the right choice was and that, no matter what she did, it was going to hurt.

All I felt was this deep, fierce ache.

Not because she was fragile, but because she was trying so hard not to be.

It killed me a little, knowing all I could do was sit beside her, hands useless, heart too full.

But she told me.

She let me in.

And I remember thinking: whatever comes next - whatever she decides - I'm not letting her walk through it alone. Not again.

39 Sam

I sat at the back table in the shop, tucked behind the espresso machine and half-hidden by the flickering light coming through the windows. It was the first lull of the day - just me, my lukewarm coffee, and the ache of everything I still hadn't said.

My phone sat face-up on the table beside me, the screen blank, but the weight of Laurel's last message hung in the air like a fog. I didn't want to respond. I didn't want to *not* respond. I just... didn't want to be afraid of the decision anymore.

You weren't perfect either, Sam.

I stared at those words. They twisted in my gut. Not because she was wrong - maybe I hadn't handled everything perfectly - but because I knew that wasn't why she sent it.

She didn't want healing. She wanted revision. And yet...

I pulled in a slow breath, letting it fill every crevice of my lungs. Then I reached for my phone. My fingers hovered over the keyboard for longer than I cared to admit.

I typed. Deleted. Typed again.

Then, finally:

> *Laurel, I got your messages. I'm not sure I'm ready to talk, but I'm not ignoring you. I just need time. Please respect that.*

I read it three times. It didn't feel powerful or pointed or perfect.

It just felt... true.

I hit send.

My heart thundered in my chest like I'd stepped off the edge of a cliff. But nothing happened. The world didn't end. My hands were shaking, but I was still breathing. Still sitting in the back of the shop with coffee gone cold and a day still left to live.

And in some small, quiet way, that felt like a win.

I shoved my phone in my back pocket and walked back to the register. The soft pop playlist I'd put on added a quiet beat to the otherwise stillness of the slow cafe. There was one other customer, a work-from-home type who had their own music - or podcast - playing through their expensive, over-ear headphones.

I hummed and began making myself a cardamom latte - something with a little sweetness, but nothing too major. Something about the day felt... lighter now. Like the absence of the decision weighing on me made the music just a tad more melodic. Like the autumn sun warming the windows was just a little brighter.

The bell.

I glanced up, careful to avoid overfilling my cup, and there stood Marcus.

His pale navy jacket swallowed him. His face twitched in a weird sort of manner that nearly made me flinch.

"Sam," he nodded curtly. "Missed you the other day."

I stiffened. My hand clenched around my cup, the steam swirling upward as I glanced at him. There was no reason to panic - none at all. He hadn't done anything. Not really.

Still, something about him scraped at the inside of my ribs like sandpaper.

"Oh… hi, Marcus." I forced a small, tight smile and lowered my mug. "I've been working different shifts."

He stepped closer to the counter, too close, and leaned forward like he wanted to whisper but didn't care if anyone heard.

"I figured," he said, eyes darting around like he was confirming we were nearly alone. "I was starting to think you were avoiding me."

If only I could, motherfucker.

I quickly cleared my throat. "What can I get started for you?"

He smiled then, but it wasn't warm. It was stretched too thin, too precise. "You remembered my order, right?"

I didn't. But I nodded anyway.

He watched me closely as I turned to the espresso machine, every movement feeling twice as loud as it should have. My hands worked quickly - too quickly - and I spilled a little milk down the side of the metal pitcher. I cursed under my breath and reached for a rag. I made a flat white on auto-pilot, completely blanking on anything helpful in the moment.

Behind me, he chuckled. "Nervous today?"

Mister work-from-home typed away in the corner, completely oblivious.

I gritted my teeth and turned back toward him with the drink. "Here you go."

He took it, letting his fingers brush against mine for too long. "Thanks. Glad to see you around again."

The door chime rang out again behind him, and I nearly sighed with relief when another customer walked in. Marcus didn't move, though. He stayed right there, his coffee untouched.

"You know," he said, voice low. "I used to think you were just shy. But I'm starting to think you're hiding something."

Who the fuck does he think he is?

My forehead and neck suddenly got clammy. I blinked at him, my stomach twisting. "Excuse me?"

He leaned in more, just enough that I could smell the artificial mint of his gum and the metallic tang of something else - something I couldn't name but made my stomach churn. "Everyone hides something. Secrets, pasts, whatever… you've got this… air about you."

I stepped back instinctively, the counter a barrier I was suddenly more aware of, more grateful for. "I really need to take care of the next customer."

He stared at me for another beat, head tilting slightly like he was trying to read a different language across my face. Then, as if a switch flipped, he smiled - too wide again.

"Of course. Another time, then."

With that, he turned and walked out, the bell above the door ringing too cheerfully for the oppressive mood he left in his wake. I gripped the edge of the counter until my knuckles turned white.

Another time.

I stared at the closed door for a long moment, the shadows outside suddenly darker than they'd been a minute ago.

• • •

I curled into the corner of Elliot's couch, legs tucked beneath me, blanket pulled high. The lights were dim, and some low-key crime doc played on the TV, but I hadn't heard a single word.

Elliot walked in from the kitchen and handed me a glass of wine without a word. He knew the look on my face by now, no matter how much I wished I was better at hiding things. He lifted my legs and settled underneath them on the couch next to me, taking a sip of his bourbon.

I took a large gulp of my wine and sighed. "Something weird happened at work today."

He sat casually beside me, arm draped loosely across the back of the couch. He didn't pry. Didn't press. Just silently waited for me to open up.

"There's this guy that's been coming into the shop… his name is Marcus. Just every so often. Gives me the creeps. He came in today…"

I glanced at Elliot. His jaw tightened, just slightly, but he still sat quietly.

"He didn't… *do* anything," I continued, like I had to preface the whole thing with a disclaimer. "It wasn't some big scene. It was just… unsettling. The way he stood too close. The way he said my name. Like he knows more about me than he should."

Elliot's arm stiffened on top of my legs. "Did he touch you?"

"No. Well… not really. Just brushed my fingers when I handed him the drink. But it wasn't the touch that bothered me. It was everything else. The way he *watched* me. The way he said he used to think I was shy, but now he thinks I'm hiding something. Like…" I trailed off. "Like he was trying to get in my head."

Elliot sat quiet for a moment, then leaned in. "You want me to come with you tomorrow? Just hang out in the shop? I can work from there."

I hesitated, then shook my head. "No. I don't need you to try and fix anything for me. I mean… I appreciate the offer, I do. But I'm okay."

I looked down at the wine in my glass and swirled it around. "I just… felt like I should tell you. That's new for me. Normally I'd keep something like that locked down so tight, I'd convince myself it never even happened."

Elliot leaned back slightly, eyes soft but steady on mine. "I'm proud of you, darling."

I let out a small, humorless laugh. "For telling you a guy gave me the creeps?"

"For not carrying it alone," he said. "That's not nothing."

I nodded, the words settling deep in my chest. He didn't question me. Didn't force me to accept his help.

Something inside me loosened. Like taking off a belt after a long day. Not because I was magically healed or because Marcus was suddenly not a problem or because Laurel's message hadn't lodged somewhere sharp in my ribs. But because, for once, it's like I didn't have to shoulder every inch of it on my own.

· · ·

My eyes fluttered open to the steady rise and fall of Elliot's chest, my cheek resting just above his heart. For a long moment, I simply breathed in time with him - wanting to soak in the quiet before the world found a way to interrupt the fragile bubble I was in.

Happy.

I was happy.

Tears pricked unexpectedly, but for once, I didn't mind. I wiped them away gently, not wanting to wake him. Something deep and warm bloomed in my chest - a strange kind of fondness, the kind that makes you want to memorize everything. Just in case.

I reached up and laid my hand over his chest, just beneath the olive branch inked near his collarbone. I didn't just want to see this moment - I wanted to feel it. To know it was real. That no one could take it away.

His lips were slightly parted in sleep, his brow relaxed. His lashes twitched faintly - like he was dreaming something peaceful.

I wanted to be wrapped up in every part of him.

Leaning in, I pressed my lips to his - soft, intentional. The closest thing to heaven I'd ever touched. He stirred beneath me, arms instinctively tightening around my waist. I felt his hand drift to my back just before he shifted to hover over me, pulling back only enough to meet my eyes.

"Well… good morning," he said, voice gravelly, teasing - but his gaze was earnest.

I smiled, small and sure.

His thumb traced a slow circle along my hip as he looked down at me, eyes flicking over my face like he was cataloging every detail. I reached up, brushing the back of my fingers along the stubble on his jaw, and felt the corner of his mouth tug upward.

"You're staring," I whispered, though I didn't really mind.

"Can you blame me?" he murmured, dipping lower until his forehead rested gently against mine.

Our breath mingled in the quiet morning. No rush. No urgency. Just the steady press of skin and the simple luxury of feeling safe in someone else's arms.

His hand slid up my side, fingertips catching on the hem of my shirt - *his* shirt - and I lifted my arms as he gently pulled it over my head, slow and reverent. My hands found the band of his pants next, fingers grazing warm skin as I eased them off.

There was nothing frantic in the way we moved. No desperation.

Just soft touches. Lingering kisses. Familiarity woven with the curiosity of something new.

I pulled him closer, and he kissed the corner of my mouth, then my jaw, then the scar on my neck just below my ear. I exhaled shakily, grounding myself in the press of his chest against mine.

This wasn't about proving anything or silencing demons.
This was choosing each other.

Letting ourselves be chosen.
Letting love live in the quiet space between breaths.

SAM

The smell of coffee filled the apartment as I sat cross-legged on the couch in one of his sweatshirts and the softest pair of boxers I could steal from his drawer.

Elliot hummed something under his breath as he poured into our matching mugs - handmade, speckled pottery he'd picked up from a market somewhere on a business trip. He handed mine over, leaning down to press a kiss to the crown of my head before plopping onto the couch beside me.

"You've officially ruined me for boring mornings," he said, wrapping an arm around my shoulders.

I smiled sheepishly into my coffee. "They're still allowed to be boring. Just not lonely."

He glanced sideways at me, that small, crooked smile I loved tugging at his lips. "You plan on making this a habit, then?"

"What, the morning-after coffee or the stealing your clothes part?"

He laughed. "All of it."

I didn't answer right away. I just tucked my feet under his thigh and rested my head on his shoulder.

Maybe I didn't have all the answers. Maybe the road ahead was still winding. But for now? For this quiet, gentle morning? This felt like home.

• • •

By the time I made it to the cafe, the morning rush had just passed. The place smelled like espresso and caramel syrup, and Bill had some old jazz vinyl spinning low through the shop speakers.

Andrew leaned against the counter, sleeves rolled to his elbows and a mischievous grin already cocked on his face like a loaded slingshot.

"Well, well, well," he said, drumming his fingers on the back of the espresso machine. "Look who's glowing like she just walked off the set of a skincare commercial."

I rolled my eyes and hung my jacket on the hook behind the counter. "You're impossible."

"Is it the coffee? The love? The, shall we say, *thoroughly satisfying* night of sleep?" He wiggled his eyebrows.

I chucked a rag at him, but I couldn't help the grin tugging at my lips. "Don't you have something better to do?"

"Not when I have front-row seats to the unfolding romance of the year," he declared dramatically. "I mean, do I *even* need to finish my screenplay when I have you and Elliot for inspiration."

I moved behind the counter and started restocking cups, but Andrew leaned in closer, his voice softer now.

"Seriously, though... You seem different. Lighter."

I paused. "Yeah… I think I am."

He didn't push. Just gave a nod, then wandered back toward his laptop.

The bell over the door chimed and I instinctively glanced up, my smile fading ever so slightly as I registered the woman stepping in.

Not Laurel.

But someone who *looked* like her.

Same build. Same length of hair. Same piercing eyes that scanned the shop and lingered a second too long. I froze, heart skipping a beat, until the woman turned away and began perusing the menu like any other customer.

Just a stranger.

Still, the unease slithered back into my chest - uninvited and all too familiar.

The warmth of the morning hadn't left completely… but something cold had crept in through the cracks. And suddenly I wasn't sure if the rest of the day would be quite so peaceful.

• • •

I tried to shake the feeling. Chalked it up to too much caffeine and too little sleep. I even managed to get through the next couple of hours without spiraling. But when I stepped into the back to grab more filters and came back out again -

He was there.

Marcus.

Leaning against the counter like he'd been coming here every day for years. Like he belonged.

"Can I help you with something?" I asked, hesitant.

Marcus ignored the question, eyes trained on me like he'd just found something worth hunting.

"Sam," he said, low and even, like he was talking to an old friend. "Glad you're here."

I stiffened, my hands still holding the filters, crinkling them in my grip. "We're busy today, Marcus."

There was no one in line.

"I just wanted to talk." His eyes sparkled with something that made my stomach drop. "It's been a while. Thought maybe you'd be friendlier after all this time."

Andrew clocked my discomfort and pulled off his headphones, rising from his seat slowly. "Hey, buddy. Can I help you with something?"

Marcus' head twitched at Andrew's voice. Didn't face him. Just made a movement like you'd make trying to keep a bug from flying in your ear.

"You're making our patrons uncomfortable," I said, my voice firmer than I expected. "I think you should leave."

"You sure it's not just *you* that's uncomfortable?" he asked, feigning concern. "You always were a little… reactive. I guess some people don't ever change, no matter how hard they try."

The fuck? Does he know something?

The air in the room felt thick. Still.

I wasn't going to give him the satisfaction of a flinch. Of a reaction.

"This isn't a place for whatever game you're trying to play," Andrew said, stepping more fully between us. "You need to go. Now."

Marcus looked like he wanted to argue, but instead, he glanced around the shop - saw the eyes watching, the way even our regulars were tense - and let out a forced chuckle.

"Fine," he muttered. "But I'll be seeing you around, Sammy."

He pushed off the counter and walked out like he'd just won a prize.

As soon as the door closed, I dropped the filters and backed toward the storage room, breath caught halfway up my throat.

Andrew didn't follow right away. He stood there, staring out the front door, perched like a predator ready to move in for the kill in case Marcus came back.

I grabbed at my necklace, trying to slow my quickening breath. I leaned against the back wall and bent slightly over, my attempt to avoid a full-on panic attack feeble at best.

When I finally looked up, finally felt my heart beating in the right direction again, Andrew stood there - arms crossed, jaw tight, and eyes filled with a quiet rage I'd never seen in him before.

"He doesn't need to come back in here," he said flatly.

"I'm sorry," I whispered.

"Don't be," he said, turning to look at me finally. "It's nothing for *you* to be sorry about. Just… tell Elliot, okay? And Bill and Jessa."

I nodded.

And this time, I didn't wait. I reached for my phone with shaking hands and started typing.

Hey. I need to talk to you. Marcus came into the shop again.

• • •

Elliot was already in the kitchen when I walked in, a glass of water halfway to his lips. The second he saw me, his eyes swept over me like he was counting visible wounds.

"You okay?" he asked, setting the glass down, voice tight with worry.

The elevator door closed behind me and I leaned against it for a beat longer than I meant to. "He was there again."

He already knew. That's why he left work early. Why he was home.

He didn't speak at first. His eyes still flicked over me scanning for damage.

"Did he touch you?"

"Again, no," I said, shaking my head. "He just… talked. Said things that made me feel like I was losing it. Like *I* was the problem."

He stepped forward, stopping just shy of touching me. "Do you want to sit? Or lie down for a bit?"

I shook my head again. "I can't sit. I can't be still right now. I feel like my skin's too tight."

Elliot waited, gave me the space to keep going. I could tell he wanted to do something - anything - but he didn't rush me.

"I think I need to run," I said eventually. "Just… go. Burn some of this out of my body."

"A run?" he repeated. Not entirely judgemental. Just surprised.

"Yeah," I said, forcing a smile. "I know it's been a while. I just - I need to move. I feel like if I don't, I might come apart."

He rubbed the back of his neck, jaw flexing again. "Okay. Main roads? And take Coop?"

"Promise."

"And your phone stays on?"

"Always."

"I still don't like it," he said, finally closing the distance between us. His voice was softer now. Low and steady. "But I know you. And I trust you to know what you need."

I reached up and touched his chest, briefly pressing my hand just over his heart. He covered it with his own, thumb brushing the scar behind my knuckles.

"Thank you. For not trying to stop me."

"Just… don't be gone too long, okay?"

"I won't," I said, already pulling away. "I just need to find a little quiet in my head again."

And then I turned, laced up my shoes by the door, harnessed Cooper up, and stepped back into the elevator - trying to remember how it felt to outrun something you couldn't see.

• • •

The early evening air wrapped around me like a breath I couldn't quite catch. Not cold. Not warm. Just unsettled.

My shoes pounded against the sidewalk in a rhythm that tried desperately to drown out the static in my chest. Left, right. Left, right. Each step a protest. A prayer. A release.

I hadn't run in weeks. My lungs burned by the second block, but it felt *good* - like I was clawing my way back into my own body.

The streets were quieter than usual. Too quiet for this part of town, even on a weekday. I clocked it, but didn't slow down.

Main roads. I'd promised Elliot. I stuck to them at first.

But there was this shortcut - a stretch behind some buildings near the edge of a park. It wasn't *technically* off-limits, just… less visible.

I hesitated when I reached the mouth of the alleyway. Looked down the cracked concrete, weeds spurting up the sides of buildings that whispered warnings I couldn't quite hear. But I kept going. Because the tightness in my chest still hadn't loosened, and I didn't want to stop until it did.

The sidewalk narrowed. My breath fogged in front of me. The echo of my footsteps sounded a little too much like someone was near, but I shook it off.

You're just jumpy. You've been through a lot. Nothing's going to happen.

My hair tossed to the side and I could have sworn someone touched me.

I whipped around, heart in my throat.

No one.

Just Cooper and shadows and wind and my own spiraling pulse.

I turned back, started to run again - faster now. Cooper trailed behind me. The burning in my calves was sharper, adrenaline surging with each stride. My phone buzzed in my pocket. Elliot, probably checking in. I didn't stop to look.

Another footstep. Closer.

Then another. Not mine.

I turned sharply, too sharply, and skidded on the gritty sidewalk.

A blur of movement.

Too fast.

Too close.

I didn't have time to scream. Just enough to scramble backward and try to turn -

Something slammed into me.

Pain exploded across the side of my head, and the world tilted hard.

My knees hit the ground. Hands scraped raw.

Everything blurred.

There were hands - rough, unkind - grabbing for my jacket. Pulling. Holding.

"No-" I choked out, struggling, legs kicking wildly against the unforgiving ground.

I clawed at the air, at the ground, at *him*, but the edges of the world were folding in too fast.

I couldn't breathe.

Couldn't fight.

Couldn't-

SAM

I always feared dying this way.

I thought about death often - how it would happen, when - but each time my mind drifted there, *this* is what made my stomach turn into knots. Alone. Cold. Miserable...

How long have I been here? Elliot will be panicking by now. Time trickles by as a hazy unknown, blurred by the pounding in my head and the seemingly spinning shadows around me. Each shallow inhale jabs at my lungs, and I will myself to stop breathing altogether, but the pain only escalates. *Fuck.*

I cough, blood spurting in droplets onto my face and the red-soaked pavement around me. Where's that even coming from? A tangled golden-brown stream of hair seems to attempt to soak up the bleeding, a foam cup trying to salvage a sinking ship as I prepare myself to drown. A hollow shiver rushes through my body. I try to scream, but no sound escapes.

He cracks the door open, peering in from the dimly-lit hallway. He checks over his shoulder and makes his way into my bedroom. I pretend to sleep, knowing it won't do any good but hoping by some miracle it works this time. He rips the covers back, grabs my ankle, and in one swift motion I'm tumbling to the floor. His boot presses into the side of my head.

A sharp pop in my ribs jolts me back to reality, and I can't tell if it's better or worse than the echoes of my past toying with my consciousness. I will myself over the edge I'm teetering on, praying that if there happens to be some sick version of a god out there he'd let me find relief in death. If life requires this kind of pain, there's no way I'm sticking around to take part in it.

I reached up and laid my hand over his chest, just beneath the olive branch inked near his collarbone. Leaning in, I pressed my lips to his - soft, intentional. The closest thing to heaven I'd ever touched. He stirred beneath me, arms instinctively tightening around my waist. I felt his hand drift to my back just before he shifted to hover over me, pulling back only enough to meet my eyes.

My throat fills with blood, and I cough some of it up again through clenched teeth. Crumpled on gritty concrete, I'm such a sorry excuse for a human. Even with my small frame I had never felt so feeble. How can I be so weak and *still* holding on? I never imagined I'd want to give up. Not after everything I'd made it through. Not after finding Elliot. But the nothingness of death would be a sweet relief.

I sob hoarsely with all the air I can muster.

"Fuuuuuu-"

Elliot

She should be back by now.

I grab my keys and press the elevator button and jab it again when it doesn't call fast enough. Before it can reach me, my phone begins to buzz in my hand. It's the front desk.

"Hello?"

"Mr. Flint, I've got Cooper here in the lobby. He showed up outside the door, but Ms. Reynolds wasn't with him." He sounds concerned.

My stomach jumps to my throat, and I almost lose it.

"I'm on my way."

I run down the stairs, too stirred up to wait on the elevator.

By the time I reach the bottom, I'm breathless and I can't tell if it's the cardio or the catastrophising. Cooper's pacing next to the doorman, whining, eyes wide, nostrils flared, hackles raised. I've never seen him so panicked.

"Thank you," I huff out, taking the leash. "Did you see where he came from?"

He shakes his head, a mix of remorse and pity flooding his face. "Mr. Flint, if there's anything I can do…"

Where could she be? What happened to her? Dammit, Flint, next steps.

I blink hard and thrust the leash back at him. I turn toward the front door, half jogging away. "Can you take him upstairs? Please? Just leave him in the penthouse, he'll be fine on his own. Thank you."

Cooper barks at me, helplessly frantic as I fling the door open. I can't bother with him right now.

I grab my phone out of my pocket and hastily dial 911.

I don't know where I'm running. I just know I've got to find her, and fast.

• • •

I pace the waiting room floor, impatient for someone to fill me in. She's back there somewhere. Pained. I'm out here, a different kind of pained entirely, but pained nonetheless. Someone had stumbled across her and called it in already. I'd flown, hazards on, barely stopping at red lights. All to sit and wait and be told there's nothing I can do right now. I can't even see her.

This place is dreadfully dull, the type of dull that drags and pulls on the clock hands. Patients and families of a number of sorts sit waiting their turn, staring at blank walls and game shows on the tv. A couple of children play at a kid's station, entirely oblivious to the ailments plaguing the people around them. A woman in the corner feeds cheerios to her toddler, and a man at the reception desk casually sips his coffee.

A woman in light gray scrubs busts through the double wooden doors, looking frantically around the room. I stand, knowing as soon as my eyes meet hers that she's looking for me. And it's not good.

"Mr. Flint?"

I nod. I can't bring myself to talk, to ask questions.

"Please, follow me."

I walk hurriedly beside her through a door she had to scan her key card to get into. We hurriedly make our way down a hall to a private room and my gait slows.

God, this can't be good.

"We're doing all we can," she started, her voice somber. "She's... not in good shape. We're trying to get her stable enough for surgery."

I know what she's saying is important, but I can't focus. My ears are ringing and betraying me by zeroing in on the distant sounds of beeping machines and chattering doctors and the clanging of medical tools.

She mentions something about her ribs and internal bleeding. A ruptured spleen. A lacerated liver. A baby. My eyes shoot up at her from their daze, tears threatening at the edge.

"I'm sorry, what?"

"I don't know if we're going to be able to save the baby," she repeats.

No.

"She... she's pregnant?"

A knowing, solemn look washes over her. "You didn't know."

I'm quiet a moment. All of life's major questions swirling in my brain. But only one matters. "She's alive now?"

"She is, but Mr. Flint, I have to warn you, the outlook isn't good."

She asks if I have any other questions. I don't. Not now. I can't think straight. Tears begin to fall as we make our way back to the waiting room where all I can do is sit. Wait.

Goddammit pull it together. She's alive now. Focus on that.

When we reach the lobby again, Ashley's there, concern plastered all over her as she paces in her white coat.

"I came down as soon as I heard. How is she?"

I break.

"Oh, Elliot," She reaches out and takes me into her arms, and I crumble like a paper left out in the rain.

I decide to keep the pregnancy to myself for now. It feels sacred somehow—like the last piece of Sam the world hasn't taken from me yet.

I pull back and wipe my face with the palm of my hand. "God, this is… I don't know what to do."

Ashley grabs my hand and takes a seat, tugging on my hand lightly to encourage me to do the same. "Unfortunately, there's nothing you *can* do. It's out of your hands right now."

"But what the *fuck* am I supposed to *do*, Ashley?" I sigh, exasperated.

She shakes her head silently, finally understanding that I meant more than just what I could tangibly, physically do in the moment.

"I just got her…" I whisper.

Ashley places her hand on my shoulder. "I know."

The chair feels too small to hold everything inside me. The tears don't stop, they just fall quieter now. More honest. More exhausted.

She's pregnant. Hurt. Fighting for her life beyond these walls.

And I've never felt more useless.

A doctor walks by, waving to Ashley with a smile that feels impossibly too joyful for this moment. His pager chimes, and I hear the words that make my blood stick still in my veins.

"Trauma team, room seven. Trauma team, room seven,"

I don't know if that's her room. I don't know anything. But worst-case scenarios flood my mind.

I've never bargained with the universe. Always felt too small for it to listen. But now I offer it everything - every good deed I've ever done, every second I have left, every piece of me - just to keep her breathing.

"Take anything else," I whisper into the hollow of my palms. "Just… not her. Not them."

• • •

Two uniformed officers pull us back into a private room. They try to ask Ashley to stand by in the waiting room, but she won't have it. Bless her.

"I already told you, I don't know what route she ran," I sigh, exasperated. "I just… Marcus. Whatever-the-fuck his last name is, I don't know. But he's been stalking her at work. You have to look into him."

One of them nods, jotting down illegible notes on a too-tiny notepad. The other stands, statuesque and emotionless at the door.

"Talk to Bill and Jessa Stone, the owners? They'll be able to give you more information," Ashley says in a calming, helpful tone.

Then, a knock at the door.

"Mr. Flint?"

I stand.

"Yes, that's me."

As soon as I see the nurse's face, my mouth runs dry. Bile hangs in the back of my throat. My legs begin to tremble under me.

"It's time."

Time? She's fucking dying and that's all you're going to give me is "it's time?"

"Time?" I choke out.

Ashley rises slowly next to me. "Elliot…"

The nurse steps closer, her expression carved from sorrow. "She's going into surgery now. If you want to see her before we take her back… this is the moment."

My heart stops. Starts again. Too fast. Too hard.

I stare at her, unable to move.

Ashley nudges my arm gently. "Go," she whispers. "She'll want to see you."

I hardly breathe the whole time we walk the hallway - just a blur of white walls, the hum of fluorescent lights, the squeak of my shoes against the polished floor. My body moves on instinct, like it always knows the way to her.

When we reach the room, she looks small. Too small, pale against the sheets, tubes and wires tangled around her like someone tried to anchor her to the world and wasn't sure she'd stay.

"Sam," I breathe, stepping closer as the nurse moves aside. "Hey, darling. I'm here."

She doesn't wake. Doesn't stir.

I take her hand anyway. It's cold.

"Don't go," I whisper, throat tightening. "Not yet. Not like this… please."

The surgical team wheels her toward the double doors. I keep my hand in hers for as long as they allow, until they pry our fingers apart gently - too gently - and the doors close between us.

And suddenly the hallway feels too quiet.
Too empty.
Too real.

ELLIOT

It had been heaven just moments ago.

Her eyes were brilliantly curious. They'd shimmer with flecks of gold when happiness found her. And, in spite of all her hurt, she did find happiness often. When her hair would hold in a messy knot on top of her head, just so. When she first smelled her morning coffee. When she watched me cook thinking I wouldn't notice. As soon as I saw it, I knew the existence of her merriment was my life's call.

She's dead for three days now.

I slouch in my library chair. Bourbon undeserving of a glass made its way to my lips. Fond memories pierce my chest. I want so badly to forget, or to be so drowned in the bottle that her memory becomes my reality. But I am painfully caught somewhere between.

How could I have let this happen?

She should have stayed. I should have made her stay. If I could go back, I would never let her out of my sight again. She'd still be here. We'd be on our way to a little family.

I begin to wonder if she'd known about the baby. She couldn't have. They'd said she was only a short few weeks along. She would have been scared shitless, but I know she would have made the best mother.

I press the rim of the bottle to my lips again. It burns less this time. Maybe I'm getting used to it. Or maybe I want it to hurt.

I stare blankly out the window across the skyline, the haze of the city glowing in the distance. Sam loved the way it looked at night - how the streetlights blinked like fireflies if you squinted hard enough.

I can't stop seeing her. Not the mangled version in the hospital. The *real* her. The one who stole my sweaters and got chocolate in the bedsheets and danced only when she thought no one was watching and hummed to make her coffee.

My chest caves in on itself.

I think of the last time she touched me - how her hand brushed my chest that morning like she was trying to memorize the feeling of being alive.

Did she know?

The elevator gears grind softly and the doors slide open. I don't look up.

"Elliot?" It's Ashley. Her voice is soft, like she's trying not to spook a wild animal. "I brought food."

I nod once. I don't think I've eaten. Maybe ever.

She steps closer and sets the bag on the table, eyes landing on the bottle in my lap. She kneels down beside me and rests a hand on my knee.

"She wouldn't want this," she whispers.

My jaw tightens. "She didn't get a say."

Silence.

"She loved you," Ashley says, voice breaking just slightly. "She would've married you. Raised a baby with you. She was… *so* happy, Elliot."

A sob shoves its way up my throat before I can stop it.

"I was supposed to protect her." The words fall like stones. "That was all I had to do. And I didn't."

Ashley doesn't tell me it's not my fault. She doesn't offer any platitude about time healing or Sam being in a better place.

She just stays.

It's not enough. But I guess now it has to be.

• • •

The elevator whirrs again, the sound crawling under my skin. I wasn't expecting anyone. Not that it mattered. Expectation hasn't meant much lately.

The friendly little *ding* feels like mockery.

Andrew storms out before the doors even finish opening, pushing past me like he owns the place. Cooper doesn't move from the couch. He lifts his head, sighs, and lays back down - grieving in his own quiet way.

"Jesus, Flint," Andrew says, voice raw. "You look like you've been hit by a bus."

The elevator doors close behind him with a soft hiss, sealing us in.

"Feels like it," I mutter.

He turns, and for a moment I almost don't recognize him. His eyes are bloodshot, hair a mess, and his hands - Christ, his hands are shaking.

"You want to explain to me how the fuck this happened?"

I stare at him, hollow. "I don't have an explanation."

He paces - back and forth, back and forth - the sound of his shoes scraping the floor syncing with the pounding in my head. "She was safe. She was *finally safe*, and now she's-" His voice breaks off. He drags a trembling hand over his face, fury and grief twisting into something unrecognizable. "You were supposed to keep her safe, man."

"I know," I snap, louder than I mean to. "You think I haven't been replaying it? Every second? I didn't let her go because I didn't care, Andrew. I let her go because I believed her when she said she'd be fine."

He slams his hand on the back of a kitchen chair. It cracks against the counter and rattles. "Well she *wasn't*, was she?"

The words slice through the air.

I take a step forward. "Don't you think I fucking know that?"

We're both breathing hard now, two live wires sparking in a room too small for both of us.

"She trusted you," he says, quieter but sharper. "She finally trusted someone."

"And I failed her," I bite out. "Congratulations, you can stop circling it and just say it."

He looks like he might hit me. For a split second, I want him to. I want the bruise, something I can point to and say *this is where it hurts*.

Instead, he deflates. "Goddammit, Elliot," he says, voice breaking. "I'm angry because I don't know what else to be. I'm angry because she was *so close* to being happy."

I glance at the bourbon bottle on the counter, its amber reflection staring back at me like an accusation. "Join the club."

He follows my gaze but doesn't comment. His voice softens "She talked about you, you know? Nonstop. Said you made her laugh more than she thought she ever would again. She was *hopeful*. I haven't seen her like that, maybe ever." His voice breaks on the last word.

I rake a hand through my hair. "I can't stop seeing her. In the hospital bed. How broken she was before they took her back and she-"

My voice cracks, too. The word won't come.

Andrew turns away, jaw trembling. "Don't."

"She was pregnant," I whisper.

He freezes. Then, sharply: "What?"

I nod, eyes burning. "A few weeks along. I don't think *she* even knew yet."

He sinks onto the couch like the air's been punched out of him. Silence swallows everything - the hum of the fridge, the soft sigh of Cooper's breath, still lingering on the couch.

"I would've married her," I say. "Tomorrow. I don't care where. Courthouse. Church. Living room. Didn't matter. I just… wanted her."

Andrew rubs his face with both hands, elbows on his knees. "You made her happy," he says, hoarse. "In a way I didn't think anyone ever could."

"I didn't give her forever."

"No." His eyes glisten, red and wet. "But you gave her peace. And she chose you, Elliot. Every damn day."

For a long time, we just sit there in the wreckage of everything she left behind.

Finally, he lets out a shaky laugh. "She'd kick our asses if she saw us like this."

"Yeah," I manage. "She'd be barking orders already."

He stands, wipes his eyes roughly. "I'm checking on you tomorrow. Don't pretend you're okay."

"I won't."

He presses the elevator button, waits in silence. When the doors open, he looks back at me.

"And Elliot?"

I lift my eyes.

"We're *going* to find him. You hear me? We're not letting it end like this."

The doors close on his words, leaving me alone in the quiet again. Only this time, it isn't quiet - it's screaming.

. . .

"Dammit, Cooper," I sigh as he lays on the couch. "It's been hours. I know you have to pee. Come the fuck on."

I wave the leash around like a madman. He doesn't lift his head. Doesn't give that quintessential tail flick he always did when he *knew* he was being obstinate. Doesn't even offer a conciliatory sigh.

I make my way over to him and clip the hook to his collar, and only then does he slink off the couch, head hung low.

And now I feel guilty. He's missing her as much as I am, and god only knows what he witnessed. I'm trying to forgive him. I really am. For leaving her there. Like that.

He did what he could. I have to believe that.

We saunter out onto the pavement and toward the pet relief area. The sun beats down, the wind blowing a dry chill through the air as winter creeps over the city.

The world stops spinning and I've still gotta take the dog to piss.

I shiver and shove my hands in my pockets.

She would have made fun of me for not wearing a jacket. I can practically hear it. *You a little chilly, Flint?*

Hot tears threaten to spill out onto my cheeks, and I sniffle.

"Would you hurry up?"

Cooper gives me a subtle side eye and lowers his head back down, taking his time sniffing out a spot to do his business.

He finally circles, lifts his leg, and does what we came out here to do. And the moment he's done, he turns back to me and nudges my shin - gentle, like he's checking if I'm still here.

I crouch down and bury my face in his fur.

"Yeah," I whisper. My voice cracks. "I miss her, too."

For a moment, the world tilts again, unsteady, unbearable. But Cooper presses closer.

And I hang on.

Elliot

I fiddle with the business card in my hand for Detective Gabby Perez. There's a bite in the air that nips at my ears and my nose. I shuffle my feet as I walk, unsure if I'd stay upright if I picked either of them up fully, and push my way into the police station.

The officer behind the desk smiles a little too bright, a little like he's bragging about the fact that he didn't just lose the love of his life to a tragic murder.

"What can I do for you this morning?"

"Find the bastard that killed my girlfriend," I snap, breezing past the reception and straight to the back to find Detective Perez's office.

Girlfriend. God it sounds so casual. So childish. Like she wasn't the entire world.

She's in the middle of a phone call when I enter the room. Her desk is covered with folders - neatly stacked, sure, but the sheer volume is chaos. Her dark eyes meet mine, irritation flickering before sympathy washes over it.

"I'm going to have to call you back…" She hangs up and folds her hands. "Mr. Flint. I-"

"Let's not do the formalities," I cut her off. "I know you're working. I *see* you're trying. But it's not enough. You've got to give me something."

She raises her eyebrows but stays measured. "Actually, Elliot, I was going to call you this morning. We've got something. Now, it's not much. But it's progress."

Progress. What a useless word.

"What is it?"

"We've been in touch with the sister… Laurel Prickett? You familiar?"

I give a half nod, stopping somewhere in the middle. "Just. Sam's… she had a tricky relationship with her."

I still haven't gotten used to her only being in the past-tense.

"She gave us some information we're going to look into. There was a man she had talked to a few times recently. Ms. Prickett didn't seem convinced he was important, but we are following every lead to try to bring some form of closure here."

I scoff. *Closure*. She brushes over it without offense.

"Have you seen this man before?" Perez lays a vague sketch in front of me.

My eyes study it deeply, and I wrack my brain for any semblance of him. Maybe early 50s. Thin but not frail. Light hair and short facial hair that wraps above his mouth and below his chin. Prominent frown lines…

I pinch the inside of my cheek between my teeth to keep tears from welling up. "No. No, I haven't. Is that Marcus?"

"No, like I said, we're running down multiple leads, Mr. Flint. And anyway, it's still helpful to know that you haven't seen him around," she offers, fully knowing it won't do anything to pacify me. "We're going to find the person that did this…"

"You *better*."

I stand too fast, the chair rattling behind me. I need air. I need out.

"Mr. Flint?" Her voice stops me at the door. I pause, hand on the handle.

"Lay off the sauce," she says, voice low. "It won't bring her back."

I clench my jaw. Swallow the scream. And leave without a word.

Elliot

A light fall of snow dusts the city outside and flurries through the air. The sky is wet. Heavy. Mourning.

What a day to put her in the ground.

It's quiet.

I haven't played music since she left. Once upon a time you couldn't find me without something playing through the speakers. Now, it just… doesn't feel right.

Cooper swirls at my feet, anxious. I'm no replacement for her. I never will be.

I kneel down beside him, smoothing a hand over his fur. His eyes meet mine and, for a moment, we just exist there - two living things clinging to the memory of someone who made us whole. "I know, buddy," I whisper. "I know."

My suit feels like a costume. Black wool, crisp collar, shoes too polished. It's not who I am, and it sure as hell isn't who she fell in love with. But I'll wear it - for her. For her chosen family. For the closure no one actually gets from days like this.

I double check my tie in the mirror. Ashley offered to ride over with me, but I told her no. I need to walk into this alone. And sober. I owe her that much.

The car ride is silent. Cooper stays home, staring at the door like he knows something important is happening and he's being left behind. I nearly break and stay. Just sit beside him on the floor and let the rest of the world keep spinning without me. But I made promises. Too late, but promises nonetheless. To Sam. To her people. And I'll keep them.

• • •

The chapel is full of unknown faces when I arrive. Some vaguely familiar, maybe coffee shop patrons. I scan each face, searching for familiarity. Or maybe some semblance of the sketch Perez had slid in front of me.

Bill and Jessa are near the front, sitting stiffly. Jessa clutches a damp tissue in one hand and Bill's arm in the other. Andrew's there too, hands clasped awkwardly in front of him, eyes red but resolute. My parents hover toward the back, sure to give distance for the sorrow we all carried. Even Perez came. She stands in the far back like a shadow, her badge tucked away, her grief at a professional level.

I make my way to the front, heart thudding, throat dry. Her photo is everywhere - at the entrance, at the front of the altar, tucked beside the bouquet that rests just beneath her urn.

God.

She's ash.

I force myself into a seat.

The minister clears his throat and begins with pleasantries that feel like splinters working under my flesh. Words like *celebration of life* and *a beautiful soul taken too soon* are spoken with delicate reverence, but none of them are Sam. Not really.

I can't focus. Not until Jessa stands and walks - wobbles - to the front.

She starts to speak and her voice cracks. But she holds steady.

"Sam was... infuriatingly independent. Fiercely kind. And the bravest woman I've ever known. She saw people. She really *saw* them. Their pain, their needs, their potential. And if you were lucky enough to be loved by her..." Her voice breaks again. "You know what I mean."

I nod, tears flowing down my cheeks freely now.

She collects herself. "There's so much I could say, but most importantly is this: Sam taught me how to love people where they are. Even when they're messy. Even when they push you away... especially then."

She leaves the podium and returns to her seat. I can see her shoulders trembling as Bill wraps an arm around her.

Then silence.

Then-

"Elliot?"

I glance up, startled. The minister is looking at me.

"Would you like to say something?"

I hadn't planned on speaking. I didn't think I could.

But I stand.

Every step to the front feels like a betrayal. Like I'm walking toward an ending I still haven't accepted. I grip the sides of the wooden stand in front of me, staring down at the paper I don't have.

"I wasn't supposed to be here today," I start, voice hoarse. "I was supposed to be at home, trying to convince Sam that we should paint the guest room. Or figure out how to screw up her coffee order on purpose just to hear her rant about it. I was supposed to kiss her before work this morning. I was supposed to *still* have her."

Silence. A few scattered sniffles.

"She was the first person who didn't make me feel like I had to have it all together. She made me realize that showing up imperfectly was enough… *That* fixed me."

I swallow the lump in my throat. Make eye contact with my mom. She tilts her head just slightly, sympathy and sadness for her youngest child - her *golden boy* - in full display.

"I lost a brother when I was young. And I thought I'd learned what grief was. But I was just a kid. Sam…" I look toward the urn, my voice softening. "Sam taught me that loss is the cost of loving deeply. And god, did she make the cost worth it. Every tear I shed is a sign that she was real, and that she was mine to love for a little while. So I'm going to keep loving her. However I can."

My voice breaks, but I finish. "I'll carry her every day. Because she carried so much she didn't deserve."

I step down. Sit. Clutch the program in my hand so tightly it nearly tears.

She'd probably tell me I looked like a wreck. Then kiss me anyway.

The service moves on without me. Music plays - something soft and vaguely spiritual - but all I can hear is the echo of her laugh, the way she'd sing off key just to make me smile.

I don't remember how long I sit there after it's over. Long enough for people to pass and murmur condolences. Long enough for the light in the stained glass to shift.

Eventually, Jessa comes to rest a hand on my shoulder. "She'd be proud of you," she says, her voice steady but worn.

I nod, eyes on the urn.

But I don't feel proud.

I just feel the weight of loving someone so much that saying goodbye doesn't feel like the end. It feels like the middle of a sentence. And I'll be searching for the rest of it, always.

•••

The last handful of guests drift away from the graveyard path, their words muffled by snowfall and sorrow. I stay back. I'm not ready to leave her - not yet.

The urn rests in the memorial wall now, tucked beneath the engraving that still feels like a misprint.

SAMANTHA GRACE REYNOLDS

1996 – 2025

A fierce and tender soul

God, she was.

I shift my weight, digging gloved hands into my coat pockets. I still can't bring myself to speak aloud. My voice doesn't feel like it belongs here - too alive for a place so quiet.

Footsteps crunch over the thin layer of snow behind me.

Laurel.

She comes to stand just behind and beside me, close enough to be seen, far enough not to be mistaken for comfort.

"I wasn't sure I should come," she says, her voice surprisingly steady.

I nod once. "But you did."

"She was my sister."

I glance toward her. Her coat is sharp - elegant in a way that clashes with the very essence of her being. Her lipstick is too dark for a winter morning. And yet, the circles under her eyes are real. Tired. Worn.

"I'm sorry for your loss," I say, because it feels like the only honest thing I can offer.

Laurel lets out a quiet breath, as if she doesn't know whether to thank me or be offended.

"She was… complicated," she says after a beat. "I think I tried to be mad at her for things that weren't her fault. And she tried to be strong for things she shouldn't have had to carry."

"She carried it all anyway," I say, voice low with a tinge of frustration. "That's who she was."

Laurel nods faintly. "Yeah. She always had this… intensity. Like she wanted to feel everything, even when it broke her."

We lapse into silence again. Her for lack of words. Me because I couldn't keep this conversation going without exploding. Laurel looks at the stone, then at me.

"She loved you, you know."

"I know."

"I wasn't always… kind to her," she says. "And I'm not going to pretend we made it right. But I did reach out."

"I know that, too."

She tilts her head, eyes narrowed slightly. "I don't expect forgiveness."

I don't offer it.

Instead, I murmur, "You're not the villain, Laurel. But you were the wound that never quite closed."

She flinches - just barely - but doesn't fight it. Instead, she straightens her coat.

"I'll go," she says.

She turns without another word, her boots crunching softly as she disappears back down the path.

I don't watch her go.

She looks good. Too good. Polished. Practiced. A walking reminder of everything Sam had to unlearn to survive.

She looks good - for wasted potential.

I turn back to the stone. My fingers rest against Sam's name. The snowfall thickens, clinging to the corners of my coat, the grooves of the lettering.

"I'll come back tomorrow," I whisper. "I don't know what else to do."

And I walk away in silence through the snow.

Elliot

The sun blazes hard on the opposite side of the drawn shades, peeking through in slivers to my otherwise dark apartment. The air inside is still. Heavy. Dry.

It's just like this now without her.

It's been a week since her funeral, and I've relived the same day seven times over. Wake up. Sob. Drag Cooper out of the house. Hole back up. Sob some more. Drink til I almost forget. Almost.

God, she'd be so disappointed in us.

The elevator whirrs, the first time today, and I brace myself for another of Ashley's drop-ins.

Not Ashley.

"Elliot?" Jessa's voice slips through the door before she does. It's like sunlight trying to press through a storm.

I stand slowly, the bourbon still warm in my hand though I'd forgotten the last sip. I don't bother trying to hide the wreckage behind me - the half-filled glass, the rumpled blanket on the couch, the silence so thick it could choke a man.

She steps in, holding a brown paper bag and a reusable mug. "I made muffins," she says as if that explains everything.

I don't have the energy to respond.

She sets the bag down gently on the kitchen counter, eyes scanning the apartment like she's afraid of what she might see. "It's quiet in here."

I offer a humorless smile. "That's kind of the problem."

She doesn't respond. Just moves through the space. Cautious. She pauses at the bookshelf and runs her fingers along the spine of one of Sam's mystery novels. I hadn't even noticed it.

She turns, her voice softer now. "You look like hell."

"That's because I live there."

Her brow furrows, but she doesn't chide me. Doesn't push. She just sits at the edge of the armchair, the one Sam used to read in with her knees tucked to her chest when no one else was home. "I know you're hurting…"

I don't reply.

She reaches into the bag and pulls out a blueberry muffin, wrapped in parchment. "She would have liked these. They've got lemon zest in them."

God. The sound of *she would have* burned more than the bourbon. And she was right. Sam *would* have loved them. That's the first pastry she ever gave me from the coffee shop - the time I couldn't make up my damn mind about what to order.

"She would've made fun of the shape," I mutter. "Called it a lopsided toadstool and eaten three anyway."

Jessa smiles, but her eyes brim. "Yeah. That sounds like her."

Silence falls between us again - this one a little softer. A little shared.

"She made you better," Jessa says eventually. "You carried each other well."

I grip the back of the couch. "It's not just losing her."

She looks up.

"It's that it didn't feel real before her. And now it does. Now it all *hurts* like it's real. Like she made the rest of my life snap into color, and now it's all bleeding out."

Jessa nods slowly. "That's what love does. And grief is just love with nowhere to go."

That cracks something open in my chest. Not wide. Just enough for air.

"She wouldn't want you to rot here," she adds gently, leaning forward to offer a consoling pat to Cooper. "I know that doesn't help. But she would want you to fight for her. The right way."

I sink into the couch finally, willing the cushions to swallow me whole.

After a long moment of silence stretches between us, "Jessa?" The *ss* sound stretches out a little too long, dripping with bourbon.

"Yeah?"

"Do you think she knew?"

Her brow lifts.

"About the baby."

She exhales, slow. Thoughtful. "Maybe. But I think she was always carrying something bigger than herself. That was the way she loved. Completely."

I nod. "I don't know how to carry it all without her."

Jessa leans forward and places the muffin in my hand. "One bite at a time."

∴

Cooper does not want to be here.

Honestly, I can't blame him.

He digs his heels in at the cemetery gate, nails scraping the gravel, giving me the same look he gives the vacuum cleaner: pure betrayal.

"Don't look at me like that," I grumble, tugging gently at the leash. My words slur just a little. "She'd be pissed if I didn't visit."

He snorts - actually snorts - and sits his ass down like a sack of wet cement.

"Cooper."

Nothing.

I drop my head back. "You're literally a German Shepherd *dog*. Why are you afraid of grass?"

He isn't, of course. He's afraid of this place. Neuroscientists could study this dog's emotional intelligence. Genius-level grief.

"I'll carry you," I threaten.

He stands immediately.

"Thought so," I say and start weaving down the gravel path, which in my current condition feels like walking on a boat made of loose marbles.

The bottle in my jacket clinks with each step. I didn't plan on bringing it. But it kept slipping back into my hand like it had something to say.

We reach her grave, and everything in me goes quiet, except the things that hurt.

Her name still looks wrong in stone. Too final, too neat. Sam was never tidy. She was a beautiful mess - chaos in a cardigan.

I sink down onto the cold ground, legs folding awkwardly beneath me. Cooper lies beside me, pressing his head against my thigh like he's trying to keep me from falling through the earth.

"Hey, darling," I whisper, voice cracking. "Sorry-sorry it's been… I don't know. Days? Years? Time's weird."

I pull out the bottle. Hold it up stupidly like I'm offering her a toast.

"I tried going without this tonight. I did. But then I had to go buy dog food, and one of your favorite songs was playing in the store. The pet store, Sam. And I'm pretty sure the worker thought I was having a stroke."

A shaky laugh, half humor, half wounded animal, escapes me.

"You would've made so much fun of me," I say. "You would've said, 'Flint, are you crying over a purple dog toy?' And I would've said yes. Because it was very cute, and I am very…" My throat closes. "Lost."

A breeze cuts through the cemetery, the kind that always made her walk a little faster. I can almost see it - see her - like a glitch in my vision.

"I don't know how to do this," I admit. "Any of it. I keep thinking I'll wake up and you'll be beside me telling me I talk in my sleep again. Or you'll text me some stupid meme you think is funnier than it is. Or Cooper will run to the door like he used to and-"

I stop.

My shoulders shake.

Cooper whines softly and nudges my hand. I scratch behind his ears.

"He's so damn loyal," I murmur. "Meanwhile I'm here, talking to dirt."

The dark humor tastes bitter.

"I don't know if you can hear me," I say. "But if you can... I miss you. And I'm sorry for every time I don't say it loud enough."

The bottle slips from my hand and rolls across the grass. I let it. I don't have the energy to chase anything anymore.

I lean forward, press my forehead to the top of the memorial wall, and the cold of it jolts something inside me. Sobering.

"I love you," I whisper. "More than my stupid heart knows what to do with."

Cooper lies down fully beside me now, curling his body around mine like he's trying to anchor me here - keep me from disappearing, too.

And in the dark, in a silent cemetery, with a dog who is grieving just as hard, I finally let myself sob without stopping.

Elliot

I made a mistake coming here.

I should've known when I stumbled my way to Biblioholic. When the hostess asked how many and I had to choke out, "Table for *one*." When I told her I changed my mind and wanted to sit at the bar. When I half collapsed into the barstool.

But I came anyway.

Memories of Sam feel like bruises I can't stop pressing - painful, tender, impossible not to touch.

The dim lighting. The hum of conversation. The sticky bartop she once wiped with a napkin, laughing because she swore she could feel every germ crawling across it.

She once sat right here and told me she didn't deserve nice things.

I remember placing my hand over hers, telling her she did. Believing it for both of us.

Now my glass is half empty, and I'm half gone, and all I can do is stare at the chair beside me and wait for her to walk in.

Then reality catches up like a steel bat to the ribs. She's not coming. Not ever again.

"We're never going to agree on this, are we?" She laughed the first true laugh I'd ever heard from her. "Nope," I said, smiling at her in that way that seemed to get under her skin. "But I love how hard you're willing to fight for your wrong opinions." Her jaw dropped. "You are impossible!" She pointed at me playfully. "And you're delightful."

Christ.

I shouldn't be here, but I can't seem to leave.

The more I drink, the longer I linger, the more memories fuel my growing rage.

I'm going to find him. I have to. But how do you destroy a monster without first losing your own humanity? I'm not convinced you can. It's criminally immoral, the ultimate desire of this feeling sitting deep in my gut. To take all he's loved and cherished and wanted, ever at any time, and burn it all to the ground.

Fucking Marcus. He took the color from the sky. The world goes on spinning, but the birds don't sing, and the air is stale, and music doesn't find its rhythm. What a constant purgatory my life has become. Just an endless gray.

Dammit, Flint. You get so metaphorical when you're drunk.

It's true, though. Life became stagnant the moment she stopped breathing.

I motion to the bartender to pour another. Bourbon settles better at home, but I couldn't bear to make it there sober, so here I sit, drinking cheap whiskey at some morning time after ten attempting to wash myself numb and plot the demise of someone I didn't even know how to find.

"You alright, buddy?"

Do I look "alright" to you?

"Fine."

"Want to talk?"

"Nope. Just want to drink."

The whiskey burns less than her silence.

Somewhere between sips, I remember her laugh echoing in the kitchen - low, breathy, the kind that made her whole body tip forward. She was wearing my sweatshirt. Humming to an 80s song she claimed to hate.

I blink hard. That sound doesn't exist anymore.

・・・

Cooper doesn't run to the door anymore. Just lifts his head from the spot on the rug and watches me like he's waiting for me to crumble. Smart dog.

I drop my keys into the bowl by the door. They clang like a gunshot in the silence.

I toe off my shoes, but don't bother unbuttoning my coat. Can't remember the last time I ate. Doesn't matter. The world feels like a watercolor left out in the rain - smudged and faded and not quite anything anymore.

I make it as far as the couch before I collapse into it, head in my hands, bourbon still clinging to the back of my throat. I think I might scream. Or sleep. Or break something.

Instead I just sit.

Minutes pass, or maybe hours. And then I see it.

On the bookshelf, jammed between a cookbook I never use and a cheesy romance I never finished - Sam's copy of *The Great Gatsby*.

God, that stupid book.

I stare at the bent spine, the cracked cover. She'd loved it because it was tragic. Because Gatsby tried so hard to remake the past. And because, deep down, she knew how that felt.

I rise on shaky legs, move like I'm underwater, and pull the book free from the shelf. It falls open like it's been waiting for this moment.

Her handwriting is there, in the margins. Little notes. Underlines. A whole world of her I forgot I still had access to.

Can't repeat the past? Of course you can.

She'd circled that line in pen. Beneath it, her messy cursive.

Famous last words, Jay. But still… I get it.

I clutch the book to my chest and fall back into the couch, body curling in on itself. The tears don't ask permission this time.

"I get it too," I whisper.

The world's still gray. But for a second, holding that book, it's not quite silent.

• • •

The bourbon sits on the dining table.

Half full.

Untouched for hours.

I stare at it like it might lunge at me, like it's daring me to pick it up again. My hand twitches toward it out of habit.

Then I slide the glass away, slow and deliberate, until it's just out of reach. I don't pour it down the sink. Not yet. But I don't drink it, either.

That's something.

Cooper sighs from across the room, curling tighter into his blanket. He hasn't eaten a full meal since she was taken from us.

I pull the old leather notebook off the shelf - the one she gave me months ago, tucked under a pile of paperwork, still with the note inside:

> *For your best ideas, your worst days, and everything in between.*
> *- S*

I run my fingers over her initial, my throat tightening. Then I flip to the first clean page. Pen in hand. No plan.

Just breath.
And grief.
And Sam.

I don't write anything profound. No masterpiece. Just fragments.

> *Her laugh at the bookstore.*
> *Her crooked smile when she beat everyone in the family at cards.*
> *The way she traced her finger around the rim of her coffee mug.*
> *The sound she made when she fell asleep in my arms.*

Memories, out of order. A flicker of Sam at a time.

Eventually, they start to form something.

A beginning.
A reason.

I'm not sure what I'm writing yet - maybe a letter, maybe a story, maybe a eulogy I wasn't ready to give. But for the first time in days, I don't feel like I'm drifting.

Still aching, but anchored.
The bourbon remains untouched.
And the pen keeps moving.

• • •

The elevator doors slide open with a creak, Ashley's soft footsteps tapping against the concrete as she came in. She didn't text beforehand. She never did anymore.

I don't look up. I'm still at the dining table, surrounded by paper and half-drank coffee gone cold. The untouched bourbon sitting further down the table, like a ghost I was trying not to look directly at.

She takes it in silently.

I hear her move through the kitchen - fix herself a glass of water. The subtle clink of ice against the glass. No judgement in it. Just life continuing, one small sound at a time. The kind of sounds I took for granted when the music played and she was here and everything was… better.

"I figured you weren't eating," she says finally, rounding the corner and leaning against the bar.

"I ate," I mutter.

"Coffee and grief don't count."

I exhale a tired breath that might've been a laugh in another life.

She crosses the room and gently slides into the seat across from me. For a long while, she doesn't say anything. Just looks at me. Looks at the pages scattered across the table, ink smudged in places where my hand shook or my eyes welled up.

"What are you writing?" she asks softly.

"I don't know yet."

She nods, the corner of her mouth barely lifting. "Sam?"

"Yeah."

Another pause.

"She'd be proud of you for this."

I finally look at her. Her eyes were tired, too, but not worn down like mine. Seasoned. Familiar with this level of pain. "It's different," I say. "You and me. I mean, when we lost-"

"Nate," she finishes for me. "Say his name. It helps."

I swallow hard, grief opening old wounds like a knife. It was something I hadn't expected - how Sam's death brought back a flood of emotions from my childhood. "Nathaniel."

Ashley folds her hands in front of her. "We were kids. I don't think I even knew how to feel it back then. I remember the funeral. The cake dad dropped. How angry mom got. But I don't remember grieving him til years later."

I stare at the pen in my hand. "And now?"

"Now... it still hurts," she says gently. Honestly. "It just doesn't own me anymore."

I close my eyes at that. "This does. Sam does. She's... everywhere. I see her in every stupid corner of this place."

"That's not a bad thing. It just means she mattered. Enough to leave a mark."

I nod slowly, tears welling up in my eyes. "And the baby... *our* baby."

Ashley reaches a hand across the table and laid it over mine. "You don't have to carry all of this alone, you know."

"I don't want anyone else to carry it," I whisper. "It's the last thing of her I've got."

Her eyes fill with tears then. The kind she rarely lets me see. "You always loved too hard, El."

"Then maybe I was never built to survive this."

"You are," she says, voice firmer now. "You're surviving it right now. And when the storm stops screaming - when you're ready - there's still more life out there. Maybe even joy. It's not betrayal to let yourself live."

I don't respond. Just stare at her. This woman who shared my blood and my ache.

Ashley squeezes my hand and stands. "I'll bring dinner tomorrow. Something *not* coffee."

"Okay," I say, barely audible.

She makes it to the elevator and presses the button before she pauses again. "Keep writing."

"I will."

She leaves, and I sit here, pen trembling in my grip.

Then, slowly, I pick up where I left off.

Elliot

I told myself I wouldn't come here again until I could walk straight.

So today - clear-headed, showered, wearing the sweater Sam always said made my eyes pop - I park the car at the bottom of the hill and make the slow climb up instead of driving. It feels… right. Like I should have to earn this somehow. Maybe a little out of punishment, but mostly out of respect.

The wind is sharp, tugging at the edges of my coat, but the sky is clear. One of those cold mornings where everything smells like pine and possibility. The mix of snow and gravel crunches under my feet as I walk, one hand in my pocket, the other gripping the flowers I brought. Some form of apology.

Cooper trots beside me, calmer than the last time we came here. Maybe he senses something different in me. Or maybe he's just tired of watching me fall apart.

We reach her spot.

I stand there a long moment, rocking on my heels like a kid about to admit he broke something valuable.

"Hey, darling," I finally say.

It comes out steady. Not perfect, but steady.

I kneel, slowly and with intention this time, and brush a few stray leaves from the memorial stone. There's a dried flower someone left weeks ago. Probably Jessa. Maybe Andrew. I don't touch it, just lay the bouquet next to it.

"I owe you an apology," I say, voice low. "For last time."

Bits of memory flash: me drunk, slurring, desperate, collapsing onto the grass while Cooper tried to drag me up by the sleeve.

Jesus.

"I'm sorry," I continue. "You deserved better than that. I guess… I just didn't know how to be in a world where you weren't anymore."

A slow breath leaves my lungs. Not a sob. Not a spiral. Just breath.

Progress.

I sit down cross-legged, letting the cold seep in through my coat and pants. Cooper settles beside me with his chin on my knee.

"I found your copy of *Gatsby,*" I say. "You left a receipt in it, by the way. From that stupid taco truck we always said we were going to get tired of but never did."

My throat tightens, but again it doesn't shut entirely.

"I started journaling," I add. "Didn't think I'd ever do something like that. But it helps. I write about you a lot. Not the bad stuff so much. The good things. The little things. I'm trying to remember you as a whole person, not just the part that hurts right now…"

Wind rustles through the nearby tree, scattering small shadows across her memorial. It doesn't feel ominous this time. Just alive.

"I'm trying, Sam," I whisper. "I'm really trying."

Cooper lifts his head, nudging my elbow, and I laugh quietly - really laugh - for the first time in maybe weeks. It surprises me, but it doesn't feel like betrayal. It feels like… surviving. Maybe healing, just a little.

"I don't know what comes next," I say, pushing a hand through my hair. "But I'm figuring it out. I just didn't want the version of me you got last time to stick. You deserved better than drunk and shattered."

A pause.

"I'm getting there, darling. I promise. It's just… taking some time."

I reach out, fingertips brushing her name.

"I'll come back soon. And next time, maybe I'll even bring the journal."

I stand, brushing the grass and snow off my coat. Cooper stretches and falls into step beside me as we walk back toward the hill.

For the first time since losing her the world feels heavy, but not impossible.

And maybe that's enough for now.

• • •

The apartment is too clean when I get home.

That's the problem with death - it scrubs everything too thoroughly. The leftovers are tossed, the laundry's done, the blankets are re-folded by Ashley on one of her recent visits… it's like trying to live inside a memory someone's already packed away in tissue paper.

I shrug off my coat and hang it by the door. The silence inside the penthouse presses against me like another layer of snowfall - cold, muffling, final.

Cooper hesitates in the threshold before padding toward the couch, curling up with a quiet huff that sounds like grief.

I know, buddy.

The bourbon still sits on the shelf, unopened since the night I found *The Great Gatsby*. I look at it now, not with longing, but with recognition. Like seeing an ex-lover at a party. You remember the pull, but not the purpose.

I pass it by.

In the kitchen, I fill a glass of water and drink it slowly. A small act. Something that doesn't destroy. I almost laugh at how novel it feels. Surviving.

I drift into the living room, standing by the balcony doors. Outside, the sky has softened to a pale gray, and snowflakes fall like whispered apologies.

Sam's copy of *Gatsby* sits on the coffee table. I reach down, run my fingers across the cover.

Cooper whines softly in his sleep, legs twitching. I imagine he's dreaming of her.

I sit.

And for the first time in days, I let myself be still without needing to shatter something.

• • •

The familiar bell above the door chimes, and I immediately regret walking in.

Not because I don't want to be here. But because everything is exactly the same.

The wooden tables. The chalkboard menu. The whirr of the espresso machine and the scent of cinnamon scones fresh from the oven.

It should feel different without her here. Wrong, maybe. But instead it just feels…

untouched. Like time had the audacity to keep moving without her. Like at any moment she might round the corner to put her apron on.

I step forward slowly, unsure what I'm even doing. My legs carried me here before my brain caught up. Maybe I thought coming here would be brave. All it feels is hollow.

The girl at the register - new - doesn't recognize me. She greets me with a polite smile that doesn't reach her eyes. I order one of Sam's recent favorites without thinking.

Cardamom latte.

The words sit bitter in my mouth, but I don't say anything else. Don't correct anything. There's nothing *to* correct.

I take it to my seat at the bar. I always watched her work from here. Watched her hum her way through making coffee. Watched her tease me, full of sarcasm and a bit of love in her eyes.

I sit there now. I don't sip the drink. I just stare at the door to the kitchen willing it to open and for her to walk through and for everything to be okay again. Try not to feel like I've broken some unwritten rule.

A few minutes pass before I hear a voice, soft but steady.

"You know, I still expect to see her, too. Playing bingo and judging people's drink orders."

I turn, and Jessa slides into the seat next to me, her eyes gentler than I've ever seen them. She doesn't smile. I'm glad she doesn't.

"I wasn't sure I'd ever come back," I admit.

"None of us were sure you'd even get out of bed again."

Her voice isn't unkind. Just honest.

I nod slowly. "It's… harder than I thought it would be. Being here."

"It always is the first time," she says flatly. "But you showed up. That matters."

I glance down at the drink. Still untouched. "Not sure what I'm trying to prove."

"You're not trying to prove anything. You're just… letting yourself keep breathing. One moment at a time."

She folds her hands around her own mug. "You don't have to bounce back, Elliot. Nobody expects you to. But she wouldn't want you to vanish, either."

I press my fingers to the cup, its warmth steady under my skin.

"She was the best part of me."

Jessa's eyes shimmer, but she doesn't cry. "She was the best part of a lot of us."

We sit there in silence. The kind that doesn't demand to be filled.

Outside, a small gust of snow swirls against the window. Inside, I take a slow sip of the latte.

It's not the same. It never will be.

But it's something.

"You know…" she says finally. Softly. I can barely hear her over the espresso machine and the music someone else obviously picked out. "Bill and I always thought we'd have kids. Came close once, but it didn't stick."

Her voice cracks slightly, and for the first time, I see it - the grief that's been living behind her eyes since the day I met her. Not just for Sam. For something older. Deeper.

"We poured everything into the ministry. Into other people's children. Into the kids who passed through the system and the ones who never quite made it out. It wasn't enough, most days. But Sam…"

She swallows and stares at something unseen.

"She made it feel like it was. Like maybe we were supposed to be *her* safe place all along. I used to tell her that she didn't owe us anything - but, god, Elliot, she gave us *everything* just by letting us love her."

I don't know what to say to that. I don't think there's anything *to* say.

"I don't know how to do this," I admit quietly after a long moment. "The part where you go on. Where you remember someone without falling apart every time they cross your mind."

Jessa lets out a long breath, and it fogs up her mug slightly.

"I don't think we ever really figure it out. I think we just get better over time at carrying what's missing. Some days are heavier than others. But we keep carrying it."

I nod, eyes stinging.

"She was proud of you, you know," Jessa adds. "She didn't always have the words, but I saw it. She *chose* you, Elliot. Even when it scared her. Even when it would have been easier to run."

I glance away, trying to steady the way her words land like bricks on my chest.

"She told me once she was afraid she'd ruin what we had. That I'd see the broken pieces of her and change my mind."

"And, I know… she didn't ruin anything," she says. "She built something. With you. That kind of love doesn't just vanish because one of you is gone."

The snow outside thickens. The coffee cools between us.

"I miss her," I whisper.

"I do, too," Jessa replies, wiping at the corner of her eye. "Every single day."

A silence settles between us again, but this time it feels like an embrace.

Not the end of grief. Not even the beginning of healing.

But a shared breath.

ELLIOT

Detective Perez's office is dim, a sliver of light cutting across the desk from half-closed blinds. The air smells like old paper and stronger coffee. I stand in the corner, arms crossed, shifting my weight from one foot to the other.

Perez finishes scribbling on a yellow legal pad and finally looks up.

"I've got good news and bad news."

"Bad news first."

She arches an eyebrow, but continues. "The lead with Prickett didn't pan out. Some guy named James? The girls' uncle. Has a solid alibi. Just thought you should know. I know you're hoping we've got something-"

"Anything. Marcus, in particular."

She gestures for me to sit. Her desk is cleaner than usual - that's how I know it's serious.

"I've got a full name. Marcus J. Price. Has a sealed juvenile record. We're trying to get it unsealed now."

"Juvenile?" I ask, brow furrowing.

"Yes. Something happened years ago. A group home, a fight, threats made. A girl reported feeling unsafe, but no charges stuck."

I freeze. "Sam… Sam lived in a group home. Briefly. After her parents…"

Perez's eyes meet mine. Sharp. Alert. "We're checking records now. If Marcus and Sam were there at the same time…"

"Then this wasn't random," I finish, voice low. "He knew her."

She nods slowly. "It's looking that way."

I breathe out through my nose, every muscle tight. "What now?"

"We're working to find him. But if he's gone underground, it might take time."

"You don't have time," I snap.

Perez's voice is calm but firm. "If we move too fast without building a case, we risk losing him altogether. I promise, Elliot. We *are* going to find him."

I nod. Not because I believe her completely, but because I need to. Because I need this part of the story to end differently than hers did.

"We pulled security footage from a nearby camera," she continues. "There's someone fitting his description coming in a few times over the last couple of weeks… lingers."

"Jesus fuck," I mutter.

Perez glances up. "We're treating him as a person of interest. Looking for him to bring him in."

My voice tightens. "He needs to pay for what he did to her."

Perez meets my gaze. "*If* he's the one who did it - we'll get there. But I need you to let *me* do this. The *right* way."

"I'm trying," I say. "But every second he's walking around free, I feel like I'm betraying her."

Perez softens just slightly. "Then let's both keep doing our jobs. Yours is to remember her. Mine is to find the person who took her away."

• • •

The sun is dipping behind the skyline, casting a dull glow across Ashley's tidy office space. I'm slouched in a chair across from her desk, arms crossed, face drawn.

It's so hard to be here. Where Sam died. But I'm supposed to meet Ashley for dinner, and she's running behind. So here I sit. Trying not to think about the last time I was here - in this building.

"You look like someone poured grief into a suit jacket," Ashley mutters, thumbing through a patient chart.

"Thanks," I say flatly.

She looks up. "You're not meant to take it as a compliment."

"Hey, I shaved today. That's progress."

Ashley stands, sets the file down, and leans her hip against the edge of her desk. "You know, it wouldn't kill you to do something Sam would be proud of."

I exhale. Hard. "Don't. Don't put that on me."

"I'm not. But you loved her. And you've been sitting in that love like it's a tomb for weeks. That's not what she'd want."

I don't answer. Just stare at the floor.

Ashley tries again, softer this time. "Remember Healing Hands?"

I look up - barely.

"You used to go every month. Sam started bringing baked goods from the cafe. You'd read to the kids… there was that fundraiser you ran into her at!"

I half-smile. "She always made me do the voices. Pick the longest books. *For the kids* she'd say."

She nudges a brochure across the desk. "They're doing a family day this weekend. Could use the extra pair of hands."

I glance down at the flyer. A happy cartoon sun and a list of activities. Bouncy houses. Face painting. Story time.

"I don't know," I say, laying the flyer back on her desk like it's too heavy to hold anymore. "I don't want to fall apart in front of a bunch of kids."

"Then fall apart afterward. But go. Do something good. Let her love live through you a little."

• • •

The first thing that strikes me is the noise.

The room feels louder than it has any right to be - voices bouncing off walls painted in too-bright colors, the squeal of sneakers on linoleum, the soft thud of plastic blocks being knocked over somewhere in the chaos. Kids dart between stations like wild pinballs. Parents hover with tired smiles, pulling juice boxes and crumpled granola bars from canvas totes. Volunteers in matching blue shirts move with easy confidence, like they'd been born knowing what to do with their hands.

I stand there with mine awkwardly shoved in my pockets, suddenly hyperaware of every breath I take. This isn't just a shelter. It's a refuge. A pause button in kids' lives that have too many hard edges.

A staffer with a warm, wrinkled smile waves me over. "You're Elliot, right? Could you read to the preschool group in five? They're getting antsy."

I swallow hard. Nod.

She places a soft, worn copy of *The Velveteen Rabbit* into my hands, its cover peeling, corners bent from years of being loved. I stare at it for a long second feeling that old, familiar tightness in my throat.

A story about a boy who loved something until it became real. A story about the cost of becoming real. God, of all books.

I walk over to the reading rug, each step feeling like trespassing on sacred ground. Tiny faces turn toward me - some curious, some bored, some already squirming in ways that suggested nap time had been an optimistic dream. They poked at each other, tugged on sleeves, fought invisible battles with imaginary swords.

And still, somehow, every single one of them looked up at me when I sat down.

"Okay," I said, clearing my throat. "This is… a story about love."

My voice cracks on that last word. I hope they don't notice. Kids are perceptive in the worst ways.

I start reading anyway. Slow at first, then with more confidence. I do the voices. Not because I'm good at them, but because the kids deserve someone who tried… and because Sam would want me to. A ripple of giggles make their way through the group when I make the Skin Horse sound like he smoked three packs a day.

Somewhere in the middle, a little girl with mismatched braids falling out into loose curls and a marker stain on her cheek toddles over and climbs into my lap like she'd done it a hundred times.

I freeze.

Just for a second.

The world tilting, something inside me threatening to crack.

Her small hand fists the fabric of my shirt. She rests her head against my chest, letting out a soft sigh, like she'd decided I was safe.

And I don't fall apart.

I don't break or crumble or run.

Instead I keep reading. Keep doing the voices. Keep turning the pages even when my eyes blur at the part where the Rabbit asks what it means to be real.

My voice never fully steadies, but I smile. Not because anything was fixed. Not because I was suddenly whole again. But because, for the first time in a long time, something in me shifted. Subtle. Quiet. Like a door cracking open in a room I'd boarded up.

• • •

I sob.

My breath catches in my throat, and I rub my hand roughly down my face - slick over the tears.

It had been so nice. So freeing to help out at Healing Hands. But the moment I got home, it all clicked.

The tiny hands. The way she leaned against my chest. The way her brown curls smelled faintly like strawberries and sunshine.

I imagine she's what ours would have looked like.

I sit down on the hard floor of the apartment - not the couch, not the bed - the floor. Cold and real and grounding.

Cooper pads over, whining, laying his head gently in my lap like he knows. Like he always knows.

"We should have protected her… them," I whisper to him like he might answer back.

He doesn't

Just me. Just this hollow echo in my chest where she used to live. Where she still lives. Where maybe - just maybe - healing is starting to sprout like grass through cracked pavement.

I lean my head back against the cabinet door and close my eyes.

Her laugh. Her book on the nightstand. Her half-used perfume still in the bathroom. None of it feels any further away. But maybe now it doesn't feel quite so impossible to carry.

Maybe tomorrow I'll show up again. For the kids. For her. For me.

But tonight… I sit on the kitchen floor, Cooper in my lap, and let the tears fall without apology.

Because this, too, is healing.

Elliot

Cooper's asleep at the foot of the couch, the only soul who seems able to rest in this house anymore.

I open Sam's laptop.

I shouldn't. I know that. But Detective Perez's words echo in my head: *a group home, a fight, threats made.*

I don't know what I'm expecting to find, but I decide it's worth it to look anyway. And when I pull up her Notes app, my heart nearly jumped out of my chest. So many journal entries. Some about me, some about groceries, some about work…

I shouldn't snoop.

But I'm going to.

I get lost in the letters, almost like I can hear her voice.

> *Elliot looks at me like he's choosing me on purpose.*
>
> *I'm beginning to think he's one of the good ones. I honestly wasn't even sure those existed.*
>
> *Fuck, I'm so happy.*

Tears rolled freely down my cheeks. God, I can't believe I get this piece of her.

I shake my head, half in disbelief, half because I know as amazing as this is I'm looking for something far more tragic.

I type *Marcus* into her computer's spotlight search bar. A Notes entry a few months old pops up.

> *Some strange guy came into the cafe today. Marcus? Pretty sure that was his name, because he freaked me the fuck out. He didn't... do anything. Just asked too many questions that felt oddly personal in the weirdest way. And what's worse is that he seems SO familiar, and I can't put a finger on why. Hopefully he's just a one-off.*

"So, this had been going on for a while, huh?" I said aloud to no one.

Cooper glanced up from his sleep, groggy and seemingly annoyed that I'd interrupted his slumber.

She doesn't write about him again, though. At least not by name. Which, at first, I think is good. Maybe he hadn't come in much after all. But then I type *group home* into the search bar. Old essays, application answers, even a few personal journal entries she'd written to herself - not a full history, just... fragments. All of it paints a picture I already knew. She hated that place. Said it was better than being abused at home, but only just.

And then I find it. Buried deep in an old entry titled *for later*.

> *There was this kid once at the group home. I tried not to remember him, but he remembered me. I think he liked feeling powerful, and I was easy to make feel small. I told Jessa he just teased me. That was a lie. He knew everything about my family. Held it over me. Got a rise out of me. One time he got so close to my face I thought he was going to hit me. Or worse.*

I sit back, breath gone cold in my chest.

Marcus.

It's him.

Of course it's him.

I sit for a long time, fingers drumming the table, until I reach for my phone. One number left that I haven't called - the one I hoped I'd never need again.

Laurel.

It rings. Once. Twice.

She answers, clipped and flat. "Elliot?"

"I need to talk to you. About someone from the group home Sam stayed in. His name was Marcus."

There's silence. Then a slow, deliberate breath. "Why are you asking me about that?"

"You were the only family she had. If there's anything - *anything* - you remember, I need you to tell me now."

She hesitates. "We didn't talk much about that time. She shut me out."

I doubt that's the full truth.

"She's not here to ask anymore."

A pause. Then: "I remember her talking about a boy. Creepy kid. Got kicked out after a month for threatening staff. Sam said he gave her the chills. She was always tense while he was there."

I close my eyes. "That's enough. Thank you."

"I didn't do right by her, Elliot."

"No," I say. "You didn't."

And I hang up.

I can't sit with this.

I stand suddenly, startling Cooper from his quiet slumber. I scratch his head quickly as I make my way to the elevator. I push the button. Then again. It doesn't make it call any faster, but it matters because it *feels* productive. The door dings open and I rush in, grabbing my coat off the hook.

Marcus.

> *"I thought he was going to hit me. Or worse."*

Fucking hell.

As soon as the doors slide open downstairs, I rush out the front of the building. Driving would take just as long, and I had too much restless energy to sit still. So I'm walking.

The winter wind is frigid against my cheeks as they burn with urgency. My hands curl and relax in my jacket pockets. I probably look like a mad man.

I am.

My boots hit the pavement hard.

Each step feels like it's not fast enough - like my legs can't keep up with the fire in my chest. She had trusted me with pieces of her past, but this - this had been hidden. Tucked away in quiet corners of her memory, where even she couldn't always face it.

The buildings blur as I push past them, wind slicing through the collar of my coat. I don't know what I'm going to say, not exactly. Just that I need Jessa. She always knew how to make sense of Sam, even when she couldn't make sense of herself.

I cut across the final crosswalk, my heart thudding against my ribs, nerves and cold making my fingers numb.

Light pours from the windows of the cafe, warm and familiar. It stings a little, walking toward something that still looks the same while everything else has unraveled.

I pull open the door. The bell startles both the new girl and Jessa as I storm in.

"We're closed in ten, you're lucky I like you," she starts to tease before she looks up and sees my face. Her brow furrows instantly. "Elliot?"

I walk in fast. Frantic. My coat still open despite the bite in the air outside. "Do you remember Sam ever telling you about a kid named Marcus? From the group home she stayed in?"

Jessa straightens, towel clutched in one hand. "That name again…"

"You've heard it?"

"Yea, of course I've heard it. Bill mentioned him after that scene in here… said he gave him a bad feeling. Why?" She's cautious. Reserved. Like I'm a bomb that might go off anytime.

I am.

"I found something on Sam's computer," I said, voice low and urgent, glancing toward the other barista who's casually wiping down already clean counters - like Sam used to. "She wrote about him. Said he used to scare her. Said he *knew* things about her - her family - and he used it to mess with her. Said he liked making her feel small."

Jessa's face drains of color. A realization.

The new girl looks up, the conversation obviously not a place for her, and makes her way through the kitchen door.

I step closer. "Did she ever talk to you about him directly?"

"She… no, not really. I asked about some of the kids when she first came around, but she always brushed it off. Called them *background noise*. I didn't press… god, Elliot…"

I nod, already pacing a little behind the counter. "Laurel remembers him. Maybe not by name, but it has to be him. Said he got kicked out of the home for threatening staff... It *has* to be him," I'm repeating myself. I don't care.

The last customer from the front corner, completely oblivious to the critical nature of our conversation, stands and waves politely to Jessa as she makes her way out. As soon as the door shuts behind her, Jessa drops the towel and grabs her phone.

"I'm calling Perez."

I put a hand on hers. "I'll go."

She stills.

"I need to be the one to take this to her. See if they've got any updates."

Jessa holds my gaze a moment, hesitant, then nods. "Okay."

She reaches up and touches my cheek gently, fingers soft with something like maternal affection. "You're doing right by her, Elliot."

I didn't feel like it. I felt like I was two steps behind a ghost and chasing guilt down alleyways. But I nodded. Then turn, coat still undone, and leave without saying goodbye.

· · ·

The police station is too bright. Fluorescents buzz above me, humming like they're judging every move I'd made up until this point.

Detective Perez looks up from her desk as I walk in. She's in plainclothes today - a slate sweater, her badge clipped to her belt - and still somehow looks more put together than I'd felt in weeks.

"Mr. Flint." She stands slowly, reading the urgency on my face. "Something new?"

"Yes," I say. "Marcus."

Her brow arches. "We've been digging into Marcus Price."

I step forward, voice lowering. "I found something. On Sam's laptop. Notes… entries. She didn't name him, but it's clear. He was in the group home with her. He tormented her there. Knew things about her past - things she said he used to twist against her. He liked control. Liked watching her squirm."

Perez sits back down, her shift in posture making room for gravity. "Go on."

"She must not have recognized him when he showed up at the cafe out of nowhere. But it's him. And I think she knew something was wrong but didn't want to admit it. Or maybe she didn't realize how much danger she was in…"

Perez opens a drawer and pulls out a legal pad. "You still have these… entries?"

"I brought them." I hand her the computer, then add, "I want to be there when you find him."

She gives me a measured look. "That's not how this works."

I rub my hand across my forehead, clammy from all the rush. "Perez, you don't-"

"Mr. Flint. That's a liability my department can't take. You did good. You gave her voice back. That matters. But you can't come with me. Besides, my team has to look over all this," she raises the computer still in her hand. "You… we have to do this right if we're gonna get him."

...

Again, it's too quiet when I get home. Still in that uncomfortable way - not peaceful, but expectant. Like something's missing. Because it is.

The elevator doors close behind me and I drop my keys on the counter, listening to them clatter into the bowl. That sound, like a punctuation mark at the end of a long sentence.

Cooper trots out from the bedroom, tail wagging half-heartedly. He's doing a *little* better as time goes. I guess we all are. He pads toward me, ears slightly lowered - cautious, almost guilty. Like he still expects me to blame him.

"Hey, bud," I say, crouching to scratch behind his ears. He presses into me without hesitation. Of course, he always loved her more. But he's mine now. Or maybe I'm his.

We sit like that for a while. His head rests on my knee, eyes fluttering closed. The silence stretches between us, gentle and aching.

I lean back on the couch and feel a knot press into my shoulder. I turn, careful not to disturb him, and dig behind the cushion. A worn tennis ball emerges in my hand, and I begin to turn it in my palm.

"She'd throw this for you til your legs gave out," I murmur. "Then she'd carry you inside like a baby. Do you remember that?"

He huffs softly, like maybe he does.

I stare out the window, still twisting the ball in my hand. The city is quiet tonight. Just a few headlights flickering by below, and the faint pulse of red from the radio tower on the far side of the skyline.

There's nothing to do but wait.

Wait for Perez to call.

Wait for justice to show up and make itself known.

Wait for the grief to dull, just a little.

Cooper lifts his head and looks at me, brown eyes soft and steady.

"You know," I say, almost to myself. "I think she'd be proud of you. You showing up here all by yourself? It helped me find her that day."

His tail gives a single thump.

"And I think… I think she'd want us to keep going."

I don't believe it yet. But I say it anyway.

Elliot

A few days of nothingness pass.

I try to be present. But I live somewhere between being caught up in the past (reliving every memory I have of her) and hung on the future (craving justice like a parched man in the desert).

I stand now at the end of a bookshelf in the used bookstore pursuing some mystery I have no actual interest in. It's just a placeholder. Something to occupy my mind. It was her favorite section. She always said the books here smelled like time itself - old paper and ghosts and puzzles to solve.

I find myself doing that more now - the things she loved. Like finally listening to that playlist she loved to play at the cafe and humming to myself while I make coffee. It makes the memory of Sam pull closer to where I can *almost* reach out and grab it. It's like hearing a song that's been stuck in your head all day - doesn't make you forget, just settles something deep in your soul.

I close the cover and exhale. The closeness I feel to her isn't enough. But it's all I have anymore.

That's when my phone rings.

I pull it out of my coat pocket. **Detective Perez**.

My thumb hesitates over the screen, breath already gone, heart in my throat.

"Elliot Flint," I manage, voice tighter than I wanted.

No pleasantries. She knows better by now. "We found him."

The world spins slightly. The bookstore around me blurs into shapes and static. I lean back against a dusty bookshelf, bracing myself. "You're sure?"

"We've verified the journal entries. One of our officers remembered a report from a nearby precinct - same Marcus. Different name back then. Long history of harassment. It's him."

A tremor moves through my chest. "Where is he now?"

"We have him in custody. Picked him up this morning. It was... theatrical, I'll say." She pauses, then adds, "I wanted you to hear it from me."

My knees bend slightly like my body isn't quite sure whether to collapse or run. I stare out past the books into the window glass fogged from the warmth inside. A couple walks past, laughing. Normal. Unbothered.

"He did it, didn't he?" I ask quietly. "You're not just humoring me?"

There's silence on the other end. Not long. Just enough to answer the question.

"We're still putting the pieces together. But this is a step, Mr. Flint. A real one."

I nod, even though she can't see me. "Thank you."

"You did right by her," Perez says. "You didn't give up."

She hangs up.

I stare down at the phone still in my hand, my reflection ghosted on the dark screen. Not smiling. Not relieved. But... something inside me shifts.

I place the book gently back on the shelf, wipe my palms on my pants, and step out into the street.

The cold meets me like a wall the moment I step outside the bookstore. The city moves through dusk around me as if nothing happened. As if the earth didn't just shift a little.

I walk slowly toward my car - it's the kind of frigid air people tend to hurry through, but I welcome the sting. My keys are clutched in my palm, thumb tracing the edge of the fob as if it could ground me.

Halfway there, I pull my phone out again and scroll to Jessa's name. Hit call.

"Elliot?" She answers on the second ring, breathless like she'd been hauling a bunch of baked goods through the shop.

"They got him," I say, the words still sounding strange in my mouth. "Marcus."

She pauses. Then, carefully: "Are you sure?"

"They're sure," I exhaled. "They picked him up this morning. I just spoke with Perez."

A long silence. I almost think she hung up. Then, "Thank god." Her voice cracks. "I... thank god."

I nod, blinking hard against the tears threatening my eyes. "I just thought you should know."

"Are you okay?" She asks gently.

"No," I admit. "But I'm better than I was."

"Nothing heavy. Just... how are you really doing?" I asked. "Better than I was?" She said it

like it was a question, but she exhaled it like she'd been needing to say it. Like she believed it more the moment it rolled off her tongue. We were sitting at the table in her apartment, eating the soup and grilled cheese she'd made. "Figuring out's a full-time job," I replied, acknowledging the hard work she was putting in. "Tell me about it," she'd said.

Jessa's voice snaps me back into the present. "Where are you going?"

I look out over the street, turn signal on my parked car still blinking from the remote unlock. "To see her."

Another pause. Then a breath. "Tell her we miss her, okay?"

"I will."

We hang up.

• • •

The cemetery is quiet except for the wind - that kind of low, constant sound that slips beneath your coat and settles between your ribs.

I tuck my hands in my pockets and step between rows of headstones. Her grave is near the willow tree.

Same spot. Same marker. Same ache in my chest.

I stand a long moment before kneeling. Breath leaves me in a cloud.

"They got him," I whisper. "Took long enough, but they did."

I look down at the engraving. The flowers someone - Jessa, maybe - had left a day or two ago. The ribbon still tied around Cooper's old collar.

"You were right." My voice is raw. "He was dangerous. And you knew it, didn't you? Even if you didn't have the words for it…"

I pull the folded paper from my coat pocket. A page I'd printed from her journal entries. The one that named Marcus without naming him. I place it gently at the base of the headstone, weighed down by a small rock.

"I'm sorry it took so long. I'm sorry you had to be scared again. I'm sorry I couldn't stop it."

The wind pushes through the trees above and they rustle like whispers. Tears flow freely now, leaving cool rivers down my cheeks.

"You didn't deserve this. Especially not after the hand you were dealt. You deserved forever. You deserved peace. You deserved safety…"

I wipe at my face, fingers trembling not from the cold.

"But we're going to get justice," I promise. "You mattered. I won't let that fade."

I stand again, but I don't leave right away.

"I don't know if I believe in any of this - heaven, afterlife, whatever," I murmur. "But if there's anything left of you somewhere, I hope you know how loved you were… are. How much you changed me."

I reach down and brush my fingers along the edge of the stone. "And I hope I make you proud with whatever I've got left."

52
Elliot

Grief doesn't end.

It changes shape.

Some mornings it wakes me before the sun. Some days it's quieter. A hum beneath the noise. A pressure in my chest that doesn't ask for permission. I don't fight it as much now. I just… let it sit beside me.

The world doesn't pause when your heart shatters.

You still have to return library books. Still have to feed the dog.

I still go to the coffee shop. Jessa always saves me a blueberry muffin, even though I barely touch them anymore. Ashley checks in every Sunday night. Andrew texts more often than he talks - but his messages make me laugh, even when I don't want to.

She's in all of it.
Not as a ghost.
As a rhythm.

She lives in the mug I reach for without thinking. In the smell of cardamom. In the copy of *The Great Gatsby*, still tucked under my nightstand. In the slow, steady way I'm learning to breathe again.

I used to think healing would be a moment. An arrival. Something final and definable - like crossing a finish line. But now I know better.

Healing isn't a destination.

It's a decision.

Every day I choose to carry Sam's memory forward rather than letting it pull me under. I still cry sometimes. Still miss her like a missing limb. Still catch myself reaching for my phone to tell her something stupid.

But when I do, I don't collapse.

Love is strange like that. It doesn't end with a heartbeat.

It lingers.
It imprints.
It softens you in some places and hardens you in others.

Losing her didn't undo me. It undid the version of me that believed life had to make sense to be beautiful.

Sam once told me Gatsby wasn't tragic because he died - he was tragic because he hoped. But she made me believe hope isn't the enemy. It's the reason I still get up.

And maybe that's what love leaves behind. Not just the ache, but the invitation:

To keep going.
To remember well.
To live with open hands - even when they're trembling.

I'll never stop missing her. But I'm learning, slowly, not to be afraid of the missing.

Sam Reynolds taught me that.

No, grief doesn't end. It just learns to walk beside you - and if you're lucky, it teaches you how to love what's left.

I'd love your feedback!

A review can work wonders for self-published authors. Tell me what you thought of Broken Pieces on Amazon or GoodReads!

Let's Be Social

Tiktok: @brokenpieces.novel

Instagram: @brokenpiecesnovel

Spotify: Abby Shrewsbury

About The Author:

Abby Shrewsbury is a storyteller at heart. By day, she works in marketing, crafting narratives designed to build trust, spark emotion, and form genuine connections with clients. In the quiet hours when the world settles, she turns to fiction. What began as an on-and-off creative outlet more than fifteen years ago grew into a refuge: a therapeutic place to explore the tender, complicated parts of being a human.

Shrewsbury writes the kind of stories she craves most - honest, a little messy, and unafraid to sit in the hard spaces. She gravitates toward imperfect characters, tangled relationships, and endings that feel like real life (not fairytales). Her narratives often center on grief, resilience, and how love has the ability to shape us into who we are.

Living with multiple chronic illnesses, Shrewsbury understands the delicate art of pacing one's life. When she isn't developing campaigns or drafting novels, you can find her recharging: unwinding with true crime podcasts, hosting low-key game nights with friends, or spending time with her loyal canine companions, Gus and Bo. She is deeply passionate about anti-trafficking advocacy and adoption initiatives, believing that storytelling can be a bridge between awareness and compassion.

Broken Pieces is Shrewsbury's debut novel, a story about the heaviness we carry and the people who help us hold it.

Preview: Deep Blue

No one could agree on why she did it, but they all agreed she did it on purpose.

Andie "Camp" Campbell. Teammate. Diver. Friend.

Dead.

The ocean is raging today. Like it's hungry and we just took its food.

The water slaps hard against the side of the boat. It's not a lapping noise so much as it is an open hand banging the hull back and forth.

She... what?

Grace is unsure if she says the words out loud or if they simply echo through her mind. Around her, the rest are trying to explain the incomprehensible. Camp had cut her regulator at the very depths of the dive. She'd fought against herself, then stilled. And now she's here, dragged up to the surface by her partners.

She lays covered by a towel. Underneath, her face is blue. Her body stiff in the wind, already the wrong color. Her dark blonde hair splays out, damp and stuck to the boat below her.

The vessel sways and rocks in the wind. Instead of calming her - the usual reaction - Grace feels as if she's about to hurl. Bile rises in her throat.

It can't be.

She leans over the side of the boat and vomits. Fish almost immediately eat at the bits. She'd experienced death before. Even seen it first-hand during her time in the Navy. She's no stranger to tragedy. But the concept of her friend - her close friend - choosing to slit the hose that held her life at 58 meters down...

Grace wipes the back of her hand across her mouth and turns back to her spot on the aft seating, staring across at her dead friend's body.

"What do we do now?" Ashton, a green diver who'd been down there with the team, asks.

"We've got to call the authorities," Grace says mechanically. "Tell them what happened. Someone… someone else has to do it. One of you who was down there."

"I will," Jeff says after a long moment of silence. He's in his forties like Grace. More mature than Ashton, more detached than Grace.

They all stand in silence for a moment, the only sound is the water pounding the boat and their breaths, less one than they started the day with.

Jeff calls over the radio and requests the Coast Guard to meet the crew at the nearest port. It's just over 20 miles to Pensacola. He sits at the captain's seat and stares at the steering wheel as if the boat might drive itself.

They ride together in silence over the choppy waves. The water is angry. Like it knows. Ashton sits at Camp's head holding the towel over her despite the wind. He quietly cries. Grace doubts he's ever experienced death before, let alone bore witness to a suicide.

Jeff maneuvers the boat with experienced ease and makes it to Pensacola in around an hour. As soon as the vessel pulls into view of the port, there's a flurry of activity. A white van waits at the dock, engine running in the heat. The words *Escambia County Medical Examiner* are stenciled on the side.

Two uniformed Coast Guard officers board the dive boat immediately, boots heavy on the deck. They don't look at Grace or Ashton or Jeff - not at first. They go to the towel, lift the corner, and nod to each other. One radios in: "Confirmed. Female, late twenties. Transport required."

Grace's stomach twists. They talk like Camp is evidence, not a person.

Statements are taken next, one by one, on clipboards. How archaic, Grace thinks. The officer never once asks if she's okay.

When it's Ashton's turn, his voice cracks. "She wouldn't have… she wouldn't have done this." His hands shake so badly the officer has to steady the pen for him. But she did.

Grace watches Jeff, stone-faced, arms crossed. He hasn't said a word since the radio call. And for the first time, Grace wonders - does he know more than he's letting on?

She feels guilty even for having the thought. Jeff has always been a kind member of their dive group. A leader, naturally. And he'd just witnessed the unconscionable actions that had gotten them here.

Still, she needed to know the details. How did Camp cut her hose? How far away was she from the group when she did? Did she even reach for her backup air? How long had she held her breath? Is there any way it could have been an accident?

Grace stared at her clipboard, empty but for a couple of dots where she'd tried to start then couldn't.

"Ma'am, we really need your account of the incident," the officer prodded.

"I... I wasn't even down there," she mutters.

"It's still important. Every detail is important."

She watched as Jeff nodded along halfheartedly to whatever the other officer was saying to him. Grateful she got the quieter of them, Grace shakily pressed the pen to the paper again, just shy of beginning to write. She needs a moment to think. The details. Small, seemingly innocuous details that couldn't possibly matter.

It's 97 degrees fahrenheit. There is a slight breeze to the southwest. Ashton fumbles with his weight belt, fingers clumsy in his gloves. He'll get it, just needs to calm down. Camp is methodical - mask defogged, hoses untangled, computer lit up on her wrist. But something's... off. Her hands linger too long on the second stage, thumb running along the hose as if it might tell her a secret. She checks her computer again, scrolling, backing out, scrolling again. "Camp, you good?" Jeff asks, glancing at her. She flashes him a quick thumbs-up, almost too quick, then goes back to her gear. It's unnerving, the way she won't meet anyone's eyes. The way she pauses before inflating her BCD to test the valve, like she has to remember what comes next.

They circle up for the final buddy check. Jeff squeezes Ashton's inflator, listens for the hiss. Ashton checks Jeff's weights. Camp is with Grace.

"BCD, releases, air..." Grace recites, hands moving with automatic precision over Camp's straps, buckles, regulator. Everything's in place. Air pressure steady. No leaks. Nothing wrong.

But there's a hesitation under Camp's skin. Her breath is slightly uneven. She doesn't say anything. God, why doesn't she say anything?

The sea churns below, slate-colored and restless.

Camp bites down on her mouthpiece, the taste of rubber and salt inevitably filling her mouth. She gives the signal. Thumbs down. And together the three of them slip into the water. Only two of them will come back.

"Miss?" The officer breaks Grace's trance. She'd zoned out, her pen drifting down the paper in a semi-straight line about an inch long.

"Oh, uh, fuck. Sorry."

The officer pulls the clipboard from her hands, removes the paper, and flips it over on the other side. He silently hands it back to her. It's a stiff movement, like he's bothered by her grief.

Grace writes her statement as thoroughly as possible. She includes the weather and the bit about Camp's inability to make eye contact. Her mind races with all the things she may have missed. Vomit creeps at the back of her throat again.

Behind her, still on the boat, a team from the coroner's office bags Camp's body as if it's just any other Tuesday. But, Grace supposes, this is just any other Tuesday for them. Death is death. And that was their life.

The black bag zipped up over Camp's face, shrouding her in the kind of darkness that would last forever. The sound echoed in Grace's ears, louder than the voices around her or the water slapping the port or the hum of the vehicles still running as if they might somehow have better places to be.

Grace quietly wonders what will happen from here. How their lives will move on while Camp is transported to a morgue, shoved into a refrigerator, and left alone for god knows how long. She questions how long it would take for them to perform the autopsy that was inevitable after such a suspicious death. What they would find.

If anything might reveal what could have possessed her friend to kill herself in such a violent way.

And it was. Violent. Some people suggest drowning is peaceful, but they've never inhaled large amounts of water before.

"Can we… go get a drink or something? I'm not sure I'm ready to go home yet," Grace says to the men as the officers collect their ancient clipboards and make their way back to their cars.

Ashton nods solemnly and Jeff shrugs. No one is quite sure what the next step is. There's a sense of morbid camaraderie between them now, and Grace is unsure that she's ready to battle the chaos of her mind all on her own quite yet.

She didn't have a partner to go home to. Nor a pet. She was utterly alone, and the fact that her friend had just left a gaping hole in her life made that all the more apparent to Grace.

The trio walked in silence, still damp in their swimsuits. They made their way to an outdoor patio of a restaurant called the Fish House. Of course, no one was hungry, and the smell of food made Grace's stomach turn somersaults again.

They order drinks. Grace a tequila soda with lime, Jeff a gin and tonic, and Ashton just a coke - he says he's too shaken up for alcohol to do any good for him, which Grace understands. She reaches a hand across the table to Ashton, which he takes hesitantly, shakily. They sip their drinks, the only sound between them the clinking of ice in the glasses. There's altogether too much to say and not enough words to say it.

Jeff pays for the round of drinks, not having it when Grace and Ashton offer to pay their own way. He says it's the least he could do, which Grace finds odd, but grief hits everyone differently. They move to leave and Jeff offers a hug to Grace and Ashton, one that lasts longer than necessary.

When she walks up to her Jeep, Grace is stunned with how normal everything had been before their dive. Her radio is still on - she kicks it off immediately. She's sure she needs the quiet lull of road noise over whatever classic rock was coming through the speakers.

Grace's stomach still spins, and the tequila sloshes with it. She swallows hard, fighting the urge to puke again. Her forehead is clammy. Her hands still shake. But she refuses to pull over and get sick on the side of the road.

It's about a 20 minute drive to her home outside of Warrington. She lived alone in an old, pale yellow house with white shutters and a small yard to the right. Her Jeep rolls into her covered porch and slows to a stop with a light squeak of the breaks. Grace thinks she'll need to think to get those checked soon, but that's the furthest thing from what she wants to worry with right now.

She pushes the gear shift into park and turns the key in the ignition to shut off the car, then sits and stares at her hands back on the steering wheel. Still shaking slightly. She takes a few long, deep breaths and squeezes her eyes shut, trying not to picture Camp's lifeless body being dragged up out of the water.

Grace finally forces herself to pull the keys free and push the door open. The cicadas buzz loudly in the August heat, an endless chorus, and for a split second she wishes she was still on the boat with the sound of waves and engines instead of this crushing quiet.

Inside, the house smells faintly of lemon cleaner and the falling mildew of old wood in the Florida humidity. She drops her bag by the door and forgets to lock it behind her. The stillness presses in, so heavy it feels like a weight on her chest.

Grace heads for the kitchen, thinking maybe water will settle her stomach. She twists the faucet on and watches it run, clear then clouded with air bubbles, before filling a glass. Her hands shake again, spilling water onto the counter.

She leans against the sink, staring at nothing. Her dive computer sits on the counter where she'd left it last night, the straps still damp with salt. Grace picks it up without meaning to. The screen is blank. She imagines what Camp's would say if anyone had the stomach to download it - depths, times, oxygen levels. Cold data, telling a story no one wants to read.

Her throat tightens. *Why did you do it, Camp?*

Grace pushes the computer away like it burns her and presses both hands flat on the counter, forcing air in and out of her lungs. But the images don't stop coming:

Camp's body being hoisted out of the water, Ashton's tears as he holds the towel over her body, the black body bag zipping over her blue face...

Grace chokes out a sound - half sob, half groan - and covers her mouth. She's not sure if she's afraid of disturbing neighbors or of hearing herself lose control.

Upstairs, her bedroom waits, but the thought of climbing into the sheets feels obscene when Camp will never climb into anything again.

Instead, she sinks to the kitchen floor, knees to her chest, and lets the silence hold her until exhaustion drags her under.

She dreams of the ocean, angry and whipping the dive boat back and forth as it carries Camp's body away. Flashes of her friend's face - swollen and water-logged - disturb her sleep. She wakes at 3:52 on the cold kitchen floor, the house dark as she hadn't turned on any lights when she came in. Grace rolls to her back and lays there rubbing a hand over her face. Her restless night on the tile, she imagines, feels somehow eerily similar to wherever the authorities had Camp, likely perched on frigid steel.

She groans as she rises from the floor, her knees and ankles popping with her weight. She needs to shower the day off. The stairs creak in the night as she climbs them. Every sound feels like a ruckus. The door tapping the stopper. The faucet handle squeaking on. The water pounding the bottom of the tub.

Grace strips off her t-shirt and swimsuit she still had on from the day. She climbs into the shower and allows the water to roll down her back, tears threatening to fall from her eyes. Her mind races with thoughts of what she might have missed. She replays the day over and over in her mind until the water runs cold.

www.ingramcontent.com/pod-product-compliance
Lightning Source LLC
LaVergne TN
LVHW041741060526
838201LV00046B/869